2 NOVELS

GREAT VALUE

HOME ON THE RANCH:
TEXAS
SECRETS

COLLEEN THOMPSON

USA TODAY BESTSELLING AUTHOR
ANGI MORGAN

PREVIOUSLY PUBLISHED AS
LONE STAR SURVIVOR AND *PROTECTING THEIR CHILD*

INTRIGUE

EDGE-OF-YOUR-SEAT INTRIGUE,
FEARLESS ROMANCE.

Harlequin Intrigue stories deal in
serious romantic suspense, keeping you
on the edge of your seat as resourceful,
true-to-life women and strong, fearless
men fight for survival.

Six new books available every month!

ISBN-13: 978-1-335-02043-7

▷ EAN

Praise for Colleen Thompson

"An action-packed, tender story about a damaged army veteran will appeal to readers, as will Ian and Andrea's sweet, intense chemistry and the powerful, gritty plot."

—*RT Book Reviews* on *Lone Star Survivor*

"Equal parts suspense and romance, this fast-paced story is filled with plenty of action and intrigue. Vulnerable, genuine characters and an interesting mystery make for a thrilling read."

—*RT Book Reviews* on *Lone Star Redemption*

"Thompson understands the heart of a hero! There's no end to the action, and the explosive climax leads to a surprise ending."

— *RT Book Reviews* on *Capturing the Commando*, Top Pick!, 4.5 stars

Praise for *USA TODAY* bestselling author Angi Morgan

"Morgan pens a lovely comeback story of a hero fighting his inner demons and struggling with PTSD. With equal parts action, romance and compelling characters, she hits all the right notes."

—*RT Book Reviews* on *The Cattleman*, Top Pick!, 4.5 stars

"From the echoing shots in a cemetery straight through the hair-raising conclusion, this story of missing memories and murders will rattle readers from the opening pages, as they guess and guess again who the real culprit is."

—*RT Book Reviews* on *Dangerous Memories*

"A great mix of drama, romance, suspense...well written, fast paced read...strong chemistry and connection that leads to some steamy love scenes... I thoroughly recommend this book to anyone who enjoys romantic suspense."

—*Goodreads* on *Bulletproof Badge*

HOME ON THE RANCH:

TEXAS SECRETS

———————— ⚒ ————————

COLLEEN THOMPSON

USA TODAY Bestelling Author

ANGI MORGAN

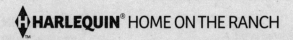
HARLEQUIN® HOME ON THE RANCH

ISBN-13: 978-1-335-02043-7

Home on the Ranch: Texas Secrets

Copyright © 2018 by Harlequin Books S.A.

The publisher acknowledges the copyright holders of the individual works as follows:

Lone Star Survivor
Copyright © 2014 by Colleen Thompson

Protecting Their Child
Copyright © 2013 by Angela Platt

Recycling programs
for this product may
not exist in your area.

Printed in U.S.A.

www.Harlequin.com

CONTENTS

After beginning her career writing historical romance novels, in 2004 **Colleen Thompson** turned to writing the contemporary romantic suspense she loves. Since then, her work has been honored with a Texas Gold Award, along with nominations for a RITA® Award, a Daphne du Maurier Award and multiple reviewers' choice honors. She has also received starred reviews from *RT Book Reviews* and *Publishers Weekly*. A former teacher living with her family in the Houston area, Colleen has a passion for reading, hiking and dog rescue. Visit her online at www.colleen-thompson.com.

Books by Colleen Thompson

Harlequin Romantic Suspense

Passion to Protect
The Colton Heir
Lone Star Redemption
Lone Star Survivor

Silhouette Romantic Suspense

Deadlier Than the Male
"Lethal Lessons"

Harlequin Intrigue

Capturing the Commando
Phantom of the French Quarter
Relentless Protector

Visit the Author Profile page at Harlequin.com for more titles.

LONE STAR SURVIVOR

COLLEEN THOMPSON

To my father, who first taught me that a true hero is not the man who talks about it but the man who quietly, steadfastly loves and supports throughout the years.

Chapter 1

Waves of searing heat shimmered above the empty road, the endless road he had been walking for hours or days or all his life. How long didn't matter, only that blurred spot in the distance, beyond the sea of dry, gold stalks, where the blazing sun reflected off what had to be a lake. The sight of it made his parched mouth ache with the memory of water, cool and fresh and unimaginably luxurious as his body slipped through it, graceful as a seal's.

While his blistered feet stumbled forward, the walker's mind returned to a jewel-bright pool of turquoise. As he sat along its edge, lush green fronds waved in the sultry breeze and giant coral blossoms spilled their honeyed fragrance. A woman in big sunglasses swayed toward him, a floral sarong molding to the sweet curve of her hips and a deep blue bikini top holding her firm, round breasts in place. But it was her smile that sent lust spearing straight to his groin, that dazzling smile so white against her summer tan.

"Ready for another?" she invited, offering him some creamy, icy beverage in a clear plastic cup. A chunk of juicy pineapple balanced on its rim, so vivid in his memory that he could almost taste it. He could almost taste *her* on his lips, too, just as he could feel the dark river of her long hair running through his fingers, gleaming strands of chocolate he'd watched her brush so many times.

He smiled, reaching for her. And felt the pain of his chapped lips splitting, tasted the thick, salt tang of blood instead of the hallucination's sweetness. The mirage teased in the distance, a lie woven from refracted heat waves. *You'll never make it back to her, not even if you walk to the earth's ends.*

But he didn't stop. He couldn't, not while every step carried him closer to the oasis he dreamed of. Toward it and toward a woman, her name as lost to him as his own.

He knew one thing, though. He'd loved her. Loved her even if… The rest shimmered in the heat and vanished, an absence permeated with the bitterness of loss. There was fear as well, the anxiety that he'd done something unspeakable to poison what they'd had. That he'd *been* someone who deserved the scorched red skin, the knotted beard and the half-healed scars he'd glimpsed in the window of the pickup that had pulled over to offer him a ride an hour earlier. Or maybe it had been yesterday. Impossible to know, since time had grown as slippery as a live fish squirming in his grasp.

A single, splintered second pierced through his confusion: the moment when he'd met the driver's eyes. Dark eyes, shaded by a broad-brimmed hat. A cowboy hat, like the ones they wore back in Texas. Like the ones he'd used to...

Before he'd been able to wrap his parched brain around the thought, those dark eyes had flared wide. The driver had hit the gas too hard, the back end of his pickup sliding around to spray the walker with pebbles. An instant later, the truck sped away in a plume of dust that he could still see hovering above the oasis.

The walker stopped and rubbed his eyes in an attempt to clear them. Because that growing smudge on the horizon—that was from now, not before. For a moment, he wondered if it could be the same truck whose driver he'd frightened away before with his appearance. Some buried instinct warned him the man might be returning to mow him down or shoot him, leaving his body to the blistering sun and the scavengers that he'd sensed watching, following his movements with hopeful, hungry eyes.

At the thought of dying here, of finally stopping, he felt an odd blend of disappointment and relief. Resignation, too, since there wasn't a damned thing he could do about it, with nothing but flat, oddly familiar rangeland on either side and no strength left to flee. So instead, the walker kept putting one foot before the other, figuring that if he died, it might as well be one step closer to the mirage on the horizon...and his memory of the poolside beauty who'd meant everything to him before he'd somehow, he felt certain, driven her away.

It was a blue-eyed man who pulled up beside him minutes later in a newer-model truck, a dark-haired man who reminded him of someone. Maybe of himself, or at least the version of himself who'd swum through cool blue waters.

Taking off his straw cowboy hat, the driver jumped

down from the cab. Tall and muscular, he wore a rolled-sleeved cotton shirt, worn jeans and a single bead of perspiration, running from his temple to his jawline. Color draining from his tan face, he stared directly at the walker, searched his eyes with an intensity that made his heart hammer.

The walker took a step backward, glancing over his shoulder, his muscles coiling as he looked for an escape route.

"I told that fool pup of a cowhand to quit talking crazy," said the driver, unblinking as he stared, "telling me he'd seen a man who looked like—looked like my dead brother out here on our land. Then I cursed him for leaving some poor, lost stranger way out here on his own in this heat, without even offering a drink of water."

"You—have w-water?" The idea of it, the possibility spun from his dreams, was so powerful that he stumbled closer, forgetting his fear as trembling overtook him.

"Yeah, sure. Here you go, man." The driver reached back inside the truck and pulled out a plastic bottle beaded with condensation. He cracked open the sealed lid and handed it over.

The walker was so overwhelmed by the cold moisture in his hand that he barely noticed the uncertainty darting through the other man's eyes or the moisture gleaming in them.

"Ian, is it really you?" he asked, letting the question hang as the walker chugged down half the bottle.

When he started choking, the driver warned him, "Slow down. Slow down and take it easy. There's plenty more where that came from. Food and clean clothes back at the house, too."

His coughing over, the walker glugged down the rest

of the bottle. When he was finished, he peered suspiciously into the blue eyes. "Why?" he asked, searching the stranger for some agenda. "Why would you do all that for me?"

"Could be one of two good reasons. Either because I don't cotton to the idea of a stranger dying on my land. Or because you're a walking, talking miracle—my only brother, Captain Ian Rayford, come back from the dead."

Andrea Warrington stared down at the file her boss, retired army colonel Julian Ross, had handed her, her throat tightening the moment she read the name *Captain Ian Rayford.*

What she had to tell the man sitting behind the battered desk, his shirtsleeves rolled up and his tie loosened against the late summer heat, would be awkward enough under any circumstances. But despite the fifteen-year difference in their ages, Andrea had recently accepted the handsome forty-six-year-old's proposal, so bat-sized butterflies attempted to flap their way free of her stomach.

Telling herself that putting it off was no longer an option, she drew a deep breath and squared her shoulders, just as she would have advised the wounded vets she counseled here at the Marston unit of the Warriors-4-Life Rehabilitation Center. "I—I'm afraid I can't take this assignment, Julian. There's something I've been meaning to tell you about myself and Captain Rayford."

"Sit down, Andrea, please." He gestured toward one of the mismatched folding chairs in front of his desk, the rich bass of his voice warmed by a gentlemanly Southern accent. Six months after the ribbon cutting that had opened this donation-supported unit, they were still getting by with whatever castoffs they could scrounge, mainly because Julian, who had been named director shortly before the center's opening, insisted on using every penny of the funds raised to provide services for their growing roster of military veterans. Though many bore physical reminders of the ordeals they had endured, the majority had come to Warriors-4-Life to deal with the fallout of combat-related brain injuries or post-traumatic stress disorder. The workload kept Andrea, the center's one practicing psychologist, along with two counselors and a psychiatric nurse-practitioner who worked under her direction, hopping, but she didn't mind her packed days—not when she knew for a certainty that she was saving lives.

Besides, the crazy hours and emotional challenges had drawn her closer to the handsome older man who had started out as her boss before evolving into much more. She admired him; she respected him, but it was love that was making the words knot in her throat.

She claimed a seat where a rattletrap oscillating fan on the desk could swivel back and forth between them. "I think I mentioned to you I was engaged before," she admitted, the breeze blowing a strand of long, dark brown hair—an escapee from her clip—into her face. "It was one of those whirlwind affairs, everything moving at light speed."

She flushed, remembering the heat of it, the passion, how exciting it had felt to be caught up in something so out of her control. But thrilling as they might seem, whirlwinds had the potential to cause a lot of damage. The kind of heartbreak she'd sworn she would never risk again.

"It didn't take long for me to realize he was lying about his deployments. There were other disappearances as well, with no warning and no explanation. I couldn't deal with the uncertainty, so I broke it off."

A smile touched Julian's brown eyes like a warm breeze from his Savannah boyhood. He'd promised he would take her one day, to see the historic Victorian home where he'd grown up before it had passed out of the family. "Everyone has a past, Andrea. I didn't imagine you'd lived underneath a bell jar for thirty-one years before you'd met me."

"Yes, but bizarre as it might seem, it was this man, Ian. Captain Rayford. He was still just a lieutenant then, and I was working on my doctorate. I—I should've told you, I know, after the news broke that he was found alive."

For weeks following his return, the "Texas miracle" was all anyone could talk about on the morning shows and social media. While Ian himself refused all interviews, the army had been left scrambling to explain how one set of charred remains could have been mistaken for another after some overworked soldier in the military's mortuary center had failed to follow proper DNA procedures to identify the body.

"So why didn't you say something?" he asked. "Surely, you can't imagine I'd hold you accountable for any of the suspicions brought up about his escape from the terrorists holding him?"

"No, of course not. It's just…" Though she couldn't put an answer into words, she felt it in the warm flush that rose to her face, the aching heaviness in her chest.

"You still have feelings for him," Julian suggested, though his sharp, brown gaze seemed more curious than judgmental. "Is that what you're saying?"

"No, it's not that." She raised her hands, not wanting to hurt this good man's feelings. "It's only—when he was reported killed in action, it brought back a lot of memories. The good, along with the bad."

Her gaze dropped, avoiding his, but because she'd learned the hard way that lies of omission could be the worst of all, she forced herself to look up. "I cried a lot at night. For months, I cried for him." Even after she'd met Julian, she'd come to work some mornings with her eyes red and swollen. His unfailing kindness, his steadiness had planted the first seeds of healing in her.

"I'm sorry for your grief," he told her. "But I assure you that I understand it. Possibly better than you can imagine. You see, the army personnel who debriefed the captain passed on his full dossier with the referral. I saw your name listed on his contact list, to be notified in case he was killed in action."

The burning in her face intensified. "He must have added me two years ago, when we were still together." She still remembered the horrendous shock that had followed the knock at the front door of her apartment back in San Diego.

"That's not my point, Andrea. My point is, I feel certain—and the army psychologist I consulted is in full agreement on this—that your past connection to Ian Rayford could be the key to recovering his missing memories."

She shook her head. "You mean he's still suffering amnesia? Was he found to have a brain injury?"

"If you'll take a look at the file—" the fan swung around to ruffle Julian's short, bronze-colored hair, a crop of silver threaded through it "—you'll see that's not the case, though he does have some residual scarring. From the torture, they believe, in attempts to extract intelligence on US targets."

"But he was cleared of those suspicions," she was quick to say. "And anyway, after a soldier's captured, codes are changed, right? Sensitive locations scrambled?" She was aware American civilians working in a war zone office had died or disappeared soon after Ian's capture, but few details had been reported, and surely, the bombing of their building could not be laid at the feet of a man who had suffered heaven only knew what torments.

Julian nodded, but his brown eyes looked troubled. "Officially, he was absolved of any responsibility in the bombing and given a medical discharge. Considering the hero's welcome drummed up by that Rayford woman's story—"

"Jessie Layton is his brother Zach's wife, isn't she? The journalist?" Andrea narrowed her eyes, trying to get it straight in her mind, since she'd never met Ian's family. They'd been estranged for years, he'd told her, though he'd avoided going into details—something that should have raised another red flag. But then, Andrea had her family secrets, too, issues so painful they'd sent her into counseling when she was in her teens. The relief she'd gotten, the insight into the dynamics that had destroyed her family, had led her to pursue the study of psychology.

Julian nodded in answer to her question. "Cutting Captain Rayford loose, giving him the benefit of the doubt, was the only thing the military could do, especially since he was diagnosed as having dissociative amnesia as a result of torture."

Andrea lifted a brow. "Not to mention all the suffering the screwup over the body caused both his family and the other soldier's. What a PR nightmare that boondoggle's been."

"So I'm told," said Julian, "which brings us back to you."

Apprehension crawled over her skin like live ants. "Let Michael take him. Or Connor. He's a real pro, and the guys love that he's ex-military himself."

"Neither of the counselors will do, or Cassidy, either, for this case," Julian said, though as a psychiatric nurse-practitioner, Cassidy had both the experience and the ability to dispense any necessary medications. "You see, Captain Rayford has refused to come here. Refused to leave the family's ranch at all. Says he's had enough of shrinks poking through his head—"

"So you want to send me, a psychologist?"

"The man doesn't need or want a psychologist right now, but a friend, he might accept. And a trained friend, someone with your sensitivity, might find a way to break through. A way to help a man whose plight has drawn so much attention—and a way to help us, too, at Warriors-4-Life."

She folded her arms beneath her chest. "Really, Julian? That's what this is all about? The money?"

He sighed. "Come on, Andrea. You know I'm 100 percent focused on these soldiers. But as director, fund-raising is a big part of my job description, and if we don't get donations up before next quarter, we're going to have way bigger problems than a broken AC system."

Worry fluttered in her stomach. "I know we're working on a shoestring out here, but what do you mean, way bigger problems? We're not—tell me we're not in danger of shutting down already. We've barely gotten up and running, and more and more returning soldiers are applying for our help every day. They need us, desperately. Where else can they go, if they don't have places like this when their lives come crashing down around them? Who else will prepare them to reintegrate into their families and meaningful employment?"

He held up a hand to stop her. "You're preaching to the choir. There's no need to sell me on what we do. I never would've come aboard if I weren't 100 percent behind it."

"I know that. I do." Like everyone else who worked at Warriors-4-Life, Julian had accepted little more than the use of one of the center's Spartan housing units and a nominal salary in exchange for his sixty- to eighty-hour workweeks. He even donated a portion of his military retirement pay to the cause, saying he couldn't encourage others to do something he wasn't doing on his own. Inspired by his generosity, Andrea gave whenever she could, as well, despite the mountain of student loans she would probably still be paying into her dotage.

"Then don't look so shocked that I'm thinking practically. I have to. Otherwise, we'll have no choice but to scale back the number of young men and women we can assist—and reduce our staff levels, as well."

She gritted her teeth, thinking of how overworked all of them were already, how many sacrifices they had made. And the look in his eyes told her that if the cutbacks didn't solve the issue, the doors they'd fought so hard to open might be forever shuttered. What would happen to their clients, then, people like twenty-year-old Ty Dawson, who'd gone missing for hours just yesterday after a lawn mower had kicked up a stone and cracked a window. He was found shaking and hiding in the darkened corner of a storage closet.

"All right," she said. "I'll rearrange tomorrow morning's schedule and try to get back by—"

"Your schedule's cleared, for the time being. Michael, Cassidy, Connor and I will all pitch in while you're away."

"Away? What do you mean? It's, what, an hour or so from here to Rusted Spur? If I leave early, I'm sure I can be back by lunchtime to help cover the afternoon group sessions."

Julian shook his head. "For the next two weeks, you'll be staying at the ranch."

"Staying at the ranch? With my ex-fiancé? Are you serious? You won't— This won't worry you at all?"

She studied his face and caught the flicker of discomfort. But he quickly squared his shoulders and reclaimed his usual composure. The composure that had made her feel so safe.

"I'll admit I was hesitant at first. You know about my ex-wife, about what happened between us?"

Andrea nodded, remembering what he'd told her about a marriage in his twenties—and a wife who'd eased her loneliness with multiple affairs during his deployments. He'd spoken of it matter-of-factly, but she had seen the hurt, the vulnerability lurking behind his solemn brown eyes. And she'd sworn to herself she would be the wife that he deserved.

He reached across the desk and found her hand, then squeezed it. "I refuse to let it change me, let that pain turn me jealous and suspicious when you've done nothing to deserve it. When I could never imagine a consummate professional like yourself—a generous, decent woman— betraying what we have."

"Of course, I wouldn't." She'd learned her lessons young; she would never be her father. "Especially not for a man who broke my heart. But I will do my best to help him, just the way I'd help any other client who was hurting."

"Then it's settled," he answered with a nod. "I'll need you to log in and update your contact records daily, but I'm told there's wireless available."

"When have I ever forgotten my logs?" It was a protocol she frequently reminded the counselors to follow, since the portion of their funding received from government grants depended on the number of recorded contact hours. The case notes themselves, however, remained password protected, covered by patient confidentiality.

"Also," Julian said, "I thought you'd like to know that when Captain Rayford's family extended the invitation for you to come, they mentioned they'd set up a suite of rooms for your use."

"A *suite* of rooms, just for me?" It sounded like paradise, since her own quarters consisted of a single bedroom in the women's dormitory, where female staff and clients alike shared a communal bath and kitchen.

"Play your cards right, and I'll throw in some bubble bath." From across the desk, he winked at her, a gesture so at odds with his usual demeanor that it made her laugh with delight.

"Ooh la la." She waggled her brows at the man who'd asked her to keep their engagement under wraps for the time being, to avoid causing any suspicions of favoritism among the staff. And given that there was no way either of them could visit the other's room without drawing speculation, the physical side of their relationship had been largely confined to their imaginations—a situation that was growing more frustrating by the day. "But it'd be even better if you could join me in that bathtub."

He smiled. "With or without strategically placed bubbles?"

"Up to you, Colonel," she teased, standing when he left his chair and came around the desk.

He pulled her into a warm embrace. "I promise you, my darling, by the time you come back to me, I'll have figured out a way to break the news to the others. And after that, no more sneaking around like a couple of teenagers."

"In that case—" she smiled up into his brown eyes "—I promise you, I'll do everything I can think of to get Captain Rayford's memory back in record time."

Chapter 2

Funny what it was his mind chose to remember, Ian thought as he curried the palomino, a sturdy gelding known as Sundance. Though Ian had been told that he hadn't set foot on the ranch since the day of his high school graduation, he remembered the order of operations he'd been taught to the last detail: currycomb, then dandy brush, followed by the mane and tail brush and the hoof pick. He remembered to lay the saddle pad over the withers and slide it back so the golden hair would lie comfortably and to walk the horse a few steps before cinching up the saddle so it would be tight enough. He knew to mount from the left side, too, just as he could still not only ride but rope a calf or cut a heifer from the herd with ease.

Procedural, semantic and short-term memory intact, one of the army shrinks had written on his report, which meant that Ian also remembered the meaning of words and could acquire new information. But it had been the next part that disturbed him, the notation: *Retrograde biographical memory continues impaired—psychogenic origin likely due to emotional trauma.*

In other damned words, they figured him for some kind of nut job. Not a veteran who'd lost his memory due to the injuries he'd clearly suffered, judging from the scarring on his back, his arms and legs, but a head case too soft to handle the stress of the ambush that he'd been told had killed a fellow soldier, along with the captivity that followed. Insulted by their insinuations and sick of being poked and prodded, he had gone back to the ranch and vowed to stay there, with the people he was learning to accept as his family…slowly.

He led the horse out of the barn and into the bright September morning, happy that last night's shower had knocked down the dust and cooled the temperature. Zach kept telling Ian he didn't have to work like a hired hand to tackle any of the never-ending chores that kept the cattle ranch's wheels turning, but he found it far easier than staying in the house to be watched, fussed over and treated like a ticking time bomb by his mother or stuffed full of pastries by their cook, Althea, who apparently took it as her God-given duty to help him put back on the forty pounds his ordeal had cost him.

His older brother was easier to deal with, maybe because he'd served as a marine corps fighter pilot before his return to run the ranch following the false reports of Ian's death. Ian had found Zach steady, supportive and respectful of his privacy, but always there if he wanted to talk or ask questions. Along with Zach's journalist wife, Jessie, he did his best to keep their little girl, Eden, out of Ian's hair, though the rambunctious five-year-old was forever finding ways to corner him and wear him out with innocently awkward questions. Questions that he couldn't answer, for the most part, no matter how damned cute she and the pair of young Australian shepherds who followed her everywhere were about their interrogation.

Mounting up, he looked beyond the ranch's outbuildings and toward the open rangeland, where a herd of red-and-white cattle grazed off in the distance. Farther afield, he'd been told one could find the fresh drilling that marked the promising new natural gas find that had recently sent the family's fortunes soaring. But Ian left the worries about the operation and the money to Zach while he focused on the hard manual labor that was not only helping him recover his physical strength but would leave him exhausted by the day's end. Too exhausted, he hoped, for the disjointed nightmares that had been waking him several times a night. Like his past, their content was largely forgotten the moment he returned to himself. But that didn't keep him from racking his brain for hours, no matter how frustrating the attempts.

He nudged the palomino into an easy lope, eager for the freedom, the peace that he found only with the prospect of a day alone in the saddle. But it had barely lasted for an hour before he spotted a lone rider making his way toward him: Zach, aboard his big bay, Ace, irritation casting more shade on his expression than the wide brim of his hat.

As his brother's mount clattered to a stop, Ian sucked a breath through his clenched teeth and raised a palm to hold off the complaint he knew was coming. "Sorry, man. I'm sorry. I did it again, didn't I?"

"Apologize to Mama, not me," Zach told him. "Do you have any idea how panicky she gets when you take off without a word to anybody? Jessie thought she was going to have a stroke when she found your bed empty after you didn't show for breakfast. Mama broke down, asking if you were really still dead, if she'd dreamed all that part about how you'd come back home."

Ian screwed shut his eyes and blew out a long breath, hating himself for causing her more suffering. "But you knew where I was, right? You told her, didn't you?"

"I told her you were sure to be around, yeah. But the fact is, Ian, I got lucky figuring out where you were because you didn't tell me, either."

"You could've called instead of riding all the way out…" But as he felt his pocket for the fancy new smartphone his brother had bought him, Ian's mouth went dust dry. "Oh, shoot. The damned cell—"

"Works a lot better when you remember to take it with you, bonehead."

Ian opened his eyes and faced his older brother's disappointment. "I know I screwed up. But I swear, I'll do better."

"Yeah, you damned well will." Zach's glare faded, his blue eyes softening. "Listen, man. I know what it's like, going from a place where you have only yourself to think of, yourself and your mission. But things are different now. You're part of a family again, with people who care, who worry about you, who want to help you finally come home."

"I *am* home," Ian insisted, the edge in his voice making his mount shuffle and toss his mane. Clutching the reins tightly to keep Sundance in hand, he added, "Against all odds, I made it."

The government's investigators had tracked his north-bound progress through Mexico and into Texas, where he'd hitchhiked, walked and at one point trailed "coyotes" smuggling their human cargo across the border during his months-long odyssey. There had been some speculation about how Ian might have gotten out of the Middle East and into Mexico, but he'd been unable to contribute anything beyond a fragmented memory of himself clinging to a coarse scrap of threadbare blanket in the dark hold of a cargo ship.

"You think you've made it, brother," Zach said, "but I'm telling you, you've still got a ways to go. Which is why you're coming back with me right now, to meet our visitor."

Ian's gut clenched. "I told you, no more shrinks. No counselors. None of Mama's preachers, either, here to save my lost soul. This range, this work, is the only salvation I need."

Zach gazed out over the undulating golden waves, over a land that looked flat to those who didn't know the deep furrows that could lead a man to its hidden places. "I remember a time when you couldn't wait to get the hell off this land."

Old resentment squeezed in Ian's chest. Because since returning, he had remembered enough fragments from their upbringing to resurrect some old grievances. "You should talk. You took off before I did. Left me here, with *him*."

At the mention of their father, Zach's shoulders fell and his gaze drifted. It served as a reminder that some of the memories Ian had recovered would be better off forgotten.

"I know, and I'm sorry, bro," Zach said. "Sorry for leaving you and Mama both behind. I was just trying to survive those years without ending up in prison. Because

I would've damned well killed the son of a bitch if I'd stayed one more day."

Ian nodded, understanding the same desperation that had driven him away from their father's brand of torture as soon as he'd been able. Like Zach, he'd left their mother here to face it, since she'd refused to admit to what her husband was, much less abandon the material comforts and social status she'd enjoyed as a Rayford. As sorry as he felt for the suffering she'd endured when he'd been believed dead, Ian still hadn't entirely forgiven her for refusing to protect him and his brother back when it might have mattered.

But there was nothing to be gained by treading that old minefield, and he quickly changed the subject. "I'll apologize for scaring Mama. I'll remember my phone next time. But I won't be coming back with you now, not unless you tell me who's there waiting."

"I'll tell you this much. It's a woman. A woman from your past."

Ian frowned, wondering which past his brother meant: the one he couldn't bear to think of, or the dark, erotic glimmers that invaded his dreams every night.

Andrea had known Ian grew up on a working cattle ranch in North Texas, but she'd had no idea that he'd come from money. Maybe she'd been projecting the hand-me-downs and frequent moves that had defined her own hardscrabble upbringing or maybe she'd judged Ian by his rare comments about living hand to mouth after going out on his own right out of high school, but the ranch itself, especially the opulent white mansion at its center, convinced her she'd had it wrong. As did the fact that a heavyset woman with her pinned-back gray hair and a starched uniform wheeled out a real, honest-to-goodness tea cart with a silver pot and baskets of delicate confections to the fussy formal living room where she waited while Ian's mother, Nancy Rayford, did her best to pick Andrea's brain.

"So, dear," said the neatly dressed, silver-haired woman over the gold rim of her teacup, "you were saying, you met my son in California?"

Andrea didn't answer, too distracted by the heat rising to her face as the maid offered her some cookies. "Th-thank you very much. These are lovely." Andrea chose a chocolate-centered square to be polite, nearly choking on the thought of how her mother, who had waited on more than a few pampered rich ladies in her day, might have looked a lot like "Miss Althea" had she lived.

The maid nodded and excused herself, leaving Mrs. Rayford to repeat her question.

Andrea nodded. "Sorry. Yes, we met on a country road not far outside of San Diego. I was out riding when the chain came off my bike and sent me flying." She shivered in the air-conditioning, remembering the moment she'd gone over the handlebars. "Fast as I was moving, it's a wonder I didn't split my skull along with my helmet." As it was, she'd been a bloody mess, with the frame of a bike she'd scrimped and saved for for two years bent so badly it was never again race-worthy.

Mrs. Rayford frowned. "You don't mean to tell me you were riding one of those noisy *motorcycles*, do you?"

Andrea nearly laughed aloud at the horror souring the woman's prim face, as if a female on a motorcycle would have been the scandal of the century. "Not a motorcycle, no. A racing bike, for the triathlons I used to compete in before that crash. I tore up my knee pretty badly in the fall. If it hadn't been for Ian pulling off the road to help me, I could've lain there for a long time before anyone else came along."

She remembered the moment she'd first seen the tall, dark-haired man jumping out of his SUV and racing toward her, gorgeous as any guy she'd ever met in real life, but in a masculine, clean-cut way that left actors and male models in the dust. Hurting as she'd been, she'd still felt sucker punched by his blue eyes, the intensity and concern in them as real as anything she'd ever seen.

"He was always a bighearted boy," his mother reminisced. "Always dragging home strays."

Jolted by her words, Andrea wondered if she'd just joined their ranks in his mother's eyes, if the woman somehow saw through the tan slacks and coral shell she wore with a light jacket, through the fake gold earrings and the thrift-store beige pumps and all the way back to the scabby-kneed, motherless girl she had once been. Telling herself that couldn't be, that Nancy Rayford only knew her as Zach's former fiancée, a psychologist who happened to work an hour away in Marston, Andrea said, "He didn't exactly drag me home, but he did drive me to the ER."

Behind her, the floor creaked, and she turned to face the man she'd met that long-ago day. Though his face was leaner and his tan deeper, she recognized those deep blue eyes and came to her feet at once. But his eyes were different, too, she realized, haunted by events he could not consciously remember.

"Ian," she managed, pulse revving as she fought an instinct to run to the man she'd once loved and throw her arms around him. "I'm so glad to see you, so relieved that you're…"

He stared into her face, his gaze as unreadable as it was disconcerting. Her stomach fluttered in response, and she felt an outbreak of tiny beads of perspiration.

"He won't remember you, of course," his mother announced. "He didn't know any of us here at all, not for days and days—"

"Andrea?" he asked, taking two steps closer. Close enough that she saw his color deepen and recognized what looked like pure relief wash over him. "Andie, is it really you?"

Andie, he had called her, using the nickname no one else did...

Before she could react, his mother scolded, "You'll need a shower before you come in on the good furniture. I can smell the horse on you from here."

Paying her no mind, Ian took two more steps and claimed Andrea, pulling her into his arms and kissing her for all he was worth.

The connection arced through every nerve ending, raising each fine hair and jolting her with memories of how incredibly well their bodies worked together. The searing contact made her ache for more, forgetting all the ways they'd wounded one another.

Forgetting, at least for a few moments, the other woman who stood gaping at them and the man Andrea herself had so recently promised to marry, a man whose face she struggled to recall.

Finally, she pulled away, a red-hot tide of embarrassment scorching her face. Shaking her head, she stammered, "I—I'm sorry. S-sorry, Ian, but what you're remembering—that was two years ago. It's been a long time since we—"

"I remember the trip we took together to Key West in

Florida," he said, the words coming in a rush as she took two steps back. "There was a little bed-and-breakfast, and you wore—there was this blue bikini. I've been dreaming of that trip, of all that color, of you for so long now."

The professional in her noticed the way his eyes had dilated and the light that had come into them, extinguishing the pain she'd first glimpsed. As much as she hated dimming that excitement, she told herself that letting him go on believing would be crueler.

"You're right," she said. "What you remember really happened. But afterward, so did a lot of other things. We're not—we're not together anymore, not in that way. But that doesn't mean I don't care about what's happened to you. It doesn't mean that I can't be your friend."

"We're not…we're not together anymore?"

Confusion shifted through his handsome features, followed by a sorrow so profound it reminded her of the day she'd told him they were finished. *Of course*, she realized, because for him, it was happening again right now, the boom lowered only seconds after he'd consciously accessed the memory of one of the happiest times of their eight-month relationship, a time before she'd grown aware that it was all built on a raft of lies.

"I'm sorry," she said, meaning it—and acutely aware of the disapproval emanating from his mother. She couldn't say whether it was because he'd made the sexual side of their relationship so obvious or because Andrea had so clearly broken her son's heart, but she knew one thing for certain: the woman didn't like her.

Andrea shook it off, reminding herself her visit was about Ian's well-being, his healing, not her comfort level. "We've been apart for two years," she said. "I have a new fiancé."

"So we're engaged—or we were?" He shook his head, offering the wry smile she'd always found so irresistibly disarming. "I must've been an idiot, letting a woman like you go."

She smiled back at him, pretending not to hear the fresh grief behind his words. "Your brother thought that we might visit for a while and talk. He thought that seeing me might help you remember."

Ian snorted. "Well, at least you're a damn sight better looking than any of those shrinks they keep pushing at me."

She sighed but realized there was no way around what was sure to be another troubling disclosure. "Do you remember why we went to Key West? What we were celebrating?"

He shook his head.

"You surprised me with the trip after I completed my doctorate."

"So you're a doctor? Like an MD?" He winked at his mother. "I always did go for the smart girls, at least, the pretty ones."

"I'm a psychologist," Andrea admitted.

He laughed, his smile turning bitter. "So that explains why you're here. One more shrink to poke around my skull. Tell me, are you working for the army these days, or the Department of Defense?"

"Neither, Ian. I'm here because I care about you. And your brother, Zach, really did speak to my boss at the center for—"

He waved it off. "I don't give a damn who sent you."

His mother looked up sharply over the gilded rim of her teacup. "Language, young man."

"I just want you out of here, right now," he finished, anger and betrayal competing in his voice.

"Please, Ian," Andrea said. "I've come a long way to see you."

"Not half as far as I've come to be left the hell alone."

With that, he showed her his back as he stalked toward the stairway. A few steps up, he paused and turned to look down at his mother, his voice gentling. "Sorry for the language, and I'm sorry I upset you earlier. I'll remember next time to let you know when I have plans."

"It's all right, Ian. It's just—" she answered nervously "—I do worry so about you, with everything that's happened."

"I'm headed upstairs for that shower now. But while I'm gone, would you please show *Dr.* Warrington the door."

On his way upstairs, he nearly ran into a strawberry-blonde woman close to Andrea's and Ian's own age as she was heading down, a purse over her shoulder and a set of keys in hand.

"Excuse me, Jessie," he said, his voice tight with impatience as he angled his way past her and the muscular black-and-tan Rottweiler at her side.

"Sure thing, Ian." Jessie raised a speculative brow as he charged upstairs. At the bottom of the steps, she paused, glancing back up toward the landing at the sound of a door slamming. "Is he mad that I sent Zach to find him?"

"I'm afraid he's upset with me," Andrea admitted as she walked up to the woman and offered her hand. "Andrea Warrington."

"The psychologist, right, and ex—the old friend." Jessie shook her hand in greeting, looking up to meet Andrea's gaze. "Hi. I'm Jessie Layton."

"Jessie *Rayford* now," her mother-in-law corrected, that same disapproval in her tone.

"I thought we'd had this discussion. Several times, as I remember." An undercurrent of annoyance rippled beneath an attempt at pleasantry. "Since I write under my maiden name—"

"But you're not writing now, Jessie. This is a social situation, and as Zach's wife and Eden's mother, I'd expect you'd want to—" Nancy Rayford cut herself off as the Rottweiler interposed herself between the women, as if to ward off her harsh words. Scowling, she added, "Really. That animal."

"Gretel, *platz*," Jessie said, and at the command—which Andrea thought might be in German—the dog dropped into the down position. "Sorry, but whenever she perceives a threat—"

"So what happens if you have an argument with my son?"

Jessie smiled at the Rottweiler. "Big traitor usually takes his side."

Eager to defuse the tension, Andrea cleared her throat. "I read the article you wrote on Ian's return. It was incredibly well done, very moving."

Jessie ducked a nod, the relief in her green eyes making it clear she appreciated the diversion. "Thanks, Andrea. It was important. To get the word out quickly, I mean. Ian might not remember why, but he's pretty paranoid these days. When he first came, he worried that someone might come take him away in the dark of night if the public didn't hear he'd come back. He's pretty short-tempered these days, too. But I guess you've already found that out for yourself."

"Please, Jessie," Nancy Rayford said. "He's been through so much. And you're making him sound like some sort of madman."

"I promise you, I'll never think of him that way," Andrea assured her. "I work with returning vets. A lot of them have anger issues, and it must be even more confusing when he doesn't consciously recall the reason why."

"It was those horrible terrorists," Mrs. Rayford whispered, tears shining in her eyes. "Heaven only knows what they did to my poor boy for almost a year. When I think of how he's suffered…"

"It must be hard for you, too." Andrea looked from one woman to the other in an effort to remind them of their common ground. "Not knowing what might set him off, not knowing what will help him."

Jessie gave her a look that seemed to weigh and judge her. "*You'll* help him. I see that."

"It's a shame that Ian won't allow it," her mother-in-law said, talking right over her. "But you heard him a moment ago. You'll have to leave, Miss Warrington."

"But I just—" Andrea started, more concerned about the swift dismissal than she was the omission of the "Dr." before her name.

"He's been through enough. We mustn't upset him."

Jessie looked down at the small, frail woman, the impatience in her expression melting into compassion. "You want him to get better, don't you?"

"I do, more than anything."

"Then can't you stick with the plan we made, you and Zach and me?"

The older woman hesitated. "I only want to be a better

mother. I swear I do, but…she *confuses* him." With this pronouncement, she pinned Andrea with an accusatory gaze. "He thinks she's still his fiancée."

This time, however, Andrea heard the fear behind the woman's words, the terror of losing her son all over again. "He knows the truth now, and if he forgets it, I'll remind him…gently, carefully. I promise you that. Believe me, I don't want to hurt him any more than you do. But I also don't want to leave him in pain the way he is."

She knew the grim statistics too well, had seen up close in her work how many returning soldiers suffering untreated PTSD chose to end their lives. Or to obliterate their pain with drugs and alcohol, which often amounted to a slower form of suicide.

Ian's mother hesitated, but for Jessie, this was apparently good enough.

"Let me show you to your room," she said. "Then, if you want, you can ride along with me to pick up Eden from her playdate, and I'll fill you in on everything you'll need to know about this family."

Andrea didn't miss the panic that flashed through Nancy Rayford's blue eyes. But for the moment, Andrea pretended not to see it as she took up Jessie on her offer and followed her to the wing that housed the mansion's guest quarters.

Still, she couldn't help but wonder, *What is it Ian's mother is so afraid I'll find out about the Rayfords? And how can I enlist this frightened woman's help to save her son?*

When he couldn't convince his brother, Jessie or even his pushover of a mother to send the shrink packing, Ian decided instead to ignore Andrea's presence. It was a hell of a lot easier said than done, though, since his mind kept replaying the warmth of her curves when he had pulled her into his arms and the strength of the connection he'd felt coursing through him that moment their lips met. The only way he could manage, could keep his eyes from locking on to every move she made, was by avoiding her as much as possible.

Over the past two days she hadn't made it any easier, "happening" upon him whenever he came inside and pretending to be no more than a *concerned friend*. But he'd brushed her off in a hurry and retreated to his room each time, not giving a damn about the look of disappointment on her gorgeous face.

What difference did it make anyway? Whether or not he ever spoke to her, she was sure to get paid for her efforts. He was a job to her, or at best some pet project, a screwed-up loser she'd dumped so she could ride off into the sunset with a guy whose brains weren't scrambled eggs.

This morning, it was the sunrise that he planned to ride off into after leaving a note in the ranch office, a space more like a studio apartment, with its own seating area, kitchenette and a small bath where Zach could wash up after getting dirty with the livestock. His brother had taken the opportunity to expand the office, which had been built into a corner of the barn after an arsonist had burned down the entire structure last year. Ian knew his family had gone through a rough stretch, a time of grief compounded by intense fear and worry, but at least some good had come of it, if his brother's relationship with Jessie was anywhere near as solid as it looked to Ian. Though yesterday he'd overheard them squabbling over Jessie's "scaring the liver out of him," as Zach had put it, with her refusal to share details of the new exposé she was working on, it was clear they loved each other deeply, and they had fun together, too.

Seeing how they worked as a team with Eden and how much joy the little girl, who'd started school just last week, brought them struck Ian with a sense of loss—and anger, sometimes, creeping up on him when he didn't expect it—for the life he'd been missing out on, a life centered on a family he'd never even known he wanted. Or maybe that wasn't true. He couldn't say for certain these days. Along with his memory, he'd lost so much more, including a true sense of who he was.

He left a brief note on his brother's desk, grateful that Zach would be running later than usual this morning since it was his turn to drive Eden into town for school. If he were here, Ian knew, there'd be another lecture and maybe an argument like yesterday's, when Ian had told his brother what he could do with his advice to quit acting like a stubborn jerk and give Andrea a chance.

He did miss his brother's coffee though, he thought as he eyed the fancy espresso machine longingly. But no way was he taking a chance on messing with Zach's prize possession, which had enough buttons and levers to rival the fighter jets he'd once piloted.

Ian thought of heading back inside to cadge a quick mug of Althea's simpler brew—and maybe a couple of his favorite raspberry thumbprint cookies—before he rode out, but that would bring the risk of running into Andrea since she'd been getting up earlier each day in an attempt to catch him alone. He felt idiotic sneaking around his own home—and more aggravated than ever with her for forcing him into it.

Which is why he swore under his breath when he saw

her standing by the hitching post, next to his saddled palomino. She held two insulated travel mugs, one of which she offered with that gorgeous smile of hers, so white it competed with the glorious September dawn. Sleek and straight, her dark brown hair had been brushed back, with a clip keeping the front sections out of those long-lashed hazel eyes he'd always loved.

"Peace offering," she said, looking more casual today in a pair of jeans that drew his eye to other favorite parts of her anatomy. Places he'd awakened hot and hard from dreams of touching, tasting and claiming as his own again.

When he reached for the mug, she didn't let go, locking in on him with a take-no-prisoners gaze instead.

"Didn't realize there'd be strings attached," he said, looking at her almost straight on, since she wore a pair of riding boots that brought her to within a couple of inches of his own six-four.

"Life is a series of negotiations, Ian. The question is, what will you bring to the table?"

He lowered his hand and shook his head. "Thanks for bringing out the coffee, but I prefer mine black, not tarted up with a bunch of shrink talk. Or any talk at all, as far as that goes."

"Then how 'bout if we ride instead? Just ride and see how that goes?"

He chuckled to himself, getting the point now of the boots and jeans. "You really think you're up to riding fences with me all day?"

"I want to try."

"Well, maybe I don't want to play nursemaid to some greenhorn. Or ride back for a ladies' room when we're a couple hours out." The moment the words were out of his mouth, he felt a stab of regret. He *was* being a jerk, he realized, punishing her for... Had she broken up with him, or was he the one who'd left her? When he reached back for the memory, he found only a black fog of loss and pain—that, and the nameless anxiety that stalked him day and night.

There's something important you're forgetting. Something so big, the weight of it will crush you flat when it finally comes.

"You don't know what you want, Ian. That's the problem. But I might be able to help you with that."

"I want to be left to my work, alone. And that's not gonna change, not even if you start staying up all night to try to catch me before I ride out."

"I'm coming with you," she insisted.

"Do you even know how to saddle a horse? Or where we keep the tack?"

She shifted uncomfortably. "Well, no. I was hoping you could help with that part."

"But you've ridden before? I see you've got the boots for it."

Her cheeks reddened. "Well, actually, Jessie was nice enough to lend me these. Turns out we wear the same shoe size. And she's tied up doing some research for a story she's been working on, so she told me I could take her horse, too. Um, Princess, I think her name is?"

He felt a tug at the corner of his mouth. "My five-year-old niece named her, which means she could've done a lot worse, considering that Eden calls the barn cat Fizzy Fuzzbutt."

"So you *do* still smile," Andrea said. "In a nice way, I mean. Haven't seen that for a long while." Emotion rippled through her words, *real* emotion as the mask of compassionate professionalism slipped a little. "I've really missed that, Ian. Missed the man I knew."

"That man's gone forever."

She nodded, her eyes somber. "You're right, I'm afraid. Experience changes people. Even experiences you're not ready to remember."

"I'm ready. More than ready. I just— It's gone, no matter what I do. No matter how hard I try." He shook his head, his sore fist curling—the same fist that had punched through the wall of his bedroom in frustration. "What the hell is wrong with me?"

"I don't think anyone has all the answers. In a lot of ways the mind's still the same uncharted wilderness it was in Freud's day. But I may have a few insights for you…if you'd like to hear them."

His knee-jerk reaction was to shut her down, to say *hell, no.* But something in the way she'd looked at him in that single, honest moment had touched off a yearning to see more of the real Andrea, the same woman who still lived in his dreams.

Besides that, he was getting sick of himself, of the way he had been acting. And if she knew something that might change that…would it really hurt so much to try?

He reached out for the coffee, their fingers brushing as he took it. Her skin felt so soft and tender beneath his calluses. So warm.

Taking a sip of the dark brew, he was relieved to find it black and bitter.

When he murmured his thanks, she shrugged. "I remembered how you took it."

"As opposed to yours…right?" he asked, as an image of her pouring cream into a porcelain mug came out of nowhere. She'd been wearing a loose white robe, her hair a jumble around her shoulders. Her lips were puffy and her smile warm, her eyes misted with a contentment that told him they'd just made love that morning.

A sense of loss sent a pang through the hollow of his chest. Of all the people the government could have sent to see him—and he felt sure they were behind this, somehow—why did they have to torture him with her?

"You're right," she confirmed, smiling sheepishly. "Two sugars and real cream whenever I can get it. I still eat pretty healthy, but I'm hopeless on that front."

"I'll saddle your horse, Andie—"

"Please, call me Andrea. All right?"

Ignoring her, he finished. "If you'll agree to wear a riding helmet. Horses can be dangerous enough when a person knows her way around 'em."

"So if I agree, you'll take me?"

"Only because I want to get my brother off my back about it. Well, that and to see how you walk tomorrow morning." Ian smiled, figuring it would be no hardship to watch the sway of her hips under any circumstances.

She winced and said, "Oh, boy. I haven't ridden very much, but I do remember that part."

"It only lasts a few days. Then you'll get used to it. Or die."

"You are teasing about that last part. Aren't you?"

He snorted. "Right. You'll only feel like dying."

He left her with a smile and went to retrieve Jessie's mare.

Chapter 3

The pinto was pretty enough to lead a parade, with bold black patches over brilliant white and a full and flowing mane and tail. But she seemed to have a mind of her own, a quality she demonstrated when Andrea tried to hold her back after she had mounted.

"You don't need to haul on the reins like that," Ian told Andrea, amusement written on his face. His own mount's golden hide gleamed in the early-morning sunlight, the well-muscled animal as handsome as his rider. "Her mouth is sensitive."

"Oh, am I hurting her? Should I— What do I do to keep her from running off with me?"

"Loosen your fingers, for starters, and grip her body with your knees, not your hands."

Embarrassed to be caught holding on to the saddle horn, she gave the reins a few inches of slack. But inside, her muscles quivered, ready to bail if Princess took a notion to gallop away.

Instead, the pinto exhaled, sounding more relieved than about to race away, and Andrea found the courage to tuck an irksome stray lock back up beneath the riding helmet and out of her eyes.

"That's a little better," said Ian. "Now breathe deeply, from way down in the bottom of your belly. And ease up on the reins a little more. Like that, yes. Now move them both to one hand. All you'll need to do is lay the reins on her neck, to the right to turn right, to the left for left, just like I'm doing here. See?"

She was grateful when he demonstrated, his amusement giving way to patience as he took her through the nudges, clicks and reining that he claimed would be enough to get her started.

As he expertly guided his mount and closed the paddock gate behind them, he eyed her critically. "We'll still have to work on your seat."

"I'll bet you say that to all the girls." Her breath caught as she reminded herself that the light teasing, the innuendo, was no longer appropriate between them.

When he laughed, though, she decided it was worth it. Worth easing her professional demeanor to help him relax around her.

"Hardly," he answered as they headed for the range, riding side by side, "but mostly because the only girls I see around here are married, five years old or my mother."

"What about Miss Althea? And there must be maids, I'm guessing?" Judging from the size of the house, it would take a team to clean it.

"Miss Althea'd crack me upside the head with a wooden spoon if she ever caught wind I was thinking about her or the maids' seats. And you're the first visitor we've had staying here since…" The spark in his blue eyes dimmed. "Since I…"

"Since you've been back?" she prompted.

She saw his throat work as he swallowed, caught his haunted look as he nodded in answer.

They rode in silence for a while, the creaking of the saddles and the clopping of the horses' hooves the only conversation. She fought back her impatience to get started with her counseling, to finish this job and head back to Warriors-4-Life, where the lines between the past and present didn't blur like hoofprints in the wind. But she reminded herself that Ian's healing was what mattered and that pushing him too quickly would only shut him down again. So instead, she took a deep breath, forcing herself to enjoy the mildness of the morning sunshine and reminding herself that the ability to wait and to listen was worth twice as much as anything a mental health professional could ever say.

She was lost in thought when Ian told her, "We'll pick up and catch the fence line I've been checking about a half mile up ahead."

"How can you know where anything is? It's like the surface of an ocean. I don't see anything but grass."

"That's because you haven't learned to really look yet, to see it like the horses or the deer or the coyotes. A lot of what's out here lies beneath the surface. There are gullies and old streambeds, hidden groves of trees and cow paths."

She looked around, still seeing nothing, then turned in the saddle and realized with a start that she'd lost track of the mansion and the ranch outbuildings, too. How was that even possible, if the land was as flat and featureless as her senses tried to tell her? "Guess you have to be born to this land. I'm so turned around, I have no idea of the way back."

"I can teach you," he assured her. "Show you, so you can always find your way back home again."

"Like you did…" she said quietly, so quietly that she wasn't certain he had heard her until she marked the way his shoulders stiffened.

"There," he said, pointing to two tufts that were a brighter green than the mostly golden grasses. "Those are the upper limbs of cottonwoods we're heading toward. They're actually good-size trees—and you see the notch between them where the creek's eroded a ravine?"

"So you go by the color of the treetops?"

He nodded. "And the time of year. Whenever you see that shade this late in the season, you know you're close to flowing water—cottonwoods usually crowd the creek beds, and the cattle like to lie in the shade beneath them."

"Sounds like an oasis."

"Oasis…" he echoed, frowning over the word as if it had stirred some dark association. Before she could decide whether to follow up with a question, he added, "It can be until a storm rips through and sends a flash flood roaring though that ravine. Then it's a damned death trap, those high walls hemming you in, heaven only knows who looking down on your location."

Andrea's stomach tensed as instinct warned her he was referring to a harsher territory. Did he himself even know what he was doing, or was she hearing from that part of him still wandering through foreign lands among those who meant to kill him, a part of him still desperate to get home?

"Thank goodness it doesn't look like rain, then." She

gestured toward the thin silvery wisps painted over the blue sky, her need to reassure him stronger than her desire to draw him out. "And no one for miles around."

"No one," he repeated, his blue eyes unfocused until he shook off whatever reverie had gripped him. "Right. Of course, you're right. Our nearest neighbor's a half-day's ride, and I always check the forecast. Every single day before I ride out."

"You used to like surprises," she said, remembering how she'd always been the one who'd wanted things locked down and certain. Remembering how she hadn't been able to deal with it when he couldn't give the security she craved.

"Not anymore, I don't."

Something in his tone had her feeling a little skittish as they rode single file down into the ravine. The narrow, crumbling walls seemed to close in on her, even after Ian stopped and pointed out a low rock outcrop behind them that marked the way back to the mansion.

Soon, however, Ian eased her worry, straightening in his saddle and leading the way with the natural air of confidence she had been drawn to from the first time she'd met him. Her faith in his leadership was soon rewarded when the ravine opened to a green and grassy hollow bisected by a swift but shallow creek splashing over rocks. The air cooled as they continued downhill, riding beneath the spreading arms of the cottonwoods and provoking a symphony of morning birdsong.

Mooing to protest the invasion, cattle rose from the hollow they'd claimed as a resting place and trotted along the barbed-wire fence line on the other side of the creek.

"It's beautiful," she said, marveling at the hidden world he'd shown her.

"Beautiful and a pain, too, sometimes. Cows are always using those fence posts to scratch whatever itches—if they're not pushing 'em over, it's some thunderstorm that's washed them out. Look, there's one now that needs attention." Dismounting in one smooth motion, he used rock from the creek bottom to brace a tilted post.

"Want some help there?" she asked, though she wasn't entirely sure she could get back on her horse without a mounting block.

"I've got it covered. Just relax and enjoy the view."

She didn't have to be told twice, her gaze seeking out one singer and then following the progress of a pair of bright red wings flitting among branches. She tracked the movement until she was distracted by what looked like the metallic glint of something moving above them on the hillside. Something that didn't belong.

She stood in the stirrups and leaned to the right, trying to see it through the branches. "What's that? I saw something move. There." Though she'd lost sight of the movement, she pointed in the direction she'd last seen it.

He looked up from the strand of barbed wire he'd been tightening, a pair of pliers in hand. "What? You mean a bird?" he asked. "Or maybe a—"

She shook her head. "Something man-made, I think. A windshield, maybe, or something metal. Could someone be—"

He swore and rushed at her, his movement so abrupt the pinto shied away from his reach.

"Get down!" He closed in, grabbing at her leg. "Off the horse now. Gun!"

"No, Ian," she said, recognizing the panic ripping through his voice, the glazed eyes seeing a time and place she knew was as real to him as this one. Clearly, he had tipped into a flashback, something she had witnessed so many times in clients. "It was only a reflection, I'll bet, maybe some piece of trash blowing in the—"

"Gun, damn it!" This time when he lunged, he caught her belt from behind, and she screamed as he pulled her down. Her terror echoed with the horses' whinnies as they bolted for the ravine's entrance, the clatter of their hoofbeats followed by a shattering boom.

Lightning strike, she thought as Ian caught her in his strong arms and started dragging her toward the shaded hollow where the cattle had lain. She'd heard of bolts from the blue, even on the clearest days.

The second blast convinced her she was wrong, the loud *plunk* as the post Ian had been working on exploded. Someone was really shooting, firing on them here and now and not in Ian's imagination. Had some out-of-season hunter mistaken them for game?

"No!" she shouted. "Don't shoot at us! We're down here!"

Ian clapped a hand over her mouth and ordered, *"Quiet. Now,"* through clenched teeth. One arm around her waist, he hauled her forward. Already knocked askew, her riding helmet fell as another shot echoed through the creek bottom. Grit spattered the back of her leg from where another bullet drilled the ground behind them, right where she'd been standing a half second earlier.

As her survival instincts kicked in, Andrea quit fighting Ian. Because whether or not this nightmare was rooted in his missing year inside the war zone, there was no denying it could kill them in the here and now.

His heart thundered in his chest, but Ian's mind dropped into mission mode as he guided the civilian with him under branches and around rocks. Because the civilian *was* the mission, her safety paramount in his mind, no matter how confused he was to have Andrea here with him.

Hadn't he left her behind in the peace and safety of Southern California? And hadn't she left him, too, a memory slicing through the darkness like a shard of broken glass, saying that she wanted another kind of life, a life without his secrets? So it made no sense that he was half leading and half dragging her here across this shallow creek, in a place where he used to hide out when his old man got that dangerous look in his eyes. But with no time to stop and think it through, Ian accepted this bizarre tangle of the half-remembered like another of his convoluted nightmares.

He searched the deepest shadows, focused on finding the one spot where he knew Andrea would be safe. A few steps beyond the water, he pointed out a horizontal shelf of weathered rock that had been undercut by past flooding. Partly filled in by damp pebbles, it would be a tight squeeze on her hands and knees, but if she could wedge herself in that space, she would be well hidden from the person up top with what sounded like a rifle.

"Crawl under there, where he won't see you."

"Down there? In that hole, you mean?" Her eyes were huge with disbelief.

He nodded. "Back yourself in, and don't come out, no matter what you hear or see."

"What about you? There's no room for both of—"

"Just do it, Andrea, and I'll come back for you. I swear to you, I will."

Their gazes locked, his blue with her hazel. And in that fraction of a second, some understanding passed between them. Face pale with terror, she blew out a shaky breath.

"You'd better," she whispered, grabbing handfuls of his shirt, "because if you leave me out here all alone, I swear to you, Ian, I will… Hunt. You. Down."

Dire as their situation was, he grinned at her bravado, then ducked his head to briefly touch his lips to hers.

Shock mingling with confusion on her beautiful face, she took two steps back and then crouched to do as he'd asked, crinkling her nose as she backed into the dank space. "There'd better not be spiders in here, especially those ones with the nasty, hairy legs."

"You'll be just fine," he assured her, not wanting to mention that a scorpion encounter was a lot more likely.

Still able to see her eyes, he dragged a tree branch to disguise the opening and moved off without another word. Stooping to palm some stones, he hurled them farther downstream, setting off a clatter.

The sniper didn't take the bait, probably wanting to get a visual before wasting another bullet. Or maybe he'd decided to cut his losses and get out, now that he had lost the element of surprise.

Whichever was the case, Ian zigzagged up the steep hillside, his progress as silent as the animals so often drawn here by the water. When he heard the deep thrum of an engine, he picked up his pace, not wanting to miss a glimpse at the SOB who'd tried to shoot them here, on his family's spread.

Remembering his brother, Ian paused and pulled the phone out of his pocket—the phone that he had, thank God, at last remembered to both charge and bring along. But down in this damned ravine, it was showing zero bars—no service. He tried sending a quick text, but it just sat in the outbox.

Jamming the cell back in his pocket, he continued his climb. With every stop, he fought to hold on to his focus, but his mind kept slipping backward, toward a past that had the blue sky above him and the brush before him fading to the ink-stained silhouettes of buildings along a blackout-dark street, where he craned his neck to see a minaret against a star-strewn sky. The crescent-moon shape at its top marked it as a mosque. He breathed in the dense smells of a city, the cooking smoke tinged with exotic spices, the animal dung mixed with burning sandalwood. A reminder that life mingled with death here, death that waited to jump out of the shadows…

As the thrumming sound receded, he wondered, by returning here to Texas, had he brought death back with him? Were the gunmen who'd abducted him heading to the house to storm its walls?

He staggered to a stop, the realization ripping through him that he hadn't lost his freedom in a remote desert ambush as he'd been told. Hadn't been knocked unconscious and captured when an explosive device overturned his Hummer and killed one of his comrades. Hadn't been in Iraq with his unit…because he hadn't been a member of an army unit at all.

The knowledge doused him like ice water, the certainty that he'd never been what he'd told his family, friends and Andrea. *So what the hell were you, if you weren't really army? And how'd you get so screwed up you'd swallow your own cover story?*

Not only that, but the army itself had backed the whole sham, sending officers to debrief him, military shrinks and doctors to poke around his head. Which had to mean they were operating under someone's orders. Or more likely, some of them had really been CIA agents, trying to determine what he knew. And whether he was capable of accidentally spilling truths they preferred to remain hidden.

Was it possible they'd sent a team to guarantee his silence? Could one or more gunmen be waiting on the prairie above, knowing he must eventually emerge from cover?

Frozen to the marrow, he was blindsided by more fragments of the past, each more horrifying than the rest. A dark cell so cramped he couldn't stand up, so rank that he could scarcely breathe. A pang of horror as the door clanked open and two pairs of rough hands dragged him out for yet another beating. A coil of loose chain in the filthy straw, dripping with his blood and buzzing with flies.

As he crouched among the bushes growing along the side of the ravine, he slowly became aware of the shifting of rock and the crunching of leaf litter, the thud of fast-approaching footsteps.

Footsteps of a new threat coming up behind him, the fate he'd let himself imagine he'd escaped.

Between Andrea's cramped, uncomfortable position and the fear that at any moment, a killer would appear and shove a gun in her face, she was miserable enough without the ants that had found their way into her boots, crawling up her pant legs and stinging her for all they were worth. She shifted her position, trying to escape them, but pinch after pinch assured her that now that they had gotten past the protection of her boots and clothing, they meant to defend their home from her invasion—to the death, if necessary.

With no other choice, she crawled out of her hiding place and brushed at, swatted and stamped out every fire ant she could get to before she was hit with more venom. Shuddering with revulsion, she took a deep breath and assured herself that the stinging devils were gone and she would be fine, save for the itchy welts that would erupt.

As she pulled her boots back on, she nervously looked around, her stomach spasming with the fear that someone might have seen her wild "ant dance" or heard her muffled yips. But she spotted no one and heard nothing, no sign of the person who'd fired on them or Ian, either.

She tried to remember how long she'd waited, still and hidden, before the stings had become too much for her to bear. Five minutes? Ten? She couldn't be certain, especially not with her heart thumping so wildly she wanted to crawl out of her skin.

She relocated to another patch of shade, where she crouched and fought to calm herself for the next few minutes. But no matter how many times she assured herself that an experienced soldier like Ian, who had survived so much, knew what he was doing, phantom worries stung every exposed inch of her heart.

Before he'd left, he'd seemed so sure of himself, so tough and so cocky, the way he'd smiled and ducked his head to surprise her with a stolen kiss. Her stomach fluttered with the memory, with the knowledge that she'd have to talk to him about it later. But other thoughts troubled her more as she recalled those moments when his blue eyes had drifted, his expression troubled as something she'd said left him grappling with memories. Memories his conscious mind remained too shell-shocked to face.

She'd seen flashbacks before, had read case reports of terrible things happening—accidents, assaults and even murders—in the wake of something as innocuous as a backfiring car, a slamming door or a loud scene during a movie. In a situation as reminiscent of wartime as this one, would Ian's struggle with the buried ghosts of his past endanger him in the present?

As more time passed, she fought to hold back the rising tide of panic, telling herself it was a good sign that she'd heard no more shots. Reminding herself of how present and centered Ian had been when he had promised to return.

But eventually, her worry overwhelmed her, and there was nothing to be done except follow in the direction he had taken. As she walked, she prayed she would encounter Ian rather than the shooter.

She prayed even harder that when she did, he would still be the man she knew.

Chapter 4

Like horses, cattle were first and foremost prey animals, ruled by their adrenaline when anything strange spooked them. A half-dozen head charged toward Ian, their eyes rolling in their broad heads as they sought a path out of the ravine, back up to a place where they wouldn't feel trapped.

"Yah, yah!" Ian shouted, waving his arms at the dumb beasts so they would veer around him instead of crushing him to the ground. Startled by his movement, they broke and headed downhill, their oversize calves bawling in protest, their hooves clattering noisily over the loose rock.

"Nearest exit's *that* way, beef-for-brains," he said, jerking his chin in the opposite direction the frightened animals had taken. But at least their presence had served to yank his mind back to the here and now and the threat that might even now be drawing a bead on him, thanks to all the racket he had just made.

No shot rang out, but as he climbed higher, he heard Andrea calling his name, her voice strained and her breathing heavy. Scanning the rocky incline below, he spotted her, except she wasn't moving his way. Instead, she was following the cattle, her attention clearly drawn by their noise.

Had nerves driven her from her hiding place? Or had something down there frightened her into leaving safety?

Strength thrumming through his limbs, he moved downhill to intercept her. Before he could reach her, though, she slipped as a patch of loose earth shifted under her feet. Sitting hard, she slid with a miniature landslide of stones, her shriek echoing as she picked up speed, hurtling toward a pile of jagged rock some thirty feet below.

Though Ian was surer on his feet, he had trouble, too, as he broke into a shuffling run. His progress sent more scree rattling downhill and bouncing toward her. Arms flailing, she managed to grab on to a jutting tree root and break her fall, only to cry out as a fist-sized stone struck her above the left eye.

"Andrea, hold on!" he called, more worried about her passing out and falling than the chance that the shooter remained nearby.

She jerked her gaze in his direction, fresh blood streaming down her pale face from a small cut above her brow. "Ian? Ian, are you all right?"

She squinted and blinked at him as he picked his way toward her, as if she couldn't focus. Concussion, maybe, he thought, cursing himself for sending the rocks raining down on her.

At last, he reached her and took her free hand. "Don't worry about me. Let's just get you someplace more stable. I know it's pretty steep here, but I'm going to help you move to safety." He pointed out a spot about twenty feet to the left. "The trick is to go slowly and slide your feet. You ready?"

She shook her head, her eyes rounding. "I'll fall again."

"Take some deep breaths through your nose if you can. That's it. In and out."

He betrayed no hint of the urgency he was feeling as he waited, though he desperately wanted to get them away from this spot where they'd made so much noise.

She darted a glance up the hillside, her nails digging hard into his palm. "Is whoever—whoever shot at us still up there? Did you see him?"

"I heard a vehicle drive away a while back," Ian told her, not mentioning his worry that someone might still be waiting above, staking out the trail they'd taken to descend into the ravine. "Would've had to be a truck or Jeep—something with four-wheel-drive—to be out here."

"So he's gone, then," she said, her grip on his hand easing.

"That's right, darlin'. Now you need to let go of that root you're holding on to, and we'll get you up on your feet, slowly."

"I—I'm too dizzy. And my head hurts."

"I know, and I'm really sorry. I think I might've accidentally knocked down—"

"Don't be sorry. Just get me back home."

He wondered whether she was referring to the place she worked in Marston, some kind of rehab center for former military, he understood from what he'd read online. Or did she mean all the way back to where she'd grown up in Southern California?

"We're going to get you out," he said, "get you help as soon as we can. All you have to do is trust me. All right?"

"Okay. I can do this." She pressed her lips together, pushing aside the fear and pain with a look of intense determination.

The expression sparked another memory of the afternoon he'd met her. Ian recalled how impressed he'd been by her courage, despite her cuts and one very torn-up knee. Rather than giving way to hysteria, she'd focused on what had needed to be done.

Now she reclaimed that survivor's strength, standing with him on her own power and carefully choosing her footing as he steadied her with an arm around her waist. Together, the two of them made their way to stable ground before heading back down to a shaded spot beside the creek.

"How 'bout you sit right there, on that boulder?" he suggested. "I'd like to wash your face if you don't mind, check out that bump on your forehead."

"This time, I'm going to check for fire ants first." She eyed the ground suspiciously, kicking at the coarse gravel around the rocks.

"Ants?" He winced at the thought of the aggressive little hellions. "Is that what happened with the place I left you?"

Sighing with relief when nothing stirred at her feet, she sat down and nodded. "You really know how to show a girl a good time, don't you? Flying bullets and stinging ants, followed by a hard crack to the noggin."

"It's a gift, my way with women. But at least I held off on the tarantulas." He smiled down at her, his hand digging in a back pocket for the clean bandanna he'd tucked inside that morning. Taking it to the creek, he stooped to dunk it in the cool, fresh water. "But then, it's always good to hold back something for the second date."

She managed a smile, but what came out was more groan than chuckle.

He squeezed water from the cloth and returned to the spot where she was sitting. "This could sting a little."

She nodded and closed her eyes, her body tensing while he washed the red streamers coating the left side of her face. He dabbed gently at the wound itself, not wanting to make the bleeding any worse.

"Do you think I'll need stitches?" she asked.

"Maybe a couple," he said, blotting the wound again. "You have a pretty good goose egg coming up, too, but that's all superficial. I'm more worried about a possible concussion. Can you tell me what day it is?"

"I'm fine."

"The date, Andie," he pressed.

She grimaced. "Everybody calls me Andrea. And it's Monday, September...the thirteenth, right?"

"The fifteenth, but we'll call that close enough, at least we will if you can tell me where we are."

She rolled her eyes. "A heck of a long walk from the mansion, since both the horses took off."

"It's not a mansion."

"Not in *your* world, maybe. But you haven't spent the past six months living in a dormitory."

"And you haven't spent the past year living in a cell." Quick and vicious as a slashing switchblade, an image of the dark and filthy hole where he'd been kept made him swallow hard.

"I'm so sorry," she said, sincerity shining in her eyes. "I wasn't thinking."

He wanted to tell her it was all right, but it was easier to change the subject. "Your idea about walking back home in the open might be a bad move. Down here, at least, there's cover."

Her gaze locked in on his. "I thought you said the shooter left."

"I *think* he did, but I'm not willing to gamble our lives on the theory." If Ian were here alone, he'd take the chance, but he couldn't bring himself to risk Andrea's safety.

He still had feelings for her, he admitted, feelings that refused to stay buried. She might have left him long ago, might be promised to another man now, but his heart and Swiss cheese memory had conspired to make all of that irrelevant. He'd tried, these past few days, to fight it, had fought to keep her at arm's length. But seeing her bruised and smeared with dirt and blood, her hair as tangled as a little girl's, ignited a fierce instinct to keep her safe.

"It makes sense that he'd leave, doesn't it?" she argued. "He probably panicked after realizing he was shooting at human beings, not a deer or something."

"It would make sense if I believed for one minute it was just some poacher hunting out of season. Or even some dumb teenager out with daddy's rifle playing Let's Shoot Anything That Moves."

"But you don't think that."

He shook his head. "I don't. Which means it's possible someone's still up there, waiting for us to make a move so he can take me out."

He went back to the creek to rinse out the bandanna, creating eddies of pink water that quickly dissipated. Wringing out the thin cloth again, he took it back and gave it to her. "You'd better hold on to this, keep it pressed to your head until the bleeding stops. Since my phone won't work down here, we could be in for a long wait before someone from the ranch comes looking."

She dabbed at the wound and frowned at him. "This theory of yours, about someone waiting for us… Is there some reason you suspect someone might be after you?"

"Other than the bullets, you mean?"

"Just now, you said *for us*. But a moment ago you used the word *me*. You said, *waiting for us to make a move so he can take me out*."

"If it makes you feel any better, he'd probably shoot you, too, to eliminate the witness."

She snorted in response, intelligence glittering in her narrowed eyes. "Witness to what, Ian? Are you suggesting some kind of a—of an *assassination*? Your sister-in-law mentioned something earlier, some worries you had when you first came back that someone might try to take you away if the public didn't know you were here."

Anger flared, like a match struck in a dark cell. "So you've been talking about me, have you? Asking family members just how crazy this situation's made me? Did they tell you it all started years ago, that Zach's and my old man beat us so often we couldn't get away from this ranch fast enough? That our mother turned a blind eye and explained away our bruises, since she didn't have any of her own to worry over."

"Oh, Ian. I'm so sorry," she said, her beautiful eyes glittering with compassion. "I had no idea."

"Maybe I am insane, to want to come back to a place with such bad memories—"

"There must be other memories, too, good memories that helped draw you back here. Or maybe you unconsciously sensed that you needed to forgive to heal. I would never call you insane for returning to your family or for worrying about how your more recent past might come back to haunt you, either."

"No, I guess you shrinks have fancier words for it. You'd call it paranoid, right? Or delusional or some other psychobabble. But I didn't make up those gunshots, did I? You heard them, too. You saw the reflection from the gun above us."

She hesitated, and his heart stumbled. He wasn't *really* crazy, was he?

She nodded, and he breathed again. "I heard the shots, Ian, and I saw something. Which means it's possible the reason for your fear might be real, too. So let's explore that for a moment—"

"I don't want to *explore* it. I don't want to *dialogue* about it, or *own my feelings*, or any of that BS you picked up in shrink school. Can't we just talk, Andrea? Talk the way we used to, back before you kicked me to the curb?"

Her cool look lasered through him. "I'm going to blame that on your memory, but the fact is, I didn't *kick* you out of my life. You made that choice, refusing to tell me where you'd been when you disappeared without a word two days before our engagement party. Refusing to tell me why, when I was worried enough to call the army post where you'd told me you were stationed, the MPs I spoke of had no record of you."

"And I said I couldn't tell you," he said, more pieces of the puzzle spinning together in his brain.

"Couldn't. Or *wouldn't*." She looked away, but not before he saw pure anguish shifting through her expression. "And all I could think of was that, for all the counseling I'd gone through, everything I'd done to start a healthy new life, I was repeating my mother's mistakes after all..."

"Your mother's?"

She nodded. "Yes, my mother's. You don't remember, do you?"

He grimaced, his mind snatching at memories that darted from his grasp like minnows. Unexpectedly, he caught one. "Your mom's dead. You found her, after. After she'd taken a whole bottle full of—"

Seeing the pain flash over Andrea's expression, he cut himself off. "Sorry. Didn't mean to blurt it out like that. It's just—when something comes back—"

"No, it's good. It's true, that's what happened," she allowed. "And I'm glad your memory's returning. That's a good sign."

He opened his mouth to ask her what their breakup had had to do with her mother's "mistake," as she'd put it. But something else occurred to him first, something he couldn't wait another minute to get off his chest. "I've remembered other things today, too, when I was climbing up to try to see the shooter."

"Flashbacks?" she asked. "I was worried the gunfire might've triggered—"

"I know the reason I lied to you in California. Why I felt I had to."

She dabbed at her dripping forehead. "I thought you might be married, but I didn't see a word about a wife or ex-wife in your file."

"You thought I might be—? Hell, no. I'd never do that. Lie to you like that, I mean. There was no other woman."

"But you *did* lie to me, about your military post, at least."

He sighed. "Believe me, it wasn't by choice. But when you're involved with clandestine services, it's easier to use a cover story than—"

"Clandestine services?" She blinked at him. "Do you mean—you were some sort of *spy* or something? Is that what you're telling me?"

"Not a spy, exactly," he said. "My work with the CIA involved cultivating relationships with foreign resources."

"So you were a spy*master*, then. Really?"

"Something like that," he admitted, though even now, with his once all-consuming career in tatters, it went against the grain to talk about his work.

"Then what were you doing in California?" she asked. "I thought people like that were all overseas or in D.C."

"Not all of us, not all the time. But as I'm sure you guessed, I was called on to travel quite a lot—especially when there was a lot of chatter about planned terrorist activities targeting our country's citizens."

"So you were overseas, then, when something went wrong?"

The dark city street came back to mind, followed by a blinding flash, a deafening boom and crumbling masonry—then nothing. "It sure as hell wasn't like the army claimed, but there was an attack when I was on my way to meet a potential asset who'd promised to turn over sensitive information. An explosion, and then…"

Overcome by a dizzying sensation, he sank down to sit beside her on the boulder. He couldn't think, couldn't speak, panic racing with his pulse as the ravine whirled around him. Panic that pushed back the onslaught of memory that threatened, the tidal wave of shame that left him shaking. If he'd only seen it coming, recognized the subtle clues that he was being set up for an ambush, he could have avoided capture and the torture that had made him—

"No wonder they want me to die," he murmured, rising to stagger away where he could retch again and again, bringing up nothing but his own icy terror. *What the hell did I do? How many deaths did I cause?*

Rising from the boulder where she had been sitting, Andrea fought to hold herself back, to give Ian the space to pull himself together. Not so much for his benefit, she realized, but because she felt so vulnerable herself. So at risk of forgetting who she was and what she'd come to do.

I'm here as a psychologist, she reminded herself, *drawing on my professional experience with PTSD survivors.* Not so much as a friend, no matter what had been said, and definitely not as Ian's lover. So why was it she ached to touch him, to comfort him not with words, but…?

No. She wasn't going to chance it. To risk confusing Ian, risk disgracing herself. She pressed the damp bandanna to the wound on her head harder than she meant to, the resulting stab of pain a penance for what she had been thinking.

No, not thinking, she realized. *Feeling.* Succumbing to memories of falling headlong into a love affair that had proved such a bad idea on the first occasion.

She walked away, holding her hands over her stomach, knowing that, in returning to him his past, she risked losing sight of her own present, not to mention the future she had planned with Julian. She fought to focus on the man she'd fallen for, the man whose vision for the center had captured her imagination. She remembered how he'd invited her to lunch at a seminar on post-traumatic stress disorder, how his passion in describing Warriors-4-Life had lured her from a better-paying job in a place that wasn't located in the dead center of nowhere.

He'd explained to her how costs were so much lower here in Texas. It was only by sheer chance that the vacant nursing facility the organization had restored had ended up being so close to the Rayford family's spread. Chance, not fate, had brought her here.

But the harder she struggled to picture Julian's face, to enumerate his noble and inspiring qualities, the more she kept glancing back at Ian, who was now crouching by the water, jeans straining against his strong thighs, his lean, muscular arms scooping handfuls to his mouth to drink. When he turned to glance back at her, the sight of him nearly took her breath away, the high cheekbones and deep tan that spoke of native blood in his lineage, the contrast of his deep blue eyes—eyes that glittered with unspeakable pain. With the need for reassurance that only she could provide.

Seeing him like that, her brain shut down completely and muscle memory took over. Her mouth drying in an instant, she started toward him. At the same moment, he moved toward her, his steps longer, swifter, unstoppable.

Helpless to resist, she hurried, too, her every cell crying out for the necessity of contact. When he took her into his arms, she felt the rush, heard the *whoosh* as her willpower caught flame, all her resolve burned to ashes the moment their mouths came together.

She tumbled to temptation, to the desperate press of lips and tangle of tongues, the hunger to taste what she'd never guessed she had been starved for. Pleasure arced through her entire body, a buzzing need that made her breasts ache for the sensation of his hands, his mouth on them. Between her legs, an even deeper yearning set in, an ache that left her wondering how she could have lived so long without his touch.

His lips slid to her neck, the hot moisture of his mouth moving over sensitive skin beneath her ear. She moaned aloud, felt herself grow hot and wet as sensation spiraled through her. Her hands rubbed at his back, pulling him even closer.

He yanked her shirttail from her jeans, then reached up beneath her top, finding and tweaking a hard nipple. She remembered how it felt—the moist heat of his mouth suckling—and the memory was so strong, her desire so sharp, that she nearly came right then. Her knees buckled from beneath her so suddenly that Ian had to make a grab for her to keep her from collapsing.

His eyes found hers, their electric blue intensity cutting through the past two years, cutting through her willpower. "I know the timing's bad—worse than bad—stuck out here with heaven knows who waiting to take another shot at us the second we leave cover. But I'm putting you on notice that I want you. I need you. And the first chance I get, the first damn moment we can find a private, safe spot, I mean to make you forget there's ever been anyone besides me. Because there damned well never should've been. It was all one big mistake."

It would've been so easy to nod her head. To forget the danger, forget herself, and give in to the chatter of the little creek, the sunshine slanting through the green leaves, the unbearable hunger building in her body and provoke him to make love to her here and now. But in the depths of his gaze, she read the terror of the unknown, his desperation to latch on to those few things that seemed familiar.

That was all she was to him, a solid rock to cling to at the center of a rushing torrent. A torrent that seemed to echo his words: *All one big mistake...*

She pulled free of his embrace, blinking and shaking her head as she struggled to clear the flood of hormones. The physical attraction she'd already allowed to carry her far past her normal boundaries.

"No, Ian. This is crazy. I don't know what's got into me to—" Seeing the hurt wash over him, she ached to return to him, but she couldn't risk the contact. "I was in the wrong here, clearly. This is totally unethical."

"Don't do this to me, Andrea," he said, his gaze a raw wound that made the cut still oozing on her forehead fade into insignificance. "Don't treat me like I'm nothing but your patient."

"But you *are* my patient, in a sense, and I was wrong to forget that for a single second." The trembling that racked her found its way into her voice. "Wrong to come here, clearly, to imagine I could put the past aside."

"You can't put it aside—can't put *me* aside—because you still love me," he insisted, "just the way I love you. Those old feelings, they're all still there. I dreamed of your face, your body for so long. I followed the memory of you home."

She closed her eyes. "Please don't, Ian. Don't put that on me. I do care for you, really. I think I always will. But I love another man now, a man I owe my loyalty—" She put a hand over her mouth in an attempt to stifle the sob that she felt coming. Because she hadn't proved worthy of the trust Julian had offered. She'd been every bit the faithless cheater his ex-wife had been. Worse yet, she'd lived up to her father's legacy—a father whose broken faith had cost her family everything.

"If you love this man so much, what are you doing kissing me?" Ian asked.

She opened her eyes, blinking away their dampness.

"Getting tangled in old emotions, echoes from the past. In my own grief after learning—did you know the army sent a chaplain and an officer to notify me you were dead?"

"Oh, Andrea. I'm sorry. I meant to change that after we—"

"It doesn't matter now, and I don't blame you. But it did tear open old wounds and make me think what might have been. If it—if it hadn't been for meeting Julian, I don't know how I would have—"

"Julian. So that's his name. The man I'm going to make you forget."

"I'm sorry, Ian, but Julian's the man I'm going to marry." A lump swelled in her throat, so painful it made her eyes brim over. "At least if he'll forgive me, after this."

"You'll tell him?"

She nodded, a yawning chasm opening in the hollow of her stomach. "Of course, I will. I won't start a life with him with secrets between us."

"Then I hope he's a jealous ass. I hope he—"

"Don't talk about him. Please don't. I feel horrible enough already. And he's a great man, really. You'd like him if you ever met him, if you heard him talk about the center, about the need to help the soldiers coming back from war with so many terrible…" She realized she'd said the wrong thing as color suffused Ian's face.

"You mean poor broken wrecks like me. Pathetic losers you would never dream of—"

"Stop it, Ian. Please, stop. Let's not make this any worse."

"I'm not sure how it could get worse," he said, "unless the sniper—"

As if conjured by his words, the rumble of an engine silenced the singing of the birds. An arrival that drove home the realization of just how vulnerable they were.

* * *

"Ian, are you down there? Dr. Warrington?"

Ian's tension dissipated when he recognized his brother's deep voice, calling him from the mouth of the ravine.

"We're down by the creek!" Ian called, watching from the corner of his eye as Andrea hurriedly tucked her shirt back into her jeans. "We're coming up now."

She looked up, catching his eye, and he noticed the flush of redness beneath her collar.

"Don't worry," he assured her. "I'm not the type to kiss and tell—even if you're still planning on it."

Avoiding his gaze, she went to rinse out the bandanna in the creek one last time. Once she was done, she followed as he retraced the uphill path they'd originally traveled, where both Zach and Virgil Straughn, the longtime ranch manager, stood outside of Zach's four-door pickup, their faces drawn with worry.

"Thought you must've run into some trouble when the horses showed up at the barn," Zach said. "I tried calling your phone—could've wrung your damned neck when I couldn't get through."

In spite of the harshness of his words, Ian saw Zach's tension in the stiffness of his shoulders, saw how badly he had scared his older brother. "I had the phone with me this time, and I swear I tried to call you. But there's no signal down there. Couldn't even get a text out."

Zach thumped him on the back a lot harder than was strictly necessary. "Thank God, you're still in one piece, man. My life flashed before my eyes at the thought of having to tell Mama you'd been…"

"That makes two of us," Virgil put in as he pulled off his sweat-stained hat and raked his fingers through his thinning gray hair. "Poor woman would've had another breakdown for sure."

Zach caught sight of Andrea pressing the cloth to her forehead. "Are you all right? What happened?"

"Just a little bump," she said, sounding surprisingly subdued. "I'll be fine, I'm sure."

"Here, miss." Virgil hurried to the truck with surprising speed, considering his slight paunch and the hitch in his gait. He opened the passenger-side front door and waved her over. "You should sit down here in the cab, and I'll get you some water and—how about some Tylenol? I think we've got some in the first-aid kit."

"That'd be fantastic," she said, heading for the pickup.

Hearing the exhaustion in her voice, Ian realized how rough the ordeal had been on her, both physically and emotionally. He'd been wrong to take advantage, to come on with all the finesse of a charging bull while she was so vulnerable.

But that didn't mean he hadn't meant every word he'd said. He wasn't sorry he had kissed her, either—a kiss that had cut through all the fog of his confusion like a beam of pure white light. Complicated as their situation was, his feelings for her were the only thing he trusted, the one thing he could see that was still worth fighting for.

While Virgil fussed over Andrea, Zach gave Ian the full big-brother stare. "So what the hell went on here? How'd you let her get hurt?"

Ian scowled at him. "I'm glad to see you, too, bro. Especially glad it *was* you and not the son of a bitch who decided to use the two of us for target practice."

"Target practice?" Zach's gaze narrowed, sweeping

the prairie in all directions. "You're telling me someone *shot* at you two?"

"I am. And as you can probably imagine, our horses took exception."

"I figured something was up when I spotted 'em making for the barn like their tails were on fire. So who was shooting? Did you see 'em? And are you sure they meant to shoot at you?"

"Damned sure, considering how close those bullets came—and how the shooter fired again after Andrea called out that we were down there." Ian's throat tightened as it hit him how close they'd both come to being killed out here. "And no, I never saw him or heard anything except an engine when he took off. Thought we'd be better off, though, waiting for help down where there's good cover."

"Smart move," Zach allowed, "and I was damned glad to find that note you left saying where you and the doc were going." He glanced back toward the truck, where Virgil was rattling around in the backseat cooler to get Andrea some ice. "That bump on her head—"

"It was a falling rock that did it, one that I'd kicked loose. We'd better take her into Marston to get checked out. I think she might need a couple stitches."

"All right, but before we go, have you come up with any idea, any theories at all, why somebody would be out to kill you?"

Ian thought of telling his brother what he'd remembered about the true nature of his work for the government, but this wasn't the time or place. "Same as I've said before," he answered. "I have this feeling not everybody's happy to have me back from the dead."

Zach's gaze zeroed in on him. "You know, when you

first came back and started talking about somebody wanting to make you disappear, I chalked it up to dehydration mostly, or the hell that you'd just been through making you a little...you know."

"In light of the fact that you invited a shrink to stay with us, I guess I do."

Zach grimaced. "Now, though, I'm beginning to see your point, especially considering how long the odds are of some random nut job coming on you out here accidentally." His gesture took in the broad sweep of a land that went on unbroken as far as the eye could see. "But why now? And why not wait to catch you alone instead of when you had a witness with you?"

"Could be that just maybe, Andrea's what set this all off," Ian said in a low voice, his gaze swinging toward Zach's truck. "Maybe whoever shot at us is worried she'll unlock something they'd just as soon stay secret. A secret—"

Zach interrupted, his face hardened as he finished his brother's sentence. "A secret so big and so ugly, someone's willing to shoot down both of you to keep it."

Chapter 5

While Zach drove them back to the house, Andrea sat in the front-passenger seat holding the ice pack Virgil had improvised for her. The cool pressure felt soothing, and it offered her a chance to hide her face—and her silent struggle to regain her composure.

It was ludicrous, she told herself, that she was far more upset about kissing Ian, now seated behind her, than she was about the fact that someone had tried to kill them. Still, she would rather dodge more bullets than try to explain her behavior to Julian.

Oh, he would be stoic about it, if she knew him, understanding even. With his own training in psychology—though he had always worked on the administrative side—he might even offer her excuses, citing her emotional trauma and her head wound, both of which had left her vulnerable to a retreat to the past. But inside, he would be devastated, left to wonder what it was that drew him to unfaithful women. Or what it was that he was lacking, when the flaw was hers alone.

As they rode, Ian and Zach discussed calling local law enforcement to report the incident.

"Not that I imagine Canter'll do much in the way of an investigation," Zach said morosely. "He's mad as hell I put a stop to him coming to Mama with his hand out every time the department needed something."

"So you have something against spreading around a little Rayford money in the public interest?"

"It's the sheriff's *self*-interest I'm worried about," Zach said. "I don't trust the SOB as far as I can throw him."

"You aren't the only one," Virgil said. "I tried to tell her it wasn't right, him coming by so often…"

Zach glanced over his shoulder, looking at his brother. "You remember Canter at all from back before we left home?"

Ian went quiet for some time before saying, "I remember a stiff-necked deputy with a hatful of attitude threatening to haul our gold-plated Rayford butts to jail when we raised hell around town. Tell me you don't mean that jackass."

"The very one. He's sheriff now, and I can tell you, he was all about kissin' up to Rayfords back when Mama was alone and half-looped most of the time with all those damned pills she was popping."

Miserable as she was, Andrea perked up a little to hear that the primly proper Nancy Rayford had had a substance abuse issue. So that was what was behind her brittle and tiresome behavior, especially toward her daughter-in-law. Andrea felt certain that the family matriarch's snootiness was nothing but a facade, hiding the flaws she feared would be exposed.

"Maybe we should just look into this ourselves," Ian suggested. "Keep him out of it entirely—and away from Mother."

"Much as I'd like to, I think we at least need to report what happened. After he blows us off, we can try digging into it on our own—"

"Or maybe Andrea can help me figure out what this is really all about…" Ian reached forward from the backseat and laid his big hand on her shoulder. She felt the warmth of him radiating through the fabric of her shirt, heard the concern in his voice as he gave her a gentle squeeze. "Almost home. You hanging in there?"

"Just trying to let everything sink in," she said. "And trying not to scratch those stupid ant bites." The itching had begun already, though she was doing her best to ignore it.

"We'll have ointment for that at the house," Ian assured her. "But we'll want to get you checked out at the nearest ER anyway."

"That's not necessary. The ice is helping, and the bleeding's almost stopped."

"Don't try to minimize it," Ian said, giving her shoulder a firmer squeeze. "I saw the way your head snapped back when that rock smacked into you. And you looked dazed or worse when I—"

She jerked away her shoulder and angrily demanded, "When you *what*?" When he had kissed her until she'd forgotten the danger they were in? Until she'd lost all sense of who she was, much less the professional and personal obligations she was honor-bound to live by?

"When I *reached* you, that's all," he said shortly. "No need to jump down my throat about it. And no damned chance of getting out of an emergency room visit, so quit arguing about it."

Zach sent a measuring look their way, his expression telling her he'd figured out there was something more than met the surface going on between them. After letting them settle for a few moments, he said, "I understand your not wanting to make a fuss, Doctor—"

"Please, it's Andrea." She'd asked the family several times to call her by her first name, just as she did with those clients she saw at the center.

"Okay. Andrea, then. But I'm going to have to side with Ian on this. There's no sense taking chances, not with a possible concussion. And since it happened on ranch property, I insist we cover the cost."

She opened her mouth to argue that wasn't the point but then realized it was useless. "I see that I'm outnumbered. But if I have to go all the way to Marston for the ER, I might as well pack my things. I'll send one of our other counselors, but I won't be coming back."

"What do you mean, you won't be coming back?" Ian demanded. "We were just beginning to make real headway. This morning, I remembered—" He cut himself off, leaving Andrea to guess he didn't want to go into his work with the CIA in front of Virgil and his brother. "I remembered so much more."

"Connor will be perfect for you," she said, pretending she hadn't heard the note of desperation in his voice. "He served in Operation Enduring Freedom, so he has a lot of personal knowledge of the effects of the war on—"

"He doesn't have personal knowledge of *me*, damn it. Not like you do, Andie."

She gritted her teeth to get past her knee-jerk desire to correct him—or tell him that his use of his old nickname for her only underscored the fact that he would never see her as anything but the woman he'd once loved...

The woman he *still* loved, she reminded herself, since he'd made it clear that in his mind, their relationship had never ended. And that he meant to do everything in his power to make her forget it had...

Even if doing so would destroy her completely. Which was why she had to get away from him the moment that she could.

Once they were back home, Jessie emerged from The Deadline Cave, as she called her book-and-paper-strewn study, and insisted on going upstairs to help Andrea clean up and gather her things. Ian had seen Zach whisper something to his wife—probably a directive to find out the real reason that Andrea was in such as hurry to leave. Seeing the fear in Andrea's eyes, Ian had already sworn that, despite what had happened, they could keep her safe here. She'd only shaken her head, her stubbornly clamped jaw telling him that she wasn't about to change her mind.

As soon as the two women disappeared into Andrea's suite, his brother turned on him and cuffed his arm. "So what the hell did you do to her, bonehead?"

Ian shoved him back, reminding the dumb lug that he might be skinnier than usual, but he was nobody's punching bag. "What makes you think I did a damned thing? Maybe she just doesn't like being used as target practice. Probably not what she signed up for after spending all those years in shrink school."

Zach mimicked an air-raid siren, a sound so annoying, Ian wanted to deck him. "You hear that?" Zach asked him. "That's my bullshit detector hittin' the red zone. Because it's obvious as the nose on your ugly face—"

"I don't care what anybody says. I don't look *that* much like you."

"—the reason she's bailing has nothing to do with bullets and everything to do with you. Or something between the two of you, more specifically. Which brings me back to my question. What the hell did you do?"

Ian grimaced and paced past the bottom of the staircase as he attempted to cool down. Much as it griped him to admit it, his brother was absolutely right about why Andrea was leaving.

"If you're going to tell me, hurry up about it," Zach urged, "before Virgil finishes calling Canter or Mama gets back from her hair appointment."

Ian blew out a long breath. "Could be I was a little too direct in announcing my intentions to make her forget this other guy."

"The one she's engaged to marry? While she's trying to help you to get back your memory? Smooth move, brother."

"I can't help it when I'm with her. Can't help the way it all comes rushing back to me—how smart and brave and sexy she is, how meeting her again brought me alive." As true as everything he'd said was, the real reason remained unspoken: how the memory of her had sustained him, keeping him safe throughout a journey that had spanned continents and oceans, how he would walk forever to get back to where they had been…even if it was a place that no longer existed.

"So that's the trouble." Zach shook his head, something between a grimace and a wry smile pulling at one side of his mouth. "You remember the rush but not the rest. Thing is, though, Ian, there's gotta be a downside. Otherwise, you wouldn't have broken up two years ago."

Ian thought of telling him why it had happened, telling him about the clandestine services career he'd kept hidden for so many years. But before he told anyone else about his CIA past, he needed time to consider whether sharing the information might prove a legal problem or, worse yet, a danger to the people he loved.

It was just as possible, though, that getting it all out in the open might prove his best defense. But at the thought of allowing the viral sensation that would follow any report of how the government had spun up the feel-good story about a "soldier's" miraculous return, his throat clenched and icy chills crawled up the column of his spine. The white marble and carved mahogany stairway fell away, dropping him back to a time and place where...

Hunger and thirst, suffocating heat and numbing cold, and the cruel positioning of his arms as they bore his weight were bad enough. But the worst part was the hood that blinded him so that he couldn't see pain coming, couldn't see the chain begin its downward arc.

He soon learned to listen for the dark chuckle or the clink of metal, to scent the sour sweat of his captors as they approached, to brace himself for the beating that would follow. But his senses failed him sometimes, leaving him in the constant torment of anticipation, holding his breath and clenching his muscles, his pulse jumping at every scrape of distant footsteps or a whisper of rats' feet in the straw.

It was the anticipation, along with the memory of pain, more than the torture itself that broke down his mind, his body, his will to resist the questions that kept coming, each one hard and unyielding as another blood-caked metal link.

"Ian? Ian, you still with me, man?" Zach's voice was

a mere echo, an imaginary strand of English woven through the rough fabric of the Pashto demands that he tell them where the listening post was.

But Ian knew it was illusion, another trick to break him, just like the hallucinations that tortured him each time he'd blacked out, impossible dreams where he'd managed to escape his bindings and strangle his guard with that damned chain. Dreams where he had somehow talked a sympathizer into helping smuggle him out of the mountains, out of the country. Where he had made his way back home…

Not to a place, so much as to a woman. A dark-haired beauty in a blue bikini, a woman who regarded him with green-gold eyes beneath the long fringe of her lashes…

"Ian!" He heard the semblance of his brother's voice again, this time coming with a hard grip that shook his shoulders.

Ian flailed to break free, his unbound arms swinging strong. His fist crashed into something solid, some*one* who shouted in surprise as he crashed backward into the banister before sitting hard on the pristine marble floor.

"What's going on, you two?" A red-faced older version of the Virgil Ian remembered stepped between the brothers, a phone forgotten in his hand. "What the hell's all this about? Show some respect in this house. Your mama could be back any minute."

Ian gasped for breath, his heart jackhammering its way through his sternum. His skin beaded with hot sweat as he looked around wildly, seeking somewhere to run before the other guards showed up to beat him, to kill him this time for daring to strike one of their own.

Before he could decide which way to run, the fog lifted, leaving him blinking down at his own brother.

At Zach, who was sitting on the landing floor and rubbing his jaw.

"It's okay, Virg," Zach said, his voice surprisingly calm for a guy who'd just gotten decked. "I've got this. You back here with us, Ian? You're safe. You're home now, and I swear to you, you're never going back."

Ian took a shaky step and bent, offering his older brother a hand up. "I'm sorry, man. I'm sorry."

"I know you are. I get it." Zach accepted his help, his steady gaze indicating that he did so more out of a desire to offer reassurance than out of any real need for assistance. Once he was on his feet, he tightened his grip. "Just let's not make a habit of it, all right? Because I can get past a sore jaw and some bumps and bruises, but what if it had been Mama? Or Jessie or even Eden?"

"I wouldn't have hit one of them."

"But you weren't swinging at *me* either, were you? Not that I don't probably have it comin' every now and then, but it was pretty clear that you were after somebody else. For one thing, you were yelling in some foreign language. Arabic, maybe? I don't know. I never had the gift for—"

"Pashto. It was Pashto," Ian told him, naming the language of his captors.

"So they were Taliban?" Zach asked him. "The ones holding you over there in—"

"I don't remember the details. And I sure as hell don't want to talk about it." It was bad enough knowing that his brother had seen the ropy, red scars across his back and shoulders. Bad enough that anyone knew that he'd been beaten.

Virgil shifted and cleared his throat, then let them know the sheriff had insisted on coming personally to take their report rather than sending a deputy to do it.

"He wanted you both still here when he arrives. I told him Dr. Warrington needs a trip to the ER before she's questioned, said I'll take her there myself."

Zach scowled, looking as if he'd rather take another shot to the jaw than deal with Canter. "What about her car, though?" he asked, referring to the old blue Honda she'd arrived in.

"I'll drive her in it and one of the hands can pick me up there later. They're always itching for an excuse to head to town anyway."

"To head to the bars there, you mean. Try and keep 'em out of trouble, will you? Or at least don't let 'em drive after they've had a few."

"As long as I don't need to stick around to keep you two out of trouble." Virgil glanced from Zach to Ian, who was still grappling with the realization that the ranch in Rusted Spur, not the torture chamber, was his reality.

"We're just fine, aren't we, Ian?" Zach said.

"Yeah." Ian blinked, then rubbed at his knuckles, noticing that one was split and bleeding. "Leastwise, I've busted up my hand enough for one day on your big mouth."

Frowning at the uneasy look that passed between the brothers, Virgil said, "I'll—ah—I'll be out in the kitchen, then. Making up a couple of more ice packs."

"Don't worry on my account," said Ian.

"Mine, either," Zach tossed in. "We're done now. Aren't we, Ian?"

"You have my word," Ian told them both.

"Then I'll be out there pinching a couple of those molasses-spice cookies I smell baking." Virgil shared a warm smile that had served as a counterbalance for their father's scowls and curses for so many years.

Seeing it calmed Ian, a reassurance that kindness sometimes outlived cruelty.

Once he'd left the room, Zach asked Ian, "You ready to talk about it now, see if the two of us can figure how your past could be connected to what went down this morning?"

"I—I don't—" Ian felt the vault of words slam shut, the lock inside him turning. He tried to struggle past it, reminding himself that his brother was on his side, but his face grew so hot he imagined he must be glowing like an ember.

"Guess not." Zach rubbed his jaw again, but not before Ian saw it was already bruising. "But if you can't talk to me, you'll better damned well talk with someone. Before whatever's bottled up inside you finds a way out we'll both regret."

"B-but Andrea's leaving," Ian choked out, "heading off to Marston and never coming back."

"Then try that other guy she mentioned. Or anybody, Ian."

"I'm not spilling my guts to some damned stranger."

"In that case, you'd better do a little quick thinking about how to change her mind."

From the guest wing, they heard a door close, but to Ian's disappointment, it was not Andrea but Jessie who came downstairs, the loose waves of strawberry-blond brushed back over her shoulders.

"How's Andrea?" Ian blurted. "Is she all right?"

Jessie shrugged. "It's hard to tell. She's being awfully quiet, especially when I mention your name. You two have a fight or something?"

Zach snorted and looked at Ian. "Didn't I tell you it was obvious?"

Ian grimaced but was saved from responding when Jessie went to her husband and reached up to touch his jaw.

"What the heck happened to you? I could swear you were in one piece when I left you."

"Just a little bump, that's all. No need to start fussing."

Jessie swung a narrow-eyed gaze from one brother to another. "Don't tell me you two got into it. *Really?* I'd think you guys would want to circle the wagons right now, with somebody taking shots at Ian."

Zach stared at her for several moments before he asked, "So what if this person *wasn't* after Ian?"

Jessie shook her head. "In what universe does that make sense, Zach? Maybe I should be loading *you* into the car to get your head scanned, too."

"Just hear me out. It could be possible that—"

"Andrea Warrington's way too nice to have made enemies, especially the kind that would come gunning for her here."

Undeterred, Zach asked, "But what if the shooter meant to kill *you*, Jessie? After all, Andrea was riding your horse."

Jessie made a scoffing noise. "Seriously, are you really back on that again? I've already told you, I'm not giving up my work. It's too important."

"It's important to me that you stay in one piece, and these people you're investigating—"

"Are going to be totally blindsided when this story hits the news. Besides, even if it did somehow get out, these guys may be slimy and corrupt, but that doesn't make them killers."

"If you're not worried about these crooks, then why keep me in the dark about what you're really up to?"

She sighed. "Because I love you, of course, and would

never want to see you accused of trying to influence—I'm sorry, but I can't discuss this. It's all irrelevant anyway. This shooting has nothing to do with me."

"What about those white supremacists you hacked off with your book last year. Who's to say those guys don't have long memories—and a longer reach? If anything were to happen to you—"

"I know you worry about me." Jessie's green eyes locked with her husband's. "But do you hear yourself, Zach? Think about it. Andrea looks nothing like me, with that long dark hair of hers."

Though Ian thought Zach's theory was a long shot, he felt bad enough about the lump rising on his brother's jaw to offer, "She did have on a riding helmet when we left. And besides, that flashy pinto of yours is recognizable from a long way off."

Jessie swung an annoyed look his way. "You might mean well, but stay out of this, or your brother won't be satisfied until he's locked me in a cage." Making a sweeping gesture that took in the entry and the living room, she added, "Sure, it's a *nice* cage, a first-class accommodation. But anyplace can be a prison, if you make the bars too tight."

"There's a big difference between being a damned prisoner," Zach told her, "and a treasure to be protected."

"Well, this *treasure's* taking Andrea to the ER in Marston. And I might even talk her into a little lunch at that cute little tea room if she's feeling up to it afterward."

"But Virgil's planning—"

"I'm sure he has better things to do," said Jessie, waving off the protest. "But the real question is, are you willing to cut me enough slack to do it?"

For several moments, the pair stared each other down,

a clash of wills that made Ian want to excuse himself before any more was said.

Zach raked his fingers through his black hair, looking as if he were considering tearing it out instead. "Yeah, Jessie. I can do that. But you'll text me, won't you? Let me know you've made it over there all right?"

Jessie raised herself on her toes to kiss his cheek, then smiled at him. "I can do that, sweetheart. And did I ever tell you how handsome you are when you're being reasonable?"

"Don't push your luck," Zach warned, swatting her on the rump as she scooted back toward the guest suites.

Once she had gone, he sighed and turned to Ian. "You ever love a woman so much you can scarcely breathe for fear you'll lose her?"

Ian answered with a slow nod, a dark void opening beneath his heart. "The thing is, there're so many ways to screw it up yourself. And if you do, you'll end up like your little brother, full of nothing but regrets."

Andrea felt vindicated when the ER doctor ran her through a few perfunctory tests, used a special skin-bonding adhesive to close the cut on her head, and pronounced her good to go. Sure, she'd been warned to return if she experienced further head pain and nausea, but the instructions sounded purely precautionary to her trained ear.

"See?" she couldn't resist asking, as they climbed into the passenger seat of Jessie's blue Prius. "It's not that I don't appreciate the concern, but I told you, Ian and Zach were overreacting. It was nothing."

Jessie shrugged as they both clicked their seat belts. "It's the way those Rayford men are made. I swear they're like my dog, Gretel, on testosterone and steroids. I'll be the first to admit it can be aggravating as all get-out sometimes. But it means they care about you, that they want to take care of you."

Alarm zinged through Andrea's system, along with worry that she hadn't done enough to make her position clear to Ian's family. "Yes, but I'm not Ian's to take care of. I'm just his psychologist—and an engaged woman to boot."

"I know you are," said Jessie as she started the engine. "But does Ian really get that? Can he, even, with his memory like it is?"

Andrea sighed. "I thought I could get through to him, but what happened this morning made it obvious he's not capable of putting our past relationship behind him."

"You mean…somewhere between the flying bullets, you two managed to—" Jessie's sharp eyes asked a question that brought swift heat to Andrea's face.

"He kissed me," she admitted in a small voice. "And heaven help me if I didn't kiss him back. I—I got caught up in the moment, the adrenaline. It's disgraceful. I'm not like this. I lo— I've made a serious commitment to my—to Julian, and I do have ethics."

Jessie was quiet for a long while before saying, "You also have a history with Ian. A history that apparently includes a good dollop of unfinished business."

"Maybe in his mind, but not in mine."

Jessie looked over at her, her green eyes sympathetic. "The words are loud and clear, Doc, but if you want anyone to hear them, you're going to have to figure out a way to keep your voice from shaking and your face from blazing red."

"I'm just— I'm tired, that's all. And maybe a little hungry."

Jessie smiled knowingly but allowed the change of subject. "All right, then. How 'bout that tearoom I mentioned earlier? We can have a nice lunch before I take you—"

"I just want to go back to the center, all right? I need to talk to my—"

"Come on, Andrea. I scarcely ever get a chance for grown-up girl talk anymore, and I swear I won't bring up Ian again or the shooting, either."

Andrea held out for a few moments before asking, "What do you mean, you don't get a chance for girl talk? I mean, with your mother-in-law right there in the house, how could it possibly get much better?"

Deadpan as Andrea's delivery was, Jessie tried to control herself, her mouth twitching before a distinctly un-ladylike snort broke free. Then both women erupted into laughter, assuring Andrea that no matter how disastrous her trip to Rusted Spur might have proved, at least she'd made a new friend.

It was midafternoon by the time she finally returned to the Warriors-4-Life Center on a grassy country road outside of town. As she pulled her suitcase from the back of the Prius, Jessie promised to have one of the hands deliver her car later that afternoon.

"That is, if I can't talk you into coming back with me to give working with Ian one more chance," Jessie added, putting a hand on the hatch to close it.

Shaking her head, Andrea glanced toward the entrance of the Warriors-4-Life Center, a long, low tan brick structure. In front of the building, a wheelchair-accessible walkway looped around a small pond partly hidden by a grove of trees. Park benches had been donated, creating a peaceful respite from the building's more institutional interior. But it was the people inside that Andrea both looked forward to and dreaded getting back to. Or one of them, at any rate.

"I have to go," she said, foreboding rippling through her at the thought of the confession to come. "Thanks for treating me to lunch. That was really sweet of you."

"Least I could do after bending your ear about my— my little issue."

"I'm not sure there's anything *little* about it, Jessie," Andrea said, recalling the dilemma Jessie had talked to her about as they'd lingered at the table once the meal was over. Though Jessie had declined to give her the specifics, she'd made it very clear that her story would open a Pandora's box that could end up hurting loved ones. But with her professional integrity, her very identity, at stake, too, there was nothing clear-cut when it came to her decision. "You clearly have some soul-searching to do before you decide whether to go forward with what you've found."

"Just tell me, tell me, please, as a psychologist and as a woman. What would you do?" Jessie pleaded.

"First of all," Andrea told her, "I don't have nearly enough information to say. Besides, I'm not you—and I'm definitely not in the business of making anyone's decisions for them. But I have faith you'll carefully think it through and figure out what's right for you."

Jessie snorted. "Spoken like a true headshrinker."

"Now you sound like Ian." Andrea's smile quickly faded. "And speaking of Ian, I'll have Julian contact your husband about the counselor I recommended."

"If this shooting business hasn't gotten him too paranoid to allow it." Frowning at the thought, Jessie added, "Though I guess it's not technically paranoia if someone's really out to get you."

Andrea felt the needle-sharp bite of fear because, no matter how enjoyable it had been to pretend that the two of them were a couple of old friends enjoying a lunch get-away, Jessie's words drove home the fact that only hours before, someone had peered down the barrel of a weapon, aimed at her and Ian, and then squeezed the trigger...

Someone who might very well do it again after discovering Ian had escaped unharmed. "No one *will* get to him, will they?"

"Zach'll see to it they don't, I promise. Ian won't be riding out alone again until we know what happened. If my husband had it his way he'd put me on lockdown, too, for the duration."

She looked so troubled that Andrea might have tried to talk more with her about it had Julian not chosen that moment to come through the front door, looking surprised to see her here, especially without her car. As he often did on days he wasn't meeting with potential donors, he wore a dark green polo shirt, the Warriors-4-Life logo embroidered over the left chest, neatly tucked into a pair of crisp chino slacks. Though he was several inches shy of Ian's six-four and fifteen years older, his warm, golden-brown eyes, his strong jaw and the dusting of gray at his temples lent him an air of authority. Fit and distinguished-looking, he strode toward her, the precision of his movements reminding her—strongly and for the first time—of the father she hadn't seen in nearly twenty years. The father she'd worshipped with a child's fervor, before she'd learned he had another family...and had left behind a third back in his hometown without troubling himself to divorce any of the women he had married.

She blinked and squinted at Julian, telling herself her suspicion wasn't true. Surely, she'd been attracted to his unwavering devotion to a greater purpose, to his leadership and kindness rather than some subconscious trigger buried in her past. She was especially sure she hadn't fallen for him because she was still pining for the father whose betrayal had shattered her family into a million pieces.

Still, nausea roiled in her stomach, her eyes stinging with suspicion.

"So that's him, is it? Ian's competition," Jessie asked her in a low voice. When Andrea couldn't find her voice to answer, her new friend added, "Guess I'll leave you to it, then."

As she pulled back out onto the road, Andrea waved goodbye before turning to Julian, dread pooling in her stomach.

"What are you doing back alrea—" The question died on his lips as his gaze latched on to the small white rectangle taped above her left eye. "What happened? Are you all right?"

She raised a hand. "Before I tell you, you need to know that everybody's okay. Doctor says I'm fine. I didn't even end up needing stitches."

He studied her for a moment before reaching to pull her to him, clearly forgetting that they might be seen by anyone. When Andrea stiffened in his arms, he broke off the embrace. "What is it?"

"Let's walk down by the pond," she said, leaving both her purse and suitcase on the first of the park benches that lined the pathway.

Though he walked beside her, he didn't try to touch her again as they descended the gradual incline leading to the pond's green-brown waters. A light breeze whispered through the tall grasses growing on the far end, and a few water lilies skimmed the surface, along with a trio of fat white ducks.

She recounted how she'd convinced Ian to take her with him out on the range that morning, saying, "It was the only way I could think of to get him to stop avoiding me and maybe open up a little."

"I had no idea you rode," said Julian, his gaze straying to the bandage once more. "Or do you?"

"Not very well, that's for certain, but I managed to stay in the saddle. Or at least I did until Ian dragged me down."

Julian stopped walking to stare at her, his face contorting. "He *attacked* you? What the devil happened?" Edged with anger, his accented words sliced like a saber.

"It wasn't like that, I swear," she rushed to explain. "It's more like Ian *saved* me. Otherwise, I might have been shot or thrown on my head when my horse spooked."

She told him what had happened, downplaying her own terror and emphasizing Ian's efforts to keep her safe and then tend to her after she was accidentally injured.

"Even after he thought he'd heard the shooter drive off, Ian insisted we stay where there was cover and we'd be safe," she said. "We waited there and talked. It was an excellent discussion, leading him to remember more than ever."

"Remember what?" Julian asked, an unaccustomed urgency in his voice. "What did he say, Andrea?"

She stopped walking to stare at him. "More about his life prior to his capture, but I can't share any details. You know that."

His face reddening, Julian grimaced. "Of course, I know you can't break confidentiality. I only— Seeing you injured like this made me worry that these recovered memories came out of flashbacks. That you might have…*exaggerated* Captain Rayford's heroism in an attempt to downplay an unfortunate—"

"He didn't hit me. I swear it." But Andrea felt her own face heat with the knowledge that, in kissing her, the handsome agent-turned-cowboy had done something far more dangerous. "We were just talking, that's all, and then his brother and the ranch manager showed up looking for us."

Her heart stumbled and she felt the prickle of perspiration beneath her top. Because in her eagerness to reassure Julian, she'd left out the fact that she and Ian had done more than talk.

Guilt pressed down on her, along with a memory of Ian leaning forward to claim her mouth. And she'd kissed him just as fervently, the memories of their original attraction igniting like dry tinder. Because when it came to the gorgeous, maddening and persistent Ian Rayford, one intimacy would always lead to another.

"All I can think of is that you might have been shot down," Julian said, wrapping her in his arms again, now that they were hidden from view by the trees. "I might have lost you forever, in a single moment."

She pulled away and resumed walking, too nervous to keep still and too disgusted with herself for words. But somehow, she must find them.

Stalling for time, she instead answered Julian's questions about what had happened with the shooter and whether Ian had any idea of who or why the attack may have happened. "I understand the sheriff will be looking into it. But unless the gunman left behind some clue, I suspect he'll get away with it."

The injustice of the thought brought with it a rush of

red-hot rage, the desire to see the guilty party punished. "It makes me absolutely furious to think that after everything Ian's been through, he'd have someone shooting at him in his own country, on his own property. How much does he have to sacrifice to finally come home?"

Julian did a double take. "You're upset. Not on your own account, but his."

"Of course, I'm upset. I care about—about my patients." She swallowed hard, a painful lump threatening to choke her. "And I can't help caring especially about Ian."

Julian stopped walking and studied her before nodding. "It's only natural, since the two of you were close once. A past personal relationship will always color—"

"The trouble is," she said, the thrumming of the blood in her veins a rushing noise in her ears, "Ian doesn't—he can't or he won't—remember that we ever broke up. It's been hard for me, too, Julian. Difficult to keep from… from being swept up in the past as I try to draw him to the present."

"What are—what are you trying to say, Andrea?" he asked, looking more concerned than ever. Or was it fear that she was seeing, a panicked pulse of déjà vu? As much as she wanted to spare him doubt or pain, she forced herself to remember how her father had once given that excuse when his acts had finally, horrifyingly come to light—and how that decision had left her mother shattered.

She shook her head. "I'm sorry, but I can't go back there. Not without risking—this morning, after we were shot at, emotions were running high. I was bleeding. He was helping me. And then—there was a kiss."

"He kissed you." Julian's voice went cool and smooth

as plate glass. But there was a spark of heat in his eyes, the telltale twitch of a muscle in his clenched jaw.

She nodded, her face blazing. "I'm so sorry. I never meant to… I thought I'd made it clear to him that I was… But clearly, it didn't sink in, and in the heat of the moment, I'm afraid—afraid I forgot myself, forgot what I was there for. And I kissed him back."

"Andrea…" Julian groaned, his eyes closing as he raised a hand to pinch the bridge of his nose.

"It's not— I love *you*, Julian. I want to be with *you*, not him or anyone else."

He blew a breath through his nose before looking at her as if she were a stranger.

Shame took root in the pit of her stomach, spreading icy tendrils. "Can you— Do you think you can forgive me?"

His lips thinned and paled as he pressed them together. But he soon regained control of himself, looking far more like the man she'd come to know, the man whose squared shoulders and quiet dignity were so much like her father's. "As you said, emotions must have been—"

"That's true, but I have to tell you, it wasn't just the moment," she said. "It was… I'd grieved this man, thought he was dead. So to expect me to be able to wall myself off from all those feelings, to forget we'd ever been a couple… It's too much, Julian. Too much to expect from me and especially from him."

"I see," he managed, looking as if the two words left a bitter taste in his mouth. "Well, I suppose I should credit you for being honest. You tried to warn me from the start, I know. But this—"

"Please don't ask me to go back. I don't want to— I

can't. Send Connor, please. I'll consult with him on the case from here."

Julian remained silent long enough for her to wonder whether he was considering or brooding. "As much as I'd prefer that solution," he finally said, "I'm afraid there are…there are other factors in play."

She stared at him, hot moisture welling in her eyes. "What other factors? You can't possibly be thinking about the money. This is—this is our future I'm talking about, Julian. And my mental health because I can't be the kind of woman who would—"

"I understand you're upset. You've been through a terrible ordeal and aren't ready to rationally talk this through, not yet."

"Talk what through? If you'd only tell me the real reason…"

"Come inside, Andrea. It's clear you need to rest now. Sleep, and then we'll talk again."

A spike of heat was her temper's only warning. "So you're putting me to bed now, like a misbehaving child?"

"I'm sending you to rest now," he said, a warning in his gaze, "because I truly do care about you. And because I need you out of my sight right now, before I end up saying something we'll both very much regret."

Chapter 6

Ian decided his brother had been right. Sheriff George Canter remained nothing but big hat and attitude, especially when it came anything to do with his two least favorite reformed hell-raisers. Tall and rugged-looking, with dark eyes and a perpetual sneer, he seemed more interested in finishing their meeting in the barn office so he could run to the house to *console* Zach and Ian's mother.

With every passing reference to their mama, the pulse point at Zach's temple beat a little harder until finally he erupted. "First of all, you've missed her. With my wife out for the afternoon, my mother was kind enough to volunteer to pick up Eden from school."

In their stalls, the nearest horses stamped and shuffled, as if they scented the tension in the air.

Canter glanced at his watch. "So what time is it that kindergarten gets out? 'Cause if she'll be back soon, it's only right that I should wait and pay my respects."

"Never you mind about that," Zach said. "You'll be out investigating the scene of the shooting by the time they're home. Before it gets dark."

Eyes narrowing, Canter pulled off his hat, revealing a full head of dark hair, highlighted by lighter patches at the temples. "Those cowhands of yours might jump to your orders, but last I checked, I work for the people of this county."

"Especially the people inclined to write checks for your next campaign."

Anger twisting in his rugged face, Canter opened his mouth to speak, but Ian broke in first.

"Let's head out now, together, and I'll help you look for shell casings. I have a pretty good idea where you might find them, after all."

The sheriff looked at him as if he were still the same dumbass tenth-grader he'd caught cutting class and drinking behind the Wheeler barn, though now he had to look up to meet Ian's eyes. Shaking his head, Canter said, "Can't have the victim along collecting evidence. Wouldn't some damned lawyer have a field day with that? No, sirree, soldier boy."

Ian's entire body clenched. "I'm not your *soldier boy*."

Canter looked him up and down. "You better damn well uncurl those fists, or maybe you'll get to be my *prisoner*. Again."

A buzzing built in Ian's head, the angry sound of a wasp's nest, as his mind whirled through several methods of overcoming and incapacitating an armed man. Methods he remembered being trained in. Methods he'd had occasion to use, even if they hadn't worked that night in Pakistan, where he'd been ambushed with another...

"Ian." Zach's voice filtered through the buzzing, and Ian recognized the warning in it. "Don't rise to the bait, man."

Zach stared at the sheriff, his voice going hard as steel. "He's a former POW, Canter. A national hero— didn't you hear it on the news? Be a damned shame not to give him the respect that he's got comin', the kind of disgrace that wouldn't look good on a campaign poster if it happened to get out."

Hero. The word lodged like a thorn in Ian's throat, as one of his captor's demands floated up from the black depths. An English-speaking captor brought in especially for this interrogation. *The listening post—you will tell us where it is. You will tell us today, or by all that is holy, you will not live to see tomorrow.*

Beyond that, he remembered nothing but a bolt of blinding pain.

Shaking if off, he grew aware of Canter, who was clearly weighing the chance of settling whatever grudge he held against the Rayford brothers and Zach's unspoken reminder that his wife was more than capable of influencing media coverage. After a bit of boot-scuffing, the sheriff said, "Don't you boys worry. I've got this covered. I should be able to find the place just fine, with those GPS coordinates you gave me. I'll head out now and collect any evidence around the rim where you said, then photograph any tire tracks, all that sort of thing."

Judging from the curdled-milk look on his face, he was none too happy about it, but at least he was willing to go through the motions.

"Track's pretty rough," Zach warned him.

"Shouldn't be an issue, with the new department SUV."

"Well, call us if you get stuck or run into any trouble. I can send Virgil or a couple of the hands out, no problem."

Canter nodded and donned his hat before leaving the barn but not before giving the brothers a look that said he wouldn't forget this indignity. The two Australian shepherds, who tagged along with Zach when Eden wasn't around, wagged their fringed tails after him, leaving Zach to shake his head.

"There's proof positive those goofball pups are no damned judge of character."

Ian laughed. "Where's Gretel when you need her? And what's the German command for 'Rip that ugly sneer off his face'?"

Zach shot him a wry grin. "She'd probably catch rabies."

"I wouldn't be surprised, but seriously, man. You need to watch your back around him. Because whatever your beef is with him, it's clear he'd love a chance to lay you low."

Zach's smile turned to a grimace. "Come here. I want to show you something. Something that might explain a whole lot."

He led Ian to the barn office and gestured toward the window. "You see that brand-new Tahoe he's heading out in? The one with every freaking option you can put on one? That was donated to the department by our mama this past November, when Jessie and I were off on our honeymoon."

"So Mama did it while you were out of sight, then," Ian said, understanding that in accordance with the terms of his father's will, he and his brother were each meant to have a vote on all large expenditures, as the three of them were equal heirs. Once Ian was reported killed in action, their mother—who despised dealing with the everyday decisions and recognized that her prescription-pill problem had caused her to make a mess of things in the past—had insisted on signing over her proxy to Zach.

Zach nodded. "While I wasn't around to guard the henhouse from one determined fox. She went all teary when I confronted her about it later, said she'd only wanted to 'give back to the community,' since we've been doing so well thanks to that natural gas find. I told her I'd be behind that idea 100 percent. I'd be glad to pitch in for a new truck for the fire department or a playground over at the school if she asked me, but no more to the sheriff. Not another dime."

"So what's his hold on her? Is it just he pays her attention, or does he have something on her?"

"He may've at one time, but that's all in the open now, and we have Eden," Zach said, referring to the dark time in his and Jessie's past that had ended up bringing them together as a family. "So I don't know what it could be. I only know it's been tough keeping them apart."

"You'd almost think he might suck up to us, too."

"Maybe he's too disgusted, remembering how he used to drag us back to the old man when we got rowdy, or he's just too eaten up with jealousy over the new money from the gas find."

Ian winced. "He wouldn't be so jealous if he knew how the old man lit into us whenever he brought us home."

"So you remember?"

"Not all of it, just bits and pieces I'd as soon've left forgotten." Only six months prior to Ian's disappearance, the old SOB had keeled over of a heart attack. Neither Ian nor his brother had attended the services that followed; nor had either one reached out to the mother who'd implored them to keep up appearances at all costs, never lifting a finger to protect them from his rages, not even when blackened eyes and broken bones were involved.

Still, for some reason Ian might never understand, this land had called him back to it, this once-shattered family drawing him the way a magnet pulled a compass needle.

When Zach said he had a call to make, Ian headed back to the house in hopes of scaring up an extra sandwich. When he'd first returned, weak and dehydrated, he'd had almost no appetite, but these days, whenever he wasn't working, he was hitting the kitchen between meals.

He forgot his hunger when he passed the little nook outside the kitchen, where he spotted Jessie at the built-in desk, completely engrossed in something she was reading. "What's wrong?"

As she turned to hide the folder behind her, he caught a glimpse of what looked like handwritten script. "Oh, nothing. Just going through today's mail, that's all. Nothing but the usual junk."

"You sure? You look a little— Is everything all right with Andrea? What did the doctors say about her head?"

"She's fine." The hand that had held the note came up empty as Jessie brushed aside his concern. "They used this glue stuff to close the cut and told her to take it easy for a few days, but she was feeling well enough to go to lunch—and I only had to twist her arm a little."

"Do you think there's any chance she'll come back? Any chance I haven't scared her off for good?"

When Jessie hesitated, he added, "I know you talked about me. I can see it in your face."

"I'm sorry, Ian." Compassion gleamed in her eyes. "I understand how confusing it must be for you, and I think it is for her, too. But it was probably a bad idea to invite her in the first place."

"I'm glad you and Zach did."

"I'm not, because it's obvious that both of you are hurting." She shook her head. "You have to understand, Ian, the way you feel about her has put her in an impossible situation. She could lose her license and hurt a man she seems to care very much about."

"I don't give a damn about him, only her. And if she can't come back to work as my psychologist, couldn't she at least come as a friend?"

"You need to understand. She's not coming back."

The pitying look Jessie gave him set his teeth on edge. He was more than just a victim—and he'd be damned if he'd be victimized by this. "What's that old saying about Mohammed coming to the mountain? Because if she won't come here, I'm heading into Marston to see her."

"I don't think that's a good idea."

"She's helping me remember. And besides, I—I still…" He couldn't get the rest out, couldn't stand to sound pathetic.

But Jessie seemed to understand him anyway. "I know you do. But you don't have a vehicle or a valid driver's license. Not to mention—"

"Yeah. Being declared dead is inconvenient that way." Ian had barely begun to tackle the reams of paperwork it was going to take to get everything sorted. "But if I didn't let those terrorists stop me, I'm damned sure not about to let a couple of small details like that get in my way."

"I was about to say, not to mention the little detail that someone's tried to blow your head off."

"I won't be caught off guard again."

Jessie frowned. "Just promise me you'll give her a little time, at least. Okay?"

"Time enough for you to talk my brother into putting me on lockdown?"

She crossed her arms in front of her chest. "We aren't your captors, Ian. But we do care about you. All of us. You're our miracle."

When he said nothing, she asked, "So are you and I good?"

He swallowed hard, then let out the breath he had been holding. "Of course, we are. And thanks, by the way, for taking care of Andrea."

"No problem. I really like her. She's smart, has a great head for people and has the driest sense of humor ever. But I'd better get up to our suite. I'm sure Gretel's more than ready for a romp outside by now. I can hear her whimpering from here."

"See you later, then."

Instead of heading to the kitchen, he grabbed this month's issue of *Working Ranch* and feigned fascination with a truck ad until he heard her footsteps heading upstairs. With Jessie safely out of sight, he went through the mail to find the note she'd hidden, but it was nowhere in the stack.

Had she slipped it under her shirt or tucked it into the waistband of her jeans? Possible, he thought, but tough to do one-handed. He took another look at the desk before trying the top drawer, though he dimly recalled that one had never slid smoothly, opening—when it did open—with a squawk of protest.

Apparently, someone had fixed it in the many years since he'd lived at home. The drawer moved freely, and sure enough, he found in it a folded piece of unlined paper.

"Gotcha," he said, but as he picked it up, a spasm of conscience tightened his gut. Did he really want to do this? Spy on his brother's wife? What if he discovered something terrible? An affair or—

No way would she do something like that, he decided, not when she was so clearly devoted to his brother and Eden. Besides, from what he'd seen of Jessie, she had way too much integrity to sneak around behind Zach's back. But he could easily imagine her trying to protect him by hiding something she thought might set back his progress, so he tamped down his reservations and unfolded the paper, then quickly read the five words someone had handwritten in block letters. Five angry words that had been clearly meant for him.

Humiliated at being sent to her room, Andrea found herself pacing its cell-like confines as the room's one window grew dark. As hard as it had been hearing the controlled anger in Julian's voice as he'd demanded she leave his sight, she'd expected—and deserved—no less. What had blindsided her, though, was his reaction to her plea to send someone else to work with Ian.

"I'm afraid there are...there are other factors in play," he'd said, but what on earth could he be talking about? Was someone pressuring him about it? Someone he knew from his former military career? Or what if he was still secretly working for the government?

She thought of how passionate, how persuasive he'd always been about the center and what he called the worthiest mission of his life. For more than six months, he'd poured every ounce of energy into Warriors-4-Life.

Difficult to believe he had room for another agenda, impossible to think his Southern honor would allow it.

But as she remembered how he'd pushed her to share confidential information, another possibility slipped like a shadow into her mind. What if Julian was one of the victims in this, a victim of blackmail? Someone might have something on him, some secret so devastating they could use it to bend him to his or her will.

So devastating he didn't care if it cost him the woman he had sworn to love for as long as he lived, the woman he wanted by his side as a life partner.

What if he'd been pressured into more than she guessed, if their relationship itself had been part of the sham? *He hasn't even taken the time from his work to pick out a ring*, some small, suspicious part of her whispered, though when he'd blushed, admitting he had found it so hard to believe a "beautiful, intelligent young woman" would accept his proposal that he'd been afraid to buy "the hardware" first, she'd blurted that she cared nothing for diamonds, only for him.

Her stomach flipped, and she told herself she was wrong, that Julian genuinely loved her. His coercion had to be more recent, for him to turn so suddenly.

When someone knocked at her door, she took a quick glance at the mirror and arranged her face into what she hoped would come off as a bland expression.

Their psychiatric nurse, Cassidy, stood there, grinning from ear to ear as she handed Andrea a key ring. "The cutest guy just dropped these off for you a while back, but I was on my way to do meds. But anyway, this cowboy? He had the whole hat, boots and license-plate-sized belt buckle going for him. Scrumptious!" A tiny redhead with a million freckles, she sighed happily and twirled one of the bright red corkscrew ringlets that fell over her shoulders.

Though she was only a couple of years older than Cassidy's twenty-nine, Andrea couldn't help but smile. Had she ever been so young or lust so uncomplicated? "Oh, yes. I remember," she said as she pocketed the keys. "They told me a couple of the hands would bring back my car." If Cassidy had gotten a gander at either of the Rayford brothers, she would have probably choked on her own drool.

"A couple? Darn it all, I only saw the one." Cassidy snapped her fingers before her smile abruptly faded. "Hey, what's that on your forehead? And what're you doing back so early anyway?"

"The short version is I bumped my head."

"I want the whole story. Come on. Dish it, sister."

Andrea looked down at the center's live wire before shaking her head. "You'd be bored to tears, and anyway, I'm exhausted."

Cassidy studied her, her eyes narrowing. "Something's bothering you. Tell me."

Though she hated to lie, Andrea pointed toward her forehead. "Kind of a bad headache. So let me rest now, and I'll tell you about the cowboys I saw on the ranch later."

Cassidy brightened instantly. "In *excruciating* detail?"

"So excruciating, you'll be begging for mercy."

"I'll hold you to that, then. Feel better."

Andrea was still smiling and shaking her head at her departure when she heard the harsh grinding of an ignition in the staff parking lot outside of her one small window. Frowning at the unpleasant sound, she peeked out from behind her curtain, curious about which staff member was murdering his or her ride.

But the SUV she saw whipping out onto the state highway was Julian's Ford Explorer. Though she couldn't see him through the tinted windows, he must be beyond upset to speed off like that. She'd never known him to be anything but a safe and cautious driver.

Could Julian be so furious thinking of Ian kissing her that he'd decided to go and confront him on the ranch? Almost instantly, she dismissed the thought. Julian wasn't the type to fly off in a jealous rage. Besides, if he had blamed Ian, he surely wouldn't have pressured her to go back into the proverbial lion's den.

Nor did she believe that Julian was so upset about her confession that he'd roar off to the nearest bar to drown his disappointment. He might have a stiff glass of bourbon in the privacy of his own room, but he was far too disciplined—and too proud—to risk making a public spectacle of himself or damaging the center's reputation.

More likely, she thought, he was desperate to speak to the person pressuring him to get inside information on Ian Rayford's progress. Though why he couldn't do it in his office, she had no idea—

His office.

She caught her lip between her teeth, thinking of how much time he spent there working on fund-raising campaigns, weighing the needs of the center's many applicants and conducting a host of other administrative tasks. Which meant, she decided, that if someone were putting pressure on him, it was the most likely place to look for evidence of whatever secret he was keeping...

Evidence she could use to save him from his blackmailer—and maybe their relationship, as well. *But is there really something left to save if you're willing to spy on him? And do you really want a man you can't be certain you can trust?*

A part of her cringed, knowing those were the questions she would ask any client she was counseling. But it didn't matter, not when the idea of getting answers had taken root so stubbornly and especially not when whatever Julian was keeping from her could be dangerous to Ian.

She slipped out of her room, avoiding her coworkers and the clients, who were sharing their evening meal in the dining room. Instead, she walked down to the building's front corridor and knocked at the door to Julian's office, as if she believed for half a second that he might be inside.

When there was no answer, as expected, she let herself in, grateful that he'd been too upset or distracted to lock the door. The office itself was moderately but comfortably decorated. Though Julian had chafed at the suggestion of putting up what he called "an ego wall," she'd talked him into hanging his framed degrees and photos of him smiling with illustrious donors, supportive politicians and several of the center's first residents to foster confidence from both the families of clients and potential contributors.

Now, though, those photographs came back to haunt her, staring down with seeming disapproval as she commandeered his leather chair and nudged the mouse of his desktop computer to wake it out of sleep mode. What came up, however, was a dialogue box asking for the administrator's password. She cursed under her breath; she had her own log-in to the network, but it was both easily traceable and useless in gaining access to his private messages.

Forgetting the idea, she started digging through drawers as she recalled the many times she'd seen him scribbling notes while he was on the phone. Surely, he must have saved some. In the top drawer, sure enough, she found a stack, each message so innocuous that she burned with fresh guilt and thought of giving up.

"In for a penny, in for a pound," she said. But it was Ian's lean and handsome face that moved her to flip through pages of Julian's calendar and then lift his desk blotter, where she plucked out a slip of paper.

Opening the folded square, she blinked and then gasped as she recognized her own passwords.

Her blood ran cold, chill bumps erupting as she realized he had not only her network and email log-in information, but passwords for the social network pages she used to keep up with old friends. He even had access to her online banking, a discovery that raised every fine hair behind her neck. She'd heard of keystroke-tracking software that could be secretly installed on a computer, but how on earth could he have gotten to her laptop? *Somehow, through the network. He must have—*

"What the devil do you think you're doing?"

She nearly jumped out of her skin at the sound of Julian's voice behind her. Hands curling into fists, she leaped to her feet, heart slamming wildly and body shaking so hard that her teeth were chattering.

"Never mind that," he said, eyeing the open drawers at the side of the desk. "The answer's quite apparent. What I want to know is *why* you're going through my things?"

Startled as she was, she could only say, "B-but I saw you race off."

"I loaned my truck to Michael. His engine wouldn't start, and he was late for what I take was a hot date with some local woman. So I ask you again, why are you spying on me?"

Swallowing back her panic, she mustered all her indignation and rattled the paper in her hand. "How *dare* you ask me that when it's even more obvious you've been spying on me for far longer than I've ever— I can't believe you. You're a total stranger. A fraud." Just the way her father had been.

At the sight of the paper, the color drained from Julian's face, his accent intensifying as he said, "No, Andrea. I'm still the same—"

"Liar," she said, flashing back to the terrible moment when she'd first accepted what her father was. Because this man, she understood now, had never been more to her than some sort of replacement for the love she'd lost as a child, though she would have sworn the wound had long since healed. "I can't believe I was so stupid to fall for your line. To imagine that I loved you."

"I still love you, Andrea. I do now and always will. But you have to understand… Marilyn destroyed me, so much that I swore I'd never again marry. So I had to be sure, dead sure, before I could possibly commit myself to—"

"Get some therapy, then. But don't count on me standing by your side while you pull yourself together. I'm finished."

"What do you mean, you're finished? Please, Andrea—"

"I can't be with you, not in a relationship. And not professionally, either. When I resigned from the youth center in San Diego, my supervisor left me an open invitation to come back if I ever—"

"You can't leave. You can't leave Warriors-4-Life. We

need you. Your clients need you. There's no one else your equal when it comes to—"

"Don't throw them up in my face," she said, yet her heart was breaking at the thought of all the vulnerable ex-soldiers she worked with, so many of them already rejected by family and friends, and the society who judged them "crazy" and turned their backs on them. And then there was Ian, caught up in a tortured no-man's-land between pain and memory.

"What about your lover?" Julian asked bitterly. "Will you really abandon him, too?"

"First of all, Ian's not my lover." Glaring, she held up the paper with her passwords as a horrifying new thought occurred. "And secondly, tell me this wasn't about him. All of it, from the start. That the rest isn't some cover story you've come up with to get to my personal case notes on him and turn them over to who knows who?"

She frowned, realizing, unlike the other passwords, her case-note log-in was outdated, since she was in the habit of changing it every week or two. "Wait— You didn't get it, did you? Not my notes." A measure of relief washed over her, a warm wave beneath a shell of ice.

"I didn't. But I'll need that password, Andrea. The latest one, right now. You can write it on the—"

"Have you lost your mind? I could lose my license, for one thing, to say nothing of betraying the confidence of all my—"

"Not all of them. Just one. The password, Andrea, before you leave this office."

She stared into his face, willing this to be a nightmare. What on earth would ever convince him to behave this way? "Just tell me, Julian, are you being coerced in some way? Blackmailed or threatened? Because if you are, I can help you. We'll call the authorities together to report it."

Standing as tall as he at six feet, she stared straight into his eyes. And saw the instant a wall slid down, cutting himself off from the possibility of redemption, of salvaging their relationship. She knew she'd never again fully trust him—or herself, around another older man. But Julian had the chance, at least, to save himself, the man whose passion and charisma had drawn her to this place…

A town only an hour's distance from the ranch where Ian grew up.

She couldn't let her mind travel down that path yet, couldn't pause to wonder if her recruitment, maybe even the establishment of the center itself, could be part of some grand conspiracy.

"You have to explain," she said. "Tell me why you'd be willing to forget every professional ethic you've ever stood for to look into a patient's confidential records."

"You talk to me about *professional ethics*—" a cold-steel hardness hammered through his words like nails driven through half-rotted wood "—when you were out there on that ranch swapping DNA with your own client—an admission that would cause you a world of trouble if I happened to report it to the state board."

"That's it. I'm out of here." She tried to step around him, but he moved to block her way.

"The newest password, Andrea. If you care about your country in the least, you have to do this for me."

"My country?" she echoed, a cold chill raising goose bumps. "Explain yourself right now."

"You'll have to trust me on this," Julian told her. "And

trust me when I tell you this is a dangerous game you're playing."

"Trust *you*, a man who's lied to me and invaded my privacy on so many levels, over someone who's sacrificed so much for his country? I saw those photos in his file, Julian. I saw what Ian's captors did to him." Tears sparkled along the lower rims of her eyes at the memory of angry, raised scars that crisscrossed his back and shoulders. Maybe they would fade with time or a plastic surgeon could diminish their appearance, but underneath, they reached to his soul, wounds to the psyche that would never go away.

"You know, Julian," she went on, "I've wondered why you've held back all this time, why you've deliberately avoided getting physical."

"I've told you why. The other employees here, the possibility of—"

"I thought maybe you were just an old-fashioned Savannah gentleman, a little out of step with the times. But now, I have to wonder, was there another reason you were afraid to get too close?"

She waited for him to argue with what she'd said, or at least to elaborate a little more. Except he couldn't. Or wouldn't, preferring instead to fall back on his most authoritative stare.

Well, she had never been one of the soldiers he commanded, so if he thought she'd accept patriotic duty as a reason without the slightest shred of proof, he'd better think again. Only inches from his face, she leveled her coldest gaze on him—partly to disguise the way her pulse was pounding. "Step out of the way, Julian, unless you want law enforcement tangled up in this, too."

"In addition to refusing your duty to your country,

you'd shut the center down? Stop all the good we're doing?"

"I'll do what I have to to get back to California—after I've warned Ian." She owed him that much, at least, even if she feared it might inflame his paranoia. Except that Jessie's words whispered in her memory: *I guess it's not technically paranoia if someone's really out to get you.* "I'm packing up my things and leaving, and if I lose my license to practice in Texas over this, so be it."

She tried again to pass him, and Julian's hand shot out to grip her forearm, hard enough that her attempts to jerk it back were useless.

Before she recovered from the shock, he spoke, his quiet words laden with an eerie menace. "If you cross me on this, I swear to you, you'll never practice again anywhere. I have connections, you see. Connections that will make certain that wherever you tried to set up shop, the charges against you will—"

"The *charges*?" She struggled again to free her arm, but his grip only tightened. "For a single kiss, shared with a confused man I was once engaged to? A man that you pressured me into seeing in the first place despite my strong reservations?"

"That's all *your* story." His gaze was as cold and level as the surface of a frozen lake. "But it won't necessarily be mine. It's counted as a sexual assault, you know, when a mental health professional has relations with a client. Especially one whose memory gaps would make him extremely vulnerable to—"

She shuddered, her skin crawling. She couldn't imagine how such a charge, without physical evidence or a client's testimony, would ever stick. But crazy as it was, even an accusation of sexual impropriety from someone as respected as Julian Ross would send her life spinning out of control. Using all her passwords, he could easily create incriminating emails, maybe even texts, too—at least enough to get an investigation started. If the media got wind of it, a female psychologist "raping" a nationally known male patient, she'd be the subject of a torrent of media and online commentary. And people would happily speculate that Ian, with his well-known memory issues, had simply forgotten what had really happened. Or enjoyed her attentions too much to complain.

"You're insane," she whispered, her tears leaking out the only warmth left in her.

"Insane?" His smile, too, was icy. "And here I thought you psychologists never used that word."

You psychologists, he'd said, as if the science were completely alien to him and not a world he'd supposedly worked with on the military side for decades. Shaking her head, she asked, "Who *are* you? Because you're certainly not my Julian."

His lips thinned and his mouth tightened, as if the question pained him. "No, I'm not. That version's gone now. Which means, my darling Andrea, that you're going to have to find a way to survive this one—you and Captain Rayford both."

Chapter 7

Ian went out to the barn office, a lump in his throat and the five words on the note echoing through his brain. He'd wanted to take it, get his brother's opinion on the handwriting, but when he'd heard quiet footsteps moving down the staircase, he'd replaced it in the same drawer where Jessie had left it hidden.

He'd retreated to the kitchen, where Althea, true to form, asked him to "taste test" the mouthwatering lemon squares she'd made a thousand times before. Unable to escape her well-meaning chatter, he smiled and made nice, praising her delicacies and gently teasing until he had the broad-hipped older woman blushing like a schoolgirl.

Then his mother came in with Eden, looking sleepy and bedraggled as a five-year-old can after a rough day in the kindergarten trenches. He'd cheered her up by sneaking her a lemon square against his mother's exhortations that she "save her appetite for supper" and telling her some silly riddles dredged up from the recesses of his memory.

Only after Eden had run off giggling to play with her dogs had he found a private moment to return to the little alcove, where he'd pulled out the drawer and found the note gone. Figuring Jessie meant only to protect him, he knocked at his brother's office door now, but there was no response. Instead, Ian found his older brother working with a coal-black filly in a nearby corral, soothing the tall three-year-old with big hands and soft words until she quit her fidgeting and trotted smoothly around the enclosure.

Not wanting to startle anyone and possibly get his brother thrown, Ian stood on the rails watching until Zach dismounted and patted the animal's sweat-soaked neck. "That's a good girl. You're going to be a real champ, aren't you?"

Ian smiled to see his brother's gentler side. "That's not the way our old man broke in young horses."

"Or sons, either," Zach said as he led the filly closer, "which is just one reason I'm going for exactly the opposite approach."

"Marriage has been good for you, ironed out some of the rough edges. Or maybe it's fatherhood that's doing it."

"Maybe it's both," Zach said, "because I'll tell you what. I had some issues of my own to work through when I came home, not the least of which was the news of my little brother's death."

He peeled off a leather glove and slapped Ian's arm with it. But Ian felt the affection in his gesture, just as he saw it in the look Zach gave him.

"So what's on your mind?" Zach gestured toward Ian's chest. "And why didn't you bring me one of those lemon squares that you've obviously been scrounging?"

Ian looked down, then brushed a few telltale yellow crumbs from the front of his shirt. "Too bad for you that Althea loves me more." The truth was, the old cook had always been more generous with her affections than their mother.

"She just feels sorry for your scrawny ass on account of you being so pitiful." Zach grinned as Ian leaned between the rails to punch his arm, a movement that had the filly tossing back her head and straining against the reins. "Come on, man, knock it off now. You're upsetting my girl here. If you want to talk, come walk with us."

Ian got serious and stepped into the corral to do as he'd been asked. Drawing a deep breath, he said, "I've gotta tell you something. Something about Jessie."

Zach stopped walking the horse to stare at him. "Just remember, that's my wife, before you start."

Ian threw his hands up. "Jessie's great, man. Really, she is. Whip-smart and beautiful and, for some damned reason nobody can figure, in love with your dumb ass."

Zach shrugged and said, "Some guys have just got it, man. I don't know what to tell you."

Ian made a scoffing sound before getting to the point. "Thing is, I saw her hiding something a little bit ago. Something I'm convinced was meant for me. She was trying not to worry me, I imagine, but after I read the thing—"

"What're you talking about?"

"It was a note, Zach, anonymous and to the point. Only thing it said was 'Your hiding days are over.'"

Zach's body tensed, a dangerous look hardening his features. Ian recognized the expression and braced himself for an explosion, but his brother's anger wasn't directed at him.

"Hold on a minute," Zach said, then raised his voice to call out, "Rusty?"

One of the younger hands looked up from whatever he'd been doing beneath the hood of an old pickup in the lee of the barn, wiped the grease from his hands and came trotting over.

"Mind interrupting what you're doing and cooling down Onyx here before you put her up?"

"Sure thing, Mr. Rayford, sir," the kid said, for Ian realized that, despite his ox-like build, the round-faced cowboy with the ridiculously tall hat still hadn't lost all his baby fat. Not that there was much chance that ranch work wouldn't melt it off him in a few months.

"You don't have to *sir* me, cowboy. This isn't the marines," Zach said. "Be gentle with this filly, though, and give her a good rubdown, too. She's just getting started, and I don't want her scared or hurt, or to have any negative associations with the barn or human handling."

The kid snatched off the ten-gallon hat, revealed an unruly shock of red-brown hair. "Yes, sir—I mean Mr. Rayford, sir." Blushing, he added helplessly, "I'm sorry. But I won't disappoint you. I promise that I won't."

Zach nodded and looked after them as the hand led off the filly.

"That horse is special to you, isn't she?" Ian asked him, taking note of the animal's gleaming jet coat and rock-solid quarter horse build.

"Not half as special as that stubborn woman of mine."

Ian nodded, his throat tightening. "I get that, Zach. I do. First the shooting, now the note. I'm a danger to your family, aren't I, to Jessie and Eden? A danger to all of us, as long as there's a sniper gunning for me. Which means, it's time to move on. I've still got my savings." Though it had been part of his own so-called estate, Zach had restored the money, along with funds from the sale of his vehicle and the furnishings from his old apartment. There would be government back pay as well, from the months he'd spent as a prisoner, and Zach was working with the family's lawyers on seeing that Ian would receive a healthy portion of the ranch's profits, too—a portion easily worth millions.

But his brother was scowling at him now, shaking his head and demanding, "Quit talking nonsense. You're not going anywhere. Mama would have a heart attack."

"You think she'll like it any better when a bullet comes flying through the window? And what if she ended up hurt, her or Jessie or Eden, or Miss Althea or Virgil or—hell, *you*?"

Zach managed a wry smile. "Glad you thought to add me in there, somewhere, bonehead. But we'll definitely be stepping up ranch security. And the thing is, Ian, we don't have any way to know if this note's got anything to do with you, not without a name or an envelope to go by."

"You've got to be kidding. Do I really need to remind you that someone's out to get me? And this time, I've got a witness to prove it's more than just my imagination."

"I realize you were shot at. But it could turn out that was some jackass kid out drinking with his buddies, thinking it'd be funny to see you and Andrea duck and cover. Or it could've been someone with an ax to grind against the family as a whole—a disgruntled former employee or somebody who's feeling resentful that the Rayfords keep getting richer while they're still flat broke."

"You could be right, I guess, but I'm right when I tell you that not everybody's happy I made it back home. I can't tell you exactly how I know it, can't remember why I'm so damned sure that whoever's responsible for that ambush is even unhappier about the fact that I'm starting to remember pieces of my time—" Ian's vision wavered like a mirage, his brother shifting, shrinking, his blue eyes going dark and hard as stone while the reins he was holding morphed into a blood-caked chain. But this time, Ian gritted his teeth and shook off the hallucination. "Of my time away. And I'm sure that this person won't care who he has to hurt to stop me from remembering the rest."

"If someone really wants you dead, why send a warning? Why not just take you out when you're least expecting it?"

Ian thought about it for a moment. "Maybe the sender changed his mind about what it was going to take to run me off. We ought to ask Jessie how and when it was delivered, take a look at any envelope, as well, to see if there's a postmark or any other clue to where it came from."

"That's a good idea. Or at least it would be if we could get my wife's cooperation."

"Even if she's trying to protect me, she'd surely be willing to confide in you. So why don't you go ahead and ask her?"

"Because I'm pretty sure my darling wife would lie to me about it."

"Lie? To you? That makes no sense as all."

Zach huffed out a sigh, his blue eyes troubled. "It makes sense if she's not trying to protect you but her career, instead."

"Wait a minute. What are you thinking? That someone's threatening her on account of her latest investigative piece?"

"Whatever the hell it is, yeah. That's exactly what I'm thinking. Wouldn't be the first time her work's gotten her on the wrong side of some very dangerous types, and it makes me damned nervous when she refuses to at least tell me whose business she's digging into."

"So you're really still thinking there's a chance that Andrea was the real target this morning, when the shooter mistook her for Jessie?" Though Ian's instincts argued against it, with no memory to back up the suspicion, he was willing to at least listen to his brother's theory.

Zach nodded. "I sure as hell do. If only I could get her to give up her crusading, settle down here on the ranch and be a full-time mom to Eden."

"We're not living in the fifties, man. What are you saying, that she should stick to shopping and planning meals with Mama?" Ian might have only met her recently, but such life choices didn't sound much like his sister-in-law's style.

Zach chuffed a humorless laugh. "Heck, no. Those two would probably kill each other, and Jessie's got too much drive and talent to be happy penning those skills up. I just want my wife, my family *safe*. We've already suffered enough with the last rabid bear she poked."

Ian hadn't heard the entire story, but what he had gleaned was enough to convince him Zach had every reason to fear for Jessie's safety as she went after corruption at the highest levels. But it was just as easy to imagine how such a spirited woman would react to her husband's demand.

Zach shook his head, clearly stewing over his frustrations and his need to keep his family safe. "I'd bet that fine filly and a whole lot more that threat was directed at Jessie, and she doesn't want me worrying about it. It's just the kind of thing that stubborn woman would do— try to take matters into her own hands."

As much as Ian hated to get in the middle of their marriage, he had to say, "I understand your theory, might even give it credence, but this note showing up on the same day someone tried to ambush me is damned suspicious."

"You've definitely got a point there," Zach said, "and I'll do my best to get the truth out of Jessie about what she's been up to. But it's bound to be a touchy subject since she's been swearing she won't talk—for everybody's safety."

"I can see why that would worry you. Wait, there she is now." Ian nodded toward Jessie, who was jogging their way, despite the high-heeled boots she wore with her jeans and a rolled-sleeved blouse.

Zach hurried to meet her, Ian right behind him.

"What's the matter? You look upset," Zach asked. "Is Eden all right?"

Jessie stopped and shook her head as she caught her breath. "Eden's fine. Nobody's hurt. It's just—"

"I'll leave the two of you." Ian stepped away, wanting to give the couple privacy. He was already wondering how upset Jessie would be with him for ratting her out to Zach about the threat.

But Jessie was raising her hands. "Don't go, Ian. This concerns you, too. It's Andrea. I just called her because one of the maids found a pair of headphones under the bed in the guest suite, but when I reached Andrea, she was so upset she could barely get the words out."

Alarm jolted through him. "Why? What's happened? Is it her head?"

"Not her head, her heart. You see, her fiancé was none too happy when she told him about what happened between the two of you."

"About the shooting, you mean?" Zach said. "I understand that, but if she wants to come back, I can guarantee him we'll be stepping up security around this place big-time."

But that wasn't what Jessie was referring to, Ian saw as their gazes locked. And so did Zach, apparently.

"This is about your crazy idea you could steal her away from him," he said.

"Or that kiss we shared down in the ravine," Ian admitted, remembering the way their contact had ignited, making him lose sight of everything else. "Because being with her—it brings it all back. For both of us, I'm sure of it."

"Well, whatever it was," Jessie said, swinging an accusatory look his way, "you've gone and gotten her not only dumped, but fired. Did you have any idea her fiancé was her boss, too?"

"Yeah, but I—I'll talk to him if that's what she wants," Ian said, "make him understand that it was all my fault."

"Too late for that now. I reminded her how the doctor at the ER told her she needed to be sure to rest, but she said she's packing up her things now and heading straight back to California. She says she'll drive as far as she can and then get a motel room."

As Ian fished his phone from his back pocket, Zach said, "That doesn't make a lick of sense. She'll run out of daylight long before she runs outta empty prairie if she heads toward the interstate."

"I tried to tell her."

"What's her number, Jessie?" asked Ian. "I never got it from her."

Jessie pulled out her own cell and showed him the number on her list of recent calls. "You can try," she said, "but she didn't pick up when I called her back. I called the main number for the center, too, but all I got was some after-hours recording. I'm really worried about her, Ian.

She didn't sound at all like the smart, together woman we saw when she was out here."

But Ian's attention was fully on his phone as he tried calling Andrea. After the call rolled over to voice mail, he tried again with the same results. This time, he left a message. "Don't you dare leave town until I see you," he warned. "I'm on my way to the center. Call me when you get this."

When he disconnected, Jessie shook her head at him. "You can't go running after her, Ian. It'll just escalate—"

"I'm going," he told both her and his brother. "The question is, which one of you is lending me your keys?"

Aware that she would have very tight quarters at the center, Andrea had sold off or given away most of her possessions before moving here from California. Yet in the months she'd been here, the few belongings she'd brought with her had somehow expanded to more than she would ever be able to cram inside her little blue Honda. She could pack far more efficiently, she knew, if she weren't half blinded by tears and having to stop what she was doing so often to blow her nose. Her head was pounding, too, in spite of the mild painkiller she had taken.

But it was worry that was exacting the harshest toll, the worry that her refusal to do as Julian wanted would come back to haunt her. Still, the idea that he would call her patriotism into question and threaten her career, even hinting that she might be putting herself in real danger unless she did his bidding had in the end done nothing but convince her she had to get away from this no matter the cost.

Unwilling to risk talking to the all-too-perceptive Cassidy, Andrea decided to leave the center's psychiatric nurse a note instructing her to take whatever she wanted and give away the rest. Adding to the hasty message, Andrea included an explanation for her own sudden departure, a lie about an emergency back home involving a nonexistent aunt's recovery from surgery.

Instead, Andrea would go to her friend Samantha's place, if Sam wouldn't mind her couch surfing for a week or two. Andrea told herself it didn't matter. She'd sleep on a park bench if she had to, whatever it took to put as many miles as possible between herself and Julian.

Was it possible he'd really go after her license as he'd threatened? But whether or not he followed through was out of her hands, she told herself as she wiped away more stinging tears. The only part she could control was her refusal to spy on Ian.

After blotting her red eyes, she sneaked another box of her belongings to the car. With the last few books she couldn't part with stashed beneath a seat, Andrea climbed into the car, relief spreading through her that she'd managed to get this far without detection. As she cranked the engine, though, her phone vibrated once more in her pocket.

Sorry that she had taken Jessie's earlier call while she was so upset, Andrea had switched off the ringer. She regretted her babbling even more when she saw Ian's name on the caller ID window, and her phone's call log told her she had missed seven calls from the same number. There were several voice mails, too, including one from Julian.

She chose to listen to that message, maybe out of the desperate hope that he was calling to explain himself at last. Instead, her eyes shot wide as his recorded voice said, "Bail on me now, and I swear you'll regret it, 'Andie,'" an ugly sneer dripping through Ian's nickname for her—a nickname she had never used or mentioned to her former boss. "But if you go and warn him, if you say one damned word to him about this, I swear to you I'll see you in a federal prison for giving aid and comfort to the enemy."

The enemy? Could he possibly mean Ian? Her hands were shaking and her stomach knotting as she powered off the phone completely and sped out of the parking lot, the acid tang of panic on her tongue.

Did Julian really have the kind of power, the authority, he implied? Or were his words no more than a last-ditch effort to control her?

And what about Ian? Could he really be the traitor Julian implied? She tried to fathom it, to picture the man she'd ridden with this morning willingly providing his captors with intelligence. Impossible, she told herself, thinking of Ian's scars, of the suffering so painful he couldn't bring himself to remember the details.

Whatever he'd done to survive, she told herself she didn't blame him or doubt his honor or his courage for a moment. She'd learned too much about the ways prisoners in captivity were broken to believe that even the strongest, most loyal person alive could long withstand the physical and psychological manipulation, the darkness, the starvation, the loneliness and deprivation. The things she'd heard in sessions with other former captives had given her nightmares, dreams so horrifying they'd had her crying out.

Nausea churning in her stomach, she fueled up at the nearest station and grabbed snacks and a bottled iced tea for what she knew would be one very long drive. More than a thousand miles, she remembered from her initial journey out here. She would have a rough time making it in one marathon session even if she were in tip-top condition. Instead, it was late afternoon already, feeling even later with the skies a leaden gray, and she was so emotionally raw that she ached with every breath. She was sore, too, from the riding, and there was a tender lump where she had opened up her forehead. All in all, she needed a warm bath and a soft bed, not a cross-country journey and a broken heart.

Just outside of town, she reached the fork in the road that forced her to make a choice. Straight on would connect her to the southbound state road that would eventually take her to the interstate she'd follow all the way to California. If she turned right instead, following the arrow with a small sign reading Spur Creek 35, Rusted Spur 70, she could be at the Rayford Ranch in less than an hour's time…could be there long enough to warn Ian—a warning Julian would have no chance of tracing through her cell phone or computer—before heading south to pick up the interstate from there and get on her way.

Behind her, a driver in a primer-gray pickup honked and glared behind dark sunglasses, alerting her to the fact that she'd come to a full stop in the middle of the road. After waving the man past her with an apologetic smile, Andrea finally made up her mind.

For Ian's sake, for old time's sake, she simply had to take the chance.

Speeding along the rural road, she struggled to calm the pounding in her chest and focus on her breathing, on the gentle rise and fall of grasslands that seemed to stretch into forever. But since her ride with Ian, she saw them differently, her gaze seeking out clues to hidden places, places that might hide either great beauty or grave dangers.

Other than the occasional distant shed, the changing

fence lines and the different types of cattle, there was little to mark her progress, and there wouldn't be, she knew, until she crossed the narrow bridge that spanned Spur Creek at the halfway point. The two-lane road was rutted and emptier than the last two times she'd come this way, and she saw far more hawks, jackrabbits and coyotes than signs of other humans.

Which was why, sometime later, she was so quick to notice the pair of headlights shining in her rearview. Headlights from a huge grill coming up behind her little Honda far too fast.

"What on God's green earth do you think you're doing takin' off in my truck like that?" Zach shouted at Ian over the cell phone's speaker. "I told you I just had to grab my wallet and I'd take you."

"Sorry, but I couldn't wait," Ian said as the big Ford roared along the ranch road. "I'll return the truck as soon as—"

"You do realize it'd make Sheriff Canter's day to lock you up for driving with no license."

"He'll have to catch me first, and it's one damned big county," Ian said. Though Canter's jurisdiction extended as far as Marston, he normally stuck closer to sleepy Rusted Spur, which had been the county seat for decades before the now-much-larger town had been established.

"Last I heard, they've opened up a satellite office in Marston—with a half-dozen deputies on patrol there. Any one of 'em would score big with the boss man by hauling in a Rayford."

"What're they gonna do?" Ian scoffed. "Prosecute a dead man?"

"Maybe not, but they can damn sure throw his stubborn ass in jail for truck theft."

"Relax, Zach. I'm just borrowing your baby. And I swear I'll return it without a single scratch or dent." As if to contradict the point, Ian took the Marston turnoff too fast, tires squealing in protest as the vehicle fishtailed around the corner. As he wrestled the pickup back under control, he heard a faint protest from his brother from the floorboard, where the phone had fallen.

"You'll be the one scratched and dented," came the tinny voice, "if you don't drive any better than the last time I remember."

"Last you remember, I was sixteen," Ian told him. "I've had a little more experience since then. Now, if you'll quit distracting me, I want to give the road my full attention."

"Just see that you do, bro. I don't want you hurt," Zach said, as his angry bluster gave way to something deeper. "And call me when you find her. All right? Then, whatever you do, try to remember that she's built a whole life since she was with you—a life you've managed to totally knock off the rails in just a few days."

"Thanks for the pep talk." A moment later, Ian's sarcasm eased into sincerity. "I will call you. Promise. And believe me, I'll do my damnedest not to scare her off this time."

The more details he remembered from their time together, the more determined he was to right the wrong that had spread like poison through his life when he'd been foolish enough to let her leave it. Sure, he'd had his job, a career he'd always thought he was damned good at, and he'd loved being a part of something that he had truly believed mattered. But with the ambush, that confidence, too, had crumbled, leaving him with nothing more than fractured memories of how fortunate, how fulfilled and whole, he'd felt when he was with her.

Thunder rumbled in the distance, hinting at the reason for the purplish gloom on the horizon. Though ordinarily, he would welcome the moisture, which would bring better grazing for the family's cattle, Ian hoped the storm would slide off in another direction or at least wait until after he found Andrea and talked her out of leaving.

Once Zach wished him luck and ended the call, Ian flipped on the pickup's headlights. Within a few miles, a light patter started, and by the time he reached the Spur Creek bridge, he was cursing the steady rain and flipping on the wipers.

His aggravation nearly made him miss the break in the narrow bridge's railing, driving past before it registered. Someone must have had a wreck there or even gone over since he'd last come through here. He was half surprised he hadn't read about it in the local paper.

Maybe because it hadn't happened prior to the last edition, some instinct told him. The same instinct that had him pulling to the gravel shoulder and turning to look back over his shoulder. But from this angle there was no way he could see the water.

You're wasting time, imagining things that aren't there. From what Jessie had told him, every second he delayed was taking Andrea farther and farther away from Marston, away from him and Texas.

Unable to bear the thought, he put the truck back into gear and sped off. As he did, the rain redoubled, every drop of it raising the level of the creek.

Chapter 8

Andrea came to with a gasp, sputtering as the cold water reached her mouth and nostrils. Reflex had her craning her neck and pushing herself away from what would drown her, struggling to escape whatever held her down. Adrenaline flooding through her, she succeeded only in gouging her own flesh with her ragged fingernails. She was going to die here, right now, her final moments illuminated by the dashboard lights.

A thought cut through her panicked scrabble. *Seat belt.* That was right. She was in her car—now lying on its side beneath the bridge railing she had crashed through, as far as she could make out. In the creek itself, judging from the water pouring into her car, rising high enough that she could only breathe by straining.

You're okay. Nothing feels broken, she assured herself, though she felt sick from the pounding in her head. *It's only panic that will kill you.*

Repeating the last part like a mantra, she found and clicked the belt latch and cried out with joy when it released. Untangling herself from the shoulder harness, she splashed frantically in an attempt to raise herself above the water level. But how would she get out, with the driver's side door pinned against the creek bottom?

Why, oh why hadn't she bought one of those escape tools for the glove box, the kind guaranteed to break out the windshield with a tap or two? Without one, her frantic attempts to punch or kick her way through the windshield were useless. And with the passenger-side door above her, she faced an awkward struggle trying to get to the latch. When she could finally reach it, she lacked the strength, or anything to brace against with her legs, to force open the door more than an inch or so.

As the dash lights flickered, she wedged a foot against the side of a seat for better leverage and screamed as the car lurched, tilting farther toward its roof. "Don't tip, don't tip, don't tip!" she begged, bracing herself in a standing position to keep her head and shoulders above the swiftly rising water.

From outside the car, she felt the rush of the current, heard its chatter as it jostled the vehicle and swept past. There were more ominous noises, too: the grinding scrape of the driver's side on the pebbles of the creek bed, the ticking of the engine and the groan of metal. Knowing that any shift in her weight could be what toppled the car, Andrea felt the water leaching the warmth from her body and understood that if she did nothing, she would surely die.

With her phone lost somewhere and undoubtedly ruined, there was no way to call for help and no time, either. There was only her strength and her courage, courage that nearly failed her as she remembered the vehicle she'd been helpless to outrace or outmaneuver, the powerful truck that had smashed into the Honda's rear tire and made her lose control.

Was the driver somewhere nearby, on the bridge or by the creek's bank? Was he waiting not to help but to kill her instead if she'd survived? Shuddering with fear and cold, she told herself that by simply waiting here to drown, she would be doing his job for him.

The dash lights gave a final flicker and then plunged her into near-darkness, making up her mind.

Bracing herself, she fought to find the focus that had once made her a fierce competitor. She might be cold and battered, her strength fading with each passing second, but she'd be damned if she let whatever government goon Julian had sent win this round and then go after Ian.

Summoning a last-ditch burst of will, she powered the door until it stood above her, open. She hesitated for a moment longer, praying for all she was worth, before jumping up to thrust an elbow out of the door.

As she began to hoist herself, however, the car abruptly shifted.

"No!" she cried, frantic to get up and get clear.

But nothing could stop the momentum that had the Honda splashing down like a dead roach on its back.

Ian didn't make it a half mile down the road before he was slammed with doubt and guilt—was he really so damned selfish he would drive right past a possible wreck? A three-point turn made him feel better. He'd go back far enough to assure himself that it was nothing and then turn around again, delaying his journey less than a minute.

Except it wasn't nothing, but instead a sight that slammed his heart into overdrive. Some twenty feet below, a dark car—in the rain, it was impossible to make out the color—lay on its side in the creek, partly submerged in the waters that swirled around it. For an instant, he took the car for Jessie's blue Prius before reminding himself that she was home and safe on the ranch.

But Andrea isn't, and her car is dark blue.

He gripped the thought like an exposed wire, the shocking certainty coursing through him, mind and body. Just as he wondered if she had survived the crash, he saw the car's door rising, lifted by someone trapped inside…

He screamed her name, turning to run down to the bank when his attention was attracted by a splashing thud. When he looked again, he saw the car's wheels pointing upward, the doors and windows totally submerged. And no sign at all of Andrea.

Rain soaking into his clothes, he raced to reach her, the steep bank giving way beneath his feet to send him sliding on his ass. But that didn't matter, no more than the current's surprising power when he dove in. It pushed him past the car the first time, forcing him to swim to shore and then make a second try from upstream before he was able to latch on to the undercarriage and position himself on the lee side of the vehicle.

Sucking in a deep breath, he dove under, feeling his way when he could see nothing…nothing until his fingers tangled in her hair.

Forced to come up for air once more, he made a second dive and encountered Andrea, her body partway through a door that refused to open wide enough to allow her lower half to get through. She thrashed and fought, jerking back reflexively when he grasped her wrist, but his attempts to pull her through the narrow gap were futile, with the door wedged against the slick rocks lining the bottom.

She's going to drown. The thought raced through his bloodstream to the frantic beating of his heart. He couldn't let it happen, refused to lose her like this.

Bracing his feet against the frame, he yanked the door with all his might. With Andrea pushing from the other side, it gave, opening a few more inches before it dug into the bottom, sticking as though cast in concrete.

The gap proved just enough, but as she came free at last, her body spasmed and went limp. Pushing off the bottom, he hauled her to the surface, then dragged her to where the bank widened and flattened out about ten yards downstream. Half crawling out, he pulled her behind him and opened her unresisting mouth, positioning her head to let the water pour out.

It wasn't enough, and her flesh was so damned chilled, the rainwater so much cooler than the mild early evening, so he tipped her onto her back and started mouth-to-mouth, his mind casting up a frantic prayer: *Breathe, please breathe.* The steps from an old first-aid class resurfaced in his memory: four rescue breaths followed by a check for a pulse at her carotid. Desperate for a sign of life, he pressed his fingers into her neck—and felt nothing but the racing rhythm of his own pounding heat.

Hoping like hell he was remembering the technique correctly, he moved to start CPR, his eyes and throat burning with an emotion that he didn't dare give in to. He couldn't think about it, couldn't doubt or hesitate a second.

Before he got in a single compression, Andrea's arms jerked, and she began coughing noisily. He turned her onto her side, where she heaved up more water, then helped her as she pushed herself back from the mess.

"Andrea, talk to me. Are you hurting anywhere? Are your neck and back—"

She held up a hand, still coughing, her body shivering violently. Her teeth chattered so hard he heard their staccato clicking.

"My phone's back in the truck," he said. "I need to call for help and see if I can find some towels or maybe a blanket for you."

"N-no call. No 911."

Breathing, speaking—now all I need is for you to start talking sense. "You need a hospital and proper warming. Your lungs could still have water in—"

"No." Her gaze found his and held it, her eyes clear and her expression urgent. "You c-call an ambulance, and I'm as good—as good as d-dead already. This w-wasn't any a-accident." She rolled onto all fours and started trying to crawl up the embankment, a scramble that felt like a knife's thrust to his heart.

Confused as she was, there was no way he could leave her alone to go and call for help, and she damned well didn't look or act like someone with a spinal injury. So instead he said, "Here, let me help you, and we'll go back to the truck and turn the heat on high."

He half supported and half carried her to the road above, finally getting her into the front seat of Zach's truck. After finding a dry towel behind the rear seat and one of his brother's old barn jackets, he helped her into the sleeves and latched her seat belt before coming around and hauling his own chilled and dripping body into the driver's seat.

For a minute, they sat panting, both of them in shock

as heat blasted through the vents. But when Ian reached forward to scoop up his phone from the floorboard, Andrea's lashes fluttered, and her eyes shot wide.

"No! I mean it, Ian. A b-big truck, or maybe it was an SUV." She was interrupted by a coughing fit, only to continue soon after. "I'm not exactly sure what it was, only that it seemed huge, the way it came roaring up behind me, chasing me for several miles. I c-couldn't get away, and I was scared to death of what might happen if I tried to pull over. Then he bumped my tire and—"

"You said *he*. Did you see a man?"

She shook her head. "I was too intent on keeping my wheels on the road to really make out anybody. But one hard bump, and I completely lost control and hit the guardrail. Next thing I knew, I was coming to with creek water pouring into my car."

"You were knocked out, too? Then you definitely need the ER. I'll drive you there myself, though. It'll be a lot faster that way."

He flipped the windshield wipers on high, but when he reached for the gearshift, she grabbed his wrist with a hand as cold as death. "We can't. I can't—or next time, I'll be dead."

His mind leaped back to the gunshots fired this morning. "Wait? Are you telling me it's all really been about you? That the sniper on the ranch this morning was related to someone running you off the road. Why?"

Her eyes widened, her face going even paler as she shook her head. "I—I have no idea. I only know this was no accident. And when he first came up, I saw what looked like a gun barrel hanging out the window. That's how I knew that pulling over to wave him past w-would only g-get me killed." A shudder ran through her entire body. "Just like it'll get me killed if he finds out I've survived this."

He sensed there was more to it, something she was too afraid to tell him. And sitting here wasn't doing a thing to get her warm and dry, so he made the best decision he could.

"Okay, Andrea, I'm taking you back to the house and getting you cleaned up and put to bed, on the condition you'll explain this later. And I swear to you, you're going to see a doctor—"

"No. Please, no. If anybody finds out and it gets back…"

Praying he was making the right decision, Ian said, "Just home then, for now, and I'll keep you safe, Andie."

She gave no answer, but instead burrowed deeper into Zach's barn jacket.

Within minutes, she was fast asleep—or unconscious. He wasn't sure which. Feeling in over his head, he called his brother and explained what he knew, right down to Andrea's terror of anyone finding out about it.

"Maybe I should be heading in the opposite direction, for the ER," Ian said, glancing over at her pale face. "If I did the wrong thing, and she ends up…" The word *dying* caught in his throat.

"There's a retired doctor from Amarillo who's recently moved back to the family homestead outside of Rusted Spur. Let me make a call, see what it would take to get him here to check her out."

"Sounds like a plan, bro. Thanks, and see you in twenty."

Once Ian ended the call, he pushed his speed a little higher, driving as fast as he dared considering the rainy conditions.

But as he neared the turnoff for the ranch, his hurry— along with, he suspected, the fact that he was driving

Zach's truck—drew the wrong attention…attention that came in the form of flashing red lights in the rearview mirror and the long wail of the sheriff's siren.

Chapter 9

As Ian bailed out of the truck, Zach was right there, his voice a low rumble. "Why the hell would you bring that son of a bitch here?"

Still muddy from the rescue, Ian shoved his damp hair from his eyes and glanced at Canter, who was climbing out of his SUV. "Didn't exactly have a choice," Ian told his brother. "He lit me up and pulled me over while I was haulin' ass to get here. Was all I could do to talk him into giving me an escort home instead of to jail."

"Last thing we need is this yahoo in the thick of things," Zach said before looking over his shoulder as Jessie came running outside, heedless of the rain.

Considering that the accident had happened on Canter's turf, Ian figured they would have ended up having to deal with the lawman one way or another, but Andrea was going to freak if she happened to see him. So far she hadn't reawakened, even when he'd shaken her to let her know they were home. "You reach that retired doctor?"

Zach nodded. "He's on his way, and Mama says you should take Andrea straight up to the guest suite, so she and Althea can keep Eden out of everybody's hair."

Jessie opened the passenger-side door, where Ian, Zach and Sheriff Canter all crowded behind her.

"Andrea, can you hear me?" Jessie was asking her. "Can you open your eyes or squeeze my hand?"

"Better let me take her up," Zach said.

Ian slipped past him and announced, "I've got this," before lifting Andrea carefully out of the front seat.

As he hurried to the front door, she moaned and murmured, "No hospital. Too many people."

"We're not at the hospital. We're home," he assured her. "I'm taking you to your room and putting you to bed."

Once he'd gotten her upstairs, Ian sat her on the bed's edge, where he moved to take off her shoes only to see she'd already lost them somewhere. "Better get her out of these wet clothes."

"Right." Zach spared Canter, who'd come up with them, an uncomfortable look. "How 'bout if we leave this part to Ian and Jessie, and you and I can head back down and keep a lookout for the doc."

"You promised to explain all this as soon as you got her here," Canter reminded Ian.

"That I did. And I will, as soon as Andrea's taken care of. And you'll get the chance to talk to her, too, but not before she's ready."

"Just see you keep that promise, or I swear to you, I'll—"

"For once in your life, Canter, can you hold off on the

bluster?" Zach demanded. "It's bad enough you're lying in wait outside the ranch grounds for a chance to pull over and harass us—"

"Now just hold it right there, mister. You high-and-mighty Rayfords aren't the only ones who pass by on that road, and I'm doin' your brother a damned favor, takin' the circumstances into account and not arresting him for—"

The argument might have escalated if Jessie hadn't come into the room at that point with a short, round-bellied man with thinning gray hair and wire-rimmed round glasses at her side. Still wearing a rain-spotted jacket and khaki pants, he carried an old-fashioned-looking medical bag at his side.

"This is Dr. Rosenfield," Jessie said. "Doctor, this is Andrea. Thank you so much for coming here to—"

Rosenfield nodded a greeting and cut in. "I'll need everyone out of the room." He set his bag on the bed and opened it. "Everyone but you, that is, Miss—?"

"I'm Zach's wife, Jessie," she said, "and of course, I'll stay and help. The rest of you, downstairs. You, too, Ian."

The others left, but Ian hesitated in the doorway.

Glancing his way, Jessie promised, "The minute we know anything, I promise you'll be the first to hear."

Zach grabbed at his arm and pulled him from the room, then gently closed the bedroom door behind them. "Come on, bro. Let's go downstairs and get out of the man's way. Or better yet, let's find you some dry clothes before Mama sees all that mud. I'm sure the sheriff can at least wait for you to do that. Can't you, George?"

To Ian's surprise, Canter looked almost sympathetic as he nodded. "Go take care of yourself, sure, as long as you're not too long about it."

Ian returned to the family room in record time, more

out of anxiety over Andrea than any worries over the sheriff's request, but Zach informed him the doctor hadn't yet come downstairs. Though Zach had filled in Canter on the basics, the sheriff asked Ian a number of questions about what had led up to Andrea's rescue and what she'd said once he had gotten her to shore.

"I understand she seemed worried about whatever had caused her to lose control," Canter said from the oversize leather sofa across from its twin, where the two brothers were sitting. Unlike his mother's fussy formal living room, this area had been decorated with men in mind—big men, clearly at home with the huge fireplace, the mounted longhorn bull's head and the weathered saloon doors that could be opened by remote to reveal an enormous wide-screen TV.

"Not whatever. *Who*ever," Ian corrected, remembering their conversation. "She was very definite about it. Told me a big pickup or an SUV, maybe, came up from behind and bumped her. Said she saw a gun sticking out the window before it bumped her."

Canter frowned, seeming to consider before he shook his head. "I know she was pretty stirred up about that whole incident this morning, too. You think it's possible she got things twisted all around and mixed up, in her condition?"

Rising from his seat, Ian paced the room, his clean boots carrying him from a spotted cowhide to the tobacco-colored wood floor. "You're saying she dreamed up this second attack? Next thing I know, you'll be telling me this morning's shooting was just thunder."

"No, I wouldn't say that. I found fresh tire tracks out there where you said, for one thing. No shell casings, but that only proves he had brains enough to go ahead and pick 'em up."

"But you're not convinced that Andrea was attacked this evening?"

"She looked pretty out of it to me," Canter said. "You can't expect too much sense out of anyone in that kind of condition. Hell, you yourself were babbling all kinds of craziness that first day after your brother picked you up and brought you back home."

Ian ground his teeth but couldn't deny it. He'd been half out of his mind, so dehydrated and overheated that no one had gotten any sense out of him for days. But the sheriff hadn't heard Andrea as she'd described another vehicle knocking her car right through the guardrail. Whether or not the sheriff wanted to believe it, Ian was convinced someone had meant to kill her.

At the sound of footsteps on the east wing staircase, where the guest suites were located, all three men went to the landing. His mother, who had been setting up Eden with a movie in the playroom, came out as well, worry lining her thin face. Though she hadn't seemed to like Andrea to begin with, it had taken her only a day or two to warm up to her polite and thoughtful houseguest, remarking—after slanting a pointed look toward Jessie—about how it was so nice to finally have a young lady around the house who seemed to enjoy listening to the more senior generation.

"Will Andrea be all right, Harold?" she asked the man who had once been her former classmate.

He sighed and said, "She's not in the kind of shape that would warrant an airlift, not that they'd fly in this weather anyway. But I can tell you if she were my wife or my daughter, I'd put her in the car and take her to the hospital myself, to rule out a serious head injury and monitor her lungs for infection, since she inhaled so much creek water. Her core temperature needs to come up, too. Poor girl's teeth are chattering nonstop."

"Then I'm taking her to the Marston ER," Ian announced, with Zach and their mother both chiming in with their agreement.

The doctor shook his head, his jowls wobbling a bit. "I wish you luck with that, young man, because she's digging in her heels and swearing she won't go."

"We'll see about that," Ian said, already heading for the stairs.

Before he reached the suite, he heard the water running. He stopped to knock at the bedroom door and then went in when there was no answer. "Andrea? Jessie?" he called, seeing neither of them, but the bathroom door was standing open, offering him a clear view of the partly fogged mirror.

He froze, transfixed by the hazy image of Andrea, her back to him as she stood nude beside the bathtub, her skin pale and her long limbs shaky as Jessie helped her step into the steaming water. He knew he should turn away, should respect Andrea's privacy, but he couldn't make himself move, couldn't do anything but stare as memories from their time together rose like whorls of mist...

Memories of a chilly night in a friend's borrowed condo on Lake Tahoe, where they'd relaxed in the hot tub and stared up at blazing stars. A night where the possibilities had seemed so limitless and his love for her so vast that his proposal had slipped out before he'd had the chance to think through how his career would affect her...

At least not until she'd looked up at him, her damp eyes gleaming, and whispered, "You know about my mother, don't you? Know what my father's lies cost my family. So just promise me, Ian, that you'll always tell me the truth. Promise me that, and I swear we'll work through whatever else this life throws at us."

His heart had been so full that night, his desire to lay claim to her so all-consuming, that he'd told her what she needed to hear, beginning their engagement with a lie. He'd make it right, he told himself, explain what he was allowed to as soon as she'd been cleared by the agents assigned to background check potential spouses, and he would make their time together worth whatever sacrifices they were making for his country.

"There you go. Careful, now," Jessie said to Andrea as she reached to shut off the water. "It isn't too hot, is it?"

"T-too hot? Is that even possible?" Weak and shaky as it was, the sound of Andrea's voice filled him with relief.

Jessie snorted. "Are you kidding? Ian'll skin me alive if I end up boiling you like a Maine lobster."

"It's not too hot," Andrea assured her before she was interrupted by a fit of coughing. "I—I'm awake now, really. So there's no need for you to babysit me."

"Sorry, kiddo," Jessie told her as she rose to grab a towel off the counter, "but you heard what the doc—" Her eyes widened in surprise as her gaze met Ian's in the mirror.

His face burned in response, as though he'd been caught peeping into windows.

"Excuse me, Jessie. I—I just thought I'd come and check on— I wanted to see about getting her over to the ER."

Jessie turned to look at him directly before she did a double take in the direction of the mirror. When she rolled her eyes at him, he sighed and threw his hands up, feigning innocence even though he knew he was busted.

To the sound of splashing, Andrea called, "Ian, there's no need for that. I'll be fine. I just need to warm up with a bath and tea or something. That's all." She coughed again.

He took a step forward. "But you could have a serious concussion, and your lungs—"

"I'll give *you* a serious concussion if you don't get out of this bathroom right this minute," she said.

Glancing directly at her for the first time, he saw her peeking over the outsize tub's edge, trying to hide herself from view.

"Or better yet," Andrea continued, "I might see if Jessie's up for loaning me Gretel to stand guard."

"Don't put me in the middle of this," Jessie said. "Didn't I tell you before you ought to listen to the doctor?"

"I'm not— I can't—" Andrea choked out, forgetting about covering herself as her hands moved to her face. "If he finds out I'm alive—"

"If *who* does?" Jessie asked her.

Andrea shook her head. "I—I don't know. I only know that someone clearly wants me dead."

"Or someone's trying to get to me by hurting you," Ian said, "but the thing is, Andrea, I'm afraid your secret's out already. After you conked out in the front seat, the sheriff pulled us over. There was no way I could get out of telling him what happened, no way to keep him from following us here to question—"

"Oh, no." There was a splash as she stood abruptly, clearly beyond caring whether he saw her glistening, pale body. But before either he or Jessie could reach her again, she sank back down, her eyes fluttering and rolling back in her head.

"Andie!" he shouted, charging past Jessie and leaning down to grasp Andrea beneath the arms to keep her from submerging.

Instead of giving in to the fainting spell, she shook it off moments later and pushed his hands away. "I—I'm fine," she said. "I stood up too quickly, that's all."

"If you're so fine," he asked her, "then why are those tears I see rolling down your face?"

Andrea struggled against the fear that whoever had been sent to silence her forever was going to strike again. But almost worse was the way she'd lost control of her life, lost everything that she'd thought had mattered, within the space of a few hours.

Too weak to continue fighting the issue, she let Jessie and Ian help her from the tub, then dry and dress her in a pair of clean sweats Jessie found for her. Afterward, she was vaguely aware of Ian carrying her downstairs and telling Sheriff Canter his questions would have to wait until the next morning or whenever she was strong enough to talk.

She drifted off again, and the remainder of the evening was a blur of time spent in the truck and another exam at the hospital before the doctor decided to admit her overnight for observation.

Each time she opened her eyes, Ian was right there, standing vigil so she could rest. When the doctor asked him to step out during her examination, he politely but firmly let them know that he was going nowhere. Now, as she looked up from the hospital bed, she spotted him beside the window, peering out into the night.

"What time is it?" she asked, her voice thick with sleep and whatever had been in the shot they'd given her.

Her guardian turned, half of his impossibly handsome face lit by the parking lot security lights outside and the light spilling from the room's bathroom, the door of which had been left cracked open. "About one or so. How're you feeling?"

She took a moment to assess, and found the pain in her head had faded to a dull ache. "Mostly guilty, right this minute. Except for when the nurse comes in to check my vitals, I've been sleeping like the dead while you've been keeping guard all this time. You must be exhausted."

"I wanted you to feel safe. That's the only thing that matters."

Warmth spilled into her chest, a brand of gratitude she had no name for. But with it came the understanding of how dangerous it was, feeling this way toward him, how it could end up getting one or both of them killed. "Sit down, at least, please. Come and sit beside me."

He strode across the room and pulled one of two chairs close but couldn't seem to settle. "Here, let's get you some water. The nurse brought some fresh a little bit ago."

Once she'd taken a few sips to appease him, he raked his fingers through his short, dark hair. "It should have damned well been me in the hospital, me in the water. Because I know it has to be my fault, the shooting, all of it."

She suspected he was right but was too frightened to admit it. If she told Ian everything, she had no doubt he'd make a beeline straight for Julian's office—and in confronting him, possibly ensure his own death or incarceration.

"Have you remembered something more?" she asked

carefully. "Something that would help explain why these attacks are happening?"

What looked like pain twisted through his chiseled features. He rose from the chair and paced, clearly unable to contain the wild energy crackling through him.

"I remember enough that it's eating me alive," he said, "everyone imagining I'm some kind of hero. When I must have—I had to have given them the coordinates. Who else could have led them to that listening post?"

Clued in by the way he'd phrased his statement, she narrowed her eyes in concentration. "You don't actually remember, do you? You don't know this for certain?"

He stopped pacing to spear her with a look. "I know enough to tell you I wouldn't be standing here today if I hadn't—if I hadn't betrayed my countrymen. You've heard there was a bombing, haven't you? I found online where it made the news less than two weeks after I was captured, an incident where five members of the US intelligence community died in a secret location in the Afghan border region."

"You *don't* know you did this," she said, making it a statement this time. "You're just assuming, exactly as you're assuming that whoever meant to kill me was doing it to hurt you."

"What? You're asking me to believe that a woman who works her tail off to help anyone who needs it has racked up the kind of enemies who would do something like this?"

"Hey, I could be complicated," she said drily. "Is it really so hard to imagine?"

He laughed. "Yeah, as a matter of fact. You were always putting yourself in others' shoes, seeing the good in everybody."

"Yeah, everybody," she said, pain reverberating through her at the memory of Julian's betrayal.

"Except for liars," he reminded her. "You reminded me of that the day we—the day you ended it between us."

"So you remember breaking up now?"

"Unfortunately, yeah, which is why, from here on in, I swear I'm going to be completely honest with you. Because whatever else I am, whether it's a traitor or a hero, I'm no longer an agent of the CIA."

"Honesty's a good thing," she said, guilt pinging inside her chest at the thought of the secrets she was keeping. "But, Ian, we're not going back. We can't unlive any of the things that've happened since then, no matter how it might seem." *And no matter how it makes me feel, having you watch over me.* But until she understood what was really going on, it was too dangerous to let him think there was any hope of a relationship.

"Jessie told me you were let go from the center. She told me this guy you were seeing—your boss, I guess—broke up with you because of what you told him about me."

"I don't want to get into that now. I won't."

"So you aren't my psychologist anymore, and you aren't another man's fiancée."

"Let's say I'm your friend, Ian. Can't we just leave it at that?"

He considered for a long time, his blue eyes searching her face until he finally nodded. "For now," he said. "But I should warn you, for your own safety, you might not even want to be that close."

She opened her mouth to argue but realized he was likely right. Aside from the physical risk of another, more successful attack, she was aware she would be risking her heart, too, to a man who might well be guilty of what he thought of as a betrayal of his country. Though she would go to the mat arguing the unfairness of blaming any victim of torture for divulging secrets, she knew he would be publicly vilified—possibly even prosecuted—if his role in American deaths became known. Could she bear to watch it happen, to see a man she would always care about destroyed?

"I'll help you get back to California," he said, "get you back on your feet with a new car and a place to stay."

She felt herself flush. "You can't be serious. You can't—"

"I can, and I'm going to. It's the least I can do, considering."

When she shook her head, his voice grew firmer. "Listen to me, Andie. If it's the money you're worried about, forget it. Please. Or if it makes you feel better, pay me back someday, when you're some fancy headshrinker with your own office in La Jolla."

She laughed at that, at the very idea that she would be the type to set up shop in an upscale community where she'd spend all day helping the rich learn to deal with the burdens of their privilege. She was instead the kind of psychologist who'd be lucky to pay off her debts and earn a modest living, the kind who'd measure her success not in CDs and stock options but in the number of wounded souls she helped avoid the despair and suicide that had taken her mother from her.

What would any of that mean, though, if I turned my back on Ian? What if his guilt turns to self-loathing, if one day he picks up a gun or sees how quickly, how easily, a lasso can be turned into a noose to end his pain?

Her heart staggered with the thought, the smile dying on her lips. She couldn't let it happen, couldn't grieve his death a second time, no matter what it cost her personally. "Thank you for the offer, for saving my life back by the creek and for staying here to help me feel safe. But I'm not going anywhere, nowhere except the ranch if you'll still have me there as a friend. Because I absolutely mean to help you remember everything."

"I'll do my best to keep you safe, hire security, whatever it takes," he vowed. "But I can't promise you won't be in danger."

"*You're* in danger, Ian. Maybe all of us are—at least until you figure out whatever it is someone wants to stay forgotten."

Chapter 10

Andrea was awakened early the next morning when someone set a tray on the bedside table and slipped from the room without a word. Nose wrinkling at the unappetizing smells from what must be her breakfast, Andrea blinked at Ian, who sat sprawled in the bedside chair, his hat tipped over his face. Sound asleep, she realized, recognizing the soft rumble that ended his every exhalation. He'd earned his rest for certain, though, since he'd remained awake and on guard throughout the long night.

But he had little time to sleep before, with a sharp rap at the door, a tall man in a khaki uniform strode in holding a hat that didn't quite block her view of the sidearm strapped to his hip. As she lowered the limp, cool piece of toast she had been nibbling, he said, "Good mornin', Miss Warrington. I'm—"

"Sheriff Canter," Ian said, coming to his feet and offering his hand so quickly that she wondered if he'd really been asleep.

The two men shook hands, each seeming to swell with testosterone as he sized up the other.

"You get the car pulled out of the creek?" Ian asked.

Canter gave a curt nod. "Had a couple of the deputies working out there half the night. Finally got some cables on it and had a wrecker drag it out this morning. No sign of bullet holes, they tell me."

"He never fired his weapon," Andrea said, nightmare images flickering through her brain like the chattering reel from an old horror movie. "When I saw the barrel, I thought he was pulling up to shoot, but instead he bumped my passenger-side rear tire. That's when my car went spinning through the guardrail and—"

"And what?" Canter asked her. "Did you see this fellow afterward, when you were down there in the creek?"

She shook her head, reaching for memories that rolled in all directions like a broken string of pearls. She could grasp a bead at a time, but the strand refused to come together. "I remember being wet, that's all. Wet and cold. My head hurt. I was trying to get out, and then the car flipped upside down, the whole world filling up with water. The next thing I know, I was lying on the bank and coughing, and Ian was there somehow. I guess he—"

Canter's sharp gaze found Ian's, suspicion rising thick as smoke. "You're saying Rayford was right there?"

Ian made a scoffing sound. "You get that badge of yours out of a cereal box, man?"

"Don't be ridiculous," Andrea told the sheriff. "He was helping me, of course. He was still dripping from pulling me out, and that same morning, we were together when someone fired at us."

Canter scowled. "Settle down, the both of you. Nobody's accusing anybody. I'm just gathering the facts. Now, if you don't mind—" he looked to Ian "—I'd like to ask the young lady a few questions in private."

"There's no need," she told him. "I won't be telling you anything I haven't already told—"

"Rayford might be a big name in these parts, but there's no way I'm lettin' one of the boys influence the course of my investigation."

"Boys," Ian echoed, looking as though he wanted to spit at the sheriff's feet.

"All right, then. Grown men now, but it's still department policy to record each witness's recollections separately."

Ian gave a terse nod. "I'll step outside and grab a cup of coffee, but, you know, Sheriff, you could've just started with that last part instead of trotting out this bad blood you've got going with my brother. Save the both of us some aggravation."

Canter's only answer was an expectant silence that sent anxiety rippling through Andrea's stomach. Once he got her alone, would he attempt to twist her words to make some kind of trouble for Ian, or would he consider her part of the enemy camp and somehow make things worse for her?

After Sheriff Canter left about twenty minutes later, Ian came in carrying a cup of coffee. "You'd tell me, wouldn't you, if he didn't treat you right? Because I'm not about to let that tin-plated blowhard get away with—"

"Relax, Ian. It was just fine," she assured him. "He asked me about the accident and what I remembered about the shooting in the ravine yesterday morning, and he was as cordial and professional about it as you could have asked for."

Well, mostly, anyway, she mentally amended. While Canter had seemed genuinely concerned about her personal safety—and angered by the thought of an outbreak of violence on his turf—he made no attempt to hide his disdain for the Rayford brothers, warning her she'd be better off steering well clear of either of them.

"Before that money came in, those two couldn't stay far enough away from Rusted Spur," he'd said when she had called him on it. "But now that the old man's gone and the place is worth a fortune, they're all over it like fleas on a hound dog, tellin' that mama of theirs who to talk to, what to think and exactly how to spend her money."

Andrea could have argued that, as far as she could see, Nancy Rayford was anything but abused and that her sons' concern for her seemed genuine, especially in light of her past issues with prescription pills. Instead, she had simply thanked the sheriff for his concern and let him go on his way, to investigate or just pretend to, depending on his mood.

"You're sure it was all right?" Ian asked. "You look a little worried."

"I have a headache, that's all."

"You need some more coffee?" he asked.

"Not if it's as burnt as yours smells."

"You're right. This vending machine stuff's pretty toxic," he said, "but there's a café just down the road. I can have them box you up a cinnamon roll, too, while I'm at it. I'd bet that ranch it'll be a hell of a lot better than whatever's on your tray."

"I didn't go to school for umpteen years to take a

sucker bet like that one, but don't worry on my account. There's no way I could eat now."

"You're feeling sick?"

"Not sick, exactly. It's the situation, that's all. But why don't you go get that roll and coffee. You probably could use it after spending all night babysitting the invalid."

"You're not an invalid, and I wasn't just doing it for your sake. There's no way I could've gone home and slept a wink, knowing that whoever put you here was out there somewhere."

She grimaced at the reminder, still scarcely able to believe that someone wanted her dead. Though the facts all pointed to it, the concept was simply too huge to wrap her mind around. What had happened to the orderly and quiet life she had been living?

Yesterday happened to it, some rational corner of her mind whispered. *And so did Ian Rayford.*

There was a quick knock, and a floor nurse, a forty-ish redhead with a harried look about her, stepped into the room. "There's a gentleman outside. I asked him to come back a little later, since the doctor's making rounds now, but he insisted I let you know—"

"Who is he?" Andrea asked, clutching the top sheet more tightly.

By the time the nurse got out the name *Julian Ross*, Andrea was shaking her head, saying, "Tell him not to bother. I don't want to see him."

A humorless smile pulled back the corners of Ian's mouth. "I'll go get rid of him. No problem."

"No!" Andrea said, thinking that Ian sounded far too eager for a confrontation. "Please don't go. I need you to stay right here."

A few minutes later, the nurse returned, gushing over

a huge bouquet of yellow roses. "Aren't they gorgeous?" she said. "There have to be a least three dozen."

"Looks like overkill to me," Ian muttered. "Like someone's compensating."

In no mood for male posturing, Andrea flashed an annoyed look his way, then plucked the envelope from the greenery. Crumpling it unread a moment later, she waved off the extravagant arrangement, not caring when the note tumbled to the floor beneath her bed. How could she believe anything Julian said anyway?

"Throw them away, will you?" she asked the nurse, pushing away the gorgeous flowers. "Or, no, on second thought, take them to someone else. Surely you have another patient who could use some cheering? Someone here on his or her own?"

"There is one older lady," the nurse answered, her expression softening. "She's buried everyone, her friends, her daughter and her husband. Poor thing."

"Then tell her the flowers are to remind her that love outlives the human body, as long as she holds the memories close to her heart."

"That's a lovely thought," the nurse said, staring at her with open admiration.

Even harder to take was the pride that Andrea saw in Ian's blue eyes, pride that made her think how very odd it was that she found words of hope to offer an old woman on a day when her own life and her future had never felt more hopeless, when she could see no future beyond the promise she'd made to help this man restore his memory.

The doctor came in next, a different one than she'd seen the night before. An attractive, dark-skinned woman who wore a white coat over a pretty, scooped-neck blue dress, she gave a foreign-sounding name that Andrea didn't catch the first time.

Flipping over the hospital ID clipped to her lapel, she pointed and repeated, "Dr. Pooja Kapur," her accent making the syllables roll off her tongue in a manner Andrea could never duplicate. "I am filling in for Dr. Collins this week. I hope this is acceptable."

Since Andrea knew neither one, it made no difference to her. Nor was she particularly surprised when Dr. Kapur asked Ian to step outside so she could complete her examination in private.

"Go ahead," Andrea urged him. "Get yourself some decent coffee, anyway."

Ian shook his head. "Think I'll hang close," he said, "in case any unwelcome visitors take another crack at stopping by."

Certain he meant Julian, she nodded, breathing a silent prayer that the two would never meet.

Dr. Kapur pulled out a stethoscope to check Andrea's lungs and heart, then asked a few general questions about how she was feeling. If some of them seemed oddly phrased, Andrea didn't think much of it, attributing the woman's way of speaking to a foreign upbringing and education.

"I'm still pretty achy and exhausted," Andrea said in answer to a question.

"This is how a person in your position should expect to feel," Dr. Kapur said with a curt nod, "unless you fail to cooperate, in which case you will no longer feel any more unpleasantness…or anything at all."

Andrea blinked hard. "I beg your pardon?" Surely, she'd misunderstood the woman.

The woman stared directly into her face, her nearly

black eyes unblinking. "Should you wish everyone involved good health, you must do exactly as I tell you."

Sucking in a sharp breath, Andrea glanced to the door Ian had just exited, but it remained stubbornly closed.

"That man, yes," said the supposed Dr. Kapur. "He has one chance, only one to live to be the big hero. And that one chance is you. Do you understand this?"

With her heart hammering like a woodpecker at a dead tree, Andrea couldn't force her brain to process. "Are you even a doctor? Who *are* you?"

"I am the woman who will save your lives, if you stop asking ridiculous questions and listen to what I have to say."

"Y-you have my complete attention," Andrea told her, and for the next few minutes, she only listened, dread tightening her stomach with each accented word.

At the end of it, Dr. Kapur reached into her pocket and pulled out a prescription pad, along with her pen. Putting both in Andrea's hand, the woman in the white coat spoke one last time.

"You will print the password here, neatly and correctly. Otherwise, the next visitor to your bedside will undoubtedly be far less pleasant."

Their gazes remained locked as Andrea drew a shaky breath and then clicked the pen's button with her thumb.

"There is no other way," Kapur urged when she hesitated.

The taste of tears on her tongue, Andrea reached the same conclusion.

The skies had brightened to a deep autumnal blue by the time Ian walked Andrea to the truck that afternoon. According to the instructions on her discharge papers, she needed rest and relaxation but no further treatment, provided there were no changes in her condition.

"I'm restraining myself from saying 'I told you so,'" Andrea said to Ian on the way home.

"Not very convincingly." He sent a wry smile her way. "But you heard what the doctor said last night. You could've had a serious brain injury or complications from near-drowning."

She didn't smile back. "*Could* have, but I didn't, and now I've cost you another fat hospital bill, along with a night's sleep. And probably a ticket, if Canter catches you driving around without a license again."

"I'd do it again in a heartbeat," he said as Marston's residential neighborhoods gave way to pastures dotted with goats and geese and donkeys, "so not another word about it, please."

"How about two instead, then? Thank you. For everything you've done."

"That's more than two, but I'll take 'em." He reached into a storage compartment and came up with a pair of Zach's sunglasses. "You should put these on. Don't want all this sunshine giving you a headache."

She shook her head. "If you don't mind, I'm going to lean back and rest for a while."

"Sure thing," he answered, sparing her a troubled glance. Since the doctor had left her room again, she'd been distracted and withdrawn, fending off his every attempt to draw her into conversation. At first, he'd worried that she might have gotten upsetting news about her condition, but when she'd finally been discharged hours later, the nurse reviewing her instructions had repeatedly emphasized how very lucky she had been.

Depends on your definition of luck, Andrea had answered with a smile that struck Ian as more desperate than reassuring.

It wasn't until they were nearly halfway home that she finally yawned and straightened. "Sorry I've been such rotten company."

"You couldn't have gotten much rest last night, with the nurses waking you up every couple of hours."

"More than you did, I'm sure. You must be exhausted by now, and if you've had anything to eat at all, I didn't see it."

"I'm fine." Behind the sunglasses he had donned, his eyes burned with fatigue, but it was nothing he couldn't set to rights with a couple hours' sack time and a visit to the kitchen. "And anyway, I'm not the one who crashed my car and nearly drowned, not to mention whatever went on between you and your boss."

Grimacing, she shook her head. "I might be the shrink here, as you'd put it, but I should really have my head examined for ever getting involved with my supervisor in the first place. Talk about putting all your eggs into one basket."

Ian chose his words with great care, reminding himself how his return had complicated her life, unraveling what she'd made of it in the two years since they'd parted. "So it didn't go over well, I take it, when you told him why you couldn't keep counseling me?"

"You know what? It's over now, and I'm finished with him. Finished with Warriors-4-Life, too, as long as he's a part of it."

"That place meant a lot to you, didn't it?" he said, hearing the regret in her voice.

She sighed. "I'm really going to miss it, not so much the place as all the people. We were a tight-knit group, and the soldiers there are such an inspiration. They keep trying for a new life, fighting their way back even when their families have given up on them and employers are afraid to take a chance on—"

"Head cases like me," Ian mused.

"They aren't *head cases*, Ian, or damaged goods, or whatever labels you've come up with to punish yourself and judge others like you. You're all just people, people who need a hand up after someone's knocked them down. It's what you're doing for me, isn't it? You don't think any less of me for it, do you?"

"Of course not, but that's different," he told her. "You were physically injured, and anyway, men are supposed to be—" His father's face forked through his brain like lightning. Dark with fury, with the spittle flying as he shouted, *Don't give me any of your sniveling, or by God, I'll teach you how a real man bears up.*

A leather belt swung through the darkness. Behind the wheel, he flinched, hearing the crack of that strap against tender flesh. Burning with remembered shame as, in his desperation to keep from crying out, he had felt his six-year-old bladder give way.

"Supposed to be what?" she asked. "Carved from stone or forged from metal?"

"My old man damned sure was," said Ian. "He wouldn't have given the enemy the satisfaction of..."

From the recesses of his mind, Ian heard a grown man's voice cry, *"I'll tell you what you want. I'll tell you anything, I swear it."*

Had it been his own, in the moment his resistance had crumpled? That moment he'd cost five others their lives?

"Of what, Ian?" Andrea pressed. "Being a flesh-and-blood human, instead of some celluloid character from an old John Wayne movie?"

"Come to think of it," Ian said, "it wouldn't be the first time that foul-tempered son of a bitch steered me wrong."

"Then maybe you should try showing yourself a measure of the compassion you've shown me," she suggested. "The same compassion I suspect you'd show to anyone but yourself."

As something shifted in his thinking, he thought how well suited this woman was to the profession she had chosen. How incredibly generous she was, to reach out through her fresher pain to try to ease his own.

They passed a little band of horses, dun and brown and gray heads that lifted from the grass to mark their progress.

"I'm sorry, Andie," he said, "sorry for messing things up for you at Warriors-4-Life." *But I'll never be sorry that I kissed you, only that I was such an idiot to think, even for a minute, that a woman like you mattered less than my career.*

She crossed her arms to rub them. "My fault. I never should've imagined I could— Let's just forget it, okay? I can't talk about this. Slow down. This is it, right?"

Leaning forward against the shoulder belt, she peered out toward the bend of Spur Creek he'd pulled her from. She was staring toward the rocks, furrows digging deep into her forehead.

"I thought it would be deeper," she said. "I remember the water pouring in, so much water that I couldn't breathe."

With no traffic behind them, he slowed the truck to a crawl. "Yesterday, it was. Water levels come up fast with a hard rain, but it doesn't take too long to drain off."

They passed an area of disturbed earth, rutted with tire marks, probably from where her poor old Honda had been pulled out and then towed away. At the center of the bridge, they passed a section strung with orange netting and a warning sign, the place where she'd crashed through the railing.

"We could've both drowned when you jumped in to free me. Could have both been in the morgue now."

"But we're here and we're alive, so how about we make it count for something?"

Not seeming to hear him, Andrea shuddered and covered her mouth to hide her muted cry. Reaching over, he squeezed the fingers of her free hand, and he wanted to tell her how damned sorry he was for somehow bringing things down on her head. But words failed him, as they often did, and all he could think of for the remainder of their journey was how he was going to do whatever it took to make sure no one ever threatened her again.

Once they arrived at the ranch, he took care to deflect his family's well-meaning concern when they came inside—well, everyone but Eden, who took one of Andrea's hands and solemnly laid it onto the back of the larger of her two Australian shepherds. "When I get scared or sad, I just pet my puppies. Lionheart—that's this one—gives the best hugs, but Sweetheart's extra good at kissing faces. Would you like to borrow one... just for today?"

Andrea smiled and squatted down, wincing only a little, a reminder of her soreness. As she stroked the young dogs' heads, first one and then the other, she said, "That's so generous of you, but both of them are so sweet, I wouldn't know how to choose. So how about I come back out and rub both tummies, once I've had a good sleep."

"And Gretel's, too?" Eden asked, pointing toward the Rottweiler, who sat politely beside Jessie. "She likes tummy rubs the best."

"Then Gretel, too," Andrea said before returning her attention to the adults and thanking Ian's mother, brother and Jessie for allowing her to be their guest again. "You're very kind to have me back."

"Of course, dear. You're very welcome to stay as long as you like," said Ian's mother, sounding as if she genuinely meant it.

"I've moved a few things into your closet," Jessie chimed in. "The pants might be a bit short for you, but they'll get you through the next few days till one of us can take you shopping."

"Sounds perfect. Thanks," she said, but her gaze was straying toward the stairwell, a hint his family took that, above all else, she needed rest and privacy.

Ian helped her settle in, bringing her fresh toiletries to get her started and asking her to make a list of anything else she would need. "Whatever you think of, please don't hesitate. I know what it's like to lose everything you own."

"I guess you would," she said with a wan smile. "But you've already done so much. And I don't want to be a charity case."

"You're not a charity. You're my friend, right? We agreed on it," he said. "And my one real shot at figuring out what it is someone doesn't want you helping me to remember."

Her worried eyes avoided his, making him wonder, was there something she knew or guessed but hadn't told him? Or was she only frightened and trying not to show it?

Instead of giving her more space, he took a half step forward and pulled her into his arms. Beneath her warm flesh, her body was as stiff as wire, so he stroked her back and spoke to her as if she were a frightened colt. "We'll get this fixed. I swear it," he said. "Until then, keeping you safe is my number-one priority."

Instead of melting into his arms as he'd hoped, she pulled away to study his face. "But who will keep you safe, Ian? Who will stop the bullets the next time they come flying?"

"We have people on it, so don't you worry about that. Just concentrate on getting stronger so you can work a little of your magic on my head. All right?"

She hesitated a moment and then nodded, her long lashes clumped with moisture. As upset as she looked, it seemed wrong to notice how beautiful she was, how much her every touch made him ache for more.

Fighting the impulse to kiss away her worry, to make each of them forget everything except the other's body, he headed for the door.

"Wait," she said. "There is one more thing I'm going to need, if it's not too big of an issue. I have to log in to my work account and make sure all the clients I've been seeing are properly taken care of."

"Sure thing. I'll loan you my laptop. You're welcome to keep it as long as you're staying here."

"Thanks, but won't you miss it?"

He shook his head. "Since Zach insisted on getting me that new smartphone, I've been using it for just about everything. And if I need something bigger, I'll just borrow Mama's—all she uses the thing for is playing online word games anyway."

After bringing Andrea the laptop, he headed downstairs to the kitchen, where he caught up with his brother while raiding the refrigerator for the leftover fried chicken, potato salad and baked beans he had missed the night before.

"Keep that up, and you'll be too stuffed for the pot roast I smell cooking," Zach warned as he watched Ian practically inhaling his first plateful. "She'll be baking yeast rolls to go with it."

Ian looked up from his chicken leg. "If you're plotting to eat my share, don't count on it, or I may just gnaw your arm off. Didn't want to leave Andrea unguarded too long, so I skipped lunch today. And breakfast."

"It's a miracle you didn't eat an orderly or something, the way you've been going through food lately, buzz saw," Zach said.

"Buzz saw," Ian said. "I kind of like that. But I'll sure miss hearing you call me bonehead."

"Don't count on it, bro." Zach's wry smile faded as he got down to more serious matters. "Just wanted to let you know Virgil's set a couple of our best hands working up around the barn for the rest of the week. He's asked them to keep a close eye out for any strangers and report back to him or me immediately. I've put in a few phone calls, too. We need a head of ranch security, and we need somebody good."

"On a permanent basis, you mean? Not just until this SOB's caught?"

His brother nodded. "That's what I'm thinking. The family was high profile enough before this gas discovery, and then your return hit the news. And wherever people know there's money, they start looking for a way to separate you from it. Everything from elaborate cons—you wouldn't believe the calls and emails I've been fielding—right down to kidnappings."

"You're worried about Eden."

"I'm worried about all of us, but, yeah. I'd be a fool not to realize my five-year-old daughter's vulnerable, especially now that she's attending public school. She loves it there, loves her friends and her teacher, and I don't want to have to twist Jessie's arm into homeschooling her just because I'm afraid."

Ian put down the chicken bone and wiped his mouth with a napkin. "I was right before. I should leave and take Andrea with me somewhere I can keep us both—"

"We've already had this conversation, and I can tell you, running off isn't the answer. Especially when I'm still not convinced this isn't somehow tied to Jessie's work."

"Not to downplay the risks involved in her career, but you're beating a dead horse, Zach. This guy who knocked Andrea's car over the bridge couldn't have mistaken her for your wife this time."

"You don't think, in a rainstorm, he might mix up—?"

"You're grasping at straws, man," Ian said. "Have you asked her about the note yet?"

Zach sighed. "Not much point in doing that unless I'm prepared to believe her answer. Maybe if I looked for it myself…"

Ian stared as if his brother had sprouted horns. And people called *him* paranoid. "That woman's the best thing that ever happened to you, and you're going to *spy* on her?"

"I went so damned long without a family, any family," Zach said, shaking his head in frustration. "The things our old man did made us—made me—so closed off, so guarded that it's a wonder anyone ever bothered cracking through to find her way in. But now that I finally have everything I really need, there's no way I'll risk losing it. No way I'll take that chance."

In that moment, Ian's brother was a stranger to him, a man who, for all his toughness, would go to any extremes for those he loved. But Ian couldn't fault his brother for his willingness to risk anything he thought might secure his family...

Not when Ian still had the sealed, crumpled note he'd picked up off the floor in Andrea's hospital room and stuffed into his pocket. Though he suspected that reading it would be a terrible idea, he hadn't been able to bring himself to dump it in the trash can either, as he'd first intended.

But whether or not he or his brother had begun to plumb the depths of craziness when it came to the women they loved, Ian wouldn't let Zach shoulder the entire burden alone.

"I'll tell you what," Ian offered. "Why don't you let me take over the job of hiring security for the ranch."

"There's no need for that, not when you're still getting your feet back under you, recovering from—from what you went through, over there."

"I've been eating your groceries and playing the lone cowboy long enough. It's time I started pulling my weight around here, and security's my area of expertise. I'll handle any strange emails you get, too."

"I still think we need somebody full-time."

"Then let me do the vetting and take care of the hiring. I have some pretty good contacts in that arena."

Zach shook his head, his eyes betraying his uncertainty. "It's not that I don't appreciate the offer, man, but you've only been back a few weeks. And you still—we've heard you late at night. Heard you shouting out with those nightmares."

"Hell," said Ian, raking his fingers through his hair. "I'm sorry about that. Why didn't you say something? I'm not—I'm not scaring Eden, am I?"

"A little bit, a couple times, but we got her settled right down."

Ian grimaced, his face heating, certain that his brother was downplaying his kid's reaction so as not to hurt his feelings. "Sorry, Zach. And what about Mom? Has she heard me, too?"

Zach hesitated before admitting, "Listen, man, she's so glad to have you back, she'd never say a word about it. It's really no big deal. Forget I brought it up, will you?"

"I will," Ian promised, "but only if you'll start treating me like a brother and a partner instead of a grenade somebody's pulled the pin on."

Zach extended his right hand, and the two shook on the deal. Later that evening, Ian packed a couple of boxes and moved over to the guest wing, down the hall from Andrea's bedroom. He told himself he was doing it for Eden's and his mother's sakes, and to be available should their guest need anything during her recovery.

But down deep, he suspected that the closer he was to the woman he would never stop loving, the less of an issue the nightmares would prove to be.

Chapter 11

After two days spent "resting" in her room, where she chewed antacids like candy to combat the anxiety chewing through her, Andrea knew that if she didn't get out of her own head, she was bound to have a meltdown—or end up back in the emergency department, this time with a bleeding ulcer.

Terrified by Dr. Kapur's implied threats if she didn't record every detail of Ian's progress, Andrea filed new logs. But instead of writing the truth—that she could barely speak to Ian for the fear and guilt coiling around her middle like a python—she had logged a fictional account of how recent events, namely the shooting and her accident, had distracted him from his work on the root causes of his post-traumatic stress.

As plausible as her logs sounded, Andrea doubted they would hold off those reading them for long. They were clearly after something in particular, she thought, some piece of information they were so desperate for her to bring to light that they would threaten, even try to kill both her and Ian to gain her cooperation. She seriously doubted that whatever they were after would be found in the logs she'd already recorded, since she'd never had the chance to make notes about his revelations the morning of the shooting…

The morning of the day my entire life went down the tubes.

Was it something to do with his CIA work or his time among the terrorists that Julian and Dr. Kapur were really after? And once Andrea did help Ian recover the memory and gave it over for the pair to see, would that be the end of this waking nightmare as the "doctor" had implied?

But as desperately as Andrea prayed the woman would be as good as her word, Andrea feared it was more likely she and Ian would both be silenced in order to keep confidential whatever volatile secret these people were hiding. Or was it possible that this was all about a public prosecution, making Ian a scapegoat for Americans killed because his superiors had failed to move their listening post after his capture as they should have?

She was losing her mind, trying to figure out which or to come up with some alternate scheme that wouldn't end up causing even more trouble.

When Ian brought a tray with lunch that afternoon, he frowned in the direction of the food still sitting on the guest room's small desk.

"You haven't even had your breakfast," he said, nodding. "And you barely touched last night's dinner, either. Are you feeling sick?"

"Not so much sick as sad, I guess. And worried about what comes next."

"Take it from me, you'll feel a lot better once you get some of Miss Althea's chicken salad in your stomach—have more energy, think more clearly. And a little shot of vitamin D definitely wouldn't hurt you, either."

Puzzled by the comment, she frowned. "Vitamin D?"

He nodded. "Sunshine, in the open air. It's a gorgeous afternoon, so how about a walk or, better yet, another riding lesson?"

"I don't know, Ian. I'm still kind of sore, and what if—if the shooter—"

"Oh, come on. I'll take it easy on you, promise. We'll stick to the corral, since Virgil has a couple of our best hands working around the paddock area to keep an eye on things. They'll do, at least until I find the right guy to take over ranch security full-time."

"You're looking for someone?"

"I've made some calls, but it's not the easiest thing on earth to lure someone qualified to a ranch that's hours from civilization."

Her lips pursed as she considered for a moment. "What if I told you I might know of someone, somebody with a background in military security? Raised in ranching country in Wyoming, too, I think, so he might fit in quite well."

"And this guy's looking for a job?"

"I'm sure of it."

"Wait a minute." Ian's eyes narrowed. "This is another of your patients, isn't it? One of your psych cases from the center."

She stared at him, astonished that he would take such a view of someone who'd suffered in the war as he had. Not exactly the same way he had, but they'd both made terrible sacrifices in the service of their country.

"If you want to miss a chance to hire a qualified candidate, that's your loss." She allowed a hint of disapproval to drip through her voice because, whether or not Ian realized it, in refusing to consider her suggestion, he was casting judgment on his own wholeness and self-worth, just as he had when he had spoken of *head cases* earlier.

A look of discomfort passed over his face, and she thought he might say more on the subject, something that would allow her an opening to draw him into conversation. *Why? So you can secretly report it?*

Instead, he shook it off and changed the subject. "How 'bout we meet outside the barn, by the hitching post in forty minutes? Will that give you enough time to finish your lunch and get yourself together?"

She looked down at the borrowed robe she was still wearing, abruptly conscious that she hadn't even brushed her hair this morning. "Sounds good," she agreed. "I guess it is time I pull myself up by the bootstraps."

He smiled. "Now you're talking like a real Texan. I'll have you chowing down on chicken-fried steak and saying *y'all* and *fixin' to* in no time."

"Heaven help us all." She faked a shudder at the thought.

Once he was gone, she forced herself to eat the fruit and half a sandwich, which she washed down with some sweet tea. Afterward, she washed up, brushed her teeth and pulled her hair into a long, sleek ponytail. She opted to wear the outfit someone had laundered for her, the same jeans and blouse she had been wearing that afternoon her car had left the road. Though there were a couple of faded stains, at least they fit well—and served as a reminder that she must soon rejoin the living and purchase herself a few changes of clothing.

Once she joined him outside, Ian smiled at her, with Eden's two Australian shepherds wagging and grinning at his side. "Looking good," he said, leading the same mounts they'd ridden on their previous outing to the hitching post. "Nice to see you back among the living."

"Thanks," she said, dropping a pair of borrowed sunglasses down to cover her eyes. "You're not looking so bad yourself, cowboy. Every day, you look like you've put back on a couple more pounds." Maybe it was the brilliance of the blue sky, the warmth of the September sunshine and the crispness of the air, or maybe he'd been right about the magical properties of Althea's chicken salad, but she couldn't help notice how well he wore the extra muscle mass.

Out of nowhere, her mouth watered at the thought of unbuttoning the deep blue work shirt he was wearing to check out his abs and pecs. Not that she'd be doing any such thing, under the present circumstances, but that didn't stop her imagination from dragging him into the hayloft. What on earth was wrong with her?

He mimicked a fork-to-mouth motion and winked at her as he explained. "It's all in the elbow action."

A bright peal of laughter slipped out of her own mouth, unexpected after days of gloom. "Well, you're looking more like your old self these days." The same gorgeous hunk of self that had practically started her drooling that first day when he had stopped to help her. "Probably feeling a whole lot better, too."

"Hang on just a minute," he said before heading back inside the barn and quickly returning with her riding helmet, along with a wooden box containing a variety of brushes, combs and hoof picks.

He taught Andrea how to groom Princess and clean her hooves, something she took to with no problem. When they got to the saddling, Andrea found it somewhat tougher, and it took several attempts for her to master the correct knot and get the cinch tight enough that the saddle wouldn't slip.

"We'll make a rancher of you yet," he said approvingly once she'd finally passed muster.

"Maybe I can write a grant to get riding therapy added at the youth center when I go back to San Diego."

At her reminder that their situation was only temporary, his smile faded. But it was only fair, she told herself, to keep him rooted in reality. He needed home and family to support his move to a full recovery. And she needed, more than anything, to put this painful chapter of her life behind her.

As she strapped on her helmet, he bridled both horses and led Princess to the mounting block. Andrea had noticed before that he didn't have to use it, but with her body still stiff and sore from the wreck, she decided this wouldn't be the day to try to climb aboard on her own.

Once in the saddle, she looked around and noticed a couple of cowboys working under the hood of a dented, rust-brown pickup not far beyond the paddock area. One had tossed aside his jacket and was working in a muscle T-shirt. Both wore boots and hats and enough testosterone to make her friend Cassidy's freckles jump right off her face.

But Andrea's gaze didn't linger, instead going to Ian's sharp blue eyes as he appraised her.

"Hang on," he said. "Jessie must've been out riding since we last went. Stirrups are too short."

In an oddly intimate adjustment, he had her move back each foot so he could raise the stirrups to adjust them for her longer legs. As he worked, his forearm brushed her thigh, an accidental touch that sent awareness rippling through her, followed by an aching need. *Touch me there again, one last time before I...*

As if he'd read her thoughts, he tensed, and a silence settled over them, a palpable strain magnified by every look that passed between them and each averted eye.

Does he already know I've handed over the password? Has he figured out I'm being threatened?

Her heart skipped a beat when Ian laid one callused hand on her calf, and the sigh that slipped from his mouth warmed the flesh beneath the denim. Or maybe that was only her imagination. But she was certain that the worry she saw in his expression was as real as the tingling of her leg and the flutter of her pulse.

"I've got a confession, Andie. I've done something I shouldn't have, and I'm scared to death you won't forgive me."

Her eyes widened. "W-wait. Forgive *you*? As kind as you've been? Are you kidding? Not to mention that you saved my life."

"Guess I do have my finer moments, but picking up that sealed card, the one you plucked out of those flowers and then dropped on the floor, wasn't one of them. I'm sorry."

"Wait. You mean the card from Julian? The one that came in the roses?"

He nodded, regret darkening his handsome face. "I only meant to toss it for you, dump it in the trash there. But I got to worrying a little, thinking he might've written something—I don't know, but you seemed so upset, and I still hadn't gotten over that moment I spotted your car in the water."

"So you took the note and read it," she said, fear rippling through her as she wondered if Julian had written something that would alert Ian to the danger he was in and possibly make things worse for them both.

"It was crazy, stupid. The kind of idiot move my brother—never mind that. I just wanted to clear the air between us and apologize for getting in your private business. Andrea—are you all right? I swear your face just went gray."

"I—I'm fine," she said, remembering to breathe again. Because, clearly, Ian was feeling guilty, not furious, as he would surely be had he had any idea that she was being coerced to share his secrets. "It's just— I'm surprised, that's all."

He looked up into her eyes. "And disappointed, I hope. Because I'm disappointed in myself."

"What did the note say, Ian? Tell me that, and I promise you're forgiven."

He turned from her but went only a few steps to mount his palomino horse in one smooth motion so that they were looking at each other almost eye to eye. Urging his horse a little closer, he dipped two fingers into the left pocket of his checked shirt to produce the note. "Here you go."

She took it from him, then drew a deep breath before unfolding it and reading.

Please come back to me. Let's talk this over and make things right.

She turned it over, looking for more, for the apology or Julian's promise to put a stop to the threats and violence. But there was nothing else, nothing at all.

Without meeting Ian's gaze, she jammed the note into her back pocket and nudged the mare's side, wanting nothing more than to distance herself from the reminder that, for all her education, she was no better than her mother at avoiding men with dangerous secrets.

Ian cleared his throat, then started giving her instructions, at times demonstrating the positioning he wanted as he made a circuit of the corral. Distracted as she was, she wasn't sure how much she got out of the lesson, other than to notice his easy athleticism in the saddle and the streaming white banner of his horse's snowy mane and tail.

For the next forty minutes or so, she did her best to follow his directions. As they worked, the conversation was stiff and formal, both of them sticking to the subject at hand. Eventually, though, she shifted in the saddle, trying to relieve the ache in muscles she'd forgotten she possessed.

"Looks like you've had about enough fun for one day," Ian noted.

"It *was* fun." *Or at least, it should have been.* "I really do appreciate the lesson. And just so you know, I meant what I said earlier about the note. I'm not upset. It's not important."

"It's important to me," he said, regret shadowing his square jaw. "Important enough to get me thinking about the man I used to be. And about the man I want to be, if I'm ever to deserve you."

She looked up sharply. "What on earth makes you believe that I deserve *you*?" If she did, she'd find the courage to tell him that because of her, someone was likely poring through her case notes even now.

He nudged his gelding's side. Closing in, he reached out to claim her hand. "Because I don't remember everything, but I damned sure remember you."

You remember someone else, someone a lot braver,

*someone who hasn't struggled to escape a car while the
waters rose to swallow her alive.* The woman who'd
emerged brought with her a new understanding of how
fragile life was. Of how willing these people—whoever
they really were—would be to kill if they were crossed.

"Why are you shaking, Andrea?" he asked her.

"I'm ready to get down. That's all," she said. "I'm
exhausted."

By the time he dismounted and moved to help her,
she was already on her feet and walking the mare back
toward the barn.

"What's really wrong?" Ian pressed, leading his own
mount beside her. "Ever since the hospital, you've been
withdrawn and miserable."

Heat rose to her face. "Seriously, Ian, how would you
expect me to behave under the circumstances?"

"It's more than that, I know it. There's something you
haven't told me."

"I'm scared, that's all, scared to stand too close to a
window. Being outdoors in the open—it's pretty overwhelming."

He pulled open the sliding door to the barn and gestured for her to walk Princess inside. As he followed,
leading Sundance, he said, "Tell me more about this man
you mentioned from the center. The one with the security background. You really think he's qualified, or are
you just feeling sorry for him because he needs a job?"

She frowned over her shoulder. "Pity's never been
part of my therapy, Ian. For example, I don't feel sorry
for you right now, just annoyed that you would ask that."

"And you're sure he's ready for this? He's not like…"
He thumped his fingertips against his sternum. "Still all
messed up?"

"I can't discuss his personal details, but suffice to say I wouldn't have recommended him unless I thought he was well qualified and capable. Your safety and your family's matter too much to me."

"All right, then. Have him email the ranch a résumé. I'll write the information down for you when we go back in."

She studied him. "You aren't just doing this to try to make it up to me for reading my note, are you?"

"You want the correct answer or the true one?" he asked, a smile ghosting through eyes the color of a field of spring bluebonnets in the sunlight.

"In that case," she said, "I withdraw the question. Because in some instances, it's better not to know for sure."

As Ian unsaddled and put away the horses, he did his best to engage Andrea in conversation. But no matter how he tried, she was so quiet that he wondered if he'd been wrong thinking there was something she was keeping from him.

"I shouldn't have pushed you so hard," he said as he closed Sundance's stall door and dusted wisps of the sweet-smelling hay he'd given each horse off the front of his shirt. "Riding was a lot of physical activity for someone—someone who was almost…" The shock of it twisted through him: how cold she'd been lying on that sandy bank, how stark-white her complexion. Combined with the bluish tint of her lips and her soaked body's corpse-like limpness, the horror of the memory was forever branded on his brain.

"I'll be fine," she assured him. "After all, Princess was the one who carried me, not the other way around."

Unable to escape the memory, he said, "I've seen dead

men before—women, children, animals—all the ugliest scenes that terrorism has to offer. But nothing's ever kicked me in the gut like thinking I'd lost you on the bank of Spur Creek. Even after I did mouth-to-mouth—"

She looked up, her face stricken. "You gave me mouth-to-mouth?"

"You weren't breathing, Andrea. And I was about to start on CPR when I couldn't find a pulse. That's when you came out of it, when you came back and it felt like—something like my own heart being restarted. *Kick*-started, like an old motorcycle with a rusty engine."

She shivered, hugging herself. "That must have been so—what am I saying? I know how it hit you. I understand exactly because I felt something inside me come alive again, too, the day that I found out you'd come back from the dead."

"Even though you'd left me and found someone else?"

It grew so quiet inside the barn that he made out the sound of hammering from somewhere outside and what he recognized as the happy, growly chuffs of the two young shepherds playing in the paddock area. There was another sound, as well, the lumbering thump of his own heartbeat, a sound that grew swifter every moment he looked into her eyes.

But he couldn't tear his gaze away, couldn't do any more than stare in fascination as she studied him, too, thoughts darting swift as swallows in the expanding darkness of her pupils. It was one of the things that he loved best about her, that sense of so much going on behind each look and every word. Maybe, as an old friend from the agency had told him after he and Andrea had parted, men with secrets like theirs were better off sticking with uncomplicated women. But he'd never wanted anyone too naive to see through his lies…

Had never wanted anyone who didn't think before she answered the important questions.

"Julian helped me through my grief for you," she finally answered. "He was good to me and kind, and we shared a passion for helping traumatized veterans—something I became intensely involved with after hearing of your…after I received that knock at the door."

"I'm sorry for what you were put through on my account."

"Don't be, because that's not my point. The thing is, Ian, Julian might've been the man I turned to. But he wasn't, he's never been, the man I needed."

His pulse booming in his ears, Ian closed the remaining space between them, his lean, work-hardened arms enfolding the sweet softness of her body. This time, when they kissed, he forced himself to hold back, to begin a wordless conversation based not on his hopeless desire to go back in time but on a wish to start anew. Only this time, he swore to himself, he'd do whatever it took to build a real relationship instead of another shimmering mirage.

He trailed kisses to the tender spot beneath her ear, making her shiver when he gently nipped the delicate flesh.

Her breathing deepening, she tipped back her head and whispered, "You, yes. Always you, except…except, Ian, there is something. Something I've been meaning to…tell…"

A word dissolved into a groan as he cupped her breast with his hand, as he pressed her up against one of the beams that separated the stalls. Right now, he didn't need or want words. He only wanted her, needed her with a fever-bright intensity that made every other consideration fall away.

Andrea's glazed eyes and parted lips told him she was swept up in the same warm current, a current that put him in mind of turquoise waters, green palms and a certain blue bikini forever imprinted on his mind.

"Later. Tell me later." His voice grew hoarse as he leaned in and their bodies came together, their movements an ebb and flow as natural and as ancient as the tropical tides.

"Ian," she murmured, her hand dropping low to squeeze the hardness making his jeans so damned uncomfortable. Moments later, she seemed to regain control of herself. "We really can't— We shouldn't. Not here, at least. And not before I talk to you about what I—what I've done."

He covered her mouth with his own, swallowing her protest. He couldn't process words now, not while he was burning body and soul with the need to lose himself in the sensation, to lose himself in her.

"Come with me," he said, gripping her by the wrist and taking a step toward his brother's office. When she hesitated, he said, "Please, Andie. Before a bunch of damned talk gets in the way of what you know we're both feeling, what we both want and need."

Her beautiful hazel eyes locked on to his, a denial written in them. But when he lifted her hand to his mouth, when he turned her wrist just far enough to taste the flesh that covered the delicate tracery of blue veins, he felt her frantic pulse slow, felt the moment when whatever resistance remained in her gave way.

Inside the barn office, he turned the lock on the door

and prayed to everything that was holy that wherever his brother was, he would stay away a good long while.

For a long time, he and Andrea kissed right there, beside the door, his hands rediscovering the hills and plains, the secret valleys of the remembered country of her body, his mouth feasting hungrily on hers. Her fingers were busy, too, unbuttoning his shirt and running through his sparse, dark chest hair, sliding her palms over work-sculpted muscle and driving him into a frenzy.

He helped her pull off her shirt, too, tossing it onto the floor in front of the oversize desk. As he reached to unhook her bra, he thought of sweeping that desk clear in a single, reckless moment, of laying her back atop its broad expanse and taking her right there. But he was distracted by the irresistible glory of her freed breasts, by an impulse so strong that he pushed her against the door to suckle first one and then the other.

"We—can't—someone will hear…" Her words dissolved into a moan. "Oh, Ian, how I've missed…"

The protests ended, and she reached for the buckle of his belt, undoing it and the top button of his jeans. Starting the zipper's downward journey, until his rock-hard erection was free of the constricting pressure.

Somehow, they made it to the sofa, a trail of clothing marking their haphazard progress. As they stood beside it, she began kissing her way down his body, his awareness of the heat of her mouth and the sharpness of her nails as they lightly scored his flesh so all-consuming that he barely registered her soft words. "Have to make it up to you. All of it, you have to forgive…"

The first brush of her lips against his heated shaft was nearly enough to set him off. But as what she'd said sank in, he put a hand on her shoulder and drew her to her feet to look into her eyes, the lashes dark and spiky with her tears.

Though it nearly killed him to resist, he groaned, "You have nothing—nothing at all to make up to me, darling."

"But, Ian, I was sent here. Julian made me come. He wanted me to spy on—"

"Guess I should pay him a visit then, to thank the son of a bitch for sending you to me."

"He wanted your—"

"Shh, Andie. I don't give a damn what he wanted, not when I'm right here wanting you more than I've ever wanted anything or anybody in my life." Taking her by the hand, he guided her onto the sofa, sat down beside her hip.

She looked up into his face and her breath hitched. She froze like a fawn when the wolf passes nearby.

His hand glided over one of her soft breasts, his fingers lingering to toy with her hard nipple. Sliding to his knees, he followed with his mouth, tempting and teasing until he heard her sigh slip free.

And then he was kissing his way up the column of her neck, drawing soft murmurs of pleasure from her. Beside her ear, he whispered, "And I want you, Andie, want to look at you, to watch your face the very moment that I slide inside you…like this."

His hand found and stroked her damp heat, his fingers dipping inside her, pumping her until she arched and gasped.

"I'm going to watch you lose control," he said, placing a knee between her creamy thighs, his excitement an exquisite torment. "Watch you come to pieces while I—"

"Now, please. I need you now, Ian." Her eyes captured his, the worry in them shifting into pure feminine desire.

He drank in the sight of her, so beautiful, so helpless with want, so completely his as he would always be hers. And then in a single long thrust, he buried himself inside her, lost himself in a rising spiral of sensation that built and built and built until she finally, fully brought him home.

Spent and satisfied some time later, he held her on the sofa, kissing the soft hair at her temple and feeling as content and relaxed as he had in the days before they'd parted. So content that he drifted off, forgetting for the moment where he was...

Until, some minutes later, the ventilation system kicked out a whiff of straw, a trace—perhaps imagined— that somehow found its way past the homey scents of horse and leather, of wholesome hay and grain. The acrid smell of fear came next, jerking him awake. He was reminded of deep shadow, deeper shame, and the deep voice he'd heard crying out beside him—a voice pleading for mercy, not for Ian, but himself.

Ian was back there again, right there, he realized as his tormentor raised a meaty fist, the end of the chain wrapped around it.

Startling to alertness, the woman beside him rolled over, staring as he scrambled off the sofa and started grabbing for his clothing. "What is it? What's wrong? Ian, can you hear me?"

His heart pounding silver nails of adrenaline through his system, he jammed a leg into his jeans. Unable to answer, to think past anything but the need to escape the tangled images ripping their way through nerve and muscle, biting into bone. They were jumbled together, shards from childhood and keen-edged blades from that place, that reeking hole beneath the floorboards, where slivers of light reached down to touch the filthy straw.

Andrea rose like a hallucination, speaking in a voice that floated across the continents and oceans. "Ian, listen to me. You're having a flashback, remembering something from the past. But you're safe now. You're with me here, in Texas. You're home, and we're okay."

He snatched up his shirt, looking around for an exit. Would there be a guard just outside, waiting for him to make a break, another excuse to lay into him? Would he have to kill again, wrapping the chain around the thick neck, pulling and pulling until he heard the crunch of cartilage?

"Can I touch you, Ian? Would that be all right with you?"

He elbowed his way roughly past the image of his Andie. The hallucination stumbled, looking both hurt and bewildered before she pulled herself together. "What is it, Ian? What's going through your mind now? What are you *remembering*?"

One splinter pierced his reality, shattering everything he thought he had known. His heart pounded and his gaze snapped to the memory of the only woman he had ever allowed himself to love. "I wasn't—wasn't there alone. A-another man—another American. He watched it. Watched me."

Two patches of color stained her cheeks, some emotion burning hot inside her. She sounded almost real as she asked, "Watched what, Ian? Watched your *torture* back there? Back before you came home?"

Ian tried to force himself back into that memory, but it was like trying to shove his entire body through a tiny pinhole. He could peek through sometimes, if the light was just right and he had the correct angle, but there was no way, no way in the damned world, he was ever going to squeeze himself into that space.

Squeezed...space. So damned dark back there, with the smell of musty straw burning in his nostrils. A deep voice, big and booming—the old man's voice, his old man's face, with the chain in his hand now.

Any minute he'll be coming back.

"Ian? Are you with me?" Andrea asked, and he noticed she was pulling up her own jeans, her top half clothed already and her now-loose hair wildly tousled.

"What?" he asked, blinking at her before his head jerked toward the low rumble of approaching voices. Male voices, sounding more casual than alarming, but Ian wanted to curse them anyway for intruding before he'd quite remembered where he was.

"Is that your brother I hear?" Andrea asked. "That's Zach out there, isn't it?"

Ian stared at her, trying to make sense of what she was saying. As the voices grew nearer, she hurried to unlock the door just before it opened.

His brother stopped in the open doorway, with a graying, goateed man visible behind him. Zach didn't come inside, his sharp gaze flicking from Andrea to Ian, his look of surprise melting into one of comprehension. There was no judgment in Zach's eyes, only the hint of a smile as he said, "Sorry to interrupt. I'll just take Doc Spencer to see to that lame heifer first and brew us up some coffee later."

They were standing in Ian's way, blocking his only exit, he realized, as reality once more spun on its axis. His vision dimmed, memory creeping on spiders' legs out of the darkness, its needle-sharp fangs dripping with a venom that burned like fire as he thought of being trapped here, trapped by the stranger in the doorway who wore his father's face.

Charging the door, he shoved his way past the first man and barely missed the second as the man jerked out of Ian's path. Ignoring their startled exclamations and the woman crying out his name, he headed full bore toward the outer barn door, the guards' furious Pashto curses ringing in his ears…

He fled the men, fled the bullets he expected to take him down at any second and raced out into the daylight, into freedom. Staring around wildly, he spotted an unsaddled horse grazing in the distance and started toward it—

Before abruptly changing course and sprinting toward an old brown truck.

"Ian!" Zach shouted, but his brother didn't answer.

Panic pounding through her, Andrea grasped his arm to stop him as he started toward the open barn door. While the vet stared after them in shock, she told Zach, "Wait. Something's set him off— He's remembering. Remembering too much."

"You stay back, too, Andrea. He looks pretty damned riled up, and I don't want you getting— No, Ian!" Zach raced outside, where Ian was running for the old pickup the two hands had been working on. The rusty hood was down now, the cowboys nowhere in sight.

She ran out after Zach, but Ian was already in the cab, cranking up the engine. For a moment, she didn't think it would catch, but an instant later, the engine rumbled to life, and he lurched off, tires shooting pea-sized gravel in their wake.

"I'll go after him, make him stop." Zach ripped the keys from his pocket and sprinted for his own truck.

Andrea was hot on his heels. "No, Zach. If you chase him while he's still trapped in the flashback, he won't get the chance to think things through. He'll just react and end up racing you to get away. Someone will get hurt."

Zach stopped short and looked after the receding truck, his handsome face contorted with anguish and frustration. "Are you sure you know what you're doing? What if we let him go now and he just keeps on driving—or worse yet, splatters his damn fool brains over the roadside when he rolls into a ditch or something."

"I can't be sure," she admitted, unshed tears making her vision shimmer, "no one can, and I'll admit that a big part of me wants to chase him down with you and drag him straight home, hog-tied and yelling his head off if that's what it takes. But my training and experience both tell me he'll wind down soon, get a grip on himself and come back once he's had a chance to process the memory that's upset him."

"What memory? Is it—what they did to him?"

"I'm not sure exactly, but it's definitely tied in with the torture." She recalled being with him, every worry driven from her mind by the kissing, touching, the way he'd looked into her eyes as he had moved inside her. She remembered, too, that moment when his body had jolted, every muscle tensing as he'd pushed himself away. He'd said something about another person, some other *American* who'd watched him *there*, which must mean the place where he'd been held and tortured. But what had Ian meant exactly? Had an American taken part in what had been done to Ian, or had he been a fellow prisoner, doomed to suffer the same torments?

Whatever the truth was, its impact on Ian had been so immediate, so profound, an insight struck her like a bolt from the blue. This had to be it, what Julian had wanted from her all along, what he and Dr. Kapur wanted. And what they would stop at nothing to keep Ian from telling anyone, especially a reporter like his sister-in-law, Jessie.

To prevent that from happening, Andrea felt sure they would do whatever damage control they deemed necessary...

Damage control that might very well include the murders of anyone who knew the truth.

"If there's anything you'd like me to do," the veterinarian said, sounding genuinely concerned, "or anyone I should call for you—the sheriff, maybe?"

"No, that's fine," Zach said. "We've got this covered. And even if we didn't, Sheriff Canter is the last person on the planet I'd ever ask for help."

"Then, I'll just go in and see about that heifer you've got penned up, shall I? You said it's the left foreleg she's favoring, didn't you?"

"That's right, and thanks, Doctor. She's in the last box stall on the left."

The veterinarian went inside, leaving Andrea and Zach to watch the receding cloud of dust that marked Ian's progress. As the truck vanished from view, Zach shook his head and swore. "I ought to beat that brother of mine senseless for taking off like that, scaring people half to death—and again, without the license."

"I understand you're worried," she said, "and I know it has to be frustrating. But he is making progress, re-membering more each passing day. Learning to handle it, to self-regulate the reactions—that's slower to come, but I promise, it *will* come."

"If he doesn't destroy himself first, you mean?" Zach's fear for his brother bled straight through his gruffness. There was love, too, in the mix, a deep though mostly unspoken bond between two men shaped by the same upbringing. A difficult upbringing, marred by their father's violence.

"I swear to you, he's not going to do that, not as long as I have breath and strength to stop it." The professional in her knew that it was reckless, irresponsible to make such a promise. But she wasn't speaking as a psychologist any longer, just as a woman. A woman whose body ached for Ian...and whose heart had no idea how to let him go.

"But there's still someone out there, isn't there? I mean, that car of yours didn't end up in Spur Creek all on its own, now did it?"

"Someone hit me," she repeated, "someone who wanted me either good and scared or stone dead."

"Then we'd better damned well hope that Ian doesn't end up running into that person before he figures this out and drags himself back home."

As the hours passed with no sign of Ian, she regretted her rash statement, along with the advice she'd given Zach that pursuing Ian would have been a very bad idea. She came to regret it even more when Zach found Ian's cell phone on the floor near his office sofa, where it must have fallen while they'd been...

The thought had regret knifing through her. Had it been the heat and intensity of their lovemaking that had somehow triggered a memory Ian clearly hadn't been prepared to deal with?

Without the smartphone, with its GPS, there was no way to track him down if need be, as she had thought at first. And no way to prevent him from somehow finding the means to keep going, leaving all of them as bereft as they'd been at the first reports of his death.

The first, but not necessarily the last.

What if she'd been wrong, if he'd really run the truck off the road as Zach had suggested? With every second that ticked past, her anxiety wound tighter, leaving her trembling with imagined scenarios where the driver who'd run her off the bridge burst out of nowhere, shooting from his window at Ian. Or what if Ian had instead regressed to the fugue state he'd been in when he'd first been found. She pictured him pulling over along some lonely stretch of roadside, leaving the door of the pickup open and walking blindly across country, continuing the odyssey he'd begun months before.

Needing the family's company as badly as they seemed to need her reassurances, she joined them that evening at the dinner table. With the exception of Eden, who was happily oblivious as she alternately shoveled potatoes, pork and peas into her mouth and chattered about a drama involving an escaped hamster in her kindergarten class, everyone else did little more than pick at their meals, each of the adults struggling with worries about what might have happened.

As Andrea watched them, she wondered if Zach's mother, his brother and Jessie were all struggling against the same fear that gripped her: the worry that somehow, some way, death had reached an icy hand through the encroaching prairie darkness and reclaimed the man who had once miraculously escaped its grip.

Chapter 12

A garish twilight glow crouched along the dark horizon when it finally came to Ian that there was no outrunning memory. No outracing it, either, especially not in a rattle-trap old pickup that was already running on fumes. He had a dim memory of pulling off to the side of one of the rutted dirt roads that crisscrossed the ranch in an attempt to pull himself together. But it clearly hadn't worked, for he was traveling down a paved road now, a narrow two-lane highway, moving toward that bloody splash to the west…

Or could it be the east? Rising on a pulse of panic, the question had him wondering if he'd lost not only his sense of direction but also more time than he'd imagined, if he might be looking at dawn's lights instead of dusk.

Breathing hard, he clenched the wheel more tightly and pulled over, staring into the dimming light until a few emerging stars convinced him it was just past sunset after all.

The first order of business, he realized, was to figure out where the hell he was and get to the nearest gas station, or he would end up adding the need to call for a ride home to the growing tally of his failures.

Though he knew he should at least set Andrea's and his family's minds at ease, it came as almost a relief when he checked his pocket and found he didn't have the cell phone with him. At least that reassured him that Zach wouldn't be jumping down his throat at any moment, demanding an explanation for what had tripped him off. Ian's gut twisted at the thought of how the memories ran together, with both his torturers and the American whose voice he'd heard, all bearing his old man's face.

Even worse than the thought of looking like a lunatic in front of his family was the idea of trying to explain the way he'd run out on Andrea after making love to her. It came to him in a rush how sad and anxious she'd looked, in the moments before he had finally seduced her, how she'd begged for the chance to "make it up" to him...

To make up the fact that—he reached back through the smoky haze of spent lust and adrenaline, struggling to remember exactly what she'd told him. Something about being sent to him, forced by the fiancé who had been her boss, as well.

He spun it around in his brain, wondering if, despite her show of reluctance, she could have been placed in his path in the hopes that pillow talk would loosen his tongue, coaxing him to reveal whatever the hell it was that this Julian and whomever he was working for were after.

They want the American, the American who watched, Ian thought, cold chills ripping through him at the hazy memory of the man who'd begged to be spared his own beatings. But as unsettling as that thought was, the suspicion that Andrea might have been coerced to sleep with him, forced against her will, turned the blood pumping through his body to ice water in an instant.

Was it possible she could have faked the cries of ecstasy, the quivering clench of her innermost muscles? Or had her reaction been no more than a physical response, one that had left her dealing with despair and shame afterward?

He ground his teeth, telling himself it couldn't be true and noticing a brighter section of the darkening sky, a glow that had him putting the truck back into gear and heading toward what he suspected must be Marston, since tiny Rusted Spur didn't have enough in the way of stores and businesses to create much light pollution.

Before he made it far enough to confirm or disprove his hunch, the truck's engine sputtered once before giving up the ghost. Rolling to the stony shoulder, Ian tried in vain to restart it before climbing out of the cab, hoping like hell he'd find a gas can in the truck's bed.

He dug through tools, old flashlights and a length of rope to find a spouted red container in the pickup's rusty toolbox. But he cursed in frustration to realize his wallet was nowhere to be found. Of course, he thought, since he'd never seen the need to carry it around the ranch.

With no other choice, he chose the flashlight with the brightest beam and started walking anyway, hoping he could prevail on someone's kindness toward a stranger in need. And praying he would be fortunate enough to come across a Good Samaritan rather than the sniper who had already tried once to shoot him—and nearly murdered Andrea on another lonely road.

An hour after dinner, Jessie was down on the floor of Eden's bedroom with her daughter, the two of them building weirdly imaginative, though oddly angular "dinosaurs" from LEGO blocks. Though Zach's mother would have wrinkled her nose at their "unladylike play," Jessie and her daughter were having a blast making their creations roar before launching them into epic battles. Both of them laughed like loons whenever a tail or claw or head went flying. Barely able to restrain themselves from joining in, Sweetheart and Lionheart played the part of enthusiastic spectators, barking and wagging hairy rumps.

Unable to resist the impulse, Jessie flipped over Eden, freshly bathed and in her pj's, and tickled her until the little girl squealed. Jessie suspected it was a huge mistake to do so this close to bedtime, but she needed the release as badly as she needed to draw breath.

Ian's disappearance, worrisome as it was, only added to the stress that had been weighing on her lately—stress and guilt about the secrets she was keeping, the discoveries she'd made. She'd wanted to talk some more to Andrea, maybe even confide about what she'd stumbled across a few days earlier while helping her mother-in-law install a software update on the computer the older woman mostly used for online word games. Jessie was still in shock over the email Nancy Rayford, a computer novice, had inadvertently left open, a message that had instantly caught Jessie's eye when the name of a target of her investigation jumped out at her.

But there had been no chance to get Andrea's take on the situation. With the exception of this evening, she'd mostly kept to her room since her return, looking so drawn and pale the one time Jessie had gone up to check on her that she hadn't had the heart to bother the woman with her troubles.

A tap at the door interrupted the impromptu wrestling match, and Zach came in.

"Daddy!" shouted Eden, springing up and running to him as if she hadn't just seen him a half hour earlier. "Read me another chapter, please. Me'n the puppies want to hear the one about the funny cow dogs."

He scooped her up for a hug, but the tightness around his eyes and his single glance at Jessie sent anxiety throbbing through her body.

Is it Ian? Is there bad news?

"I'll tell you what, Eden," he said, his deep voice taking on the tones he used to gentle a frightened young horse or soothe an injured calf. Big and powerful a man as he was, he never used his size or strength to command respect, but there was a core of strength there that made nearly everyone, from the ranch's dogs and horses to the roughest-natured cowboys, obey him without question. "If you'll pick up your toys while your mom and I go and talk for a while, I promise you, I'll come and do just that a little later."

"*Two* chapters," said Eden, whose unerring child's instinct told her she was in a position to bargain. "Two chapters, and bedtime fifteen minutes later?"

"Pick up your blocks, and we'll see about the rest," he said, the somberness of his words making Jessie's stomach flutter.

"Listen to your dad," she said.

Eden glanced from one parent to the other. "Okay, Daddy. I'll do it." She smooched his stubbled cheek. "And then you won't have to be a grumpy face anymore."

"Thanks, Glitterbug. You're the best," he said, bending to put her down. "I'll be back in a little bit."

He held the door open for Jessie and then closed it behind the two of them once they'd stepped into the hallway.

"What is it? Is it Ian?" she whispered urgently.

Zach only shook his head and nodded in the direction of their bedroom. Hurrying to keep up with his long strides, she felt an ominous weight squeeze the air from her lungs, certain that the news was as dire as any of their fears.

Inside their room, she glanced anxiously at the dark windows. Away from the ranch's security lighting, the blackness would be almost complete, the distant stars and thin sliver of moon offering only the barest scintilla of relief. "If you're scaring me like this for nothing…"

"I can tell you this much—Ian hasn't wrecked the truck somewhere on the road to Rusted Spur or Marston. About a half hour after he left, I sent Virgil off in one direction and those cow-patties-for-brains hands who left the keys in the truck's ignition in another to check the roads—and Marston's beer joints, too, as long as they were at it."

"I thought you said Ian's not a drinker."

"He's not—or hasn't been since the two of us stirred up so much trouble back when we were looking for ways to punish the old man…not that that ever worked out so well for either of us."

She caressed his forearm lightly, her heart twisting at the thought of the violence that had defined his early years. It made her proud, too, of Zach's efforts to be a far different type of father than the sorry example who had blighted both brothers' childhoods.

The question was, was she willing to allow the late John Rayford's sins to open up a fresh new set of wounds with the publication of her story? But the thought of hiding the man's low character, of letting her target get away with outrageous behavior didn't sit well with her, either. Nor could she bear the idea of letting Zach try to remake her into the kind of woman she would never be, even if he did so in the name of love.

"Just wanted to rule out the drinking," Zach explained, "because whatever he's remembered—if you'd only seen the look on his face. It was like he was still back there. It was the kind of pain a man might do any crazy thing to numb."

She nodded, feeling terrible for Ian. "Sometimes I wonder if he'd be better off keeping those demons buried."

"We both know that's no good, either, because buried or not, those damned memories have been eating him alive."

"He's been a little better since Andrea, don't you think?"

"Better, yeah—or just more focused on her than his own problems. From what I've seen, it's not entirely one-sided, either."

She smiled, once again touching him lightly. "So you're just now noticing that?"

He shrugged and stalked in the direction of the bed he'd had built for them, a bed that she sometimes joked could only be owned by a cattle rancher or a king. Between its massive proportions and its dark headboard shaped to resemble the spreading, hand-carved horns of a bull, it might have been ridiculous if Zach weren't able to deliver on the virility it promised.

But boy howdy, did her husband ever deliver, in more ways than even he might guess.

"I'm too busy thinking about cattle prices, cowboy grudges and natural gas leases to notice that kind of thing."

"In other words, you're a man."

He shrugged. "A man who also has to keep an eye out for whatever mischief you and that daughter of yours are getting up to."

"Oh, so she's mine when she annoys you?" Jessie said, lightly but delicately. For biologically, Eden was related to Jessie, through her own twin sister, and not Zach—not that he'd ever treated her as anything less than a natural daughter.

"And mine whenever she's an angel," he said. "Ask my mother if you don't believe me."

She snorted, relieved that she hadn't said the wrong thing after all, but as they sat down on the bed's edge, she couldn't help noticing that his smile was strained and his touch distracted when he patted her hand.

Apprehension fluttered in her stomach, but she told herself he had no idea what secrets she was keeping. "So where do you think Ian's gone?"

He shook his head. "I'm out of ideas, but he couldn't be too far. He left his wallet behind, for one thing, and Jimmy says there wasn't much fuel in that old gas guzzler."

"Ian's made his way home once. He will again." Despite her reassuring words, worries wriggled beneath the surface like mosquito larvae in a stagnant puddle.

"I imagine he will when he's ready," Zach said, his gaze cooling. "But I didn't bring you in here just to talk about that."

"What is it then? You're making me nervous."

His scowl did nothing to reassure her. "I need you to finally come clean with me about how this new story of yours affects us as a family."

"I told you, it's nothing to worry about," she said, nervousness pulling the lie from her, though she knew that in the long run, it was only going to make things worse.

"Then what about this—what I found hidden in your office?"

When he pulled a small packet of folded papers from his back pocket and slapped them down on the bed between them, her jittery stomach threatened a full-scale rebellion. As guilty and regretful as she felt, she jumped to her feet to face him, the first words uttered coming out completely wrong.

"My office is my private workspace, so what on earth have you been doing in there, snooping through my research files?"

He unfolded the pages and laid them down, one after the other. And Jessie held her breath as he displayed the four notes she'd found these past three weeks, tucked beneath the blade of her car's windshield wiper or, once, left on her front seat, though she could have sworn she'd left the car locked when she went inside the school to speak to Eden's teacher. After the fourth sheet, Zach stopped, staring at her as he waited for her explanation.

Which meant, she hoped and prayed, that he didn't have the printout she'd made of his mother's incriminating email. Didn't have his finger on the trigger of a weapon that would wound.

Or kill, Jessie thought, laying her hand protectively over her roiling stomach. And wondering if Zach could have been right when he'd suggested that the attacks on Andrea and Ian both traced back to a secret she had no right to keep.

Chapter 13

The darker the sky outside her bedroom window grew, the blacker Andrea's suspicions became. *He's not coming back. He's walking.* She pictured him blindly stumbling, tripping over rocks and grassy tussocks, saw him tumbling down the side of a ravine and splitting his head. Or maybe he would suffer the same fate he'd saved her from after falling into a creek, drowning between a pair of sandy banks. The thought sent panic churning through her, flooding her brain with vivid memories of the moment her car had rolled over, filling with water so quickly she'd barely had time to snatch a breath of air and hold it.

Heart thumping, she paced the room, remembering his eyes, his voice, his heated touch. What if death was even now cooling those hands, that mouth, the whole of his magnificently sculpted body? If something she had done or said had provoked the flashback that drove him from his home?

Done...or said.

She stopped short, thinking of the way Ian had looked at her when she'd tried to explain to him what Julian had forced her to do. *Guess I should pay him a visit then, to thank the son of a bitch for sending you to me.*

Was it possible he might recover from his shock enough to do so? That he would go, not to *thank* Julian as he'd said, in his eagerness to soothe her aching conscience, but to confront him about what was going on?

If Ian suddenly showed up at the center, demanding explanations or hurling accusations, would he, too, suffer an accident, just as she had? Or would he once again go missing, never to return?

Furious with herself for not having thought of it earlier, Andrea left her room and trotted down the staircase in the hope of finding Zach—or anyone she could convince to loan her a vehicle or drive her. Downstairs, the house was quiet and dark, other than a few dim lights that had been left on, which had to mean that everyone else had gone upstairs, at least for now.

Her teeth worrying her lower lip, Andrea remembered spotting a rack hanging in the mudroom, with a number of key rings dangling from its copper hooks. But was she really so ungrateful a guest, after everything the Rayfords had done for her, to take a set of keys without permission and steal a vehicle?

Her heart thumped at the thought of it, but with her mind full of Ian, there was little room for uncertainty and no room at all to worry over whatever consequences she might suffer. For there was absolutely nothing worse than the thought of losing the man she loved—the man she could only now admit had always and would forever own a piece of her heart.

Standing near the back door, she was lifting a key ring when she heard a jingling sound behind her. Pulse racing, she whipped around, only to see close to a hundred pounds of vigilant Rottweiler standing in the doorway, her deep brown gaze fixed and her broad head lowered.

"Nice doggie. Good Gretel." Andrea used the same soothing tone she reserved for troubled clients, but she suspected that the well-trained animal scented her nervousness like a raw and bloody steak. Andrea waited for the curled lip or the growl that would indicate the dog was about to punish her transgression, probably in a manner that would involve another visit to the hospital.

Instead, the Rottweiler looked over her shoulder, where Jessie was standing in the shadows.

"What are you doing with my car keys?" she asked.

"Oh, you surprised me...." Andrea stalled while her mind raced to come up with a halfway plausible explanation. "I was thinking that the other day, when we went out to lunch, my lip balm might've rolled out of my purse. I didn't want to bother you about it, but I thought I'd go and check under the seat."

"You're worried about *lip balm*? When you lost the whole purse and everything you own in Spur Creek?"

Gretel's low growl barely registered. Did the animal somehow sense the lie, or was she mirroring Jessie's skepticism instead?

"It was recovered—the purse, I mean. Dripping wet with most everything inside it ruined, but..." Andrea let the story wind down as Jessie stepped into the light, her eyes damp and her face blotchy. "What's wrong?"

Jessie wiped at her eyes. "Other than your lying to me, you mean? Nothing."

"Now who's lying? It's not Ian, is it? You haven't heard anything?"

"It's not Ian. It's Zach. I just had… We were discussing—" Jessie heaved a sigh. "I thought I was sparing him, sparing all of them by keeping my investigation into North Texas campaign fund-raising tactics to myself. But all I've done is screw things up. Zach's already livid that I've dug into his mother's donations—he thinks I'm doing it for spite and not because I care that some sleazy local politician's milking her for whatever he can extort. And once Zach finds out the rest, he'll—"

She dug a tissue from her pocket and turned away to blow her nose.

The car keys still in her hand, Andrea stepped closer to lay a hand on Jessie's shaking shoulder.

"I'm such a colossal screwup," Jessie said. "I just wanted to— I thought I could use my investigative skills to solve one family issue, not create a dozen more."

"If it makes you feel any better," Andrea told her, "you aren't the only one to foul up. I was about to take off with your car."

"Why would you do that?" Jessie looked more confused than angry. "I'm going out on a limb here, but I don't see you as the type to take a joyride in my Prius."

"I had an idea, a crazy idea, maybe, about where Ian could be heading."

"Where?"

Andrea drew in a deep breath. "Back to Marston, at the center where I worked. And I think he could be heading straight for trouble."

"But it's an hour away. Shouldn't we just call the satellite office over there and have them send a deputy to head off trouble?"

"No," Andrea said firmly, convinced Ian would run at the first sign of a patrol car. And heaven only knew where he might go after that. "But if you'll lend me your phone, I'll try calling a friend of mine who works there and have her keep an eye out for any trouble."

"I don't understand. Why would Ian go there in the first place? I mean, that's the reason we had you come here to work with him, since he refused to leave the ranch for counseling."

"This isn't about counseling, but it could take a lot of explanation. And I'm afraid we don't have that kind of time, not if I'm going to keep Ian from making the worst mistake of his life." *Or maybe even the last.*

Jessie stared another moment before making her decision. "Then let me grab my purse and leave a note for Zach, and we'll talk on the way. But first, give me those car keys. And don't you dare try to take off before I come back."

She gave a quiet command in German, then left the Rottweiler watching Andrea with an intent expression.

Grimacing, Andrea called after her, "Wouldn't dream of leaving."

Gretel seemed to smile at her, exposing a row of shark-like teeth.

Ian took it as a good sign when the headlights coming from behind slowed instead of speeding up and gunning for him. An older, red Corolla pulled up and the driver put down the passenger-side window. "Saw your truck back there. Need a lift into town?"

Ian took in the clean-shaven face of a male in his late thirties, a sandy-haired man who was giving him the same cautious appraisal, probably hoping he hadn't just offered a ride to some psycho killer. Nodding, Ian said, "Thanks. I'd sure appreciate it."

After stowing the gas can behind the front seat, Ian climbed in next to the driver and buckled up.

"I'm Connor." The driver reached over to shake his hand. "Connor Timmerman."

"Good to meet you. Ian Rayford, and I feel like the biggest idiot in the Panhandle for running dry way out here."

"Wait. You're *him*, Captain Rayford, right? Yeah, of course. I recognize you."

Ian winced as it dawned on him that with all the publicity Jessie's story had generated, he was probably as close to a celebrity as it came around these parts. Though he'd declined the scores of requests for on-camera interviews that followed, it hadn't prevented anyone from digging up whatever old photos they could find. "That's me, yeah." *Unfortunately.*

"Awesome. I was just talking to some guys about you."

Ian tensed. "What guys? Who was talking about me?"

Timmerman shrugged. "Just some of the veterans I work with. You're an inspiration to them, man. They would absolutely love to meet you."

"Veterans… Wait. You're not the same Connor that Andrea Warrington mentioned to me, are you? Over at Warriors-4-Life?"

"One and the same. Big fan of Andrea's," Timmerman admitted before his smile faltered. "I understand she was working with you at the ranch for a short time before she decided to leave the center."

"She *quit*?"

"That's what we're hearing, and I can tell you, it's a real blow, losing her. Hard to believe she'd bug out on her clients, on all of us, without a word of explanation. I tried calling her a couple times, but her voice mail box is full."

"She's back at the ranch," Ian said, "recovering from a wreck she had the night of the storm."

"She was in an accident? Is she all right?" Too distracted by the news to drive, Timmerman left the car in Park.

Judging the man's surprise and concern to be sincere, Ian said, "The car was totaled, but her injuries weren't serious. She's already back on her feet. It was no accident, though."

"No accident? What do you mean?"

"I mean, a larger vehicle ran up on her and forced her over the Spur Creek bridge. She damn near drowned before I happened on the scene and pulled her out. And if I ever get my hands on the bastard responsible—"

"Does Julian know all this? Julian Ross, our director?"

"Absolutely, he does. He came to visit when she was under observation at the hospital." Wondering what else he might get out of Timmerman, Ian didn't mention that Andrea had refused to see Ross.

"I can't believe it. Why on earth wouldn't he have told us, unless—"

"Unless what?" Ian asked when Timmerman abruptly cut himself off.

"He's seemed kind of *off* lately, and he got pretty short with the staff when we tried to press him about why Andrea would leave. You have to understand. Julian's a good administrator and a real rainmaker when it comes to funding, but Andrea's the one most of the clients and the staff would throw themselves on a grenade for. She's the heart and soul of that place."

Ian let the words sink in, judged them to be genuine. "Yet Ross wouldn't give you any explanation?"

Timmerman shook his head. "He just said it was a personal matter and ordered us to drop it, giving us this no-bull army glare that made everybody back down."

Ian perked up. "So the man's ex-military?"

Timmerman snorted. "Retired army colonel, yeah, though he doesn't like to talk about it."

Ian ran it through his mind. When he finally spoke again, his voice was grim. "Sounds like there are a lot of things this boss of yours doesn't like to talk about. So how about you and I forget the gas station trip and go try and get some answers out of Colonel Ross now instead?"

Convincing Timmerman took a lot more talk, but the counselor started driving anyway, turning onto a road on Marston's outskirts rather than continuing toward downtown. But by the time he turned into the drive of a low brick building fronted by a Warriors-4-Life sign, Timmerman was shaking his head and sounding more uncertain than ever.

"I don't know about this, Rayford. I consider Andrea a good friend. I mean, she was the one who convinced me they really needed a counselor with my combat experience to give the program credibility, but still…"

"Don't you want to know why Ross fired her, then? Because that's what Andrea told my sister-in-law happened, just before her car was forced off that bridge."

As the car glided to a stop, Timmerman jerked his head to stare at Ian. "You aren't suggesting that Julian had anything to do with that, are you? Because whatever the deal is between him and Andrea—and the whole staff's figured by now there was something going on between them—I don't peg him as the type to fly off the handle and do something crazy. He's just—he's more methodical, you know? More measured in the way he deals with issues."

"Is that your personal or your professional opinion?"

"Both. You have to understand, I work with a lot of seriously volatile people, people who have hell on earth bubbling up inside them looking for a place to boil over."

"People like me, you mean."

"I don't know you, Captain Rayford, and you have to understand, I'm not passing judgment on you. I'm the last person in the world who would, considering what I've been through personally. But, yeah, from what I've read and seen about your situation, I'd be damned surprised if you didn't have some issues."

"But Julian Ross doesn't? That's what you're trying to say to me?"

"I'm sure he does. Doesn't everybody? But not the kind that involve the kind of craziness you're talking."

"I appreciate your take on this." Ian reached for the door handle. "But if you don't mind, I'll need to get some answers for myself."

They both climbed out of the car, and Ian hesitated. "Before we head inside, can you tell me which vehicle is Ross's?"

Timmerman scanned the parking lot, which was lit by a pair of security lights. A moment later, he shook his head. "That's odd. I don't see his Explorer. He must've run in to town to pick up something. But don't worry. I can't imagine he'll be gone long."

"Then I'll be waiting for the colonel by the time he makes it back. Can you take me to his office?"

Timmerman nodded. "That'll work. He's sure to stop in there to check for messages, and I do have a key. But still, I can't just— I have a lot of clients counting on me here, especially without Andrea around to counsel them."

"Don't worry. There's no need for you to be involved in this. I won't mention that you let me in."

"These questions you're here to ask my boss," the counselor asked as he studied Ian intently, "can you promise me that's all you're here for? Nobody's going to get hurt, are they?"

"Someone already has been," said Ian darkly as he thought of Andrea. "But I'll give you my word, I'll do my best to keep things safe and civil."

"And afterward, you'll fill me in?"

"I'll definitely find a way to do that. For one thing, I'll still need a ride to grab some gas—and maybe to borrow twenty bucks, if you can spare it, since I lit out without my wallet." As much as Ian hated to admit it, he figured such a request deserved some explanation. "Damned flashback got the better of me."

A look of understanding crossed the older man's face, and once again, he offered a firm handshake. "You've got it, Captain. For Andrea."

"For Andrea," Ian echoed.

Jessie glanced over from behind the wheel of her car. "So tell me, Andrea, why are we heading out now? And I still don't understand why you were so dead set against taking the dog."

"Because that's not a dog. It's a T. rex in a dog suit," Andrea argued. "I'm already nervous enough."

Jessie shook her head. "What the heck is going on with you?"

"I could ask you the same thing," Andrea said, concerned about how troubled Jessie had seemed. Whatever was really going on between her and Zach must have been pretty serious to strain a marriage that looked so solid.

"You first," Jessie said. "It's only fair, since I'm taking off to drive you without a word to Zach, which, I guarantee you, is going to cause an issue."

"So why do it, then?" Andrea asked. "You could've let me borrow your car."

"You've got to be kidding. After what you did to the last one you drove?"

Andrea smiled though it was clear to her that Jessie had wanted out of the house. "You did say you left him a note though, right?"

"Yeah, right on his pillow, where he should see it after he's gotten Eden down for the night. But trust me, he'll still be furious. So spill it, Andrea."

"Let me make that call first to my friend at the center?"

"Only if you promise you'll answer my questions when you're done."

Once Andrea agreed, Jessie pulled her cell phone from her purse and handed it to Andrea. Soon, she managed to connect with Cassidy at the center.

"I need you to do me a big favor," Andrea told her. "No questions, no arguments—just take my word that it's important, and I promise you, I'll introduce you to some of the most gorgeous cowboys you've ever laid your eyes on."

Jessie jerked a curious glance her way, but Andrea shrugged it off. "Okay, now. I need you to head straight out to the parking lot. You may want to take a flashlight with you."

"These better be some seriously prime cuts of beef

you're talking about," Cassidy grumbled. "I just got out of the shower, and I'm a dripping mess. And maybe you can tell me, what the heck happened with you, anyway? One minute, you're off doing some one-on-one with a client, and next thing I know, you're gone—poof, and Julian's shooting the atomic death glare every time your name's brought up."

"I'll explain everything later. I promise. But for now, you need to tell me, do you see an old brown pickup in the parking lot?" Andrea described the truck Ian had been driving as best she could but didn't know whether to be relieved or disappointed when Cassidy didn't find it.

"No."

"What about Julian? Is he there?"

"His Explorer's gone, in case you were wanting to come by to pick up something you left."

"Great. I'm on my way, but I need you to call me back at this number if you see any sign of either Julian or Ian Rayford."

"Ian Rayford? The guy you were counseling? I don't understand. Why would he be here, and what's this have to do with Julian?"

"Just promise you'll call me, and I'll be there as fast as I can."

Andrea ended the call and laid the phone in the car's center console.

When Jessie glanced over at her this time, the soft glow of the dash lights highlighted her impatience. "Okay, now explain, with no more stalling. I'm not going to be put off a second longer—unless you're a big fan of long walks."

Andrea nodded, dragging in a deep breath. "The truth is, my being on hand and available to work with Ian was no coincidence. Someone appears to have gone to a lot of trouble to put me in place before Ian's return."

"I *knew* it." Jessie popped the steering wheel with one hand. "I've been saying the same thing to Zach from the start, how it seemed awfully convenient. He just said we shouldn't waste too much energy questioning good fortune."

"It did seem odd to me, too, but I was so shell-shocked after hearing about Ian's return that I wasn't seeing the forest for the trees."

"I imagine it's been as overwhelming for you as it has for Zach and his mom," Jessie said.

Andrea shook her head. "I should've known something was up when Julian insisted that I come out here to counsel Ian in the first place. When I told him I didn't think it was a good idea because I'd been in a relationship with Ian, Julian already knew all about it. He said the only thing that mattered was getting Ian to open up, and I might be the key to his healing."

"He might've had that part right. Ian didn't exactly rush across the room and kiss the daylights out of the last couple of psychologists the government sent to look under the hood. My mother-in-law's still in shock over it. Though you have to understand, the woman practically passes out over the kissing scenes in Eden's princess movies."

Andrea made a face at the memory. "I thought I was going to pass out from embarrassment myself that day, considering how hard I was working to convince her I was a professional."

Jessie laughed. "You convinced her you were Eve offering the serpent's apple, trying to lure her poor boy from the garden. But she got over it pretty quickly. Nancy really likes you."

"I like her, too, though I can imagine she's not the easiest person in the world to live with."

"You could certainly say that, but then, rumor has it, I'm no pushover myself."

Andrea's smile was fleeting. "I was so caught up in my own emotions, I still didn't understand there was something going on with Julian, at least not until I went back after the shooting and refused to keep working professionally with Ian. We'd been too close, and it was obvious he wasn't able to keep his feelings for me in the past."

Jessie glanced over as they turned onto the state highway. "He wasn't the only one having that problem, was he?"

"He wasn't." Andrea recalled riding her bike in one of California's inland deserts, a desiccated, brown landscape she'd revisited days later only to find it filled with vibrant blossoms in the wake of a spring rain. With her training and her books, she'd thought she understood something of the human psyche, so how was it she hadn't comprehended that emotions could lie as dormant as those withered plants, that all the love she'd ever felt could burst forth no matter how she fought it? "Or he isn't, I should say, because I've... I'll always care for Ian. Love him, even when I have no right to."

"Why would you say a thing like that?"

"For one thing, Ian's memory's not right. He's nowhere near right, not yet. And as a psychologist, I should be able to divorce myself from my feelings, keep everything professional—"

"Professional ethics, rules in general, can't stand up

to fate, Andrea. And anyone with eyes can see that you two belong together."

"*Fate*? I've heard too many people use it as a handy excuse for caving to their own selfish desires." Her father, for one, Andrea remembered, thinking of how he'd explained his serial marriage habit as something that was *simply meant to be*.

"You have a point there. But what you have with Ian, it's not just fate, it's love, isn't it? The kind of love a person's lucky to find once in a lifetime."

Andrea sighed. "I thought I loved Julian. I did. Maybe in a different way, but—"

"That must have been one tough conversation when you told him."

"I would've understood if he'd been so jealous he'd wanted to lash out at me. But his reaction was a mix of that and something scarier, something I couldn't—I kept it secret because I was so scared and ashamed."

Jessie looked over at her, her voice tightening. "What did he do to you? If he hurt you, I swear we'll find some way to make him pay."

"He didn't hurt me," Andrea said. "Not physically, at any rate. But he threatened to have me charged with unethical conduct, to ruin my career, if I didn't—if I wouldn't keep acting as his spy."

"His *spy*?" Jessie shook her head. "I don't understand, unless—who is this Julian, and what does he really want with Ian?"

It came as a relief when Andrea told her what she knew of Julian's military background, and how she suspected that the government might have a hand in what appeared to be a plot to acquire intelligence about what had really happened during the months Ian was in captivity. She detailed the threats he had used against her, followed by the visit from the mysterious Dr. Kapur.

"What I can't understand," Jessie said, "is why they'd come after you on the road like they did? Killing you wouldn't have gotten them what you're saying they were after."

"I'm a little shaky on that part myself," Andrea admitted. "Best I can come up with, they were trying to keep me quiet after I refused Julian that afternoon. Either that, or it was meant to scare me into helping them, only the warning got out of hand."

"Maybe, if they put some hothead on it. Unless—you don't think it was Julian himself, do you?"

"Before I would have said no way, but now—now I wonder if I ever really knew him. He played me for such a fool. I can't believe I bought that compassionate, dedicated act he was selling."

"Don't beat yourself up. It sounds to me almost like these people went out of their way to find out what made you tick and came up with the kind of man that would be guaranteed to attract you."

A chill swept over Andrea, and she nodded in agreement. "They caught me at a vulnerable time, too, while I was grieving what everyone thought was Ian's death."

"Not everyone, I'm betting. Julian and whoever's running the show—the army, I'm guessing—must've suspected he was alive and headed home months before any of us had any inkling. They knew it and said nothing, while they plotted out this operation when they couldn't find him."

Andrea hesitated, uncertain whether she should say more, especially to a reporter, who had both the power and the inclination to spill dangerous secrets. Finally, she said, "Can I tell you something with the understanding that all this is off-the-record?"

Jessie thought about it for a minute before nodding. "You've got it. But only because I care a lot more about my family than any story."

"*Your* family," Andrea echoed.

"Yeah, mine," Jessie said, comprehension dawning in her face as she nodded. "They're my family now, too, and as important as my career is to me, they're what really matters in the end."

Hearing the sincerity in her voice, Andrea told her, "Ian isn't army. He never really has been."

After Andrea explained it, Jessie gave a low whistle. "Wow. Talk about a bombshell, especially with the military participating in my whole heroic soldier story. But it explains a lot, too. This long-range plot has spy secrets written all over it."

"What scares me to death," said Andrea, "is worrying over whether spy secrets might become *deadly* secrets if Ian shows up and starts demanding answers out of Julian."

Engulfed in the darkness of Julian's office, Ian flicked the fading yellow beam of his flashlight over photo after photo hanging on the ivory walls. Most showed a fit-looking man in his midforties with dark eyes and a military bearing. In some of the shots, Julian Ross wore tailored, dark suits as he glad-handed the presenters of oversize checks. In others, he was more casually dressed as he cheered on a group of young men participating in what looked like an outdoor team-building exercise.

Show photos, Ian figured, meant to convince the world he was a real-life humanitarian rather than the kind of man who would force a woman he had claimed to love into an impossible situation. Determined to find out what Ross was really after, Ian pulled papers from the file cabinet, scanning before scattering them as he proceeded.

His cursory sweep turned up nothing of interest, only the logs, files and handwritten notes he would expect to find. After sitting in the wheeled, leather desk chair and switching on a small lamp, Ian methodically pulled out the contents from one drawer after another, caring only about finding whatever leverage he needed to get answers—and shut this SOB down.

Hidden beneath the false bottom of the top, left-side drawer, he found not the evidence he'd been looking for, but a different form of leverage. Carefully, he lifted the .38 automatic he recognized as an antique collector's model.

Before he had the chance to see if it was loaded and operational, he heard swift-approaching footsteps in the hallways. Rather than getting up and hiding, Ian opted to stay seated, concealing both hands and the gun beneath the level of the desk.

As the door opened, the same man from the photos stood there staring at him, another pistol in his right hand…

But unlike the century-old Colt he'd found, Ian would bet his bottom dollar that the gleaming new SIG Sauer Julian Ross was holding was in perfect working order, with a bullet in the chamber.

Chapter 14

"Captain Rayford," Julian said as he casually approached his desk. Except there was nothing casual about the way he held the pistol, not pointing it at Ian but slanting it slightly downward, where he could raise it in a hurry. "What a pleasure it is to finally meet you."

"Wish I could say the same," Ian told him, not moving from behind the desk or showing his hands, either. "But I'm hardly ever pleased when I encounter a man holding a gun."

"Just as I'm rarely pleased when I run across someone going through my desk drawers," Julian countered, his Southern accent as smooth and deep as well-aged whiskey. "Would you mind showing me your hands? Then perhaps we can dispense with all this hardware and talk this through like gentlemen."

I doubt that very much, thought Ian, trying to figure out what Andrea might have seen in this old man. Sure, he appeared to be in good shape, with intense brown eyes and a full head of hair, as far as Ian could tell in the dim light beyond the desktop lamp's range, but there was something that rang false about him, something that had unease churning in Ian's stomach.

Allowing that a man in his midforties wasn't exactly geriatric and he would probably hate any man who had ever touched Andrea, Ian laid both hands on the desktop. But he left the antique gun pinned against the seat by his own thigh, where he could quickly grab and fire it if need be—provided the old pistol was operational. "There you go. Now how about yours?"

Ross went one step further than Ian had dared to hope, clearing his gun's chamber and ejecting the magazine before laying it on top of the clutter of strewn papers. Raising his palms, he said, "There you go. So tell me, Captain, what brings you here to see me?"

"Are you sure you're not a shrink, too, *Colonel*? Because you've got the moves down pat."

Ross laughed. "I'm not, I assure you. But I've spent enough years administering mental health services that I suppose I've picked up a few of their tricks."

"I don't want to be soothed. I want to understand this. What do you want out of me? And why did you feel the need to threaten Andrea to get it?"

"Threaten Andrea?" Julian's jaw unhinged, his gray-brown brows rising in an almost theatrical display of shock. His accent growing even more pronounced, he asked, "Why on earth— What are you talking about, Captain?"

"Your fiancée told me all about it, how you threatened to destroy her career if she didn't do your bidding."

Ross moved forward to the edge of his seat and slapped a hand down on the desktop. "Destroy her career? She's all but done that herself with these outrageous lies."

"You'd better damn well watch who you're accusing."

"Who *I'm* accusing? I don't know what that woman's playing at. For one thing, she's no fiancée of mine. I'd never get involved with a subordinate. It's completely unbecoming."

"Maybe in the military it would be a problem, but out in the civilian world—"

"And I've never threatened anyone." Ross's face grew redder with each word. "My reputation—the people here—mean everything to me."

As angry as the man's words were making Ian, Ross's Southern accent was burrowing even deeper under his skin. Or maybe it wasn't the accent, exactly, but the timbre of his voice, the way he strung his words together. "You brought her flowers at the hospital, tried to go and see her."

"Of course I did. I felt bad that we'd parted on bad terms. I was hoping we could smooth things over…for her clients' sakes, not mine."

Ian shook his head. "A man doesn't bring three-dozen long-stem roses to an employee—"

"We really need her back here." Ross shook his head. "But if she honestly believes the things she's saying, then she's even more unstable than I feared."

"What the hell? You two—you were getting married. She told me."

"Have you ever seen any evidence of this? A ring, perhaps, or another individual who mentioned this *engagement*?"

Ian turned it over in his mind and shook his head. "I don't need proof. I have her word."

"The word of a woman who's been terminated from her position here for increasingly erratic behavior?"

"That's insane. If she was so erratic, why would you send her to see me?"

Ross winced and sighed. "Because I was asked to do what I could for you by a former superior—and because she truly is an excellent psychologist when she's taking her own medications."

"And here I expected you'd try to make out like I'm the crazy one." A wild energy crackled through Ian, making him feel like leaping across the desk and putting this liar in a chokehold.

The older man shook his head, his expression filling with what looked like real regret. "You should know that people with psychiatric issues aren't crazy. When correctly treated, they can lead fulfilling, useful lives, have productive careers, be loving family members."

Beads of perspiration broke out on Ian's forehead. The accent threw him off, but that voice, those words…or was it something in the man's face that seemed so familiar. Had he met the army officer through the agency during his days working in D.C.? Or had it been somewhere abroad? "Andrea's not crazy. But you sure as hell are if you expect me to believe—"

"A tendency toward delusional behavior under extreme stress is often passed down through families, you know. Did she ever mention her mother's suicide?"

"Yeah, after her father was exposed and the family publicly—"

"Psychotic depression, triggered by the unfounded belief that the father had taken on *shadow families.* None of it was real, of course. There's no evidence at all he was some sort of bigamist. No archived stories in the hometown paper. Look it up yourself. It's all—"

Ian snatched up the antique gun, rising from his seat to glower down at Ross. A trickle of hot sweat rolled down the channel formed by his spine. "Your technique's giving you away, the way you're weaving a complicated web of lies to sell your story. Anything to confuse the target enough that he'll dismiss his own perceptions and grasp on to your version."

Ross remained seated, looking into Ian's face instead of at the gun. "What are you suggesting?"

"That you're not working for the army. For all I know, you never were. You've been forcing Andrea to feed you information about what happened to me so you can pass it on to—"

"You do want these people punished, don't you, not only for your suffering but for the bombing of our listening post in—"

"You're part of the intelligence community, aren't you? CIA, NSA or maybe FBI."

"Take a step back from this—this paranoia. Have a seat, and put the gun down. It isn't loaded anyway. Check it for yourself."

Ian pointed it at Ross's head, his hand steady but his anger and confusion growing. Because his theory *did* sound crazy, even to his own ears, and Ross's calm demeanor was so damned reassuring, his smooth Southern voice both calming and disturbingly familiar.

Another drop of sweat broke free from just beneath the hairline, but as the stinging moisture ran into his eyes, Ian didn't make a move to wipe it away. He couldn't, with the kindness on Ross's face morphing into the remembered cruelty of Ian's father. With the memories jumbling his senses, raising the reek of rotting meat and old blood, the shadows of silhouetted figures...the sounds of clinking chain and desperate pleas.

Let me go! I'll tell you! I'll tell you anything you want! Just don't—I can't take another minute!

Desperate words, spoken by a desperate American, a captive stripped of all defenses, of his accent—one of many learned with the assistance of a dialect coach the agency had contracted—to the expert disguises he so often employed.

Ian's mind was swirling, churning, the cone of light from the desktop lamp burning into his brain. The gun in his hand rose, seemingly of its own volition, his finger squeezing the Colt's trigger.

As they stood in the center's parking lot, Andrea turned to Jessie. "If I'm not back within ten minutes, I want you to call 911."

"To report what?"

"Anything, as long as it'll bring a lot of lights and sirens in a hurry."

"Just what're you expecting to find?"

Andrea shook her head. "I don't know for certain, but the last time I was here, Julian surprised me. He'd loaned his Explorer to one of the counselors, so who knows if he's really here?"

"If you think this guy is dangerous, maybe I should come in with you."

"What I'm really scared of is Ian confronting him, so I'll be safer if you wait here and try to hold him off if he shows up. But if it comes down to it, Jessie," Andrea warned, "don't stand in Ian's way."

"You aren't thinking he'd be dangerous? To me, I mean?"

"I know he would never willingly hurt you, but you didn't see him earlier, in the grips of that flashback. It's possible he's confused."

"Like he was when Zach first brought him home? You

don't think he's back in that state, do you? Or, worse yet, violent?"

"I don't know what to think. To tell you the truth, I'm grasping at straws to even imagine he'll come back here. For all I know, I've dragged you out tonight, gotten you into more hot water with Zach, and all for nothing."

"Don't you worry about my marriage. I'll find a way to make things right with Zach—for our sake and our children's."

Andrea froze in place. "Your *children's*? You aren't saying that you're…"

Jessie nodded. "Almost three months, but I've been afraid he'll seize on it as an excuse to try to stop me from my work."

"You'll figure it out, the two of you, as long as you keep loving one another."

Jessie said nothing for a moment. "Just get inside and make sure everything's okay."

Andrea gave her a spontaneous hug before trotting to a side door, where Cassidy was waiting to let her inside, her red ringlets dampening the shoulders of a sweatshirt that swamped her pint-size body.

"He's here," Cassidy warned, her voice low and her eyes wide. "Julian, I mean. I guess Michael has his Explorer again, but I spotted Julian heading for his office. If you're looking to avoid him while you check your room, I can keep watch for— Hey, where are you going?"

"I need to make sure Ian isn't with him," said Andrea, her longer strides quickly outpacing the younger woman's. "Finding him is too important to pussyfoot around."

"I'm not so sure Julian's going to be happy to see you back. The way he was acting earlier when we asked about you—"

"I'm miles beyond giving a damn what makes Julian Ross happy."

Cassidy staggered to a stop, sounding uncertain as she called, "Andrea, please."

Andrea broke into a run, her pulse thrumming an urgent warning. But the intuition that had her in its grips came too late, for as Andrea approached the door to Julian's office, a crack of gunfire broke the evening stillness—the sound of a bullet as it pierced wood, then ripped a white-hot channel across her upper arm before it slammed into the wall behind her.

An SUV pulled into a space, and a smaller man with a short beard climbed out and headed inside. From what Jessie could make out from where she was crouched behind her Prius, the guy looked too young to be Ross, but she checked out the vehicle anyway and found it was a dark gray Explorer.

Reasoning that Julian must have loaned out his SUV again, Jessie wondered if it was possible that this same vehicle had been used to knock Andrea's car off the Spur Creek bridge? Walking all the way around it, Jessie used her smartphone's flashlight to check for any dents or paint damage.

Finding nothing other than a thin layer of road film, she let out a deep breath just as her phone began to vibrate in her hand. She groaned, heart thumping as a photo featuring Zach's handsome grin popped up to identify him as the caller.

"Betcha any money you're not smiling now," she murmured, since she'd already ignored several calls from his phone. Bracing herself for the chewing out she knew she deserved, she put her thumb over the green button to answer.

Instead, she flinched, startled by what sounded like a

backfire or a single clap of thunder. Except, she realized, it had come from the direction of the building.

And her every instinct screamed at her to duck and dial for help.

The blast rang in Ian's ears. The smell of gunpowder filled his lungs, and from the hallway just outside, a shrill scream had his blood freezing in his veins.

Had the shot he'd deliberately aimed high found an unintended victim? An innocent woman, whose blood was on his hands?

Seized with horror, he barely reacted in time to avoid Ross's leap across the desk toward him, a move that sent the lamp tumbling to the floor. Glass shattered, plunging the room into darkness as Ross shouted, "Drop it, Rayford! Drop the weapon—before somebody gets hurt!"

Heart pummeling his chest wall, Ian heard the clatter of other desktop items falling to the floor—or was it Ross fumbling to reload his own weapon? Uncertain whether he might be shot at any second, Ian took what little cover he could find behind the filing cabinet, the antique pistol hot as a glowing coal in his hand. Or maybe it was only his guilt as he wondered if some poor woman was bleeding, dying—or maybe even dead already in the hallway.

"Toss the gun and lie facedown on the floor!" Ross ordered, his voice deep and commanding.

"I know that voice. I know *you*." Though Ian knew he would do better to keep his words from giving away his position, adrenaline tore the memory from his mouth. The memory of a man who'd bargained for his own freedom after being forced to witness Ian's beatings. Willing to do anything to save himself, his fellow agent, who had looked very different with the darker hair and thick gray beard he'd worn to blend in for his overseas work, had given up information that had cost five Americans their lives. Lives Ian had had on his own conscience, certain that he had been the guilty party. "It's over now, you traitor. I'm not taking the blame for their deaths anymore."

"Put the gun down now," Ross repeated. "You're having a psychotic episode." Raising his voice, he shouted in the direction of the door, "We'll need restraints! Connor, Michael, anybody! Get Cassidy in here right now with something to calm this man down!"

Realizing that Ross was going to try using the same tactic he'd attempted to discredit Andrea, Ian crept forward, intent on jumping the man, subduing him until his own memories could be verified. But the door opened, spilling light from the hallway into the dark room.

Andrea leaned around the door's edge. "Ian, put the gun down! Before someone else gets hurt!"

His gaze locked on her blood-soaked upper right sleeve, where she tried to stanch the flow by clamping her left hand over the wound. As the realization that he'd shot her hit Ian like a closed fist, Ross slammed him down backward, sending the antique pistol spinning from Ian's grasp.

He landed hard on his back, his breath violently forced from his lungs as Ross came down on top of him. Ian flipped the older man off him but was soon distracted by his own struggle to draw breath. The harder that he fought to fill his lungs, the more painfully they spasmed.

In his peripheral vision, he caught sight of the old Colt where it had come to rest underneath the desk. But he could no more reach the gun than he could sprout wings, not laid out as he was, unable to do so much as cough.

For one adrenaline-charged moment, Ian imagined his rib cage crushed by the fall and pictured himself turning blue, then dying where he lay, with Andrea looking on in horror. He heard her screaming, saw her pushing past Ross to get closer to him. As Ian's gaze connected with hers, his breath returned in a dizzying rush.

With the sudden flow of oxygen, a roaring noise filled his brain, one quickly drowned out by a jumble of urgent-sounding voices, male and female, Pashto and English. Andrea was pulled away, and the terrorist's vicious threats dissolved into a nightmare haze, leaving behind a reality that was just as disconcerting.

He fought to sit up, to get away from several people who surrounded him while Julian Ross yelled, "The shot. Give him the needle," Ross urged, "before he hurts anyone else."

Strong hands held him down, and Ian saw that one of the two men was Connor Timmerman, who had seemed so damned friendly when he'd picked him up along the roadside, who *sounded* friendly even now, as he said, "Don't try to get up, buddy. Don't fight this, and you'll be safe."

But Ian didn't feel safe, not when he spotted a petite red-haired woman holding a hypodermic needle, her gaze flicking uncertainly from Julian Ross to him.

"What are you waiting for?" Ross demanded. "Give him the damned drugs."

"I don't need meds." Ian's gaze sought Andrea's. "I just need you to listen. Please, Andrea. Tell them how he's threatened you, how he's tried to force you to spy on me for him."

Her face was white as paper, her bloody arm dripping onto the carpet.

"I'm so sorry I hurt you," he said, darkness fizzing through his vision, "but you can't let them do this. Can't let Ross get away with—"

"I know you didn't mean it," she said, her face drawn

and pale as she shook her head. "I know you'd never intentionally hurt me or anyone."

Ian turned to glare at Ross. "*You* told me it wasn't loaded, you lying sack of—"

"You can see, he's highly agitated." Ross told the woman with the needle. "A danger to himself and others."

Ian bucked against Timmerman's grasp, fighting to catch Andrea's eye. "It was him, Andie. He was captured with me and held in that same cell. Only instead of beating him, too, they forced him to watch my torture until he broke down, until he was willing to tell them anything to keep from getting a taste of it himself."

Ross surged forward, shaking his head. "The shot now, Cassidy. Don't you know classic paranoid delusions when you hear them?"

"Ian," Andrea said. "Please stop fighting."

"It was him. I swear it," Ian repeated. "Haven't you ever wondered why he brought you all here, where he could watch and wait once he was tipped off that I'd escaped?"

Ross swore, his face reddening, but Cassidy ignored him to stare a question in Andrea's direction. But Andrea was watching Ian, her eyes wide, her mouth slightly open. In shock from pain and blood loss, he thought, or was it uncertainty he read in her face? Did his accusations sound so outrageous, or could she really be buying Ross's self-serving garbage?

Ian fought free of Timmerman's grasp, throwing the counselor into the tiny redhead. With a startled cry, she fell, the needle rolling from her hand.

"Stay down!" Timmerman shouted at Ian as he and a younger man with a short, dark beard made a grab for Ian's arms.

Scrambling to his feet, Ian ignored Andrea, who was

helping Cassidy up, to point at Ross. "This man's name is Davis Parnell, and he's a traitor to his country! He's a missing CIA agent, a master manipulator, and he'll say anything, hurt anyone to save his own—"

"Give it back! You're not allowed to do that!" Cassidy told Andrea.

"Let me. He won't hurt me," she said, and it was then Ian realized that Andrea had picked up the fallen hypodermic needle. The needle loaded with enough drugs to ensure that he woke up in a freaking psych ward in restraints.

At the thought of being tied down, panic pounded through him. He'd die before he let them chain him in that dark hole, where rats crawled through the musty straw…the smell that took him back to a child's spiraling terror at being bound with ropes and left alone inside a pitch-black feed room, a punishment for some childish transgression.

As he flung off the bearded man, Ian saw out of the corner of his eye Ross's hand dipping into the pocket of his jacket. Certain he was going for the gun, Ian opened his mouth to shout a warning, but Andrea stepped in, the hypo in her bloody hand.

"Time to sleep now, Ian," she said, those long-lashed hazel eyes he loved shimmering with tears. "Time for you to lie down, where I can keep you safe."

Inside of Ian, something fractured, broken beyond repair by her betrayal, but he couldn't bring himself to shove her away. Couldn't do anything but stand like a dead man as she ignored Cassidy, who was warning that Andrea could lose her license by dispensing medication, to push the needle toward the inside of his arm.

Chapter 15

Andrea's heart broke at the look in Ian's eyes, the look that told him he believed she had turned against him. There was more working as well, for she'd recognized the signs of flashback in his glazed look only seconds earlier as the past and present came together in one perfect, deadly storm.

In this state, he was dangerous, as he'd already proved with the gunshot that had creased the outer layers of her upper arm. Sure, the shallow cut stung like a thousand wasp stings, but it was nothing compared to what he could do if he blindly swung his fists or made a sudden grab for her throat.

Press the plunger, and he'll be safe. He'll go down and sleep, and Julian will take his hand off that gun I know he's holding, the gun he'll use if it's what it takes to end this now.

A flash of insight raised the fine hairs behind her neck.

No wonder he's been so desperate to make me his eyes and ears at the ranch. All along, he's been trying to figure out whether he'll have to kill Ian to protect his own secrets. Now that he knew that nothing short of death would ever keep Ian quiet, Andrea was terrified that Julian would find some excuse to pull the trigger—and silence the threat forever.

"There you are," she said, turning her body so the others wouldn't see that she was only pretending to inject the drugs into Ian's arm. As the plastic slid harmlessly past his inner elbow, light flickered through his blue eyes, followed by a dawning comprehension. "Rest now, Ian, and you'll feel so much clearer when you wake up. Everything will make sense, and *everyone* here will have a chance to calm down."

Careful to keep the hypo out of the view of those behind her, she clasped his arm, willing him to understand that this subterfuge was for his safety—and hers as well, considering that Julian must have already tried to kill her at least once, on the bridge.

Ian pressed his lips into a grim line, nodding his agreement but clearly none too pleased with the idea. "I think— I'm just so tired. Everything's so mixed up."

"Let Michael and Connor help you, then. Let them help you to lie down."

Rebellion sparked in his eyes, a quick grimace that told her his mind was fighting the idea of lying prone and helpless.

"In the chair, then," she suggested, leading him back toward Julian's desk. "Just sit and lay your head down."

As they moved in that direction, Connor righted the fallen chair and wheeled it back into place.

"Sorry if I hurt you, man," Ian told him. "I didn't want any of you hurt. I just couldn't—couldn't let him—"

Connor helped him into the chair. "I understand. I've been there. We're all on your side here."

As Ian slumped forward onto the desk, Andrea's attention was drawn by movement of the one man who definitely wasn't in Ian's corner. "Where exactly are you going?" she asked as she moved between Julian and the office door. In her uninjured left hand, she kept the needle behind her hip, wondering if it was possible... *Even if I pull it off, you'll still have time to put a bullet in me—and possibly everyone else in this room.*

"Someone should check on the clients in the game room," he said. "They were gathering to watch a movie, but if any of them heard that gunshot..."

As ploys went it was a good one, Andrea decided, a reminder that Ian wasn't the only person on the premises whose PTSD might trigger flashbacks. But if Julian escaped this room, she knew there was a good chance he'd head to the parking lot and take off to stay one step ahead of Ian's accusations.

"My gosh, Julian," Cassidy scolded. "Don't you see her standing there, bleeding like crazy?" Marching toward him, she caught his sleeve. "Here, let me have that jacket. It's got a big rip in it already, and we need something to wrap up her arm and apply pressure before she passes out."

He jerked his arm free of her grasp. "Not my jacket. I'll be right back with bandages, towels, whatever you need."

But as Andrea's gaze locked with his, they both knew he didn't give a damn about giving up a ruined sports jacket. It was the gun inside the pocket he couldn't afford to part with, the gun and wallet and whatever else he'd need to put distance between himself and the truth.

As much as she hated the idea, it would be safer to let him go, to turn over the job of capturing this traitorous coward to the authorities instead of risking her own, Ian's and her friend's lives in some desperate gambit. But when she opened her mouth to tell this man who'd used her so cruelly, this monster willing to kill to keep from accepting responsibility for his own cowardly actions that he could leave now, the only words that came out were, "So tell me, where're you really off to in such a hurry... *Davis Parnell*?"

Even at that point, Ian thought later, things might have still turned out all right. The man calling himself Julian Ross might have simply pushed past Andrea to make a break for it, escaping, maybe, but at least no one would have died.

Instead, the sound of sirens outside caught everyone's attention, the flashing of red-and-white lights shining through the window.

Ian opened his eyes just in time to see Ross grab Andrea by the neck to pull her in front of him, his other hand coming up to point the SIG Sauer at her head.

As Cassidy screamed, Ian dropped behind the desk, groping desperately for the antique pistol—a pistol that Timmerman must have picked up earlier, for he came up with it, shouting at Ross, "Let go of her, Ross! Let's talk whatever this is through!"

Hiding behind Andrea, Ross turned the gun toward Timmerman. A split second later, Ian caught the blur of Andrea's bloody hand as she jabbed the needle hard into Ross's thigh. Ross screamed as it stabbed his leg, but jerked away from her so quickly that Ian doubted that she'd managed to get much of the drug into his muscle.

It wouldn't have mattered anyway, with adrenaline propelling those next few split seconds. As Andrea tried to jab him again, Ross grabbed her hair and swung the gun back toward her skull.

Bellowing to distract him, Ian charged, Timmerman right behind him. As Andrea twisted away and out the door, there were two loud cracks, followed by a third as Ross began to crumple, the first geyser of blood already spouting from his chest.

But he had strength and will enough to squeeze off a final shot, and he pointed the SIG Sauer at Ian.

A final shot he aimed…except not well enough.

Chapter 16

Andrea sat at the back of an ambulance, where a paramedic wrapped her arm, since she had refused transport to the hospital.

"I'm not making a third trip there this week," she told the kind-eyed woman as she improvised a sling, "not for a cut on my arm and a h-handful of torn-out hair. And especially not when—when Cassidy will never..."

Andrea dissolved into sobs, her vision filling with the image of Cassidy sprawled on the floor, her beautiful ringlets soaked with blood. Andrea knew instinctively she would never forget the stricken look on Ian's face when he knelt to check for a pulse. "I'm so sorry, but she's gone."

"If I hadn't fought him, hadn't stabbed him with that needle," Andrea had stammered.

Ian shook his head. "It was me. He meant to shoot me."

Connor, too, had looked ill as he'd stared down at

the two guns he'd set down on the desktop: the one he'd picked up off the floor, meaning to defend Andrea, and the one he'd pulled from Julian's still-twitching hand before Ross had spasmed and gone still, without anyone making a move to try to help him.

As Andrea wept, Jessie came and wrapped a protective arm around her waist. Ian and Connor were still inside going over what had happened with the chief deputy, who'd taken control of the scene until Canter could arrive, but Michael stood near the ambulance, as well, his fingers repeatedly running through his short beard and his eyes glazed with shock.

Through her tears, Andrea noticed that the other staff members and most of the residents had ventured outside, some of them staring at the flashing lights of the ambulances, fire trucks and sheriff's department vehicles that had responded to the call Jessie made on hearing the first gunshot. A few of the patients were pacing wildly and one appeared to be talking and gesturing to himself.

Someone should be helping them, talking them through the strategies she, Michael and Connor had been teaching them to cope with flashbacks. Someone better equipped, but who else was there, really, with all of them in shock?

While the paramedic questioned Michael, one of the center's clients walked up, a wild-eyed man in his latter twenties, who was chain-smoking away his restless energy. "Is she really dead? Miss Cassidy?"

"She and Julian Ross both are," Jessie answered for her, the words echoing through Andrea's hollowed heart.

"Colonel Ross?" The chain-smoker, Kris Vargas, asked Andrea. "But why? What happened, Doc? Is it—it's the war again, isn't it? It's just like Ty said. It's followed—followed us back home."

As he wandered off without an answer, it occurred to Andrea that he was right, that every one of these men and women, along with Ian and Julian, had carried home a piece of the war locked inside their minds. For Ian, that memory had been overwhelming enough that his psyche could only deal with bits and pieces at a time. For Julian, it had been so unbearably shameful that he'd been willing to create a new identity and threaten or even kill to keep the secret instead of turning himself in or dealing with the psychological torment he had been exposed to.

Intellectually, she understood it. Emotionally, she knew she never would. But that didn't mean she had to allow herself to become another victim, not when there were people here who urgently needed her help.

She came to her feet, intent on answering Kris, though he had already wandered off to shout the same questions at Michael.

"You need to sit down. You're hurt," Jessie told her.

"We're all hurt. Every one of us. The question is, what do we do with our pain?"

"Andrea, you're in shock. The psychobabble can wait for someone else to—"

She wiped away her tears, swallowing back her pain. "They need me now, someone they know and trust to help them. And if I'm to make it through this night, I'll need them just as much."

Jessie looked as if she might argue, but Zach pulled up in his truck, then jumped out and ran to his wife.

He pulled her into his arms, relief and worry mingling in his expression. "What the hell's happening? Are you all right?"

"I'm fine, and so's your brother. He's inside, talking with Canter's second in command about the shooting that happened here tonight."

Zach pulled back to stare a question at his wife. "Shooting? What the hell?"

Leaving the couple to their discussion, Andrea went to see if she could roust Michael from his shock and grief to help him. It took a few minutes, but she talked the younger counselor into refocusing on the center's mission.

"It's what Cassidy would've wanted," she told him, "what she would have found the strength to do if it had been one of us."

"You—you're right," he said, giving her a hug and pulling himself together.

For the next hour or so, the two of them kept busy, recruiting support staff to do a head count and organizing client teams to offer mutual support and redirect their individual thought patterns. Ignoring her throbbing arm and aching head, Andrea spent time, too, talking to Kris and one female patient who'd been especially close to Cassidy, helping relieve their heightened states of anxiety.

Time seemed to slow down, the lights blurring and the voices growing muffled as she worked on. She didn't see the tall man coming up behind her, didn't hear him even when he called her name. When finally, he caught her by her good arm and turned her toward him, she startled and cried out.

Then she saw that it was Ian and buried her face against his broad chest, her shoulders shaking as she leaned into his strength.

Ian stroked Andrea's back and hair, holding her tightly as she wept against his chest. As the evening wore down, a front had dropped the temperature and kicked up a cool wind. He felt her trembling with the chill—or possibly pain and exhaustion. Considering all she'd been through, he'd been amazed to find her out here in the first place, going from one group to another with her bloodstained arm in a sling. One of the most traumatic nights of her life, and she was pouring every scrap of her strength into helping those around her. But that strength was spent now, and she needed him, whether or not she would admit it.

"Come on in with me now," he said, slipping out of his own jacket to wrap it around her. "We need to get you warmed up, and anyway, Canter's swearing he'll come hunt you down if that's what it takes to get your statement."

She shook her head. "Then let him. I'm not coming in while there's still one client unaccounted for." In spite of her insistence, her voice was as brittle as the dried leaves rattling past their feet. "Ty Dawson's practically a kid, one of our most at-risk."

"Blond guy, right? I heard about it, but Timmerman and Michael are almost sure he'll be found holed up in some dark corner until things quiet down. Apparently, he's done this sort of thing before."

"He has, several times, but it's still possible he could've been drawn outside by all these lights."

"The rest of the staff has stepped up and some of the patients, too, checking room by room for any sign of this guy. Zach's in on the search, too, and Jessie's taken charge of brewing coffee in the dining area. You could go in and keep her company while she—"

"That's all great, but I'm the senior staff person now. I need to make sure everyone's safe."

"Listen to me, Andrea. You're cold, you're hurting and you're heading in now, too—unless you're looking to spend another night at Marston Regional. Because I swear I'm hauling you over to the ER to get that arm looked at if you don't at least sit down and let me get you something hot to drink."

She pulled away from him, her brow furrowing. "This is exactly what Jessie was saying about you Rayford men. Give you an inch, and you want to take over a woman's whole life. No wonder she's been reduced to hiding her work from—"

"I wouldn't *have* to take over if you knew enough to take care of yourself."

"Are you suggesting you know better than I do about how I should get through this night? Exactly what is it that gives you that expertise, the Y chromosome or the Rayford blood? Or is it your vast experience in handling your own trauma?"

Temper burned through his restraint. "You act like you forget, but I was in that room, too. I was there when Ross, Parnell—whatever you want to call the bastard—pointed that gun at me and missed. So before you start acting like you're sorry that he did, maybe you should rethink lashing out at someone who only wants to help you."

She sucked in a startled breath, gaping as though she had been slapped. "I'm not—not sorry he missed you. How c-can you even think that?"

"I don't. Of course, I don't. I'm sorry. It's only— It's been a horrible night for both of us. Let's say we don't end it by wounding one another."

She wiped at her eyes. "I'm sorry, too. I didn't mean to say such hateful things. I don't even know where that came from."

"From a place of pain. And I do know from experience. After all, I've been lashing out at everyone, acting like a jerk since I set foot on the ranch."

"Everybody understood," she said. "Even if they didn't love the behavior, they loved *you*."

"And I love you, which is why—"

"Why you're backing off right now, Ian, and leaving me alone."

"Until you do what? Fall down with exhaustion?"

"You don't understand. If I stop, I'll have to—" She ground her knuckles into her forehead. "It keeps replaying through my head, how furious it made him when I jabbed him with the needle. It was why he pulled the trigger, why poor Cassidy's lying in that—"

"Listen to me, Andie. We could stand here arguing all night about who set what off back in that office— whether it was me remembering that Ross was really Parnell, you reacting the way you did, Timmerman grabbing the gun, or Michael, who's beating himself up for freezing at the crucial moment. The fact is, there's only one guy who pulled the trigger, one man who used the master manipulator skills he developed in clandestine services to hide his shame. Parnell shot her, no one else, and he paid the price. Sad as it is, that's where this story needs to end."

"But it's *not* over. It can't be, because Cassidy is gone forever— She's *dying* forever, in an endless loop each time I stop for a moment. And I'll always know I could've changed the way it ended. One little movement, one shift in my reaction, and I might have—"

"You might have *died*, or maybe me, or one of your other friends in that room. Or all of us or maybe no one, but it really doesn't matter because things played out the way they played out, and no amount of reliving them in your head is ever going to make it different, just like it will never change what happened to me in that cell hidden in the mountains. It will never fix what snapped inside Parnell when he was forced to watch."

Andrea shoved her hands into the pockets of his jacket and made a sniffling sound. "I know I've said those same words, or something like them, to so many others. And in my head, I know you're right."

Ian stepped back to cup her face with both hands, forcing her to look into his face. "I need you to understand this, not just in your head, but in your heart before you fall into the same trap I did, blaming yourself for something totally out of your control, running it over and over in your mind how you should've been stronger, smarter, luckier or faster. How you don't deserve to be the one who walked out of there alive. Because it's not about *deserving*, Andie, and even if it were, I'd take a hundred bullets myself if I could only guarantee you'd come through this unscathed."

She pulled out the flashlight he had in his pocket, and flicked it on to look at him. "And all this time, Ian Rayford, I've imagined you were the one who needed my help…"

Shielding his eyes from the beam, he said, "Don't sell yourself short. You've helped more than you know. And now it's time for me to return the favor."

She winced and blew out a long breath. "I just need to call—C-Cassidy's family in Colorado. How will I ever tell them?"

"It's all taken care of. I helped Timmerman locate her personnel file in the office, and local law enforcement there is notifying her father and her brothers. So let's go in now, Andrea. Let's get you off your feet."

As she nodded, he felt her pain so acutely it was like

a stone bruise to his own soul. He felt, too, the horrific waste of the young nurse's life, a sense of loss magnified by the grief of those who had loved Cassidy.

He put a protective hand behind Andrea's waist to guide her to the building's side doors. She trudged forward like a zombie, not seeming to see anything around her—at least not until she swung the light's beam to the left and muttered a choice word under her breath.

"That woman—do you see her? It's Dr. Kapur, from the hospital."

"Who?" Ian couldn't recall hearing the name.

"Julian sent her there to threaten me. She forced me to give up my passwords."

"When?" he asked. "How did she get past me?"

But Andrea was already making a beeline toward a woman wearing a navy suit with what looked like a laminated ID badge clipped to her lapel. Ian pegged her as federal government before they made it within ten feet of her. Had she forged an alliance with a former colleague, or was her relationship with "Julian" personal?

"Dr. Kapur," Andrea called, clearly beyond caring that she was interrupting the woman's conversation with one of the deputies.

Kapur turned toward her, jaw dropping as she took in Andrea's sling. "Miss Warrington, I hadn't heard you were hurt. Could I get you some—"

"It's *Dr.* Warrington," said Andrea, moving close enough to glare at her. "And your partner's dead. Did you know? Or maybe the right word isn't *partner* but *accomplice*?"

"If you mean Julian Ross, I've been briefed about what happened—" Kapur nodded her thanks to Chief Deputy Browning, who tipped a nod of his own before walking off to talk to one of the men he supervised. "And I'm terribly sorry to hear about tonight's tragedy. We'd very much hoped to have him in custody before it ever came to—"

"In custody? Who *are* you?"

"Special Agent Neela Chapal," she said, the accent nowhere in evidence as she held up a laminated ID badge on a lanyard. "Federal Bureau of Investigation. I've been part of a joint task force looking into the bombing of a listening post in—"

"You *threatened* me—threatened to kill Ian if I wouldn't cooperate with Julian's—"

"I'm very sorry I allowed you to believe that." Chapal spared Ian an apologetic look and shook her head. "But what I actually said was that giving me those passwords was the way to save his life. By then, you see, we strongly suspected Ross was missing clandestine services agent Davis Parnell. We just needed to prove it without tipping him off and letting him escape again—to see what he was seeing and track how he was reacting so we could arrest him before he resorted to violence to protect his secret."

"But he did, and now—now he's killed Cassidy!" Andrea surged toward her, so upset that Ian wasn't certain what she would have done had he not caught her around the waist to stop her.

Frustrated, she turned her fury on him. "Stop it, Ian! Let go of me."

"Not until I know you're not going to end up spending tonight in jail for assaulting a federal officer."

But as the heel of her shoe connected with his shinbone, Ian began to wonder if he was the one who was going to end up bruised.

Chapter 17

Andrea had promised to come inside once she had cooled down, and Ian finally, reluctantly backed off. She saw him gritting his teeth, clearly fighting his natural inclination to take care of her, but at least he had the good sense to know she was in no mood to be managed.

The woman who had called herself Kapur too excused herself, saying she had to step inside out of the wind to phone in a report. As the chief deputy held the door for a pair of men wheeling a gurney toward a dark van, Andrea stood alone, a sick feeling in her stomach as she watched what was clearly a body being loaded through the vehicle's rear doors.

Was it Cassidy or Julian, or would both of them leave together, separated only by a pair of body bags. At the thought of it, pain sparked in Andrea's chest, a white-hot anger so consuming that she had to turn away.

In the tail of her vision, she caught a fleeting movement from between two parked vehicles, a flash of what she could've sworn was light blond hair ducking down and out of sight. Breath hitching, she jogged after the person hiding from view.

"Tyler—Ty, is that you?" she called. The wind gusted, sending dried leaves skittering across the concrete surface. Imagining she heard receding footsteps, Andrea flicked on the flashlight again and slipped between a parked pickup and an SUV bearing the markings of the Trencher County Sheriff's Office.

As she hurried after the sound, her beam swept across the dark brown Tahoe's gleaming front fender. But something about the reflection was *off* ever so slightly, something that had her stopping in her tracks.

She turned, her pulse drumming a rapid-fire warning that she shouldn't be out here alone. But that was ridiculous. With Julian dead and Kapur a legitimate government agent, Andrea told herself she no longer had anyone to fear. And Ty Dawson was no danger to her or anyone, just a troubled client in need of guidance—a boy, really, not even old enough to drink. She tried to move forward, telling herself she'd lose his trail if she didn't hurry, but some instinct kept her rooted to the spot...

An instinct that sent apprehension skittering on spiders' legs along her backbone, whispering that it hadn't been what she'd seen reflected that had triggered her alarm at all but instead the *nature* of the surface. Taking a deep breath, she turned the flashlight's beam back toward the Tahoe's fender. Only this time she registered the slight dimpling of the metal, along with a patch of paint that didn't quite match.

As if someone had inexpertly repaired body damage

in that one spot—a bad fix on a vehicle that otherwise looked pristine.

She told herself that it was nothing, that law-enforcement vehicles were probably involved in accidents quite often. Still, why would someone try to cover it on the sly instead of taking it back to the dealership or at least a paint-and-body guy who knew what he was doing?

Foreboding contracted low in her gut, an instinct that had her remembering something Jessie had said about her investigation into some *sleazy local politician*. Sheriffs were elected, weren't they? And wasn't there already some kind of bad blood between Canter and the Rayfords?

An image, sharp as a knife's edge, sliced away reality. As the night around her fell away, she saw a dusky sky made darker by the pouring rain outside of her car's window, saw the side-view mirror with the dark grill bearing down. She recalled jamming hard on the accelerator, shooting toward the bridge, but her pursuer was closing in too fast. His front fender slammed against her rear tire with a crashing crunch that flung her like a tin can into—and through—the bridge's guardrail.

She shivered, staring at the fender, suddenly dead certain that if the paint was flaked away from that faulty paint job, she'd find another splash of color underneath it—the blue of her own car.

"But why my car?" she asked herself. "What would make him want to kill me?"

A twig cracked just behind her, and a deep male voice said, "Because I've always considered myself a truck man. Those damned little foreign cars all look alike to me."

In the dining area, Ian poured a cup of coffee, as determined as he'd ever been in all his life.

On her way past with sandwiches, Jessie stopped and did a double take. Setting the tray on the nearby table-top, she said, "Whoa, Ian. Are you all right? Because I haven't seen a look that intense since I came downstairs right after you slugged your brother that morning at the house."

"I'm not slugging anybody, but if Andrea thinks I'm giving up on her, she's got another think coming." He dumped enough sugar in the mug to make up for the lack of cream. *If the mountain won't come to Moham-med, then Mohammed's heading to her—armed with fresh, hot caffeine.*

Frowning at him, Jessie appeared not to notice his brother walk up behind her, the Rottweiler padding at his side.

"But she's asked you for some space, right? Space to wrap her head around what's happened?"

Zach stopped, with the half sandwich only inches from his mouth.

"Yeah, she has. And before you start on me about how I'm smothering her like my brother—"

"Trust me, you don't want to do that. You don't want to scare the woman so much she runs straight back to California to get away from the bad memories."

"If she does, I'll follow her. I'll find work out there. I'll do anything—"

"Or frighten her into entering the witness-protection program to get away from a psycho stalker. And in case I'm losing you here, Ian, I mean you, the way you sound right now."

Did he really sound that unhinged when it came to Andrea? "Is it really so bad, Jessie? Knowing someone loves you so much that it's making him a little crazy?"

Zach grimaced at the question, a pained look on his eyes as he awaited Jessie's answer.

"I—I love your brother with all my heart and soul," Jessie said, her words tinged with sadness. "I can't remember how I ever lived without him, can't imagine how I ever would again. But it *is* scary, wondering how far love can go before it's all-consuming. Especially with— I haven't even told Zach this yet, but…"

Ian waited patiently, but Zach's restraint crumbled. "Told me what, Jessie? If your career means so much to you, please forget I ever said anything about you quitting. Let me work with you, find some way to help you make things safer for all of us, with no secrets and no holdouts. I know I've been an ass at times. I know I've been demanding. Just don't leave me, Jessie. Give me another chance to get the most important thing in my life right."

Jessie's surprise at seeing him eased into a softer emotion that sent a flush rising to her cheeks. Slipping into his embrace, she said, "Of course, I'm not going to leave you, you big lug. What with all my deadlines and keeping up with Eden, *somebody's* going to have to pitch in and take his turn changing diapers."

Zach pulled away to stare at her face. "Diapers? Eden's a long way past—"

She looked up at him, her green eyes glimmering. "I know I might've been a bit hard on you lately, but in my defense, the hormones—"

"Diapers?" Zach repeated, as if the word were foreign to him.

Ian laughed at the expression on his big brother's face. "Who's the blockhead now? She's telling you she's pregnant. Sounds like Eden's going to be a big sister pretty soon."

Jessie was nodding, smiling at him. "Lots and lots of diapers, Zach. At least, that's what the doctor said when she found the heartbeats." She held up first one and then a second finger. "Two heartbeats, two babies. But I guess you knew that twins run in my family."

Ian clapped his dumbstruck brother on the shoulder before leaving the two to a joyful celebration.

He had a woman of his own to find, support and some-day very soon claim for all of their forevers.

But first, he meant to get a cup of hot coffee in her, a reminder of the one she'd brought to begin their dialogue.

As Sheriff Canter moved in closer, Andrea reflex-ively backed away until she stood trapped against the SUV's front door. The cut on her arm, the older bumps and bruises from her car wreck, all throbbed in time to the breakneck drumming of her heart. She fought not to look down at his hands, at least not at the one holding his drawn gun.

Canter clenched his jaw, his face looking monstrous with her flashlight illuminating his features from below. "It should've been mine, all of it. The natural gas find and the cattle, the house and all the land. *I* was the one who took care of her, you know, who saw to her all those years after those two good-for-nothing hell-raisers of hers lit out like the punks they were."

"Wh-what are you talking about?" she asked, knowing that her best chance, her only chance, was to keep him talking, make him feel that he was, perhaps for the first time, being heard. From what Ian had told her about the Rayford family's history, Andrea had no doubt, either, that two abused teenage boys, unable to get their mother to speak up on their behalf, had done what they'd had to to survive. "You took care of— You're talking about Zach and Ian's mother?"

His mouth twisted as he fought some internal battle. "Who else was there for her to call on, once the *lord of the manor* turned to roughing her up after those two losers were gone?"

Despite the icy terror ripping through her, Andrea felt a pang of sympathy for the proud and fragile Nancy Rayford. "So that was when he started hurting her, after the boys left?"

Rayford's lip curled, revealing long, white teeth, along with his disgust. "Back when I was still a deputy, I got a disturbance call from The Cattleman in Marston— 'bout the fanciest restaurant in these parts. He'd been in a mood over something, had gotten sloppy drunk before the bill came. When she tried to calm him down, get him to lower his voice and stop botherin' everybody, what do you think that SOB did?"

She loosed a shuddering breath, his unfocused look telling her he didn't really want an answer. That he had been biding his time for years, waiting for a chance to tell his story.

"He doubled up one of those big fists of his and popped that tiny woman, not a hundred pounds, in the eye. She cried and carried on but wouldn't dream of pressing charges. She said later, though, how she'd liked the way I'd handled him, how I'd talked sense all respectful-like and without hurtin' his pride so much he'd feel the need to take it out on her later."

Canter closed his eyes, lost inside a memory. But when Andrea dared to take a step, the dark eyes widened, and his left hand shot out to block her escape. With his right, he pressed the barrel of his weapon against her ribs, aimed at her pounding heart.

She scarcely dared to breathe. *One wrong move, and I'll be the next one leaving in a body bag.* Leaving the center and all the people here who needed her, but it was the image of Ian's handsome face that filled her with regret for what might have been, if the two of them had only had time.

"I gave Mrs. Rayford my personal number that night," Canter said. "And afterward, she called me now and then when things were getting out of hand."

"Are things getting out of hand now, Sheriff Canter?" Andrea asked quietly. "Because I'm thinking there could be another way. A way to back this off, let everybody breathe a little like you did with him so well that first night."

Canter scowled down at her and shook his head. "You don't even look like Zach's woman at all, not really. It's just, what the hell were you doing out riding her horse anyway? And that car's the same damned color. When I followed it off the ranch road, I thought—"

"But why Jessie?" Andrea asked, the fine hairs rising behind her neck. "Why would you want to—"

"Woman's been asking questions all over the county, digging into things that're none of her damned business. Not only that, but Nancy's pretty sure the little bitch had been nosing through her emails, including one where I reminded her just how far I was willing to go to—to make sure he never beat on her again."

Andrea stared at him, remembering having heard that Zach and Ian's father had died of a heart attack about six months before Ian had gone missing. But something in Canter's phrasing, in the hard look on his handsome face, struck her with the certainty there was far more to the story.

"The bitch has figured it out," Canter said. "And I see it in your face she's told you, hasn't she? She told you all about it."

Andrea shook her head emphatically. "The only thing Jessie said was she'd been looking at some campaign finance stuff on some North Texas politicians. But when I asked, she said she had nothing on you. Nothing."

At his hesitation, a cold thrill chased through her nervous system. *You're thinking it though now, just how and where you want to kill me. Because I might've bought Jessie a reprieve, but you have to know you can't possibly let me go. Not without risking everything.*

Grabbing her by the arm, he ordered, "Open up that back door. We're going for a little ride."

"No!" she said, "That's not necessary. Listen, Canter, I know how to keep my mouth shut. And anyway—"

He let go of her long enough to pull open the Tahoe's back door. Long enough for her to glimpse the steel-mesh cage separating the SUV's rear from the front-seat passenger. A structure meant for prisoners, who would have no access to door handles or window controls. Who would have no way of escaping as they were taken to the Trencher County Jail.

But Andrea had no illusions that she would make it that far. A man who'd spent his life patrolling this mostly rural county was bound to know of any number of rugged tracks and cattle paths, places where a body might lie undisturbed by anything but the buzzards and coyotes.

"Get on in there," he said. "Don't make this any harder than it has to be."

Still resisting, she made a wild guess. "I think I understand. A person's loyalty should be rewarded, right? And after you got rid of John Rayford for Nancy—"

"He had a heart attack. He really did. It was his own damned fault he happened to be stuffed inside a closet gagged and handcuffed when it happened. It was the only way to keep him from killing her without taking him to jail."

"And Nancy Rayford knows about this?"

He nodded. "It was her idea to take off the hardware and the gag, give the man a little dignity in death. Spare her the embarrassment—"

"And spare *you* any kind of inquiry."

Canter's scowl deepened. "Get in now." He shoved her toward the open door, pushing her hard enough to bang the side of her head.

That was when the first rock cracked against the driver's side window. As Canter spun around, a second stone the size of a man's palm smacked into his temple, eliciting a shout of pain and rage.

Andrea didn't stop to question the miracle or wonder where the easily spooked Ty had found the courage. Seizing on the distraction, she bolted, making for the wooded area surrounding the pond. Between the trees and the darkness, she figured she might just stand a chance—at least if Sheriff Canter didn't shoot her in the back.

"Go get help, kid, right now," Ian had whispered urgently to the scared and skinny blond who'd come upon him in a panic. His stutter was so severe he'd gotten out little more than Andrea's name before half dragging Ian to the parking lot, where Ty pointed out Canter having an intense conversation with Andrea next to the Tahoe.

"Find the deputies or another counselor," Ian instructed as the two of them crouched behind a pickup, "anybody you can get out here in a hurry. If you can't get the words out, just make some noise or knock someone down, anything to get 'em chasing you. You got that?"

Ty nodded and took off, but as squirrelly as the kid seemed, Ian had no idea if he'd go for help or race off to find another bolt-hole.

Tossing aside the mug of coffee he'd been carrying, Ian crept in closer, adrenaline flooding through his system. He couldn't be sure what Canter was so angry with Andrea about, but clearly something was very wrong— something the lawman would just as soon keep to himself, judging from his furtive glances around, as if checking to see if anyone was coming.

When Ian made out the word *bitch* and then the sharpness of Andrea's refusal, it was enough to get him moving, looking for sticks or rocks, anything he might use for a distraction. He hauled off and threw two good-size stones, giving Andrea the chance she needed to take off running.

"I'll kill you!" Canter bellowed, blood trickling from his temple, as he spun and looked around wildly for mere seconds before cursing and then abruptly sprinting after Andrea instead.

Racing after him along the sidewalk, Ian could only hope the sheriff didn't turn around and fire. But he'd rather take a bullet than allow the lawman to catch up with Andrea. Canter was so out of control that Ian had no doubt of his intention to kill or hurt her or anyone who got in his way.

Canter charged forward like a maddened bull, shouting at her, "Hold it now, or I swear to you I'll—"

A security light gave Ian a glimpse of Andrea leaving

the sidewalk that ringed the pond and making a beeline for a thick, dark grove of trees. But Canter clearly saw her, too, stopping to take aim at her back.

"No!" Ian bellowed, racing forward to leap at him.

Distracted by his shout, Canter whipped around and took a wild shot, close enough that Ian saw the flash and felt the bullet buzz past his ear like a wasp straight out of hell.

Before Canter could fire again, Ian struck him at chest level, taking them both down hard and knocking the gun out of Canter's right hand. As he grabbed for it, Ian pounded his face, slugging him repeatedly and rolling both of them downhill and then into the cold water.

Canter used his legs, flipping Ian over. Catching him by the throat, he shouted, "Rayford!" before driving his head beneath the shallow murk.

The water wasn't a foot deep, but it would be enough, Ian realized as he bucked and flailed to free himself of the hand gripping his neck. Fighting for the surface, he instead sucked in a muddy mouthful and heard Andrea, far too close by, screaming, "Let him up! Let him breathe!"

Why the hell wasn't she running, going to get help?

Choking and coughing, he wanted to shout at her to get out before Canter could finish him and then kill her, too. But Ian couldn't do anything but thrash more and more weakly—until a last-ditch swing connected with the side of Canter's head.

The lawman let go of Ian's throat, allowing him to come up, still coughing. Canter scrabbled for shore, crawling on hands and knees for the gun knocked from his hand earlier.

Seeing his intention, Andrea, too, lunged for the weapon. But even if she reached it first, could she really bring herself to do what it would take to stop a man intent on killing them both?

A deep snarl was the only warning either of them had before a huge black-and-tan blur leaped at Canter. The Rottweiler clamped down on the sheriff's arm, attacking with a ferocity that had him screaming as he fought to protect his face and neck—all thoughts of his weapon forgotten.

Andrea darted in to claim it, just as Jessie shouted, *"Aus! Hier!"*

Zach, standing just behind her, called, "Gretel," and the dog broke off her attack and ran back to the two of them.

Chief Deputy Browning ran up behind them, his own weapon drawn as he yelled, "Hands up, all of you! Grab that animal before I shoot it, and drop that weapon, Dr. Warrington!"

"Shoot them, Browning!" Canter shouted, bleeding from a dozen places. "Kill every one of them right now!"

The deputy swung an incredulous look in his direction as two more of his fellow officers, along with Special Agent Chapal, hurried into view.

"I've got a better idea, Sheriff," Browning told his superior, his voice as grim as the look etched on his face. "Why don't you go ahead and raise those hands where I can see 'em, at least until we get all this sorted out."

Then and only then did Ian finally release the breath he had been holding.

Chapter 18

Two months later...

A hard lump formed in Andrea's throat as she hung up the phone in the small reception-area niche she'd claimed as her temporary headquarters. Fighting back tears of frustration, she wished she had a door to close so she could pull herself together—with deep breathing, loud cursing or perhaps a headlong dive into the stash of delicious European chocolates some anonymous angel kept adding to her bottom desk drawer when she wasn't looking.

After "Julian's" office had been restored to order by contractors from the insurance company, she had made what she believed to be the sensible decision to use that more private space as she'd worked to undo the damage done by all the negative publicity, but it was hopeless. Every time she walked through the door, she was overwhelmed with nausea as the events of that horrific night replayed in her mind.

The irony hit hard that she was experiencing so many of the same symptoms as those she sought to help, from nightmares and hyperreactivity to loud noises to extreme watchfulness. Certain she ought to know better, she'd forced herself to focus on the needs of others, refusing to take time to talk to the new counselor Warriors-4-Life's umbrella organization had sent to help with what the national director was now calling "the transition."

A transition he had just confirmed would end with the Marston center's permanent closure, in spite of all the endless meetings and phone calls she'd put in trying to forestall it.

She heard the footsteps before she saw them, her stomach tensing as she recognized the sound of Ian's boots against the tile. "Hey, Andrea."

"Hi, Ian." She turned her head just enough to glance and nod at him. Any more, and she feared he would see her face and ask her what the matter was. Then she'd fall apart for certain, before she'd had the chance to speak with the staff or anyone. "Here for your appointment?"

A few days after Cassidy's memorial service, Ian had blurted an awkward proposal, begging her to join him at the ranch and put the tragedy and all of Warriors-4-Life's headaches behind her. Feeling overwhelmed and fragile, she had turned him down—on three separate occasions—before finally insisting that he needed to work on learning the difference between real love and a fixation.

If that's what it takes to convince you, then sign me up, he'd told her, and since then, he'd been coming to the center three times a week to meet with Connor. He'd stopped proposing, too, though she wasn't certain whether he'd lost interest or was simply biding his time, waiting for her to come around.

Her stomach fluttered at the thought, though she told herself it was a good thing she'd found a way to put distance between them. All too soon, that distance would be physical—and permanent, as she looked for another way to continue working with the veterans whose welfare meant so much to her.

"Just finished up my session," he told her, "and I was hoping I could lure you away from your desk for a little walk."

"I'm— I really don't have the time now."

"C'mon, Andie. Come celebrate with me. It's a gorgeous day and—"

"What exactly are we celebrating?" asked Andrea, who felt less like celebrating and more like drowning herself in the chocolate drawer with every passing moment.

"Connor thinks I'm ready to move from individual to group sessions." Ian flashed the open smile that reminded her so much of the man she'd first fallen for. Only now, there was a gravity behind it, a steadiness and patience that had convinced his brother to let him take over the management of the family's increasingly complicated finances. According to Jessie, who had stopped by a couple of times after visiting her obstetrician, he'd made amends with his mother, too, both he and his brother forgiving her for covering up the circumstances of their father's death. And she was so thrilled about the prospect of becoming a grandmother to Jessie's twins that she had made peace with her daughter-in-law, too.

Moved by accounts of Nancy Rayford's abuse, a Trencher County grand jury had refused to indict either her or former-sheriff George Canter on charges related to John Rayford's death. But that hadn't prevented the panel from indicting Canter on multiple counts of attempted homicide against both Andrea and Ian, along with additional charges of public corruption for extorting "campaign contributions" from Nancy Rayford and other citizens and using much of the money for his own personal gain.

"That's excellent news," Andrea said, coming out of her chair to give Ian a spontaneous hug. "I'm so glad to hear you're making such great progress."

He lifted her jacket from the back of her chair and held it out for her. When she hesitated, he asked, "Then why are you standing there looking at me like the saddest, most stressed-out person on the planet?"

She jammed her arms into the jacket's sleeves and started walking quickly. If she was going to lose it— and the tears were coming now, unstoppable—better she should do it outside, away from where any client, staff member or visitor might walk past and see her. For his part, Ian didn't try to stop her; nor did he call after her demanding answers to explain the emotional tsunami...

A tsunami spawned not only by the loss of the center that meant so much to her, but another reality she hadn't even begun to wrap her head around.

She walked beside the center's pond, tears streaming as she made three circuits and then five of the same place where she'd watched Canter shove Ian's face beneath the water. It was a moment she'd never forget, a memory that rose like muddy bubbles in her dreams every night. Only in her nightmares, the horror didn't end with Gretel's attack and the arrival of the deputies and special agent; instead, Andrea woke screaming at the sight of Ian's body floating facedown, his dark hair matted with algae, his strong hands limp and swollen.

Finally, she stopped, then closed her eyes and listened

to the sound of approaching footsteps. The dogged, determined footsteps of a man too foolish or too stubborn to ever give up, even if she walked as far as he had to return from the dead.

Turning around, she slipped into his strong arms, those arms that had been waiting so patiently for her to finally admit she needed his strength.

"They're shutting the place down next month," she said, "claiming they need to distance the organization from the *Julian Ross legacy* before the decline in donations forces them to close other centers, too. After all the work I've done, all the people I've met with—but who am I kidding? I'm no fund-raiser, no administrator. I'm just a broken-down shrink who can't even fix herself."

He looked into her eyes, his gaze reading far beneath the surface. "There's nothing broken down at all about you. You're just tired, that's all. Exhausted from working your tail off to help everybody but yourself."

"But what good have I done, Ian? The patients whose families didn't pull them after the shooting will be split up and sent to other facilities, sure, but how far will some of them regress with the new location and new counselors?"

"You've done wonders, Andrea. Look at Ty. I know you're still working with him personally. I saw him today. He was talking up a storm and laughing—really *laughing*—while he and a few of his buddies played basketball in the gym."

She smiled, though she couldn't help worrying over how hard it was going to be for him to leave the one place where he felt safe before he was fully ready.

"And look at me," Ian said. "Thanks to your expert advice, I've got my memory back, I'm handling stress a whole lot better, and—this next part's the most important—I even made my counselor sign a note to prove it to you."

"To prove what?"

He dug into his pocket, and a plastic bag of chocolates, each piece wrapped in gold foil, fell out. As he scooped it up and stuffed it back inside, she laughed.

"*Busted*, Angel of the Bottom Desk Drawer. And thank you, from the bottom of *my* rapidly expanding bottom. Seriously, Ian, I've put on five pounds since you've started with that. *Five*."

Dashing a hellion's grin against the talk of angels, he took a step back and spun her around by the shoulders. Once he had her turned away from him, he leaned close to her ear. "I'd say they look good on you. Damned delectable, in fact."

The warmth of his breath sent a tingle of pleasure through her, though she tried to hide the way he made her shiver. She had to focus, to remember she would soon be tucking her tail between her legs and heading off to work at whatever veteran's program would have her. But one of his hands slipped to her waist, making her desperate for distraction.

"So what about this note from Connor?" she blurted, stepping away and turning to look at him from a safer distance. "What was so important?"

A smirk slanted across Ian's handsome face, and he pulled out a sheet of paper, unfolded it with a flourish and presented it to her.

She squinted at the spiky print she recognized as Connor's, her lip quivering as she read aloud:

"In my considered professional opinion, the client, Ian Rayford, now completely and accurately distinguishes between the concepts of 'real love' and 'fixation.'"

Looking up at him, she asked, "And you honestly figured this was going to cut it?"

He shrugged and said, "Why not? I bribed him extra to throw in a couple of two-dollar words, you know, on account of you having your doctorate in head shrinking."

She snorted and then broke out laughing at his good-old-boy act—especially because she knew darned well that Ian had a couple of degrees himself, in global politics and finance.

"I was hoping it might at least break the ice that's built up the past couple of months between us." His voice sobered as he explained, "Because I can honestly tell you, you were right. I *was* fixated on a mirage, just the way you said, an image of a perfect woman who never really existed anywhere except in my imagination."

Andrea gave a shuddering sigh, pleased that he had made so much progress but aching with the realization of what stepping back as she had, letting him grow away from her, might have cost.

"But the thing is," he went on, "these past two months, I've had the opportunity to get to know the real you, the one who sees a need, realizes she can help and throws herself into it with a passion I can only envy…a passion I'm finally truly free to pursue, since serving my country in the covert operations is no longer an option for me."

"I'm sorry that was taken from you, Ian."

He hesitated for a long while before taking her hand. "I'm not, not anymore. Because that brand of passion, that kind of life left me no room for anyone else. No room for the family I need or the very real woman I want to walk the next part of my journey with."

Her throat tightened and her vision blurred. "You understand I'm leaving, don't you? That I'll be hunting up a new position as soon as I make certain all the clients are placed and the members of this staff won't be tainted by their association with this center."

"Why should they be tainted? They weren't responsible for Parnell's actions. None of you were. All of you do great work here. The kind that really matters."

She shook her head. "Tell that to the donors and the Warriors-4-Life board."

"They're running scared, that's all. Not seeing how this bad publicity can all be turned around."

"Turned around how, Ian? I've done everything I can to convince people—and get reporters interested in covering the good we do."

"You have done all you can, but *I* haven't even started." He beamed at her, his smile warmer than the autumn sunshine. "Trust me on this, Andie. Once the reporters show up for tomorrow's press conference—"

"What press conference?"

"The one I've conned Jessie into setting up. That woman's called in more favors—she swears she'll have national network news on this, the big cable outlets, too, not to mention about a dozen influential papers."

"For what? I don't get it."

"For Captain Ian Rayford's first live press conference since his return."

She gaped in amazement, her heart twisting at the thought of him giving up the privacy he'd insisted on all along. "But you—you've told everyone you weren't going to be anybody's show pony."

"What I said was I wasn't about to let the government trot me out to sell some pack of lies to cover up *their* cover-up. But what I will do is say thank you to an organization—and a woman—who've made all the difference in my life. And why not do it in a way—one that will come with a very large check from the newly established Rayford Foundation I'll be running—that'll raise awareness of the issues PTSD-affected veterans are facing...and with any luck touch off a landslide of donations?"

Bouncing on her feet, she threw her arms around him. "Oh, my gosh, Ian! Thank you! That's incredibly generous of you."

"Not entirely," he admitted, slanting a look down at her that sent a shock of energy straight to her libido. "I do have ulterior motives..."

"What motives are those?" she asked, pretending that she couldn't guess.

"I want to keep my wife close," he said, "because the idea of a long-distance marriage doesn't work for me."

"So that's what all this is for, then? The press conference and the big donation? Just to convince me we should get hitched?"

He shook his head. "The chocolate might've been a bribe, but not this. I meant what I said. Whether or not you ever say yes to my proposal, I'm making that donation—all seven figures' worth—and doing the press conference, as long as Warriors-4-Life agrees to keep this center open."

"I can't imagine they'd do anything but jump at the opportunity."

"What about you, Andie? What would you say to the opportunity to live together, love together, build a family together as we both work at something that changes people's lives?"

"You're talking about commuting to and from the ranch?" As much as she wanted to believe it was possible, that there was a way to make things work between them, the idea of the hour-long commute each way was less an issue than the thought of intruding on what felt like Zach and Jessie's home and family.

He shook his head. "I mean building our own house in Marston, someplace where we can have the privacy we need to focus on our work…and each other."

"And our own growing family," she added, warmth flowing through her as she finally allowed herself to think about the doctor's appointment she'd finally had the nerve to go to just this morning—and the confirmation that his test had provided.

"Growing… Wait. You don't mean…?"

She nodded. "I figured there was probably a reason most of those five pounds I've gained seem to have gravitated to my breasts."

"Oh, baby…" he murmured.

"Oh, yes," she told him. "*Yes* to everything…because it seems as if the coming year's going to offer a bumper crop of little Rayfords. And most of all because I love the man you always were and the man you've grown into."

"I know you shrinks are really fond of talking," he said with a wry smile, "but if you don't mind, darling, I'm itching to put those lips of yours to better use right now."

And so it was that a walk that had begun with tears ended with her laughter, followed by a kiss that tasted sweeter than the fine chocolates in his jacket…

Chocolates that were crushed and melted by the time the two of them finally made it back inside.

* * * * *

USA TODAY bestselling author **Angi Morgan** writes Harlequin Intrigue novels where honor and danger collide with love. Her work is a multiple contest finalist, RWA Golden Heart® Award winner and *Publishers Weekly* bestseller. When not fostering Labradors, she drags her dogs—and husband—around Texas for research road trips so she can write off her camera. See her photos on bit.ly/apicaday. Somehow every detour makes it into a book. She loves to hear from fans at angimorgan.com or on Facebook at Angi Morgan Books.

Visit the Author Profile page at Harlequin.com for more titles.

PROTECTING
THEIR CHILD

ANGI MORGAN

Cheers to "the magic room" and the countless twenty-minute sprints. A big thanks to Tenia, my mom and Aunt Peggy for helping me work out the kinks. And a special thanks to Baxter, who said it was okay to blow up the chopper as long as he wasn't in it.

Chapter 1

"Your wife is a dead woman." Jorje Serna left the court-room a free man, pointing directly at Cord McCrea.

The evil words closed Cord's throat in a moment of fear. A moment that pierced him as fast as the bullet that had broken his back. The ache around the scar was real enough. He recognized it. Fought it. Shoved it aside.

Free on a technicality after three years in prison, short years for the crimes Serna had committed. Incredibly long years while Cord's life as a husband and Texas Ranger unraveled.

"He's serious, you know." The lead prosecutor, Paul Maddox, tapped Cord's shoulder with one hand and dialed his cell in the other. "You and Kate should take extra precautions."

"Get her protection. The local sheriff can get to the ranch faster." Cord pulled his phone from his uniform pocket. "We may already be too late."

"On it. Go. You can meet them there."

Cord hit his speed dial as he turned toward the back stairs. "Come on, pick up."

No answer. He began running. Pain jarred him to a slow jog, and taking the stairs slowed him to a limp— the angle going down was torture.

"Kate. No time to explain. Get out of the house and call me."

He hadn't accepted a phone call from her in five months and doubted she'd reciprocate, but maybe she'd listen to the message. *Why?* You *don't.* That inner blabbing in his head kept at him until he pushed the exit door open.

The small county court appearance equaled close parking. Cord was in his truck within minutes of Serna's promise. Even at high speeds and running a couple of stoplights, he was at least forty-five minutes away from the ranch...and Kate.

Coming from a member of a vengeful gang with long tentacles in West Texas, Cord had no doubts the words were a serious threat.

He dialed his ex-wife's numbers again. Landline, cell, ranch foreman. No answers.

Cord wished the next hour would be the longest of his life, but it wouldn't be. He could recall every grueling minute after they'd been ambushed and shot. Each moment of his wife driving the opposite direction down this same road, yelling at him to stay with her, that he dare not leave her alone. Every tortured second of the next week as he mourned the loss of their unborn child.

Yeah, minutes crawled by, stuck in a hospital, unable to walk through a cemetery to bury your partner, his wife or your daughter. They completely stopped when he'd realized he could no longer protect Kate and must let her go.

The bastard Serna wouldn't take anything else from him. He flipped the radio on and listened, petrified he'd hear a notification by the Sheriff's department. Then he heard the dreaded words.

"Shots fired. Ambulance and backup needed at Danver Ranch."

Serna's men had probably been waiting at the ranch.

The truck skidded turning onto the gravel drive. Cord yanked the steering wheel the opposite direction, forcing the car to move straight. He punched the gas pedal to the floor. Sixteen minutes. That's as fast as he'd ever driven the private road to the house.

"Don't be dead, Kate."

Two cars, lights swirling on top, sat near his ex father-in-law's front porch. The closer he got, the worse the fear grew. He couldn't swallow. A fear he didn't understand gripped his heart and wouldn't let go. He slid to a stop, slammed the truck into Park and didn't bother to kill the engine or shut the door. "Kate!"

Two officers stood on the porch, one kneeling over an inert male, the other with his shotgun resting on his shoulder. He recognized Griggs, a deputy who'd been around the county five or six years.

"Where is she?"

"Shot this guy making a run for it from the house. He must have surprised Frank in the barn. We found him beaten, throat slit."

"Where is she?"

"No one else is here, Cord."

He recognized the voice of the guy kneeling, Sheriff Mike Barber, but Cord wasn't looking anywhere except inside the open door. "You're certain? Searched the sheds, the storm cellar?" he shouted over his shoulder.

"All clear. Car, two trucks still parked out back."

"No one took her? He didn't have a partner who may have abducted…" He couldn't finish the thought, but the horrific image of what Serna would do to her was already in his mind.

"Griggs came from the east and I came in from the west. One road in, McCrea, and it was empty." Barber had followed him inside the house. "Take a breath, Cord. She wasn't here. She's still safe."

"Serna seemed certain she was…that she'd been…" His unsteady legs threatened to buckle under him. He locked his knees, standing next to the desk used by three generations of Kate's family for ranching business. "Were the ATVs out back?"

The sheriff shoved the curtains aside on the nearest window. "Only one. Do they have a pair? Is David Sr. in town?"

"Her dad's up with David Jr.'s family. Been there since a colt broke his arm in September." He might not talk to Kate directly, but he'd overheard his physical therapy doctor mention the break at the clinic. And how stubborn David Danver had been about resting the compound fracture. "It's possible she's out checking fences. Where does she keep that dang schedule?" He flipped through the stacks of papers. "Come on, Kate."

"Griggs, wait on the coroner," Barber called over his shoulder. "We'll take your truck, McCrea."

"Quickest way is the four-wheeler, Sheriff. Faster if I go after her. I can still find my way around here." He scanned the work schedule Kate's father had been meticulous about keeping. "Got it. Should be in the northwest quadrant today. I'll call as soon as I find her and get back into cell coverage."

"You sure you're up to it?" the sheriff asked. "That's an awful lot of ranch to cover."

"I got this."

He didn't wait for permission. He didn't need explanations of what had happened when the sheriff and his deputy had arrived. He didn't care. Serna's assassin was dead, but he'd send another. And another. Until Kate was dead.

It didn't matter to the gang that they were divorced. The soulless hatred Cord had seen staring at him throughout this week's proceedings confirmed that a war of sorts had been declared. A war that wouldn't end until Cord had been stripped of everything he held close and then was dead himself.

Revenge was a powerful venom. Since no attack had happened in the past three years, Cord had accepted Serna wanted it delivered in person. Damn all technicalities and the scumbag lawyers who found them.

He snagged the keys from the peg at the back door, along with a thick coat. Jumping on the ATV, he gunned the engine and shot around to the front yard to his idling truck.

"We'll be a while," Griggs said from near his vehicle. "Got an extra rifle in the trunk. Think you'll need it?"

"You never know." Cord cut his engine and retrieved his own 9mm from the lockbox under his seat. Grabbed his hat, cell and extra clips. "Make arrangements with Maddox for Kate's protective custody. I want her out of here fast."

"You got it. Hey, watch your back, McCrea. This guy

came out the door shooting. We didn't have a choice taking him out."

"Thanks for getting here fast." He tossed his keys to Griggs and took the offered rifle. "Lock those inside the house, will ya?"

"Anything for you guys."

Cord knew that look. Pity. He'd faced it for the past three years. Everywhere he went in town, all the interviews and therapy sessions to make sure his head was screwed on straight. How could it be? He'd lost his unborn daughter and his wife. Nearly lost the use of his legs, his job, his life.

He straddled the seat, powered up again and left before anything else could be said. It was easier to leave with a curt nod of acknowledgment. After about a year he'd learned what to say to get around the questions. Learned how to avoid the dialogue.

At least with everyone except Kate.

He couldn't fool Kate.

He couldn't protect her before and now she was in danger again.

"No more!" he shouted down the trail, to God and anyone else who could hear. "This is going to end!"

Today was like every day on the ranch but then it wasn't. Kate McCrea finished the repair on the barbed wire, picked up the tools and put them back in the satchel on the four-wheeler.

She'd grown up stretching and repairing fence, taking care of the stock, cleaning and cooking alongside her mom for a houseful of men. Not that her brother didn't have to jump in and help with the biscuits or bacon.

The thought brought a smile to her heart and curved

her chilled lips. A welcome change after the week of tense updates regarding Jorje Serna's appeal.

Working the fence was solitary and peaceful. Lord knows she got enough of that around the house, but it was different with nothing else except the base of the Davis Mountains in sight. The wind was the only roar in her ears. No airplanes, no tractors, no whine of the refrigerator driving her crazy.

Silence.

Completely interrupted by a racing engine heading toward her. She missed using horses to ride the fence, but they'd made the switch like most ranchers.

"Dang it, Frank. I told you I could handle this today." She complained into the chilling wind, watching the approaching four-wheeler bounce across the pasture a little faster than usual.

With her extra scarf wrapped back around her neck, she pulled on warmer gloves, shoving the worn leather work pair deep into the pockets of her work coat. "Gosh darn it, I really wanted to be alone."

He must have news about the trial since she was explicit about her return to the house. She'd had a feeling when Jorje Serna's case had been accepted for appeal that he'd be released. His threats scared her to death. Frightened her enough to consider leaving the ranch. But the only way to keep her father from mending fences with a broken arm had been to send him to her brother in Colorado.

She debated whether to go or stay every day.

Especially now.

She had another life to think about. Even through the thick jacket she could feel the small swell to her belly. She wouldn't be able to hide it much longer. Her family knew and she'd be forced into a face-to-face confrontation with Cord soon since he wouldn't return her calls. Even their lawyers couldn't get a response.

She couldn't believe he knew and had rejected them. No matter what had happened and the chasm that had grown between them, they were going to be parents. In spite of their differences, he was a good man. Stubborn, silent, stoic…but a good man who would be a great father.

The far pasture had been perfect today for thinking. Pondering big decisions and the advice from everyone who wanted to help. It was up to her, though. She was alone with this decision, especially since Cord wouldn't talk to her.

The sting of tears heated her eyes and cooled her cheeks. Too often, too fast and too much out of her control. She turned back to face the mountains, swiping at the tears, getting herself in hand.

The engine grew louder, idled a moment and cut off.

"What's happened?" she asked.

"Kate?"

Cord? So Serna had been released. That was the only reason he would come here. Today. "Frank shouldn't have told you where I was."

"Kate, Frank's dead."

She couldn't move and grabbed the fence post for support. "Serna?"

"One of his people. He was released going on three hours now."

"I'm surprised he waited this long to make a move." She wiped the tears for Frank off her face. The last time she'd seen Cord she'd been crying, silently watching him stand in their doorway as she drove from the house. She refused to face him again still falling to pieces and pushed her sunglasses into place. There'd be time for tears later. "Frank was a good man. He'll be missed."

"Kate—"

"Don't. Let's just get back. I have to call Dad and the guys. How soon can we have the funeral?"

"You won't be here."

She couldn't avoid looking at him any longer and couldn't believe what he was insinuating. "I'm not leaving everything and running away."

"Protective custody isn't running, Kate."

He was closer than she had anticipated. Only a couple of steps separated them. His six-foot-two shadow fell across her eyes, thankfully hidden behind dark glasses. He couldn't see her notice how lean he'd become.

He'd traded out the Ranger hat for his favorite Stetson, held now in his ever-polite hands. His hair was department-regulation short, just like when they'd met, fallen in love, married and been happy. Completely different than their last night when she'd shoved her fingers through the longish length. The day before the divorce.

No matter what the circumstances, watching him stand on his own two feet gave her a lump in her throat. "I see you're back in uniform, but you need to remember you can't tell me what to do anymore. We're not married."

"I could never tell you what to do, babe."

Habit. Wanting to run to the protection of his arms was just a habit that needed to be broken. *No sniffles. Stand strong.* "Let's go. I have things to do."

She stepped toward her ride and his hand wrapped around her upper arm. *Keep it together.*

"I mean it, Kate. I can't protect you and take out Serna."

He's going to kill him.

"First off, I can protect myself." She pulled her arm free. "And you can't possibly think you're going to win this thing. Are you planning a suicide run to 'take out Serna,' or depending on another verdict that's supposed to keep him in isolation the rest of his life so the rest of his gang doesn't come after us?"

She threw his words back at him. She'd known Cord for seven years, been married to him for five. The determined angle of his head slightly cocked to his right, that sharp-angled nose of his pointing over her shoulder. Straight, full lips pressed flat across his teeth. All signs he was making a stand.

Was he even aware his body shouted his intentions? She knew him better than he did. His nonanswer confirmed her fear, adding fuel to the apprehension she'd been fighting all week.

"Dad blast it, Cord! I'm not going into protective custody. There are plenty of places I can be safe. Davy's house in Colorado is a fortress."

"It's temporary. Maddox is arranging it."

"And are you going?"

"We don't have time to argue." He snagged her arm and gave a gentle tug. "Come on."

"No." She yanked free a second time, stepping back out of his long reach. "I'm not going anywhere until you give me your word."

"It's the only way you'll be safe."

"Like Sarah and Shane? Like a week after you were in the hospital?"

A direct hit below his belt. She knew it was a low blow as soon as the words spewed from her fear. He felt guilty enough and none of it had been his fault. He'd just been doing his job.

Both Rangers had been with their wives when the double ambush happened three years ago. Shane and Sarah never had a chance against Jorje Serna when they'd pulled away from their favorite restaurant. Serna's younger brother had caught her and Cord on the ranch drive, shooting Cord before he returned fire and killed him. It was still hard for her to make the drive to town without reliving that traumatic emotion.

The wind whistled through the tall brown prairie grass, vibrating the fence wire, echoing the void that had grown between them. There was so much they'd left unsaid.

"I didn't mean that." She advanced a step toward him but he backed away before she could touch him. "You have to believe that I don't blame you."

"Not a problem. Let's get out of here."

She'd known the dangers of his job when they'd decided to marry. "I didn't mean to lash out, but I won't trust the police with my life."

"Shane and Sarah were ambushed just like us. This is different."

"Not really." Her hand went protectively across her belly, always remembering the feeling of emptiness after losing their unborn daughter.

Cord was face-to-face with her in a blink of an eye. She couldn't back away again. In spite of everything, she needed him. She felt so all alone.

"Trust me, Kate."

His touch, wiping yet another tear from her cheek, forced her to look closer at him. The strain showed in his eyes. The hurt she understood too well. There was so much to say…

And if she were in protective custody, the words would

never happen. There was no guarantee when she'd be back or if she'd ever see Cord or her family.

"No. I'll go to Davy's. He can send someone to get me."

"Dammit, Kate. This is not the time to be stubborn."

"I've made up my mind." She climbed on the four-wheeler. "No more discussion."

"You aren't going back to the ranch house then. It's one thing leaving with security, but you can't wait for David Jr. to come collect you at a place Serna's already attacked. Successfully." He pulled his cell phone from his shirt pocket. It was the first time she noticed that he actually had her father's work coat on. "Just verifying there's no coverage."

"I have a hand radio, but if Frank's—"

"Right. No one's listening at the ranch. So we punt. We'll spend a couple of nights at Caliente Lodge until we know for certain when your transportation is showing up. They have a working ham radio up there, right?"

"I assume so. The guys check it out every fall when they restock the supplies. They went up three weeks ago. We'll have to have horses to get up there."

"Horses at the line shed?"

"When have they not been?"

"Who's there?" His eyes were scanning the horizon. Making certain no one had followed him?

"Juan."

"I'll take the lead. When we get there, Juan can take a message back to Griggs or Maddox with the new plan." He swung his long legs over the seat as naturally as mounting a horse. No awkwardness from a man who couldn't walk two-and-a-half years earlier.

"No chance you'll change your mind?" he asked in his deep, low voice.

"None."

"We're taking a huge risk getting to the lodge." He replaced his hat and shoved the top closer to his ears.

"I know, but if we leave now, we'll make it just after dark. Cord?" He acknowledged her with a pause while buttoning the jacket. "Your word, please."

"Want a Scout's honor, too?" He started his four-wheeler.

"Just your promise. And I know you were never a Scout."

"No protective custody." He revved the engine, obviously angry. "I promise." As soon as the words were said, he shot forward in a cloud of dirt and grass.

"I promise, too, kiddo." She tilted her head, comforting their unborn baby. "I'll keep you safe or die trying."

Chapter 2

Even on ATVs, the trail to get the horses took a little over an hour. Kate's back killed her from the bouncing around, but she knew it didn't hold up to the pain Cord must be experiencing. He stopped once to make certain she was okay and she could see the strain on his face. The wheels were chugging along behind those dark brown eyes in that investigator-problem-solving mind. After seven years, parts of him were obvious. Or so she thought. Some stayed completely hidden.

The Cord McCrea who couldn't walk for eight months. *That* man had shut himself behind a door she'd never been able to open. One who she'd waited for, given up on, and two years later finally asked for a divorce.

"Is that Juan's truck?" he asked, stopping and killing his engine just out of sight of the line shack.

"It's Dad's old Chevy."

He stiffly climbed off the four-wheeler and pulled his

weapon, checking his ammo. "Keep your rifle ready to fire, Kate."

"You can't possibly think someone's beat us here. How? There's nowhere to hide a car and it takes much longer than an hour to drive. It's safe."

"Griggs had to kill the man who shot Frank. There wasn't a vehicle. And it's been closer to three hours since that happened. Took me a while to find you." He dropped his hat on the seat. His familiar short hair barely had a dent from the impression. "Didn't take much training to see the man wasn't alone. I didn't get a look at Frank, but I can't imagine they were able to pound your whereabouts from him. But we don't know. Too many uncertainties. If you won't go into protective custody, then we trust no one and take nothing for granted." He nodded to the rifle strapped behind her. "Get it ready and stay out of sight."

He darted into the brush and the sparse trees. She followed him with her eyes, unable to look anywhere else. She didn't hesitate and followed his instructions to unstrap the rifle, bringing it across her knees. She wasn't leaving the ATV, though. It was her only means of escape.

"You've made me a paranoid scaredy-cat, Cord McCrea," she said to the wind.

Prepared, not paranoid.

There was a difference. The security detail assigned to protect her had gotten lax after eight days. Both men had lost their lives because they hadn't been prepared. She might not agree with his orders, but she'd brought the rifle and two boxes of shells with her on the chance Serna was released today. Prepared.

"Shoot, Frank. I sure wish you'd heeded my warning. I'm sorry you died because of me," she whispered, and dropped the sunglasses into her pocket, pushing away more tears that blurred her vision.

The minutes ticked slower and slower as Cord crept closer to the line shack. One room with one door, one window, one cot and an outhouse that she needed badly. What was she doing? Risking everything on a man who had mentally walked away from her and wasn't approved for active duty, that's what.

She stood to watch him check out the shack by looking through the window. The door opened and Juan stepped outside. Cord waved her forward.

"Guess that was the all clear." She replaced the rifle, fingering the safety back on. "I know, baby. I might as well face that it's going to be a rough couple of days. Maybe years."

She pulled up in front of the shack just as Juan was pulling away in the truck.

"Where's he rushing to?"

"I filled him in and sent him back with a message for Maddox." He stretched his back and started down the dirt ruts they used for a road.

"Wait, I can take you back."

"We're not staying, but it might be better to put out Juan's fire and eat the chili he told me about."

"You sure you can make another two hours on a horse?" His back must be cramping; her muscles sure were.

"You paid a lawyer good money not to worry about me anymore, Kate. No reason to start again."

Probably to prove a point, he took off jogging over the rough terrain. The man wouldn't let her see him limp. Nope, he would never be vulnerable. Not with anyone and especially not her.

"Okay." She sighed. "A very *long* couple of days."

* * *

"The horses are saddled." Cord entered the shack, tossing his hat in the corner at the foot of the cot. When he turned to unbutton David's coat, he finally caught a glimpse of Kate. "What the…you're…you're pregnant?"

"Obviously." Kate pointed to her belly, showing beneath the tight layer of thermals.

Jealousy shot out from his gut, twisting Cord's insides. Was it someone he knew? Jenkins had helped her while he'd been in rehab. He knew Nick helped her at the ranch. Had she gotten back with her old boyfriend? God, please don't let it be someone he knew.

"Why so surprised? When you wouldn't talk to me, my lawyer sent you a registered letter. I explained everything."

He commanded his voice to remain steady, no inflection, nothing accusatory. Hard to do when you're thinking of your wife with another man. *Ex-wife*. "Who's the lucky dad?"

"Really, Cord? Was your phone off for five months and three days?" She sighed, extended and heavy with exasperation.

"But that's the day we…the night before the divorce?"

"That's right." She raised her chin just a hair and compressed her lips. "Mr. Sixth Generation Texas Ranger Cordell Wayne McCrae is…" She paused, and her bottom lip began to shake.

"A father?" he finished for her.

His legs wouldn't work. He took a step toward her, but the wobbly things wouldn't hold him upright and he knew his body sort of hit the door and slid to the floor, even though feeling really hadn't set in.

"Cord!"

Kate was closer. His hand smacked the bed on the way down and his hat fell to the floor beside him. A soft hand swiped his face, a strong one shook his shoulder.

"Are you okay?"

"I'm great, just tripped." The fall added another bruise to his wounded pride. "I was sort of surprised."

"So surprised you fell down."

"Why didn't you tell me?" Dad-blasted humiliating sticks for legs were tingling under him like they were asleep.

"Think about the hundred or so messages I've left for you, Cord. You never listened to any of them?"

"I couldn't." Meeting her perfect sky-blue eyes didn't work. He was ashamed of himself. She'd needed him and he hadn't been there. Hadn't been for three years. "I had no idea that's why you were calling. This changes everything."

"Hold your horses, cowboy." She stood, leaving him next to the drafty shack door. "Nothing's changed. Nada. Zip. I'm still going to Davy's."

"I disagree. Everything's changed." His whole world had changed. Hadn't hers?

"I'm pregnant, not incapable of—"

"Just stop a minute."

Every emotion he'd buried for the past three years screamed to surface. He pushed himself to his feet, struggling to keep steady, determined to keep his mouth and opinions shut. He couldn't. That was his child, too.

He leaned against the door, clawing his hair, indecisive. His attention splintered between convincing Kate he couldn't protect her alone and protecting her himself by getting her into the mountains as soon as possible.

Kate continually made him lose focus.

"You promised." She divided the chili into two bowls already sitting on the two-foot log table.

It had always amazed him that she could hold an argument or discussion or share intimate stories while prepping dinner or making a bed. Even trimming trees. She just pushed right through whatever she was doing, barely pausing for responses, just expecting a nod or acknowledgment that he was listening. This time he had an opinion and she wouldn't change his mind. She…they— there were two of them now—needed protective custody. Maybe permanently.

"I promised before I had all the facts. Completely voids the agreement." He stated the facts. How could she be so calm about having a kid?

She's had five months to get used to the idea. He had less time to think about it before the baby arrived.

"You can't pull that reasoning on me. I thought you knew about the baby." Her movements might have reflected ordinary things that needed to be done to eat, but he could see the strain, the tension just under the surface.

"I didn't."

She stood straight, faced him, tummy between them. The urge to pull her close had his hands tangled together behind his back to stop himself. *Are you happy?*

"Nothing's changed. It's still safer to get me—" she put her hand over her small belly "us—to Davy's than anywhere else. All of us, even you."

"No."

The one word shooting across the room caused her shoulders to drop and had her sighing in disappointment. He knew all her sighs. A habit she'd tried to break for years but could never conquer. Her eyes dropped to his hands when he removed his gloves. He should have taken off his wedding ring long ago. Somehow, he'd never felt comfortable without it on. He pulled it and shoved it on his right hand.

"And that's your final word? You won't come with me?" she asked, seeming fairly certain of his answer.

There wasn't a choice for him. No options. No way out. "I'm not leaving this unfinished." *Not again.*

"It's suicide."

She was right, but he had to protect his family. He hadn't before, but this time would be different.

"We better hit the trail before much longer."

"I'm hungry and not going anywhere while there's a drop of this chili left. Juan's a pretty good cook. He must have made this at home to bring with him. So sit down, enjoy it as much as possible and rest your back. I know it's hurting."

She was right. Dang it. The muscles were aching like an entire string of curse words. He hadn't favored it, so how had she known?

Hell, she always knew. Nothing ever got past her.

They both sat at the small table tied together with horsehair. He leaned over it, sitting in a stiff bodark chair while she sat on a mattress that he knew was very comfortable.

Didn't matter if Juan was a good cook or not. He couldn't taste a thing. His memories had him twisting in his seat and he wasn't likely to enjoy anything. They'd experienced several nights on that dang mattress.

Several nights enjoying the rustic line shack far from cell reception, from last-minute on-call duty or surprise leads in the investigation. He was headed for a tailspin if he didn't block those thoughts. Wouldn't look good to walk it off outside since she'd just let him know he'd be a father.

Sheeze... I'm going to be a dad!

Unable to speak or actually think of anything appropriate to say, he spooned several bites of chili into his mouth hoping not to choke. He hadn't thought he'd ever be around Kate without thinking of her as his wife. And he hadn't accomplished that task yet. One of the reasons he hadn't listened to messages or opened envelopes was simply to stop thinking about her.

Stop thinking of the long, silky curtain of hair draped across his chest when she rested her head in the perfect spot. A spot she'd taken months to find so she could stay in his arms all night.

What happened with them now? Was he supposed to ask? Was it too soon? Was he supposed to tell her how happy he was at the thought of being a dad? Or how terrified he was that Serna would take her away from him permanently?

Push the emotional subjects aside. He had to clear his head and decide what they needed to accomplish today. First priority, get Kate out of here...alive.

"You know I hate it when you call me Cordell." He blew on the chili and shoved another couple of bites down.

"I still think it's funny how upset you get at Chuck Norris's character having the same name. As much as your dad pretended to dislike that show, he watched the reruns every day. You should be honored he was consulted about it."

"I know."

"Did you ever order him the DVD set like we'd talked about?"

He put a bite of chili in his mouth and shook his head.

She set her bowl on the table and leaned back against the wall. Sighing. A short one, mainly through her nose. And, yeah, he knew how to interpret that one, too. She was ready to talk and let him have it for not visiting his father. She probably knew he hadn't really seen anyone except the shrinks and physical therapists for close to two years.

"You haven't talked to him, have you?" she asked.

"Don't start, Kate." He knew she knew the answer. They'd been together too long. Or *had been together*.

She crossed her arms and tipped her chin into the air in a determined show of downright stubbornness. She was about to let him have both barrels. Then all her reasons and frustrations—whatever they were—would tumble out. He'd listen and wouldn't interrupt since she'd be right. Then it would be too dark to leave till morning. And then they'd be sleeping here on that one mattress. 'Cause he was certain he wasn't sleeping on the cold, drafty boards forming the floor. No, sir, now wasn't the time to hash out how stunted his emotions were.

Remind her how dangerous the situation is.

"Don't get me wrong, Kate. I know there's a lot to talk about. Now's just not the best time." He dropped his spoon on the table. "Serna probably has someone watching the ranch house. The longer we stay here, the more likely the bastard will get curious about why we're not heading back. Hell, he might already know where we are 'cause Juan showed up."

"I understand all that. I didn't say a word. And it's amazing how you can't unless you're issuing orders." She grabbed her bowl and ate.

The silence grew.

He turned his bowl up to his lips and spooned what

he could in his mouth, chewing the rest as he stood and stretched his aching back. This afternoon had been the most activity outside of physical therapy that he'd had in three years. He was not looking forward to a couple of hours on horseback over rocky terrain, in the dark.

"Leave the dishes in the well bucket. I'll put out the fire."

She didn't argue, just dropped the metal bowls with a clunk into the only water inside the shack. He pulled the extra blankets off the shelf, rolling them tight for their saddles—just in case they didn't make it to the cabin.

Man, he needed the dad-blasted water to put out the fire.

Slow on the uptake. That's what he was. She'd known and that's exactly why she hadn't made a different suggestion. He might be a Texas Ranger, investigating drug cartels and other illegal activity, but his wife would always be a whole lot smarter.

Kate's family had kept the line shack simple. She loved the hand-assembled furniture put together from boredom by ranch hands over the years. Some of the cast-iron pots had been used on cattle drives a century ago. There was no way she'd let it rust. She scrubbed and oiled the old Dutch oven while Cord made a trip to the well to water the horses they'd leave behind.

Keeping it simple kept the shack an unattractive place for people passing through their property. Nothing of real value to steal or carry off. Her family and all the ranch hands had to accept the fact people were going to cross the land. There was a lot of acreage, making it impossible to monitor one hundred percent of the time. A plus on their side was that the land wasn't desirable for much.

It had only been in the past five years that they'd cleared and widened the trail so a vehicle could drive here. About the same time they began utilizing ATVs. That was a long and muscle-aching project. Every free day Cord had off from duty that summer was spent moving rocks and smoothing the road. Her dad had loved how his son-in-law had just assumed he'd be there to help.

Kate swiped the back of her hand across her eyes. No crying. Nope. Nope. Nope. There were things to do and definitely places to go.

Everything was stored. Supplies were sealed away. She pulled her sweatshirt on and packed herself in her winter garb. She'd just stepped out the door with the rifle when the muffled sound of an engine caught her attention.

Then it was gone.

She ran the short distance to the corral and opened the gate. She didn't have to see a vehicle to know whoever had driven up wasn't on their side. Whoever "they" were, they had stopped far enough away to hope for a surprise attack. She pulled the cinches and shooed the extra horses into the open field.

"Kate." Cord's voice was deep and low, barely audible. "You ready?"

She slid the rifle into the center of the blanket he'd already tied to the back of her saddle and stepped into the stirrup. "I am now."

His arms were right behind her, circling both ends of the saddle, his body close enough to touch her leg. She wished she could brush his smooth cheek with her fingers. His left hand landed on her thigh and gave her a comforting pat. "Stay low and get out of here as fast as possible. Don't look back."

"I'm not leaving you behind." She pulled tight on the

reins, holding the sorrel under her in check, searching Cord's eyes to see if he was saying goodbye.

He'd done that before and she'd refused to let him die on her.

"Leave. Your job's to protect the…the baby." He tapped the horse's rump and she skittishly jumped forward.

One last look at the father of her child, then she clicked at Candy and they flew.

As fast as her horse could cover the hills stretching in front of them, she put more and more distance behind her. The riding was hard. Slumping low in her saddle wasn't the easiest, most comfortable way to ride. How she wished she'd heeded Cord's need to hurry. What price was she going to pay for the foolish sentimental value of a Dutch oven?

"Come on, Candy girl, get us out of here."

She heard the pop. She knew what it was. Knew the long echo of the sound bouncing through the low hills to the far canyon walls. She'd heard it for the first time when she was six years old and her father had taught her which end of a gun was what.

She waited.

"Come on, Cord."

Candy kept moving forward, and Kate twisted in her saddle, looking.

No one followed. Then, after what seemed an eternity… more gunfire.

"Daddy's alive, munchkin. Just delayed while he kicks some ass."

Chapter 3

No fire. No camp. No Cord.

Kate searched behind her, confident that Cord could follow the trail she'd left. If he were following. If he weren't injured. If he weren't dead.

"Dumb, Kate," she whispered, her breath forming a little fog in front of her. She couldn't let herself think that way. Of course Cord was on his way. He'd make certain he wasn't being followed and when he saw the trail veer off, he'd make certain no one else would see where he'd headed.

The clear, beautiful night did nothing to calm her nerves. Stars shone in the midnight black, but not having even a sliver of the moon made seeing difficult. She took a deep calming breath of chilled air. She'd done it a thousand other times during her life in West Texas. Just like camping, riding, shooting and waiting.

She should have stayed to help. But the scared look

in Cord's eyes made her let him jump into action while she ran. He wasn't thinking of himself, just her and their child. What if…

"I will not let my imagination run all over the country. He'll be here," she whispered to the baby, her hand searching for it under her coat. "He'll know where to come."

Deviating from the plan to go to the lodge seemed right. Once the gunfire stopped, she couldn't bring herself to potentially lead anyone following her straight to the only safety net they may have left. They needed that radio. One night in the open cold couldn't kill her, but being trapped by Serna's men certainly would.

Candy whinnied. Short and sweet, as if calling to another horse. Kate quickly stood, pulled the saddle girth, draped the reins over the sorrel's neck and mounted. All the while searching the darkness for a white Stetson. The rifle was in her hands, safety off before she thought twice. She heard movement just below her, but still couldn't see anything—or anyone.

She'd chosen a spot a horse couldn't reach easily. Familiar to her and Cord. He'd proposed here. Under the stars, a brilliant, clear summer night that seemed lifetimes ago.

"You really need to stop talking to yourself." Cord's voice cut through the silence. She saw his short brown hair pop up behind their rock. "Heard you clear at the bottom of the trail."

She dismounted Candy and looped her reins around the bottom of some scrub, keeping the rifle in her other hand. Not wanting to talk about her concern for his safety. No matter how much she still cared for Cord, they couldn't be together. "You all right?"

"Yeah, just sore. Lost Griggs's rifle on the rocks. He's going to be irritated."

She didn't need much light to see his pinched expression, the tightness in the way he moved, the slowness of each step leading his horse, Ginger, up the steep slope.

Cord plopped down on a smooth surface. She stuck her hand out for Ginger's reins and he couldn't raise his arm.

"What happened? Where are you injured?" She quickly staked his horse, clicked her safety on the rifle and knelt beside him.

His hairline was covered in sweat as if he'd been running, which she hadn't seen since before… Well, running wasn't a plausible explanation when he'd brought a horse. He might say he was fine, but he couldn't hide that he was in pain.

"Don't lie to me, Cord. We'll get through this situation—and stay alive—a lot faster if we agree to just say what we mean and be honest."

"Okay." He unbuttoned her father's work coat, pushing down the left sleeve.

"Were you shot?"

"Not hardly. You know, for some would-be assassins, those guys stink. Couldn't hit the shed or a moving six-two target."

She searched his arm and each movement caused a grimace. "There's no blood."

"I tripped. Wrenched my shoulder out of place."

"We need to get you to the hospital."

Cord looked at her like she was from a different planet. His lips compressed as if he were gathering strength or holding back his real opinion. "What we need is to get to the cabin and the radio. We're one hour ahead. Two if we're lucky. I slowed down two of them, can't guarantee they aren't out of the picture permanently. The other two left in the Chevy."

"Dad's truck?"

"Right. Juan's either working with them, or they were waiting for him. Either way, we can't risk going back to the ranch. You have to help with my shoulder, babe."

Her heart did a little flip at his endearment while her stomach churned at having to pop his shoulder into place. *God, give me strength.*

Juan working with Serna? Juan telling Serna they were headed to the cabin? A two-hour lead? Frank dead? No one knew where they were? The thoughts shot through her mind at lightning speed, but why had her sure-footed, boot-wearing ex-husband "tripped"?

"You're not talking."

"I'm concentrating, trying to remember the last time, if ever, that you've tripped." She pulled her gloves off, dropping them to the ground. "I also have a very vivid memory of the last time I tried to pop your shoulder into place."

"Right after the touch football game on the Fourth of July in Valentine."

"As I recall, it didn't turn out well and you spent three days in a sling." She shoved his coat off his right shoulder with just a bit too much enthusiasm and he growled. "Sorry."

"I understand why you're angry."

"No, you don't. I don't understand, so how could you?" It was natural to care about the father of her child. The tension from the past several hours hadn't lessened just because he was safe. She had to think of what would happen next. And she might be a little bit mad at herself for not having thought about anything except Cord. "Let's just fix your shoulder and get out of here. Okay?"

Drops of sweat beaded on his brow. She wanted to gently wipe them away, take him to a doctor and…and… She shook her head and swiped the stones from directly behind Cord.

She pulled her jacket off and laid it behind him, along with his own. The ground was uneven and rocky. She'd been shifting on it for an hour waiting on him to arrive and knew how uncomfortable it was.

"Lie down on your jacket and walk me through this. I've never done it correctly before."

He caught her wrist in a solid grip. "Kate. I'm sorry you worried."

Did he really think that's all it would take for her to forgive him? They were so past those words. Stupid hormones caused her to consider just how sorry he was.

"You ready?" she asked. *Please don't let me mess this up.*

He lay back, his voice strained as he told her step-by-step how to put his shoulder back in its socket. An old injury from before she'd known him. A bad fall in a college football game. Tech vs. Texas maybe? That's all she knew. He rarely talked about his past and she'd most likely heard a version of the story from his father or mother.

A solid pop, a loud grunt through clenched teeth and Cord rolled to his side away from her, holding his shoulder.

"I'll make a sling from a blanket."

"No." He gulped a couple of times and stood, rotating his arm, the pain clear with each forced movement. "No time. Let's hit the trail."

"We can wait a few—"

He took her shoulders in his strong hands, jerking her to a stop. "Serna is determined to kill you, Kate. He wants to take you from me like I took his brother from him. Believe me. There's no stronger motivation for revenge. We can't wait around. I need to get you out of here. The faster, the better."

"Still no chance you're coming with us?" She knew the answer before she saw the look in his eyes.

He understood revenge. He wanted it for Sarah and Shane and even a daughter he'd never held.

Cord turned to his horse and rested his head on the saddle a couple of seconds before lifting his hand to the saddle horn and pulling himself up top. He had to be in terrible pain, but they'd gone through worse.

Much worse.

"There has to be aspirin or something around here."

Kate had been opening and banging cabinet doors for ten minutes. Cord didn't know how to calm her down. At least he was consistent, 'cause he'd never known what to do or what to say.

"It's okay, babe. Come on, sit. Rest a minute."

"Stop telling me what to do and definitely stop calling me 'babe.'" She wrapped her arms around her middle, giving herself a hug, and crossed the room to the rocker.

He couldn't start the lodge generator. They wouldn't be able to hear anyone coming. So they were wrapping up in heavy blankets. Fortunately, there were flashlights and extra batteries so they could at least see a little.

"Wish I could start a fire for you. You've been cold a long time."

"Don't worry about me." She rocked furiously, determined in whatever her thoughts were at the moment. She blew on her hands, rubbing them about as fast as that rocker was rocking.

"Why don't you catch some winks. I'm not sure how long we can stay. If they followed—"

"There you go again." Rocking, she threw a hand in the air, waving at him as if he knew why she was so totally out of sorts. "There weren't any horses for them to follow with. And since we didn't come back, don't you think that Maddox and the Sheriff's office are just a bit curious as to why? Don't you think we have till morning to make a decision?"

"I was just making a suggestion, ba—Kate. I'm sort of tired myself."

"Then *you* take a nap."

"I'm not the one who's pregnant." That must not have been the right thing to say.

"Men." The one word ended on a long huff.

Man, he needed aspirin. Not only was his body rebelling at the fall and horseback riding, his head ached from trying to keep up with Kate.

"Do you mind getting me the small Philips head? Remember where the tools are?"

He remembered. Tools were in the bench seat by the front door. Extra blankets in the cupboard between the bedrooms. Towels on the shelves above the bathtub. No hot water unless the generator was running or you heated it up in the cast-iron pot in the fireplace.

The cabin looked the same. Simple. Clean. Neat. No real valuables. No personal mementos since multiple families used it year-round. Fewer people during the winter since the road wasn't easily accessed and ended four hundred feet below. It was officially on Danver land, but could only be reached by car from the ranch to the northwest, Nick Burke's place.

Kate slowly stood, wrapped a blanket around her shoulders and sat at the table in the corner.

"This dang radio should work. We should have already sent a message to my brother or father, who would be rallying the troops to get here. We should have notified Maddox about the attack. What's wrong with the stupid thing?"

He handed her the pouch of small household tools. She was crying, swiping at tears of frustration with the back of her hand. What were you supposed to do when your ex-wife cried? Comfort her? Keep your hands to yourself? Definitely keep your hands to yourself. Except this woman also carried his child. The situation was complicated so he kept his hands on the flashlight and the beam of light where she was working. Ignoring how upset she was, ignoring how he felt.

Department-forced therapy had made him think. As much as he wanted to shrug suggestions and thoughts away, he couldn't. If the shrink didn't approve him service-ready…he'd be behind a desk for a long time. So he'd recently been thinking more about the past three years than he wanted. Watching Kate get more upset and frightened brought each of his wrong turns into his mind, but he couldn't see the solution.

So he held the flashlight.

"Why does every plan we have go wrong? This should have been a safe way out." She unscrewed the back panel of the radio. "There's no way to fix this—it's missing tubes. The hands didn't say anything about needing parts or I would have ordered them."

"Who brought up the supplies?"

"Juan and Bernie."

"Juan again. Something doesn't feel right, Kate. Serna's men couldn't have predicted that we'd come here. Why sabotage the radio? Is anything out of place?" He searched the neat room with the limited lit view. Nothing seemed wrong.

"Honestly, I don't know. I haven't been here since that last time with you. Don't go jumping to any conclusions. I just haven't had time and there hasn't been much of a reason to lately." Her hands protectively caressed their child. "We rarely use this place anymore. Dad hasn't hunted since Davy left home seven years ago."

Before, he would have come up behind her, slipped his fingers through hers and just stood there, holding and loving her. He'd thought that had been enough. Guess nothing was enough when you couldn't defend your family.

"Tear the place apart. The radio parts have to be here." *Or something else showing us what's going on.*

They searched. Methodically. Silently.

Beginning with the east side of the cabin, they opened each door, taking everything off shelves, checking the backs of closets and the pantry. He searched the fireplace, the potbellied stove, the mattresses for new threads or lumps. Each quarter hour he swung outside to look and listen. Nothing and no one.

Cord's back ached, reminding him he needed to stretch it out flat and relax. He couldn't. He had to be missing something.

"There's nothing here," she said, putting her hands on her lower back and stretching side to side. "I'm exhausted."

"It's after midnight. With no radio, we should ride down to the road, cross over to Nick's place and make arrangements for your dad to come get you. You catch some rest on the couch, I'll wake you at first light. And that wasn't an order, Kate."

"I know. I'm just cold and tired."

She was right. Serna's men would have already been here if they'd had access to horses. And if they'd determined they'd gone to the cabin, a little smoke wouldn't alert anyone. He brought in more wood and, without any discussion, lit a fire. The living area warmed immediately. He pulled the couch closer and Kate snuggled beneath several blankets.

The thought of warming his wife—*ex-wife*—throughout the night made all the aches take a backseat to the craving his body had for her. But he was a McCrea and could keep his distance, even if that meant holding Kate tight.

Determined to do what was needed and not what he wanted, he grabbed a pillow off the bed, switched off his flashlight and waited for his body's need to defuse.

"Promise me it'll work out," she said softly from the couch.

"I promise." *No matter what needs to be done. I promise.* "Move over."

"What? Why?"

"You know why. It's in the teens outside, not too much higher in here. It's a lot warmer on the couch than on the floor. I gotta be able to move tomorrow."

"I don't think that's a good idea."

"It's the only option. Now move over."

She crowded to the cushions, tucking a blanket around her back. If he'd wanted something to happen, that thin layer wouldn't stop him. He was more concerned with keeping her warm, relaxing his back and listening for signs of Serna's men.

"Good night, Cord."

He may have grunted a bit when she shifted once or twice. Her breathing steadied and she was out within a couple of minutes. Something she'd always been able to accomplish. She told him it was her clean conscience. If that were the case, no wonder it took such a long time for him to fall asleep.

The fire had died down.

4:00 a.m. He'd dozed. Last time he'd looked at his watch it had been just after two.

He shifted away from his hold on Kate, reluctantly removing his arm wrapped around the baby. Good Lord, she was pregnant again. He pushed the thoughts of three years ago away, burying them deep so he could think how to get them to safety and keep them that way.

Sitting on the hearth, he dropped a couple of logs on the fire, building the heat back up, casting a glow across the most beautiful woman he'd ever known. Her pale yellow hair seemed to sparkle as much as her eyes when she was ticked off at him. He could think of a couple of times her anger and frustration had actually turned into a nice romp on a bed, or whatever else was handy.

The thought made him laugh out loud but didn't wake her.

The cold, flat floor called to his cramping back.

He checked the horses through the window, examined the open terrain as much as possible in the starlit night. Nothing.

Why not come after them? What did Serna know that he didn't?

Cramp. Floor. Stretch. Relax.

When the pain had subsided to a dull throbbing, the fire popped, drawing his attention. Cord looked at the back of the old couch—or under it. The boards where the heavy log frame had been sitting were uneven.

"Right under us the entire time." He pulled the bench seat open and grabbed the ax. Using the blade he pried the wooden floor panels loose.

"What did you find?" Kate aimed the flashlight where he worked.

"I'm not sure, but I think…"

Sticking his hand under the boards, he didn't have to search long before his hand snagged a large bag. He knew without looking it was drugs.

He popped up more and more of the loose floor.

"Oh, my God, Cord."

"There are at least twenty bags here. Serna's men made use of your family's absence. This is the perfect place to hand off drugs to suppliers without authorities close by watching."

"How long do you think they've been using it?"

"How long has Juan been an employee?"

"At least five years."

"I bet Serna's been laughing at how close I was to everything and could never gather enough evidence for a conviction. Dammit, we stumbled right on top of his operation." He could beat himself up later. He opened a large bag, shoved a smaller one into his pants pockets and began replacing the boards.

"You don't know how long this has been here."

His gut knew. Serna had taunted their investigation by keeping the drugs under their nose. Then ambushed their families to get them out of the way. "We need to get everything back to exactly where it was."

Kate laughed. "Sorry, what do you think they'll do if they discover we know? Try to kill us?"

She had a point, but it might buy them some time. Either way, she folded the blankets and put things in their place. He finished the floor and moved the heavy furniture back, even moving the dust around so they couldn't see the drag marks.

"If they assumed we were coming here…" Kate hesitated while dousing the fire. "Do you think they've created another trail this direction that we didn't see in the dark?"

"Worse."

Cord held her jacket and she slipped her arms inside. "I don't understand."

"We had suspicions that Serna's operation was using planes to get drugs farther north. Flying under the radar so they couldn't be tracked."

They left the cabin, not trying to hide their presence, but at least it didn't look like they'd found anything of importance. The horses were rested enough for a trek to Nick Burke's place. If they pushed hard, they could get there late tonight, but it would be a difficult ride, no stops, out in the open. Plenty of places a chopper could fly in low and pursue them.

"There's no way Serna could have built a landing strip without us knowing," she said, once they had their saddles and gear packed.

"It's wide open for choppers, babe." They both swung onto their horses' backs in time to see the first edge of pink on the horizon. "Five will get you ten, they have ATVs hidden somewhere nearby to get them in and out fast."

"If they do, there's only one place they'd be able to hide something that large." She clicked to her horse and took off away from the trail, toward the ridge. "We'll get to Nick's a lot faster on ATVs and they'll be on foot."

"Kate, no!" He clicked his heels into the horse and caught up quickly. "We can't look for a drop zone or four-wheelers. That canyon is a three-sided death trap for us."

"We're sitting ducks on horseback. You know that. It would be safer doubling back across our land than getting caught in the open. Those ATVs would catch up with us no matter which way we choose. This is the only logical thing, Cord."

Smart woman. Too smart for her own dang good.

"Logical doesn't mean the safest." Like that would deter her once she'd thought it through.

"I'm not changing my mind. We can find those ATVs or whatever they use." She didn't slow her horse, either.

"I can't allow—"

She turned in her saddle to face him. Old jacket, beat-up scarf wrapped around her neck, determined look in her eyes piercing his heart.

"Don't say that, Cord. This is my fight, too. It always has been."

Chapter 4

Galloping with the father of her child. It should have been a pleasant experience, not a petrifying one. He shouted again and she pulled on the reins to slow a bit. The terrain demanded a slower pace. Cord wanted her to stop, talk about what they'd do, think about their options. They didn't have any options. They needed to beat a chopper to the nearest landing site.

Thinking that idea was possible seemed completely ridiculous. They'd be outmanned and outgunned. But if the two of them could get there, they'd have surprise on their side. She was certain it was the only way. And certain that Cord would find a way to deter the men wanting them dead.

One thing about riding at this speed and direction, it didn't lend to much chatting. It took a lot of concentration. Cord was more of a doer anyway. She'd always liked that about him until the shooting. A piece of him had shut down and never come back to her.

With each hint of sunshine peeking over the hill, she heeled Candy just a little faster. It was a risky gambit. One she needed to play if her family was going to survive. She couldn't live fearing someone waited around every corner. She didn't want to live constantly wondering if Serna or his gang members would make that day her last.

"Come on, Kate! It's too dark to be taking the trail like this," Cord shouted from behind her.

Thank goodness the path wasn't wide enough for the horses side by side. If she looked at him…well, she just wouldn't look at him until it was too late to back out.

"Kate! Think what you're doing!"

"I'll wait for you at the vista," she shouted over her shoulder. The wind was so strong she'd be lucky if Cord understood anything. She reined Candy off the trail leading down the mountain and headed for the closest place this high a helicopter could land. Slowing over the rocks for the horse's benefit, she was still way ahead of Cord.

To her knowledge, her ex-husband hadn't been on a horse since the shooting. And he'd never been on Ginger's back, so he couldn't be certain of her abilities.

Cord kept within shouting distance. Probably mad, but he followed. He didn't have an option, since Kate knew he'd never leave her unprotected. They may be divorced, but he was an honorable man. Sometimes too honorable.

It would be so easy for Kate to push Candy just a little harder and leave Cord in the dust. This ride in the dark was dangerous as it was without her ex-husband getting more worked up. Candy broke through the scrub and they were in the open at the edge of the incline. Down into the box canyon or around the top of the ridge.

"Are you crazy? What if you'd fallen? Or your horse had stumbled, sending you into the rocks?" Cord's deep voice stated on an offended breath as he pulled Ginger to a stop.

Her heart still raced as fast as the horse's. She dismounted, looping the reins around some juniper. Cord was one step behind her, fisting Ginger's bridle in his hand.

She turned to face him, completely uncertain about the next step and totally unwilling to acknowledge his worry. "What do we do now? How can we stop these guys? You're trained for this, right?"

"All of my training told me to head to Nick's, not into a gunfight or barreling down a dark trail with a pregnant woman."

Uh-oh. That's why he'd been shouting. Sometimes she forgot she was pregnant. The doctor said to go through her normal routine, normal exercise, and that riding—within reason—was good for her. "I got it. Sorry."

"Can you see anything?"

Cord wasn't looking along the horizon. His search was below them, in the small canyon—if it actually qualified as one. Kate followed him to the edge of the rock face and searched. "I can only see two possibilities. If they've hidden ATVs or a vehicle, they'd be closer to the rocks. But there aren't any caves in this area to hide anything."

"There." He pointed to an unnatural outcropping of rock. "At first glance it looks like part of the sloping wall, but it's not. It's been camouflaged."

"You're right."

"Gotta be a vehicle of some sort under there since I

don't see any fence or hay for horses. Will you let me handle this alone?" he asked with a quick look at her belly.

"No."

"I didn't think you would." Cord looked away, seemingly focused on the fake rock lean-to.

"Someone needs to have your back." She watched him
stiffen as he stood taller. "I mean, I should help. You
shouldn't do this alone."

"You're right. I'm heading down the rocks and you
stay here to cover my back. I'll need eyes up top."

He faced her, one straight brow slightly arched. She
could see the triumph in his eyes. He'd tricked her. She'd
demanded to help and he'd agreed and kept her up here
out of the way.

"Just because I'm pregnant, doesn't mean—" Her first
instinct was to argue, but he was right, she did need to
think of the baby. "Okay, I'll be your eyes. What's your
plan?"

"Shh. Do you hear that?" His hand cupped her shoulder as he froze.

The distant whomp-whomp-whomp of a helicopter
bounced around the hills and she couldn't discern which
direction it came from.

"No time for discussion." He shoved the reins in her
hand and handed over his hat before skidding down the
hill in his boots. "Just stay here. No matter what!"

Five minutes. They needed just five lousy minutes to
beat those murderers.

"And just how am I supposed to warn you if anything
goes wrong?" She raised her voice, confident no one else
was there yet. "Wait, Cord! Maybe we should go straight
to Nick's?"

"Keep those horses out of sight."

Where? The juniper trees were a bit thicker behind
them where they'd ridden, so she backed them up and
tied Candy in place. She wouldn't go anywhere, not with
a saddle on her back—she was too well trained. Ginger
was her exact opposite and would bolt at the first distraction, so she took her scarf and covered the horse's
eyes. She headed back to the ridge with her rifle and
extra shells in tow.

While moving the horses, she'd lost sight of Cord.
She'd seen the evidence that his back was hurting him
with every movement, but he hadn't let it slow him down.
Neither had his shoulder. She lay on the rock path perfectly still and watched the lean-to. She pinpointed Cord
by seeing his arm a couple of times outside the camouflage. If she hadn't known he was there, he would have
been invisible.

Hopefully, someone else would have to look twice to
see either of them—her dirty work coat was the same
color as the red-and-brown stone but her hair… She
pulled her neon-colored knit hat off and stuffed it in her
pocket. She'd been hunting enough to know how to blend
into the scenery. She pulled her pocketknife and whacked
the bottom of some brush, shook off any attached critters
and set it over her head to hide the blond.

What is he doing?

Helicopter sounds grew louder. It must be flying close
to the ground. She couldn't see it, but that was the logical assumption. It shouldn't be there and no one had reported seeing or hearing one to her. Then again, if Cord's
insinuations were correct, Juan might have been coordi-
nating arrivals with the dates he was at the line shack.

The helicopter topped the vista and swooped over the
edge with a practiced flair. It swirled around, sending

dust and small rocks in every direction. Tiny whirlwinds of dust shot into the air near Cord's location.

I need you alive, Cord.

The camo hid more than just the gang's transportation. Cord discovered a small man-made cave where supplies and gas cans were stashed. Sheeze, there was even a table and chairs. For what?

If they used the cabin, like he suspected, then why a second unloading area? One look at the box contents and the pieces of a five-year investigation were beginning to fit together. He heard the chopper landing and squeezed his sore body uncomfortably between the rough rocks and a couple of crates marked Hazardous.

Cord had suspected that Serna's gang must have used the cabin for years. It was Serna's style. Break the law in plain sight. It's exactly why he'd shot Kate himself instead of sending minions. And why he'd gone to jail. But he and Kate had stayed alive for three years. Cord half expected, half hoped for the gang leader to be on that chopper.

This could end real fast if he was.

Stuffed like a sausage behind the crates, he couldn't see a dang thing outside. He could hear a guy complaining about unloading the chopper by himself. Heard the whine of the chopper blades slow to a halt. Several Spanish curse words mumbled loud enough for others to respond and tell him to stop his whining. At least three men, two most likely ready for an attack, covered the one unloading.

Four to one.

And him in a cave. All they had to do was wait for them to leave. Kate would never wait. She'd fire and take at least one out, one would keep him pinned down, and another would go after her.

You should have just slashed the tires.

Then there would be no doubt he and Kate were close by. What could he do?

Gas cans.

Lots of gas cans!

It was risky. A logical assumption that they'd fill up the ATVs before heading out. He inched the crate toward the cave entrance, just enough to give him room to dive for protection. Waiting for unloader man's return to the chopper, he quickly moved, unscrewed the lids of the front two gas cans and scooped handfuls of sand inside. One good shake and he was set.

Back behind the crates, he waited for the next trip and repeated the procedure with the next two cans in line. Then he moved farther away to wait.

Please wait, Kate. Be patient.

Cordell McCrea, what are you waiting on?

He couldn't get out without being seen. How was she supposed to warn him after they'd already landed? She couldn't. He'd known that.

Rifle ready, she slid along the path until she lined up a better shot. She'd have his back…and his front. Her daddy had shared his gift of being a marksman.

"Ouch. Shoot." A piece of dried cactus had lodged itself in her jacket, and one of the thorns had stuck through the material and scraped the skin of her arm. She hurriedly knocked it away with her hand, catching another thorn in her thumb. She'd known better but just wasn't slowing down to think. She wiggled her fingers, attempting to keep the tense nervousness in check.

The pilot stayed put while three men jumped from the chopper, ducking low with the blades still rotating above their heads. One had a rifle leaning on his chest. The other two headed straight for Cord.

Any second.

Nothing.

Where had Cord gone? The man with the rifle stood at the helicopter like nothing was wrong. Voices, strong, angry words in Spanish. The pilot was still inside, but the blades were slowing—he'd cut the engine.

Four to two. Not such bad odds.

Could she do it? Could she shoot a human being?

The picture of Cord's bleeding body rushed before her eyes. He had bled from multiple bullet wounds these men—or men just like them—had put there three years ago. It was hard to forget him attempting to say goodbye to her while rushing him to the hospital. Instead, he'd coughed up blood. He'd come so close to being killed by those monsters.

Yeah, she could defend Cord and their child. She funneled her anger into concentration. She took aim, keeping the barrel trained on the man with the gun who seemed to be searching the rim. One man unloaded boxes from the rear seat, disappearing under the camouflage.

If she could take out the one with his finger on the trigger of a machine pistol first, the odds might be better for keeping Cord alive.

Still nothing.

Kate only had a clean shot for the guard. She couldn't act with Cord trapped wherever he was hidden. So she had no choice but to wait, hoping and praying that the men in the helicopter were the only ones around. She was a sitting duck for anyone approaching behind her.

A clear day with lots of sunshine. She'd soon be a little warmer lying on the cold, rocky earth. If they could time this correctly, the men would be completely blinded by the sun rising over the rocks.

Maybe I should have talked things through with you, Cordell.

The men unloading and seeming to gripe about every trip back to the helicopter finished and chugged bottles of water. It wasn't hot, but in the high desert most kept themselves hydrated. As thirsty as she was, she would not move until Cord was out of that canyon.

The pilot finished whatever he'd been doing on the opposite side of the helicopter. The echo of him slamming something back in place bounced around while he wiped his hands and wandered to stand by the guard. He shoved the red work rag in his pocket, elbowing the assault weapon slung across his back, out of the way.

Still no sign of Cord or that he'd been discovered. There must be a cave entrance hidden by all that camouflage.

What were all the supplies for, and if they had this place, why use the cabin to hide the drugs? These men were packing weapons ready for a battle. They didn't need to be good shots with machine guns. Just point and shoot. Both she and Cord had limited ammo but were excellent marksmen. And they still had surprise on their side. That had to be in their favor.

Outgunned and outmanned. Yeah, I should have talked through some plans with Cord. What did I get us into, baby?

Chapter 5

Desperate times called for desperate measures.

He'd heard that saying throughout his lifetime. Each member of his family had bragged on how they'd made it through the Depression, more than one world war. Men and women had sacrificed so he could walk the land he worked every day.

This barn had been erected by his father and fellow ranchers. A monument to the prosperity of the times. The tack room had been his refuge growing up. Now the whole place housed more broken-down junk and car parts than horses. And at the moment, Serna and two of his men.

It didn't matter how bad the situation had become, no one from any part of his life would approve of the lethal men he was "in bed" with now. Drug gangs. Murderers. Men who didn't think twice about taking a life and leaving the body somewhere to rot.

He knew the risks. He also knew what would have happened if he hadn't agreed. *He'd* be one of those bodies rotting somewhere to be discovered by a stray desert hiker.

He watched Serna's show from the corner of the tack room, careful not to turn his back on his partners of the past four years. Hopefully, they didn't notice how tense he stood waiting to be spoken to. Probably never noticed that he kept his .357 shoved under a pile of broken harnesses, easily within one step.

Watching this gang leader lose control reminded him of what type of men his "business" partners were. He didn't trust any of them and wanted out. Hell, he'd never wanted in. Another saying of his grandmother's popped into his head. Bargain with the devil—or his agents—and you're gonna get burned. But that was the price you paid when things were going belly-up and there were no options left.

"They couldn't have disappeared. I told you, they were going to that thing they call a lodge," Serna spit into the cell. The newly released state felon ranted, waving his arms in his sharply pressed striped shirt. Ironic that the stripes were heading the opposite direction than the prison bars he'd been wearing until yesterday.

If McCrea was at the lodge, he wasn't worried. He hadn't wanted a money trail and had accepted payment of another kind. His personal stash of heroin was hidden but no one had found it for four years. Nothing to pin him to the gang once he got rid of the burner phone.

"I told you McCrea is the number-one priority. Doesn't anyone listen to me? No! Bring him to me alive. I want to rip his head from his freakin' Ranger's neck and spit down his stinkin' throat." Serna clicked more buttons and finally slid the new phone into his back pocket.

He stood there. Waiting for Serna to state what he needed.

"Those incompetents working for me will receive the same if they don't find that cowboy and his whore soon. The entire schedule will be thrown off. They should have waited and taken them all out at the ranch."

He waited for one of Serna's men to answer or explain why that had been impossible after Serna had threatened McCrea at the courthouse. No one dared.

And neither did he.

Serna might not kill him, but pissing him off right before this last shipment wasn't part of the plan, either. Making a boatload of money and blaming someone else—the Danvers were as good as anyone else. *That* was the plan. And if poor little Kate got caught in the crosshairs again…so be it. No skin off his nose.

"What? No one feels like talkin' to me," Serna declared with no question in his angry bellow.

"We're waitin' on orders, Boss," one young man in the back sheepishly mewed.

"I order you out. Go! Leave!" Serna touched the handle of his pistol tucked in the front of his pants.

The lead minion couldn't find the door handle fast enough before the four men bunched to a stop trying to figure out how to get out. Serna threw back his head, laughing. The heavy wood swung shut on its own accord.

Serna sauntered toward him. "So cool. Never acting afraid."

He stood in his corner, forcing his expression to remain the same. He shifted his weight closer to his weapon, itching to take it and shoot the scum dead. But he was a necessary evil to finish his plan. He'd dealt with middlemen while Serna had been in jail. Things had gone easier after Serna had gone to jail and vowed to kill Mc-Crea. On a personal level, he only wanted the Ranger out of the way so Kate would be gone, too.

Dealing with this mad dog in front of him had grown tiresome fast. Mad dog? Yes. Continuously high on a cocktail of drugs, consistently popping more pills. It was amazing Serna had ever accomplished any type of work-able drug smuggling across the border. And nothing on the scale of what they were attempting.

"Do I have a reason to fear you?" he asked more coolly than he'd thought. The sweat under his arms and the line gathering to trickle down his spine physically showed the truth.

"My friend…"

I'm not your friend.

"Things have been going good, yes?"

"I'm not complaining."

"Did you know about the little—" he pursed his lips together and shrugged "—shortage I was told about last week?"

"No shortage. You were told where the drugs are. We thought it better not to go in so close to your hearing." *It was also part of the plan.* "We'll move it with the rest."

"Then why not continue our arrangement? So much time and energy wasted finding a new route."

"You know why, *friend*. The DEA is getting too close for horseshoes and grenades."

"They haven't discovered us in four years' time." Serna's eyes were dilated and when he faced the early-morning sunlight, he pulled his mirrored shades to his nose. "What makes you so certain that they're getting… closer."

The drug addict patted his shoulder in a demeaning way, fingering the grip of the gun at his waist. Trying to command the situation. Serna had no idea he'd been used in this carefully constructed relationship.

When the DEA found the cave—and they would find the cave—the gang would take the fall. A means to an end to restore his financial stability. An end he'd wanted for many years.

I'm a small pawn in the overall picture and Feds will love to give me immunity for what I know about your organization. Serna, you are so screwed.

He wanted to shout the truth. Wanted to bark it back at this doper just what kind of a mistake he'd made forcing him into this situation. He kept his voice low and calm, saying, "Let's get this shipment taken care of and worry about the rest later."

It was dangerously close to the time hands would begin showing up for work. Should Serna be reminded he didn't want to be seen here by anyone? Five more minutes and he'd have to tell—or ask—him to leave.

"I agree, *amigo*. But first, we take care of our runaway couple. Edward!" Serna faced the door, waiting on one of the men to reenter the room. "This is exhausting for me."

"You need something, Boss?" The youngest, who'd dared to speak earlier, kept one foot out of the room.

"Time to get moving." Serna spoke more Spanish, lower, loud enough only for Edward to hear, nod and leave. "McCrea will be found and dealt with. You're certain they'll head across the mountains?"

"Everyone knows David's at his son's place. If they need help, that leaves the friendly neighboring Burke ranch. We wouldn't be looking for them if your guys had taken them out at the shack."

The look of hatred on Serna's face accentuated the prominent lines of droopy skin, the yellowish tint of his eyes. He wasn't healthy, but of course, he was a drug addict of the worse sort. The question wasn't his physical health…just his mental. Was he stable enough to finish?

"Do not piss me off, *amigo*." Serna paused his exit, slowly sliding his arms into his jacket, always playing the role of some huge crime lord. How laughable.

His jaw popped as he gritted his teeth, his eyes narrowed to slits. "Nothing else matters to me until that bastard is dying a slow death while he watches me kill the one thing he loves more than his own life."

"I have no problem with that. If McCrea's alive, the operation is at risk."

No problem at all. He was only here for the money.

Chapter 6

Cord had never been good at waiting. For months doctors and physical therapists had instructed him to be patient. Don't rush things. Don't push his legs too far. Even his father and mother had warned him.

The minutes ticked by. No one reached for the gas.

His legs cramped. The shaky sticks weren't one hundred percent. He hadn't passed the physical test to requalify but none of that mattered. If he failed, Kate would die.

Their child would die.

So to quote whoever said it first, "failure was not an option."

Option one—sand in the gas tanks, seize up the engines. ATVs couldn't follow when they rode out on horses. Chopper still could. He'd take out the pilot or engine with rifle cover.

Then run to the top of the ridge? On these legs?

What was he thinking?

Option two—shoot everyone. There couldn't be that many—they'd come in a chopper loaded with extra weight. Three or four men tops. What type of weapons did they have? Was Serna with them? Could he even get to the entrance without being seen?

I'm blind in this cave.

Option three—wait. Not his favorite option. Kate was most likely going nuts on the rim. Would she wait? He'd reminded her of the baby; maybe she would listen this time. Unlike getting out of the car when they'd been ambushed three years ago.

Damn...not now.

The memory of the shooting rushed into his mind. Once there he couldn't get away from it. It was so real, taking over his optic nerves and replaying in slow motion in front of him. He saw the gun barrels. Heard the shouts to shoot Kate. Yelled at her to get down. He turned to protect her....

Searing fire in his back, then nothing.

Kate screamed, kept screaming his name. He could still move his hands, his fingers still gripped his weapon. "Roll me over, Kathleen."

She'd nodded, the fright vivid in her beautiful, tear-filled eyes.

"Wait until he's on top of us," he whispered.

Concentrating only on Kate's face, he'd stayed conscious for her. She rolled him. He'd ignored the pain but could remember it now, wincing at the vivid memory. Then he'd squeezed the trigger, shooting Ronaldo Serna between the eyes. The second man with him must have been stunned, pausing just long enough for Cord to get a second shot off, severely wounding him.

No repeat performance. Kate was screaming now. She was up on a ledge waiting for him. He would get out of this bear hole without being shot. He wasn't doing that to Kate or his child. He just needed options.

A real shot echoed through the box canyon. Men scrambled. Bullets connected with metal.

Kate hadn't waited. Or she'd waited long enough. He rolled over the crates and prayed his legs wouldn't buckle when he hit the earth floor. They held and he shoved his back to the wall at the cave entrance.

First guy through the entrance he coldcocked in the face. Out cold on the rocks.

Second guy backed through the entrance, tripped over the body of the first and raised his face into the barrel of Cord's weapon. He raised his hands in the air, letting the machine pistol hang across his shoulder.

"Drop it."

The guy shrugged.

"Don't let the uniform fool you. This is personal and I'll drop you like the jackal you are. Now take the strap over your head and stop pretending you don't understand."

The man complied and Cord kicked the gun into the sunlight. He used his belt to immobilize the man's hands and feet and dragged him to the back of the cave by the gas cans. He lacked time to do anything else. He slung the machine pistol across his chest and positioned himself behind the ATV. Still hidden to the chopper pilot, he heard Kate's rifle between the rapid firing of another automatic.

There were shouts in Spanish calling from the chopper to the cave asking where they were. The gunfire didn't stop. From his view he couldn't find Kate on the ridge.

* * *

One lone shot pierced the silence and then nothing.

"Cord!" Kate shouted. "Are you alive?"

"I'm good." He kept low to the ground and zigzagged to the chopper.

"Good. I think I… I killed him." Her voice shook— he could hear it even at this distance. "He's not moving. I haven't seen him move."

One glance at the pilot and he didn't need to take a pulse. He'd been shot in the throat. He waved his arm at Kate. He still couldn't see her. He couldn't find the fourth guy. Where had he run? And if the man had heard him shouting at Kate…

Rapid gunfire from the cave took down the pole and the tarp collapsed. He fell flat and used the chopper as cover. The edge of the tarp dropped and blew across the ground, but bullets pummeled the rock face behind him. He lifted the machine pistol and pulled the trigger, hearing his own spray of bullets bite through the camouflage. A short curse and then silence.

They'd broken free inside the cave, found another weapon and now were dead. He checked the bodies for a pulse. None. And no ID. Where was the fourth man?

"What the hell does Serna have planned?" No more time to search the crates. He had to find that fourth guy. They needed to get out of there and fast. It would take them several hours to get to Nick's without a vehicle. They could have used the water for the horses, but he had no way to carry it up that ridge. They'd have to take the trek slow, hiding their movements.

When he edged from the cave, he saw the bastard picking his way to the top of the ledge.

"Kate!" he shouted, running to the bottom of the trail.

Maybe she'd seen him, couldn't get a shot from her angle with the rifle. Cord aimed the MAC-10, squeezed the trigger on the inaccurate weapon and nothing. The magazine was empty. He wasn't close enough to use his 9mm so he had one choice. Climb.

The steep incline he'd used before would be easier but longer. Straight in front of him, there wasn't a path, but the incline wasn't completely perpendicular. He could get there before the fourth man.

He pushed hard. No sound from Kate. His blood pumped hard from the strain. Little sleep and hours on horseback had taken its toll on his body, but he pushed up the hill, shouting for Kate and not receiving an answer.

A cramp seized his back. He bent forward, stretching and praying for it to end. He had to get back to Kate but he had to stop this man first. He pushed harder and evened up with the man on the side of the canyon. He ran toward the guy, ignoring when his feet slipped on the uneven hill. The small pebbles were dangerous, but he dug his boots into the soft earth, maintaining his balance.

As soon as he was in range he pulled his weapon from his waistband. "Hold it."

The fourth man pivoted to escape.

"Come on, man, you've got nowhere to run! Drop the gun."

Fourth guy stopped, began turning, but his hands weren't in the air. Cord dropped hard to his knees, steadying his weapon. The fourth guy began firing as he turned. Cord pulled the trigger, hitting his target and planting his face in the dirt until the machine pistol was silent.

He looked up in time to see the fourth guy tumbling down the incline to the canyon floor below. The body rested at an odd angle and didn't move.

Even if he had time to check the crates or hide the bodies, he didn't think he could make the climb up again. He had to think of Kate. No more delays.

His body felt as tough as a marshmallow. He took the remainder of the easier trail as fast as his wobbly legs would carry him.

"Kate?" She didn't answer. He knew what was wrong as soon as he topped the ridge and saw her lying on the ground. She was still under a bush, still gripping the rifle, finger still on the trigger. Her grip released as soon as he touched the barrel. She covered her face with her hands, dropping her head to the dirt.

She'd shot a man.

Dead.

Cord stretched out beside her, pulling her to him, ignoring the rocks, his shaky muscles and his sore shoulder. Even ignoring that he hadn't held her in his arms for five months and how much he'd missed her.

It wasn't about him.

She'd just killed a man.

"Kate, honey, you did what you had to do. Those men would have killed us."

"Is he really dead?" she asked between soft hiccups.

His Kate always got the hiccups when she cried.

"Don't lose any tears or sleep over this guy, Kate. He's not worth it."

"Every life is worth it, Cord." She shoved him an arm's length away. "*Every* life."

"Go ahead and get mad at me if that's what it takes." They sat up, shoulder to shoulder, looking toward the high plains and Davis Mountains. "You can't be certain it was your bullet. Could have been mine."

"You were firing?"

He hadn't been. He'd never admit it, but nodded affirmation.

"I thought…before it all happened, I was so confident. I didn't think I'd…but when he turned toward you, I couldn't just watch you get shot again." She dropped her face back into her hands, drawing her knees to her chest. "I just couldn't go through that again. So I pulled the…you know."

Cord watched the little involuntary jerk her torso did when she was holding in the hiccups. He'd always thought it was cute before. Had teased her about it relentlessly. Now all he could do was rub her back.

"You did what you had to to protect yourself and the baby."

She hurried to her feet, heading down the trail where she'd hidden the horses from view. Cord followed.

"So how do we get down to those ATVs?" she asked.

"We don't. We're stuck on horseback."

"I don't understand." She dusted off her work pants, stowed her rifle and adjusted her saddle.

"I put dirt in the gas." The trail was narrow and he passed on the opposite side of her horse, removing her scarf from Ginger's head and hanging it across Kate's saddle.

"You put—dirt, huh? I don't guess you've learned to fly a helicopter in the past five months?" She tugged Candy's cinch tight and rested her forehead against the leather. "You were going to wait it out, weren't you? If I'd known, I wouldn't have started shooting. If—"

"Don't do the 'what if' thing, Kate. They would have left someone behind. The results would have been the same. You saved my life." He heard his shrink's voice rolling inside his ears. *Admit your mistake. Maybe it will help.* "Okay, I was wrong for not having a plan before I took off."

There, he'd admitted his feelings out loud.

"You certainly were." She looked down on him from high on Candy's back, having mounted while he had his back turned.

"Wait a minute! Aren't you going to admit that *you* were wrong for getting us into this mess?"

"Me? So *I'm* responsible?"

Had he just accused her or defended his actions? Whichever, he couldn't take it back. She closed her eyes and sighed. The long one where he was totally on her bad side until something else happened to change her attitude.

"Come on, Kate. You know I'm talking about right here, right now, this particular situation."

"Really? Would it have happened at all if you'd been able to walk away from the Serna investigation when the threats began?"

"We don't have time for this." He pulled the saddle cinch, wanting to be eye level for where the next words would take them. He knew what was coming. What should have come a long time ago. She'd never accused him. Never yelled at him. Never told him he was responsible.

"You've never chosen to discuss it. That's why I divorced you." She turned her back to him, clicking to Candy to start moving.

"Right."

How many times over the past three years had he heard the words *if you'll just talk to me.* About what? They both knew what had happened when he'd gotten shot and, more important, when she'd lost the baby. Bottom line? He'd paid the ultimate price for not being there to protect her—he'd lost his family.

Talking about it wouldn't make it any better. He'd never understood why she thought it would. What more was there to say?

"Yeah, fall into that same old habit, Cord. Lock down and don't say another word to me. It's a long way to Nick's place. Good thing you decided a long time ago talking is one thing we can live without."

She heeled her horse, not waiting for him to mount, not heeding the potential danger still out there waiting. And not before he heard her mumble, "Thanks for the reminder."

He stepped into the stirrup and took off down the trail after his wife—ex-wife—began the all-day trek to her closest neighbor and high school sweetheart.

"Dammit."

Chapter 7

"Do you see that, Cord?" Kate stretched tall in the saddle but couldn't see who was coming toward them.

They'd been riding the fence separating the Danver and Burke ranches for at least an hour. Cord had wanted to just cut through, but she'd refused. He'd given in when she reminded him that it was faster to get to the next cattle guard and follow the road. That had been the only conversation. They'd been in a hurry with a storm moving in and had taken very few breaks for the exhausted horses.

"Do you think it's Burke?"

She leaned forward, patting Candy's neck. "Can't tell. They're on the road from his place."

"It's unlikely Serna would send his men that direction. Logical to assume Sheriff Barber asked if we'd shown up there."

"If you say so."

Cord took the lead the last hundred yards to the gate. It didn't pass her notice that he'd brought the empty machine gun pistol around from his back for show. Or that he pulled the pistol from his waist. He rode Ginger with one hand on the reins and looked like a weathered cowboy in her dad's old coat.

The sorrow at taking a human life hit her chest right along with the fright of who was in that vehicle. Her mouth went drier than it already had been. She stuffed her gloves into her jacket and pulled her rifle to lay it across her lap. The apprehension made her belly turn over a couple of times, just like the first days of morning sickness.

Cord slowed to a standstill, waiting for the car to top the next rise. He didn't give any indication of what to do. Typical Cord. But he didn't have to. Candy whinnied at the tense hold of her reins. Kate tightened her thighs around her horse, who was ready to bolt.

"The dust is still flying so they haven't stopped. That's good. They had to have seen us. Stay alert, Kate. Tell me if you don't recognize someone."

Cord's voice had a dangerous, low warning tone, easily recognized from all the trouble they'd experienced together. She was glad for it, at least as much as she could be while waiting to see who would top that hill—gang member or close friend.

"That's Nick's Jeep."

"Yeah."

"Mr. Cauldwell's driving." Every muscle in her body melted. She relaxed Candy's harness and they ambled forward in line with Ginger.

Cord pocketed the pistol and grabbed her thigh. "Don't

talk about it. Not a word to Nick, his foreman or anyone else. It's important. We can't trust anyone yet."

"Don't be ridiculous. You know Nick and Mac Cauldwell. They wouldn't hurt me."

"I don't know anything."

That cold steel edge in his voice pierced her heart, sending a shiver up her spine. He meant it and she should remember. *Don't trust anyone.*

"What about the drugs? Are you calling the Ranger headquarters or DEA or whoever you were working with? If they know about the cabin and the canyon, can't they arrest Serna? Wouldn't we be safer then?"

"I'll take care of the phone calls. Just don't give details to anyone. Period."

"Kate! Thank God!" Nick jumped from the doorless Wrangler and opened the gate for the horses. "We've had teams out looking for you since early this morning. It's lucky we found you, there's a bad storm moving in, shutting everything down. Some flash flooding is expected."

They dismounted while Nick was talking. Cord gave her strange looks when Nick hugged her.

"Where have you two been?" Mr. Cauldwell asked, his arm casually draped over the steering wheel.

"We didn't see anyone. Some rocks blocked the trail to the lodge so we trekked over here. Got a way to recall those searchers?" Cord sounded cordial enough from his horse's side, but Kate could feel the tension zinging from his actions.

The machine gun was gone from around his chest. When had he—and where had he—hidden it?

"We're dog tired, Nick. Got room in that thing for our gear?" she asked. She didn't want to be rude, but Cord had said not to talk about the details. "We've been riding on these dang horses much too long, I'm afraid. Hey, Mr. Cauldwell, I see you've taken up a much cushier ride."

She received the chuckle she'd hoped for from the older foreman, who didn't ask for more details. There was no one in Jeff Davis County that was faster throwing a rope around a steer. She'd known the man her entire life. Things wouldn't be the same when he retired.

"Here, let me help," Nick said as she lifted her leg over the saddle.

Before she could say no, he'd slipped his hands around her waist to help her down. As if she'd ever needed help.

Turning to face him and be polite with a thanks, she caught his expression of disillusionment. She'd completely forgotten no one outside the family knew she was pregnant.

"How's your dad doing, Nick?" She tried to act normal and hoped he wouldn't cause a scene.

"Always thinking about others. He's holding his own, Kate. In fact, he almost got dressed to come search for you himself." Nick's words were nice, but his questioning look toward her belly confirmed that he'd felt the baby. "So you guys are back together. You sit, I'll get your saddle. Mac will send someone for the horses when we get back."

Cord darted a look and a shake of his head, reminding her not to impart information. There weren't answers anyway. They were forever together in a sense. Whatever happened, they'd both be involved with the upbringing of their child. Not if Cord had his way and she disappeared into a witness-protection program.

Leaving her family? Her friends? Her heritage? Could she do that?

Suddenly very tired, all she wanted was a hot, soaking bath to ease the ache in her muscles. And just a few minutes forgetting what might happen to the rest of her life. A little peace after a phone call to her dad. *Oh, no.*

"Does my dad think we're missing?"

"You can use my cell as soon as we hit coverage," Nick said, stowing her stuff. "No one mentioned him, though."

"What exactly have you heard, Nick?" Cord asked, joining him with the saddle from Ginger. "How about you, Mac?"

Mac shrugged. "Nothing much. I do what I'm told these days."

"The sheriff called, said you'd gone missing in the mountains and taken Katie with you."

She hated being called Katie. It was such a sissy name. She'd given Nick more than one bloody nose before they were in their teens for using it.

"I'll borrow your cell now."

Nick joined her, handed her the phone and leaned closer. "I'm going to assume this has something to do with Jorje Serna's release and that McCrea doesn't want you to talk to me. But if you need anything, and I mean *anything*, including getting away from your ex... I'm there for you."

Why did the offer send more *heebie-jeebies* up her spine?

As he watched Kate's high school best friend and prom date lean in, essentially trapping her to the side of the Wrangler, his fists clenched. And not from the normal pain in his backside. He fought the urge to grab Burke by his coat collar and connect his knuckles with that artificially tanned face. But he was more than a little tired and would end up losing. If you're going to fight for a woman, you at least need to win the battle and look good. Right?

Kate had made it very plain he wouldn't win the war no matter what kind of shape he was in. He clenched his fists and shoved them in his pockets. Drawing on every Ranger discipline he knew—and a few shrink techniques—he cloaked his anger with blandness.

Kate shot him a questioning look as Burke put her in the front seat.

"I think I'll drive back to the house, Mac," Burke said.

Mac Cauldwell rolled his stiff old body from the Wrangler, popped the seat forward and crooked himself in back without a word. Unfortunately, Cord felt as old as the foreman he sat next to looked.

Burke stuck to the trek everyone referred to as a road, hitting every hole and rut along the way. Cord's back cramped more with each one the Jeep found. At least on the horse he'd been able to stand in the stirrups and relieve the pressure.

By the time they reached the main house, Nick had jabbered about the thunderstorm warnings and given them a play-by-play on the search for both them and Serna.

The gang leader should have been arrested before he left the courtroom. The lack of preparedness on the DoJ's part just confirmed that Serna had someone on the inside. He was missing something obvious. Had to be.

He'd been over the case files a hundred times. More than a hundred if the truth were told. Lord knows he had the time. Kate assumed he was back on the job, but he'd only been allowed back in uniform for court. There wasn't a desk for him in Valentine, Texas. Only desk work in Lubbock or El Paso. He wasn't ready to move

and give up the daily reminder of what life could have
been like before Serna had destroyed it.

Searching the case file for something he'd missed had
become his routine while sitting in their empty house
waiting. Waiting to leave for therapy—mental or physical. That was a fairly accurate description of his life.

Sleep avoided him most nights. Or he avoided sleep.
Dreams plagued him.

If the darkness wasn't filled with demons from the
shooting, they were filled with thoughts of angels holding their little girl.

His thumb wrapped around his fingers again. The fists
rested in his lap. They passed the cattle guard, pulling
around to a row of cars and trucks to park. Mac patted
him on the shoulder. When Cord caught his knowing
look, the embarrassment made him physically relax his
body but didn't help with the jealousy he tasted.

"I'm going to call my dad now," Kate said, jumping from the Jeep as if she'd been on a picnic instead of
twenty-four hours of pure stress.

Cord recognized that tone in her voice. Burke had
made two mistakes. One—she hated being called Katie.
She'd told him that her father had chuckled when her
brother had teased her with it while they'd grown up.
Probably still did.

And the second was assuming that he'd told Kate to
do anything.

Yeah, he could count on Burke getting a cold shoulder for the next couple of hours. It wouldn't be long afterward that they'd be gone. Of course, he didn't plan on
letting Kate out of his sight very long.

But Kate didn't need to know their time schedule.
Not yet.

"Dad? Yes, we're fine. What did they tell you?" Kate didn't head to the house. She took off toward Mrs. Burke's garden, her rifle in hand.

Nothing much there this time of year except privacy.

He threw his saddlebags over his shoulder and followed at a distance. Far enough away to not hear their conversation. Close enough to tell when she'd finished up.

"He wants to talk with you."

He took the cell and Kate walked to the kitchen door. He hadn't spoken to any member of the Danver family since before the divorce and had no idea what to expect during this conversation.

"Hello, David. Before you waste time complaining about the danger I've put your daughter in, understand that nothing will happen to her under my protection."

"Right now, Cord, you're the only one she trusts. Just get her to the airport tomorrow. They're telling us there will only be a short window between these merging storm fronts. We'll call as soon as we're allowed to lift off."

"That's not what I have planned, sir."

Silence.

Cord looked at the phone to make sure they hadn't been disconnected. "I don't believe it's safe to wait."

"I see. You think he's coming after you?"

"The less details I share with you, sir, the less danger your family's in." It wasn't that Cord didn't trust Kate's father. He just didn't know how thoroughly Serna's men had infiltrated the local area.

"You'll notify me?"

"Yes, sir." Cord had a few other things to say to convince David he was right. He hadn't planned on one hundred percent cooperation. Made for a shorter call.

"I'll tell your parents you're both all right and that you'll call when you can."

What an ungrateful son. He hadn't even thought about calling his parents to let them know he or Kate were okay. The Rangers had probably contacted his dad as soon as Serna was freed.

"Thank you for that." He paused. "And for your trust."

"Goes without sayin'."

The old man had thrown him off his rehearsed dialogue. He would never have thought David would openly support his decisions. "Wish there were more time to bring you up to speed, but—"

"Yeah, Kate told me a bit about the cabin and confrontation this morning."

"She didn't hesitate."

"That's what's bothering her, son."

"Sir? I…" Cord knew he needed to say the words. There was a chance he'd never see David Danver again. He owed him an apology. The shrink had stressed that ignoring everyone in his life for the past three years had hurt them. He knew that without the shrink's constant discussion. "I wanted to tell you—"

"This isn't the time for regrets, son. I would have kicked your ass a couple of times already if Kathleen hadn't stopped me. Take care of my little girl."

This time there was a distinct click as David Sr. hung up. Cord dialed his parents' house phone. They should hear from him directly. His mom was probably worried sick. The call went straight to voice mail.

"Hey, Mom. Just wanted you to know we're okay and I'll be keeping Kate safe for a while. I'll call as soon as I can. Just borrowed this phone so there's no reason to call back."

He had a few more phone calls to make. He stuck the phone in the bag still hanging on his shoulder. Man, he was tired and starving and filthy.

Time to face Burke's mom and crew, get cleaned up and maybe—just maybe—give his aching back a rest. Their host was right about one thing. The storm moving in would complicate everything he had planned.

Nick's mother was a sight for very tired eyes. Juliet waved her inside through the back door.

"Oh, my dear, don't take this the wrong way, but you look awful." She pulled out a kitchen chair and gestured for Kate to sit.

"I probably do look a wreck." She removed the scarf and work coat and collapsed on the seat cushion.

"You sit down here at the table." Juliet tied her apron and paused. "Want coffee or hot chocolate?"

"Your famous chocolate, please."

"My grandmother said everything could be fixed with a good cup of cocoa and, after living so many years in this desolate backcountry, I tend to agree with her. Of course, I make Alan a cup every afternoon." She removed milk from the fridge and turned to the stove. "Not instant, mind you. I hate instant. Don't you? Well, even if you preferred it, I'd have to make it on the stove because I don't have any. Instant, that is. I don't like it so I don't buy it."

"How is Mr. Burke?"

"Staying busy. A rancher's work is never done. He rests a lot, though. Takes things slower." Juliet wiped the corner of her eye with the back of her hand as she gathered more chocolate ingredients.

Tears? So maybe the rumor she'd heard about his remission was true and he wasn't doing well at all. How terrible for Juliet and Nick.

Hearing Juliet's voice reminded her how much she missed her father being around the house. This was exactly how he talked when he made his enchiladas. The one dish he excelled at and had perfected. He explained everything he did, each and every time.

Then it was her turn to cook and he'd chatted instructions nonstop until the pan was in the oven and the cheese bubbled to perfection. She'd asked him why when she was about seventeen. Being a smart-assed teenager, she'd patiently explained to him that she'd heard the recitation once a month her entire life and could repeat it by heart.

Of course, the next batch was the most horrible enchiladas they'd ever eaten because she'd had to prepare them on her own. After that, they cooked enchiladas together with her father talking her through every family secret along the way.

"Kate?" Cord was seated at the table with her. He nodded toward Juliet.

"Hmm?" She'd been so lost in thought, or so dang tired, she hadn't heard him come in the door.

"Toast or biscuits?" Juliet asked, looking concerned. "Are you too tired to eat, dear?"

"Oh, sorry. No, I'm starving. Food first, please."

"Toast, Mrs. Burke."

"Then I'll have to make biscuits for dinner. Now that I put the thought of them in my head it's the only way to get them out."

"I'm going to check in with Mac's men. Find out if they saw anything." Cord stood, scooting the chair across the wooden floor that was older than everyone in the room added together.

"You go right ahead, dear. I'll have everything ready to throw in the pan when you get back. I'm just going to fry up some venison sausage."

The uniform pants didn't fit him as snugly as they had three years ago. He'd lost weight and gained a lot of muscle even over the past five months. It had felt really good on that couch, backed against his chest. Having his warm breath caress the back of her neck had caused some additional tingling that had kept her awake long past him falling asleep.

Before the shooting, his occasional light snores would wake her and she would shake him to tell him to go back asleep. Last night, she couldn't close her eyes until he was relaxed and breathing deeply.

Kate didn't want to be rude, but watching her ex-husband walk to the bunkhouse comforted her and she really couldn't concentrate too much on what Juliet was saying. She listened to the stories, remembering how many times she'd sat at this same table.

"Do you remember the first time we met, dear?"

"Yes, ma'am. Mom brought me over after you bought the place from Mac. She was the self-appointed, one-woman welcoming committee to Valentine."

"That's right. She brought us her homemade bread. I was so impressed she showed me how to make it on the spot. Said she got tired of running to the store when your brother used all the bread to feed the baby chicks. Did she ever break him of that?"

"Not until he stopped feeding the chickens as one of his chores." She laughed at the memory. "Angering mom to get out of the chore may have been the only reason he used the bread. Davy still hates feeding chickens."

She wiped her hands on her ruffled apron and held

them out to Kate. A serious look consumed her normally cheery face.

Kate held on to Juliet's strong embrace. "I miss her."

"I do, too. I only bring it up because I want you to know if you need anything or need to talk to anyone, I'm here." Juliet looked directly at her stomach. "When I was pregnant with Nick…well, I missed my mother more at that time than I normally did."

"So you know about the baby?" Kate hadn't removed her jacket, uncertain if she wanted to share her news with anyone. She shrugged out of the work coat and let Juliet hang it on the back door hook. But it was time to stop avoiding what people would say. Maybe it was because Cord knew now.

"David told me. I hope you don't mind." She set the toast and homemade jam on the table.

"Not really. It's not like it's a secret. Everyone will know soon enough." She caressed the swell that would soon make her barrel-size.

"I may have complained when we moved here about this being a desolate country, but it's become my home. All of our friends have become family. So if I can help, I want to be there for you. And for your mom."

Kate was touched. She'd been so isolated on the ranch. She hadn't really spoken much with her father since he'd gone to her brother's. She hadn't wanted to bother him with ranch details. And she especially hadn't wanted to hear the worry in his voice.

"I know this is butting in, but you don't have anyone to push their nose in your business." She smiled. "You should tell that man how you really feel."

"Cord? He knows."

"He doesn't. He's all confused and worried. It's as plain as the whiskers on his face."

"I'm not the one who has him turning in circles. It's Serna and not knowing. *That's* why he's so worried."

Juliet released her hand and picked up the corner of her apron to move the hot pan back to the burner. She began turning the bacon. "You can trust me on this Kathleen Danver McCrea, that man does not think you love him."

"But… I don't." *I can't.*

"I had my hope of you falling in love with Nick and I think for a little while, so did he. But those days have long passed. I never thought twice about it after Cord came into your life. You look at him, well, just like your daddy looked at your mama."

Chapter 8

They were stuck at Nick's overnight but Kate wanted to be on her way. It was hard to sit still. Hard to relax when Serna and his men were out there waiting. The unknown had never appealed to her. She liked family. Loved working the ranch. And had discovered she loved running it even more.

One of the many reasons she'd refused to run away before Serna had been released. She couldn't run—with the exception of away from Cord. But that was different.

She wrapped herself in a towel reluctantly, leaving her extended soak. Clothes presented a problem, but Nick's mom had loaned her some pajamas and all Kate really wanted was to slide into the comfy queen-size bed, curl up and sleep until the thunderstorm was over. Then it would be safe to drive without the threat of falling rocks or flash floods.

She pulled the drawstring tight on the bottoms and heard a soft knock on her door that was already swinging open. Cord leaned in the doorway holding a blanket and pillow. Hat pushed back on his head, still dressed in his uniform, he hadn't cleaned up a bit since they'd arrived at Nick's ranch.

"What have you been doing?"

"Hate to ask this, Kate. I know you're tired. Can you let me use your shower for a couple of minutes?" Her ex-husband was already unbuttoning his shirt, assuming she'd say yes.

"And what was wrong with the main bath Mrs. Burke told you to use?"

"Didn't have time."

"Too many secret phone calls trying to get us out of here sooner?" She crossed her arms over her braless breasts that he kept glancing down at. "What's wrong with the hall shower?"

"Actually, I was sitting outside your door, waiting. Probably nothing wrong with that shower. Better if I'm here."

Had he become a delusional paranoid? "Really? You think someone's going to attack me in the guest bedroom?"

He shrugged his shoulders free of the drab beige color and tossed it on the back of the chair.

"Just stay awake five minutes. Then I'll take care of watching over things." His hands went to his belt buckle.

"Don't you do that, Cordell." She waved her hands. His eyes dropped to her breasts again. "Oh, go on. But hurry."

Cord laughed at her embarrassment heading to the bathroom. She hadn't heard him laugh in so long, turning a bright red was worth it. She checked the mirror just to verify that, yes, she had changed to a *sunburned palomino* as Cord had nicknamed her.

The shower spray came on. She grabbed a throw blanket to cover her shoulders and shut the bathroom door. *Just like old times.*

"Ouch." She shook her thumb where the dried cactus had lodged. It was irritating more than painful, something that had happened more than once in her youth. She could see the thorn just under the skin and she needed a needle or tweezers. Each time her thumb scraped something it brought her back to pulling the trigger...

She wanted the reminder gone.

Creeping like a thief, she opened the bath door. Cord had his back to her, and she could see the white suds from the soap still clinging to the gorgeous muscles. She didn't blame them for wanting to try. Ignoring the body on the other side of the curtain, she slowly pulled open the medicine cabinet. No luck. Then the drawer. Yea, pin cushion.

"You don't have to be so quiet. You aren't disturbing me." The water shut off. Cord shook his head and drew the curtain to one side. He pointed past her. "Want to hand me that towel? Or I could stand here and let you have a longer look-see."

"You...that was fast."

"Towel?"

"Oh, yeah, sorry."

Her *ex*-husband reached around her to grab the matching towel to the one wrapped around her hair.

What was wrong with her? She'd seen a naked Cord many, many times. Her nipples tightened as did many other places in her body. "I, um, needed a needle."

Wow, thank goodness he wrapped the lower half of his body. That just left the desire to sleuth off those beads of water from his shoulders and chest. If she didn't watch it, she'd be breathing hard soon. She was just tired. They both were.

"You done with this?" He tugged the towel from her hair and hung it around his neck, using the ends to absorb some of the drops. "What happened? Want me to take a look?"

Without waiting for permission, he brought her thumb closer to his sharp brown eyes. He didn't release her hand when she tugged.

"I can do it."

"I'm sure you can, but it would be easier and quicker if I helped. Then you could hit the hay faster." He took the needle from the cushion. "This is in there sort of deep. When did you get it?"

She didn't want to say it aloud. She'd killed a man.

"Humph."

He could tell. He'd always been able to read her, especially when something was wrong. If only he could talk through a problem as well as he could spot one.

"Ouch!" She jerked her thumb away from where he'd stabbed it.

"Don't be a baby. You know this is how you get a thorn free."

"It hurts."

"Of course it hurts. You have a piece of cactus stuck in your thumb." He swiped his hands on the towel hanging around his neck and adjusted it to cover most of the skin.

The sweet strawberry-patterned towel blocked her from seeing most of the muscles he'd developed in the five months they'd been apart. "You mashing and prodding won't help."

"Let me see it." He drew her hand closer to his eyes

again. But he didn't look; he had them closed. He wrapped his lips around her thumb and sucked.

Oh, wow.

"Cord McCrea, stop that. What do you think you're doing?"

"Just softening up the skin so it won't hurt as much."

"It's plenty soft."

"Yeah, I remember."

"Cord, I'm—we can't—"

"I'm not." He teasingly smiled at her.

"Yes, you are." She jerked her hand to behind her back, protecting more than just her thumb from him. She didn't need much of an imagination to know what was going on under that towel at his hips. She'd experienced it and her muscle memory was playing havoc with her restraint. Her body was desperately ready to see if she remembered anything about sex.

He rolled the needle between his fingers and held out his left palm. "I promise to behave. Now give me your thumb."

Reluctantly, she placed her thumb in his care again. But she didn't know if she was reluctant because he might break his promise or that he might keep it.

Chapter 9

"They're here."

With all the hands called in for the search and now back at the ranch, it was difficult to find a place to make a very private phone call.

"What do you mean? Where's 'here'?" Serna's voice showed his frustration.

"At the ranch. They're cleaning up."

Together. Same bedroom. Good. Serna's punishment will mean more if they're together. Divorced or not.

"How long? Did they say where they've been? My men haven't checked in from this morning."

Hadn't the man learned anything? McCrea was good. Too good. That's why he had to be taken out before he was reinstalled to the task force. Something that would have already been taken care of if it weren't for Serna's personal vendetta. The man should have been killed while he couldn't walk and defend himself.

"Knowing McCrea, you should send more men to the cabin. The others are probably dead." He pulled the phone away from his ear until the string of curses ceased, then continued, "We need that chopper. And he hasn't said anything about their activities."

"I want them dead."

"I know what you want and that's your problem. I've kept my end of the bargain for over four years. I'm taking a big risk calling you with so many people around."

"Your end will come much sooner if you don't deliver them to me."

He bit his tongue instead of explaining why it was useless to threaten him. Serna would be gone along with everyone else.

"The storm's going to delay everything in the operation. You have time to get the chopper and get the McCreas before they leave."

He disconnected the line. The storm actually made his part to take down Serna, frame the Danvers and succeed much easier. Of course he'd deliver the McCreas. They'd ridden their horses right where he'd hoped.

Serna's men were lax and took too much for granted. The ones on the mountain were also probably dead.

Dance with the devil and all that.

"Good grief, just be still and let me finish."

"Ow." She stuck the pad of her thumb in her mouth, her pink nail a slightly darker shade than her lips.

"There. All done. I see you're still having your nails done." Cord looked at her toes, perfectly manicured, just like her fingertips.

No matter how much she worked on the ranch, she didn't miss her appointment for a mani-pedi. It was almost a ritual for her. He'd teased but never asked her to stop, because he liked it.

"You always made fun of my nails."

He did like it. Liked that she took time for herself. She deserved it.

So tell her. That shrink voice nagged him. His sessions were full of reasons he'd pushed people away. And every session ended with a question about Kate. The same question nagging him to answer right now.

He'd avoided thinking about why he hadn't contacted her since the divorce. Then during the last session his shrink had thrown out this thought-provoking moment: *You know you can't move forward until you face the past. And Kate is your past, Cord. If you expect change, you can't continue to walk through life. Letting her go is necessary and it's going to be painful.*

"What is it?" she asked. "You *do* think my nails are silly. Well, I don't care. When all's said and done, I still like to feel nice." She pushed at his chest, trying to move past him in the little bathroom.

His hands fell to her middle, holding her in place. "It's not that. I was thinking about something else. Kate, I— Holy cow, what was that?" His hand was on the side of her belly. "I thought we just ate. That was a heck of a stomach gurgle."

"Cord, I think that…that's the baby." She put her hand over his, shifting his touch more to the center. "There. Feel that."

Their eyes met and all he could manage was a nod. He'd just *thought* the baby was real before. The depth of emotion welling inside him was about to erupt like the volcano that formed the mountains around them. He couldn't label them or put words to them, but he knew they were there.

"Is that the first time she's moved?" he asked.

She. Daughter.

That eruption knocked the barricade he'd stashed his numb heart behind. He'd thought he'd hidden it deep under a cover of recovery. The tears welled in Kate's eyes, her lower lip rolled between her teeth and she swayed backward.

They'd shared something special, something only they could understand. And he'd screwed it up. Twisted it with a memory of pain.

Say it. Tell her you're sorry for being an insensitive jerk.

He could fall to his knees and beg for forgiveness. Or he could ignore another moment she seemed to be waiting for words he didn't have. How long had the minute lasted? Sixty seconds that time? Or three years of hurt?

The amazing woman sighed—a new one he didn't know. Then she squeezed his hands. Move on? It's okay? God, he wished he was better at this.

"It really is amazing. I'm glad you were here. Why do you think the baby's a…a girl?" She stumbled over *girl* but recovered. "My bet's on a boy. The McCreas always have a son to pass the Ranger badge to. Don't they?"

Was it wrong not to want a boy? There couldn't be a replacement, but he wanted that little baby girl. He wanted to rock her in the antique crib Kate had found. She'd talked the dealer in Fredericksburg to lower his price and had scraped every spare dollar they had together for the purchase. The yellow-and-brown baby comforter was still hanging on the side.

He clasped Kate's free hand, bringing it to his lips. "That was quite a wallop of a kick."

"Or just a flip. I think she's done now." She moved away from him. "We need some rest."

"Right. As soon as the storm passes, we gotta move." He stepped back, wanting to pull the woman carrying his child into his arms. He didn't know what to think or assume. Didn't know why feeling his child move made him want to make wild love to her. "You go lie down."

Kate walked away, not looking pregnant at all from behind. But he liked the pregnancy. It looked as good on her as the nail polish. Okay, not a perfect comparison for such a beautiful woman. He knew what the crazy thoughts firing through his mind meant. The same reason he couldn't discuss Kate with his shrink. The same reason he hadn't accepted Kate's phone calls or texts or letters or heard her name without aching for the part of him that she'd completed.

She's not your wife anymore. She'd divorced him the morning after they'd made their baby. He knew that. He deserved that.

He caught himself from falling with a hand on the counter. His legs were tired, but it was the scar that ached like a deep, wrenching wound. No physical reason that it should. The doctor said there wasn't a reason for it. But there were three strong reasons: Shane, Sarah and a baby girl who never drew her first breath.

He'd almost forgotten to cover the scar when he'd left the shower. Hopefully, Kate hadn't noticed since he hadn't faced her straight on. He pressed his palm into the scar, trying to ease the hurt.

"Thanks for the hospitality, Juliet. I can do the laundry. Just point me in the right direction," Kate said from the other room.

He stood straight, surprised at Kate's voice. He looked at his red-rimmed eyes and turned on the cold water to splash his face.

"I won't hear of it," Mrs. Burke answered. "You both get some rest."

That's what happened when he let emotions get caught in a loop in his head. His training dropped to nil. He hadn't heard the door open. *Pull yourself together.* He sucked it up, stowed the distracting thoughts in an imaginary box and tucked the towel at his hips tighter.

Get Kate to safety. First priority. Only priority.

She was curled on top of the bed with a light blanket covering her. He wasn't looking forward to the small desk chair in the corner where he planned on spending the afternoon.

"You going to lie down in the other room?"

"Go to sleep," he directed. "I'm staying right here."

"In the chair?"

"Yeah. I don't want to leave you alone."

"Then come lie down."

"That's not a good idea." Just the thought of her spooning that pretty bottom into him got his blood flowing faster.

"Good or bad, I'll sleep sounder if you're next to me and you'll sleep better if your back is relaxed."

He lacked the ability to say no. As much as he wanted those emotions to stay under lock and key…they weren't. He was just too tired and sore. He needed the comfort of stretching out and relaxing if he were going to fulfill his promise.

But he wasn't lying there naked. He'd already visited Burke's bedroom and lifted some jeans and a T-shirt.

"What are you doing?" Kate asked on a gasp.

He turned around, stretching a leg into the stiff jeans. "Getting dressed."

She was leaning on one elbow. Her eyes were huge and her mouth a perfect O.

"You've seen all this before, babe."

Tears dropped to her cheeks. She was seriously crying. What the h…? He zipped the loose pants and rushed to sit on the edge of the bed.

"I didn't mean to upset you. I didn't think about getting dressed. I mean. I didn't think you'd get mad about it. I sort of didn't think about it at all."

"Shh. You didn't do anything. It's just that… I've never seen this." She caressed the bullet scar in his chest with the tip of her finger, then down and around his side, leaning behind him. "Or this."

"Man, I'm sorry." He tried to stand to get the shirt but Kate held him where he was.

No one besides the doctor and nurse had ever seen let alone touched his back since the shooting. Certain, methodical hands he handled without a second thought. Their praise at how well he'd healed always left him hollow. He didn't feel healed. Not by a long shot.

Whisper-soft strokes soothed him in a way he didn't know existed. Kate's fingers barely skimmed the puckered and stitched scars he had memorized in his mind. The places he couldn't physically feel were worse. The touch disappeared, reminding him of so many times he'd yearned for it.

Too emotionally raw to take any more, he jumped up and grabbed his shirt.

She didn't beg him to come back, just stretched her hand out in a gesture for him to return. And he did.

For the first time since his partner had been murdered, he needed to trust those around him to keep watch. He drew the drapes to darken the room more than the storm already had and tried not to bounce the bed too much as he lay down.

He put his arms under his head on the pillow and stared at the ceiling, careful not to touch Kate. But she had other ideas. She scooted that luscious bottom next to his hip.

A familiar hand touched his side, tugging, wanting him to do what he feared the most. *Snuggle.* He turned, meticulously keeping his hands to himself. Kate laced her fingers with his and placed his palm on the baby.

"I know it's not forever and I hope you'll forgive me for asking it of you. But right now, this minute," she whispered, "I want to dream of our family."

God help me, but I'm going to let you.

Chapter 10

"Thanks for putting us up, Mr. Burke," Kate said when they entered the dining room. She could smell fresh bread every time the swinging door opened and someone brought another dish to the table.

Cord followed her. Everything was ready for six people. Ron was seated at the head of the table, buttering a famous homemade biscuit. She was so hungry it was like she hadn't eaten a huge plate of scrambled eggs and bacon before they'd cleaned up.

"I think Juliet and Nick had a little more say in the matter than I did, but you're welcome." Mr. Burke bit into the biscuit, so hot the butter oozed out and dripped onto the plate.

Ron Burke was a little younger than her dad and probably should lay off the butter considering he'd had a major heart attack the year before. Sometimes a wake-up call and sometimes not. He looked the same though, a tough old coot who had been a businessman before turning rancher.

Being here brought back a rush of memories. When her mother had been alive, the Burkes had gotten together with her parents every other week. They'd shared so many stories about ranch work not being what they'd expected. Laughing about their missteps in taking over the ranch had been a weekly topic. After her mother died, the dinners had grown fewer and dwindled down to not at all.

The sad part was that they'd bought this ranch from Mac, one of her dad's best friends. Mac had withdrawn after taking the job of foreman here, in charge of the land that had been in his family for several generations.

Standing at the door to the kitchen, Mac helped Mrs. Burke carry the rest of dinner to the table. Kate was glad to see him join them. There had been so many years where he'd been too embarrassed over losing the ranch to associate with any of the families in Valentine.

"Hey, Mac, glad you could brave the weather to come for dinner." She liked Mac, always had. "There isn't a better cowboy in the county, or the next, or the next."

"I think someone's probably passed me up by now. These old bones just ain't what they used to be."

"Never," she said faithfully, but didn't receive a crack of a smile from him.

Everyone joined Ron at the table. Nick had been silent in the corner, waiting with his arms crossed. He pulled out her chair, but Cord seated himself at her side. She didn't want to giggle, but it was sort of fun to have them competing for her time again. Mrs. Burke gave her a knowing smile and Mac just shook his head.

"You going to tell us what's going on?" Ron asked,

loading his mouth with a bite of pork chop, his plate already laden with food.

Cord shrugged. "You know the basics. Jorje Serna vowed to kill Kate and then me. He was released yesterday and Kate needs to get to safety."

"Why didn't you head back to your place? I mean Danver's, or utilize the sheriff? Seems like that would have been faster than crossing the dang mountain," Ron stated. He didn't even look at them. "Took all the hands from their work to search for you."

"Dad, give it up," Nick insisted. "It wasn't like they could do a lot with the threat of the storm anyway. We got everything ready yesterday."

"Aren't you curious?" Ron asked his son.

Mac and Juliet silently ate their dinner, either ignoring or totally used to the father-son arguments.

"Cord's a Texas Ranger, sir," Kate explained, hating that everyone thought they had a right to know, for some odd reason. "He can't really talk about his investigations. It's always been that way. So naturally, we shouldn't say what we saw or what happened."

Did anyone else at the table notice her voice change? Maybe Juliet, since she'd actually looked up. She sounded so full of regret and sadness. If she wasn't careful, she'd remember everything that had happened this morning. She wanted to forget. She could still feel the Remington's reverb against her shoulder. She rubbed it and was surprised at how bruised she felt.

"Sorry, Ron. It's simple really," Cord said. "Coming here seemed a safer option than returning to Kate's."

Her husband had never wanted to discuss his cases with her. Had always thought it was too dangerous. Then they'd been threatened. And threatened again. And ambushed. And he'd still held back details. The thought should make her angry—angrier—but she wasn't. She was proud that he'd kept his oath to the Rangers. But the world had changed. There wasn't honor among thieves and there were no boundaries on the casualties of war.

"The news said Frank Stewart was murdered." Nick put his fork across his half-eaten plate. "That true? Someone got the jump on Frank?"

"Shame about Frank. Now there was a good man. Your daddy liked him a lot," Ron said, and added another bite of gravy and biscuit to his mouth.

As good as she knew the food to be, it tasted like dry, lifeless cardboard. *Oh, good Lord.* She was about to lose it. She tuned everyone at the table out. Concentrated on the fork. One bite. Just one.

Too many thoughts swimming in her head. Regrets or mistakes? Death. Killing. She bit her lip to stop. Took another bite of biscuit and thought she'd choke. Half a glass of water, Frank's name, a chuckle, the words "was such a good man." How could she get out of here?

Cord was relieved the conversation had turned reminiscent and the focus was off what had happened on the mountain. Curious how no one had asked if they'd run into trouble. Of course, Kate had sort of told them not to.

"Now that dinner's over, I for one would like to know what really happened out there. Why did you insist on talking to the sheriff alone, McCrea?" Nick Burke looked between Cord and Kate.

Spoke too soon. Kate stiffened beside him. Others might not see it, but he did. Her eyes were too shiny. Tears. She was about to cry. Had to be because of the pilot, the guy she'd killed. The events of the past two days were catching up with her. She couldn't do this to herself. He couldn't let her do this to herself.

"Thanks for a great dinner, Mrs. Burke," he said, pointedly ignoring the question about their activities. He pushed away from the table and tugged on Kate's chair.

"Now, Cord, if you don't start calling me Juliet, I'm going to get a complex."

Probably the most genuine person in the room, Burke's mother reminded him a lot of his own. He'd love to pick up the phone and tell her about the baby. Shoot, maybe she already knew. Shake it off, man. Get Kate out of here.

"I'll say it again, but I hope I can make gravy like that one day," Kate said, placing her napkin on her plate.

"Just come over a couple of more times and Mom can give you lessons," Nick spouted, covering Kate's hand and squeezing.

She's your ex, and can leave her hand wherever she wants. Get over it.

"A lesson would be nice. Maybe after all this is over and done with I'll have some time."

Kate looked up at only him, expressing a pleading look of "save me." Was it his wishful thinking that she didn't want her hand under Burke's? Or just didn't want to make small talk about gravy lessons? Either way, the strain and tears were still in her eyes. Time to go.

"Sorry again to impose on you like this, but it's much appreciated. I'm done in. How 'bout you, Kate?"

"I hardly slept last night. I think I'll say good night." She finally stood and joined him.

Cord had his hand on her lower back, guiding her to walk into the hall first when Burke reached out. The sturdy control on his forearm wasn't a casual stop. Neither was the look from Kate's former beau.

"Mom said the guest room's ready."

"Not necessary since I'm not leaving Kate's side."

"Listen, McCrea." Burke stood, facing him toe-to-toe, dropping his voice to a threatening whisper. "Next time you want some pants, just ask."

Cord replied with a raised eyebrow. Let Burke interpret it any way he wanted. Kate was waiting in the doorway. Cord turned back to Mrs. Burke, pulling free from her son's grip. "If it's okay with you, Juliet, I might just have seconds on those biscuits and gravy later."

"That's fine, dear. Just fine. Glad you like 'em."

When he looked back at Kate, it wasn't the threat of tears he saw in her eyes. Nope, that long sigh and the slight shake of her head meant she was disappointed. Again or always.

He closed the bedroom door behind them and turned the lock. Not real protection, but it would have to do. Kate's hands were balled and planted on her hips. He knew the routine and it wasn't something he wanted at the moment. Arguing about his behavior would just avoid what she needed. Yeah, that pattern was something he'd become an authority on in the past three years. He'd mastered the process to perfection.

"You didn't ask for his jeans?"

"No."

"Your mother would be so embarrassed. *I'm* embarrassed."

"Well, don't be." He shrugged out of the button-up he'd been given to wear to dinner. "As you're constantly reminding me, we're not married anymore."

"Get out. Go sleep in your own room. I'm perfectly safe here."

"We need to talk, Kathleen."

"Right. You mean, you have instructions to give and I need to listen."

"I know you're upset."

"You bet your patootie, I'm upset. The Burkes have been nothing but gracious to us and you stole Nick's jeans."

"You shot a man."

"Oh." She swiped a pillow off the bed and sat in the desk chair, wrapping her arms around the softness and hugging herself. Visibly deflated and dejected, her shoulders dropped. The fire left her eyes and yet they sparkled as they filled with tears. "What's going to happen?"

"Is that what you're really worried about?"

He waited. If there was one thing he'd learned after a year of therapy, it was that whoever was asking the questions waited until they were answered. You couldn't rush the conversation.

"No."

"It couldn't be avoided."

"I still killed a man," she whispered.

He hooked her hair over her ear to see her face more clearly. "Does it scare you more that you *shot* a man or that you don't regret it?"

"I regret it! I do." Her head jerked up, but her face wasn't full of indignation, it was full of questions.

"There's probably truth in that and there should be. What you have to hold on to and remember is that he would have killed me. And he would definitely have killed you." He gently moved the pillow to smooth her shirt over her belly. "Snuffing out two heartbeats with one shot if he'd had the opportunity."

"I know all that." She tapped her temple. "But how do you live with it every day? You never talked about this part of your job."

"I guess I never did. If I'd ever had to shoot someone, maybe I would have. I don't know."

"Wait. You never—before that night—?"

"Nope. And I don't remember shooting Serna's brother. The first guys that I can remember happened this morning. And you're right. There's a touch of regret for the loss of life, but I'm right. We didn't have a choice. They would have killed us or taken us to Serna, who would have done worse."

There were worse things than dying. Watching someone you love suffer or, worse still, be tortured. Surely that was worse than losing your life? He never wanted to find out.

"Thing is, babe…" He took a knee next to the chair so he could see her downcast eyes. "I wouldn't hesitate to protect you again. Not a second. Let another bastard try."

She tossed the pillow to the floor and wrapped her arms around his neck. He felt the hot tears on his skin. Man, she smelled good. Holding her felt good. Didn't matter why he was holding her. She belonged in his arms. He let her cry and when she was exhausted and the hiccups began, he lifted her, keeping her tucked close, and took her to bed.

As much as he ached for her, she was no longer his, and holding her would have to do. But they'd traveled through an impasse of his making. Maybe the shrink was right. Maybe they could talk through that night and what happened after. It wasn't something he looked forward to, but maybe, just maybe, they'd taken the first step on the journey back to each other.

Chapter 11

They were up from a second nap, rested and hungry again. The storm was letting up and it was pitch-black outside. As soon as Cord could, they'd snatch a set of keys from the rack and borrow a car. When they reached Kent, he'd "borrow" another one. His only plan at the moment was to keep them moving so Serna couldn't find them.

"I thought we were getting dressed for a midnight snack? Why are you packing?" Kate asked.

"I don't think it's a good idea to hang around." He hedged, since he hadn't told Kate her family wouldn't be at the airport. The subject would come up soon enough and the thought of flying tomorrow seemed to ease the tension for Kate. If Serna knew no one could fly in, it also meant that they couldn't use any airstrips to escape. So he'd be watching the roads even closer.

"Sorry, but we're here for a while. The weather front is not cooperating with your timetable, Cord. A front in

Colorado is headed this way with possibly additional
fronts pushing into the area from the west late tomorrow. Dad said they couldn't fly until after the snow. It's
okay to wait here and be safe."

Not okay with him. As for being safe? Well, the
Ranger task force were certain Serna had an inside man
at most, if not all, the ranches in this area. It was one ex-
planation why they'd been using the mountains so openly.
And successfully. No matter how much hospitality the
Burkes showed them, he didn't trust Nick.

He had to obtain the right vehicle and drive her somewhere safe. As soon as he figured out where that could
be. He'd confirmed a time to call David. If he didn't, it
meant they were in trouble. Kate's father was the only
person he trusted beside himself to keep her safe. The
man didn't need much explanation or convincing. He'd
been begging her to get out of Texas for weeks.

If anything went wrong, Cord was solely responsible.

Her father agreed that Cord should get her out as soon
as physically possible. They couldn't wait patiently for
police protection, at the ranch or at a secret location.
There was no secret location. Not where Serna was concerned. And they couldn't hang around the airport waiting on the chance the weather would clear before Serna
found them to take his revenge.

"The longer you stay here, the more danger you're
in, Kate."

She walked from the bath where she'd been dressing,
holding a large Texas Tech sweatshirt—Burke's. "Why
do you hate Nick?"

"I don't hate Burke." He intensely disliked the man.

"You don't like him," she clarified.

"He doesn't really care for me, either."

"You think he's attracted to me? Still?" She laughed, pointing to the swell in her stomach, very apparent again under the thermal shirt.

"Darn certain he is." He sounded just like the jealous husband. Damn. He was the jealous ex-husband.

If Kate had attended Tech in Lubbock instead of UT in Austin, their paths would never have crossed. They'd never have met and he wouldn't have taken this assignment to stay in the area. She'd be the younger Mrs. Burke by now. She wouldn't be in danger. And she wouldn't look at him with those disappointed sighs gracing her luscious lips.

"You shouldn't dislike him because we were good friends growing up."

"That's not the reason. Let's drop it." *The man's still in love with you, Kate. Can't you tell?* Tell her. Say it out loud. Tell her how you've missed her, how your arms ache to hold her every night.

"Right. Nothing's changed," she said.

No, nothing about his feelings had changed. He pulled on his boots, wishing he'd had something with thicker, sturdier soles for climbing earlier in the canyon.

"What's going to happen to us here?" she asked with her fingers paused on the doorknob.

"Put on your boots."

"Really? I wanted to keep my toes near the fire and get some more hot chocolate and biscuits."

"We need to be ready to move. I don't trust—"

"Anyone."

"Now's not the time to explain."

In spite of the disgust he heard in her voice, she grabbed her shoes and sat in the chair to tie them. He'd protect his family no matter what she thought about his *trust* issues.

"Set the phones on the table, will you?"

"We can't take them?" she asked, standing near the end of the bed, dragging a finger across the rifle barrel currently wrapped in a towel. "Where did you get the backpack?"

"I kept the SD cards." He gestured to the pack. "Mrs. Burke thought it would be easier to carry our stuff. I left the saddlebags with our tack."

"She didn't see the machine gun, did she?"

"Nope. Not unless you showed her."

"Right. Are those boxes of cartridges? Nick gave you—"

He stiffened at the word "gave," giving himself away.

Realization spread across her face. "Good grief, Cord. You broke into his gun cabinet?"

"He should have better security. Too easy. I used a pocketknife."

"I cannot believe you'd do such a thing."

He stopped her from pulling the door open. Then stopped her from talking by slipping his hand over her lips. "You made me promise. I gave my word to protect you and the baby. Do you honestly think we're safe here?"

She shook her head and he dropped his hand. The fear of what Serna would do to her shook his core. He blocked it from his mind. If he got emotional, he'd lose focus. He needed to focus. Have a plan and a backup plan and a backup plan to that.

"Is this going to end, Cord?"

The words were on the tip of his tongue to tell her everything would be okay. Things would change. They'd be fine. He wanted to lie. He couldn't. Not to Kate.

Her arms wrapped around his neck, pulling him to her in a moment of frightened clarity. When she looked up at him, tears pooled in eyes that never deserved to cry but had too often. He bent closer and captured her lips.

Five months, five days without feeling the surge of power he'd always experienced with her kiss. A strengthening power that recharged his entire being. Knowing that she was the only person who'd ever made him feel... anything. The knowledge floored him. Knocked his feet out from under him when he realized he may never feel that again. She kept him from losing control.

No one except Kate had been able to catch him in a free fall. She'd been the only woman he'd wanted since they met.

The natural hunger from her startled him. His brain screamed at him. Go further. Take more. You want her and, more important, you need her. Her body melted into him. Why had he wasted the past several hours on sleep?

Their tongues tangled, desperate for each other. Logically, it wasn't a good idea, but with Kate in his arms he couldn't behave logically. He just wasn't that strong. Only his body was reacting. And right then, the loose jeans he'd borrowed were getting pretty dang tight.

Man, he needed her. He cupped each side of her face and devoured her lips. Every aching, hungry attack was countered with her own. Her hands were on his chest, raising his shirt, skimming along his rib cage. When he hesitated, her mouth sought his. They collided together, twisting closer. The back of his knees hit the edge of the bed.

"I can't..." She stopped, pushing back. "We can't go there. This can't happen. I'm sorry."

Cord released her as if she were a hot branding iron.

He commanded his body to relax. Almost. He shoved the second box of ammo into the pack along with water and food he'd taken when Mrs. Burke wasn't looking.

"Cord…" Kate wrapped her fingers around his shoulder and he jerked away.

"Don't. I get it. We're divorced."

"I don't want to hurt you."

He stood straight, threw the strap over his shoulder and forced his voice not to shake. "We're past that."

You can't hurt someone who's already dead inside.

Kate followed Cord from the bedroom, where they'd spent a few peaceful hours. The storm had taken a south turn toward Marfa and was easing up a bit. The brief hail that accompanied it had awoken her from a sound sleep before dinner. One of two she'd had safely wrapped in Cord's arms.

It brought memories of happier times before the shooting, but not as much as the kiss. Oh man, to be kissed like that every day again. Cord was such a good kisser.

And such a good lover. She missed him so much, but she couldn't go back. It was impossible not to wonder if she'd ever feel safe without him. Shoot, it was impossible to be with him and wonder if she'd ever feel safe. Now she had another life to think about.

It was so sad to admit they were finished. Maybe if she weren't pregnant she would give him a second chance. Perhaps. But the baby changed everything. If Serna weren't the problem, some other gang Cord investigated would be.

Seven years ago, Cord's life had seemed exciting, adventurous. Now she knew it was just deadly. Being a Ranger was bred into Cord. It was a part of him, just like breathing was to a normal man. She placed her hand on their baby. Right now she needed lots of normal.

She wished with all her heart that they were secure, but as Cord continually reminded her, they weren't. Her strong Texas Ranger was prepared for an assault. And that's the reason she'd wanted his promise to protect her himself. He really was the only one she trusted to think of her first.

"Where is everybody?" Cord asked, leading the way to an empty TV room.

"Juliet mentioned they were heading to bed soon after we went to our room. It's after midnight, and this is a ranch with chores at the break of dawn. Most people are in bed. But speaking of dinner, I'm starved again. Leftovers are in the fridge."

He'd shut down and wasn't looking at her. Not ignoring, just not looking.

"Perfect. Leave it wrapped up and bring it with us."

"If you have some type of master plan, now would be a good time to fill me in on it."

He whipped her around, cupped her chin to meet his eyes, his jaw clenched tight in Ranger mode. "Trust me."

Two could play that stubborn game. She knocked his gentle grip away. "I do trust you, Cord. You are absolutely one of the few people I completely trust with my life. But don't take that as compliance and a reason not to keep me in the loop. We both know how *that* turned out this morning."

"I'm sorry, but we're leaving. Now." His voice was low and very determined.

"That's ridiculous. Dad can't get here until late tomorrow." She'd spoken to her father, had confirmed with

Cord that they'd wait until the storm front cleared Colorado.

"Your dad's not coming. We're meeting him somewhere else. I spoke with him, too. He agreed it's too dangerous to wait."

Even trusting Cord's experience, she was not a child. The men in her life didn't get to arbitrarily make decisions for her. "You should have discussed this with me. I'm not asking why you didn't, but do you think you could disclose this mysterious location?"

"Dammit, Kate. We need to move. I'll explain on the road." He swung the pack over his shoulder, then grabbed all the key rings, sorting them into two hands.

"Are you serious? What are you doing?"

"No keys, no one can follow."

"These are the good guys, Cord. What if we need their help?"

"Grab the food and let's get out of here." Cord threw her jacket and Nick's sweatshirt at her.

"I need my cell phone."

"We're leaving them here. We can't risk being tracked that way."

Trust him, he knows what he's doing. She hurriedly pulled both on, not looking forward to the downpour of rain that was about to soak through all of it. In spite of her indicating he couldn't order her around, she'd go. She had to. She grabbed the plate wrapped in foil and the extra biscuits from the stove left in a ziplock.

"Can you tell me where we're going and at least grab a car with a heater?"

The next couple of minutes were a blur. Between the rain and Cord being her human Kevlar, she didn't see much. She watched the ground where she was running, trusting that he could see the rest of the yard and bunk-house where the men could be. He dropped all the keys inside a car once he found a Wrangler with four-wheel drive.

They left like thieves without anyone running down the drive after them.

"Before you get all curious again asking a ton of questions, help me watch the road. Will ya?"

He laughed when she acknowledged him with a low growl of her own. The man was so very frustrating. She waited. Not patiently. She cranked the heat up, tapped her wet shoes on the floorboard, removed her jacket and stared at the barely visible wet gravel.

If her behavior annoyed him, he didn't show it. When she glanced in his direction he had a smile on his face. A very frustrating man.

"North. Definitely not the shortest route to civilization," she stated when he turned onto the main road.

"Nope, but it's the shortest to Interstate Ten and New Mexico. Rain's letting up."

"Can I eat now? I know you can't, but I'm starving." She didn't wait for approval, glad that the pork chop was something she could hand him later to eat on his own. "Juliet was nice to make us homemade biscuits. I haven't had peppered gravy like that since high school."

"Trying to torture me with talk of food? I snuck an extra one when I grabbed the water. Got some of that gravy, too."

Frustrating. Now all she could think about was thick peppered gravy. The exact type her mother excelled at and she couldn't personally ever get right. What she wouldn't give for her mother to be here when the baby came.

No tears. Anything could be on the road now. She

needed to see and shouldn't get all emotional. *Just eat and watch.*

Living in the mountains, you got used to traveling cautiously around curves and inclines. There were enough of both to slow you to a snail's pace with even a smidgen of bad weather. Cord was a great driver and wisely braked at the right places.

A lot of time had passed, but they hadn't driven far in the rain, looking for fallen rocks and debris. Kate had been watching carefully but was scared witless when Cord brought the Jeep to a skidding halt on a desolate stretch of road.

"Should I ask what you see that I don't?"

"Backup lights around the next curve."

"Someone's waiting for us? How did they know?" She saw his raised eyebrow with the glow of the dash lights until he pushed the button cutting everything off. "This doesn't mean anything, Cord. Nick's place is the closest around. They must have been watching. No one there called Serna's men."

"Right."

It wasn't the time to tell him his I'm-a-Texas-Ranger-and-know-everything attitude didn't help their relationship. Or get a cooperative attitude. So it was up to her to just ignore it. She could do that.

"How do we get around them?"

"We can't."

"Then we turn around? Just tell me what your plan is. Good grief, Cord, you are so frustrating."

"We walk," he said, backing the Jeep to the side of the road.

"You think they've got someone waiting on the south road, too." Leaving the car was insane. How could he possibly think they'd be successful? What were the odds they could be? "You're serious that we should walk?"

"You know I am."

She did know and didn't argue. "It's going to be a tremendously hard hike. Cold, muddy…it may continue to storm, maybe snow. We have no camping or climbing gear. Shoot, we don't even have raincoats. And you want us to hike straight over a mountain—in the dark?"

"Don't forget, Serna's men will probably follow us."

"Sounds like fun," she said with as much sarcasm as she could muster.

"Glad you agree."

If they headed west, they'd be completely in the open and easily seen in daylight. So east over the mountain was the only way. In normal weather and daylight, the hike might take them several hours. Probably an entire day. Under these conditions and without the proper supplies…

"Cord?"

His hand covered hers, stretched over their child. "I know. I won't let anything happen to you, babe. Either of you. But it's our only option."

She put on her outer coat, scarf and gloves, attempting to keep as much warmth for as long as she could. She popped the door open and Cord pulled her around to face him.

"I swear it, Kathleen."

The raw promise in his eyes gave her the confidence to take the first step on a hellish journey.

Chapter 12

What the hell had he been thinking? When he watched Kate's feet slip on loose rocks, his heart paused, taking a full second to catch up with the realization that she hadn't fallen. Ten or fifteen minutes and the stress began taking its toll. He could only imagine what this hike would do to Kate. They couldn't afford to stop and discuss how the near misses were affecting her.

Near misses? This was nothing. This was a path at the bottom of the hill that was at the bottom of a steep grade to the top. To avoid the steep rock faces, they'd have to walk a couple of miles either direction.

Kate stopped and began stretching her back. "Sure wish we had a flashlight." She waved her hand at him and caught her breath. "Oh, I know we couldn't use it now. They'd be able to see it from the Burke's ranch house. But I wish we had one for later."

"Do you think I should go first?" he asked, uncertain

if it were safer to climb in front and check the path or behind her in case she fell.

She threw her gloved hands in the air. "I'm moving as fast as I can," she said, the frustration of talking to him plain in her voice.

"That's not why I asked."

"Oh. Well, I don't think there's a good—or safe—way to accomplish this, Cord."

He looked back to the Jeep as he had every two minutes. A car dome light flickered on and off. "They found the car."

"We should get moving. Any idea where we're heading? Especially without our cells?"

"We couldn't use them without being found, babe." The familiar endearment slipped out before he caught himself.

"There's nothing on the other side other than the state park and observatory."

"Then that's where we head. The observatory has satellites. People equal phones and they have a field for a helicopter to land."

"Good grief, do you know how far that is? What's wrong with hitching a ride to the highway?" She rolled her shoulders, swung her arms back and forth as if she were warming up for her workout video.

"Not safe. We don't know who's in the car—driving or holding a gun to the back of their head."

She shared a deflated long sigh. "You're right. I don't want anyone else hurt. But you know we're headed to the highest point in the mountains and there isn't *anything* between here and there. No ranches, no Ranger stations and we have no cell phones."

The heavy mist that would have eventually soaked them turned into bigger plops on their jackets. Kate got hit in the face. All she had was that old crocheted thing she'd made with her mother many years ago. When he'd "borrowed" his jeans and shirt, he should have found Kate a suitable brim to keep the rain off her.

"Better get after it then. Wait." He placed his favorite hat on top of her worn cap. She gave him a genuine smile with lots of white, straight teeth and didn't argue.

Kate set a steady, careful pace. Easy for him to follow and keep watch for men who might be following. So far there weren't any lights flashing around below. Their mud-caked boots—neither pair made for hiking—contributed to the consistent slipping, adding another layer of danger to their journey.

Within minutes they were soaked. The temperature had to be just above freezing. Cord glanced at his watch again. They'd been climbing forty-five minutes with very limited headway. Kate slowed for another short catch-her-breath minute. They'd taken several and his back was more thankful than his lungs.

"There's too much rain to locate our position," he shared. "Think we should use a compass?"

Even at the slow pace she'd maintained, Kate huffed a couple of times before answering. "At this point, using a compass is pointless. There's really only one path—even though I use that term very loosely." She put her head down to avoid the pelting rain and took another step, falling to her knee, then waving him off. "I'm okay. Better get used to it. A scraped knee will soon be the least of our worries."

She pointed to the rock face just above them. This little trek wouldn't get them over that. They'd have to climb.

God help him, but how had things come to this? *He* was the one putting his wife in harm's way now. *Ex-wife*. The shrink's voice popped into his head. *She's forever tied to me now*, his own voice replied. Family. He could think of his child and his child's mother as family.

"We can't attempt to climb in this weather. I don't think anyone's following—they probably haven't been since they didn't know which direction we'd taken off."

"And this isn't the logical choice."

"Nope." He pointed ahead. "There enough trail to make it to the bottom? Might find a bit of an overhang for protection. If we stop here, we're fairly exposed to the elements."

"I can make it, Cord. Don't worry about me." She turned and got going.

From the looks of things, they had at least another hour and a half before hitting the base. He stretched his back, swung his arms a bit slower than Kate had. The pain shot up his spine with the first step.

"I know you can make it, superwoman," he mumbled to himself. "It's me I have doubts about."

"The ranch hands were told that the McCreas left the Jeep when they were picked up by the Sheriff's department." He leaned against the post in the bunkhouse, crossing his arms, looking—if not feeling—like he was unconcerned.

The hands had gone home when the rain let up. He'd lied as a couple passed the unattended Jeep, bringing attention to the missing couple. If it hadn't been for his warning, Serna's men would have been caught standing there with their thumbs tied to their automatic weapons.

"And they bought it?" Serna asked, demanded and shouted all on one long exhale.

The idiot had arrived shortly after the hands had left. He'd be lucky if no one in the main house noticed the lights out here. If they did, he'd explain it. He always did.

"Why wouldn't they? They don't suspect anything." He relaxed his face as soon as he realized he'd been scowling. He didn't appreciate being constantly questioned. It irritated the hell out of him, and it killed him to hold his tongue.

"We should send the men out to hunt them down like animals." Serna paced the length of the room like a caged mountain cat, a disgusted look on his haggard face as he passed each of the six men trying to dry off.

Serna's boys looked like drowned Chihuahuas. It took a lot of control not to laugh at their ruined expensive shoes. He covered his mouth with a hand, determined not to make a bad situation worse by taunting their stupidity with a smile. They were in the damn mountains dressed in slacks and imported footwear.

"Waste of time right now. Your men ain't experienced and you have no idea which direction McCrea took off. Best to just use the chopper."

Serna slapped the old pine table in the middle of the room with both palms. "We don't have another pilot here till morning. You said it would take another hour to get him to the canyon and then there are repairs."

"Yep, there is that."

Serna fingered the butt of his handgun while getting close enough that the stinking, stale smell of cigarettes drifted from his heavy breathing. "Be careful of your tone, my *friend*. Have you forgotten our deal?"

Such a jackass.

He stood straight, pushing himself closer. "I haven't."

A gun was pulled to his left. A loud warning to back off. The kid Serna had chastised that morning was just new enough to think he might be making a place for himself if he pulled the trigger. Drawing a deep, silent breath through his nose, he reminded himself of his endgame. The money. Serna was just a bad card necessary for the first round. But, unlike the unknown card he might be dealt, the winning pot was within his grasp.

He just needed to hold his tongue a little while longer.

"Can you remind your boy we're on the same side? Guns make me nervous." Far from it, there was a fully loaded peashooter in his inside jacket pocket.

"You're in the wrong line of work, friend."

"Edward, go sit with Ricky." Serna waved off the kid, who retreated. Then gestured to the table. "Come, sit. We'll relax."

"Radar said snow's likely. Just a suggestion, but you might consider leaving while you can still get to that pilot of yours." He opened the door next to him.

"Always thinking. Nice." Serna's words didn't reflect the anger trapped in his eyes.

The man wants to kill me as badly as I want him out of the way.

But he left. And thanks to the storm, no one at the house heard their jacked-up cars start or leave. If they had, there would be lights and coffee. The others wouldn't hesitate to ask what was going on. There had already been too many questions about why McCrea had left without telling anyone.

Fortunately, it had been written off as part of the Ranger's overcautiousness concerning Kate.

Two days. That's all he needed. Just two days. If the weather cleared and held, he'd be free of this pompous jackass, the men with imported shoes and, most important, the distraction the McCreas were causing.

Chapter 13

"This is good, Kate," Cord called from the first level spot they'd come to since they'd run out of path.

Kate could see a slight—very slight—jutting of rocks that might block a smidgen of the rain. She got another handhold, positioned her right foot and used what was left of her biceps. Her arms shook. The rest of her body felt like deadweight as she tugged and searched with the toe of her boot for the foothold she'd spied a few minutes earlier.

"I swear, Kate, this is as far as we go tonight," he demanded, his hands resting on his waist, legs spread to support him, and his serious face tipped up. "Promise me!"

She knew he was shouting. It was the only way to be heard between the cracks of thunder. The lightning didn't worry her. During one of the flashes, she could see that the cars next to Nick's Jeep were gone. Hopefully, so were the men.

But she was cold. Wet. Exhausted. And tired of the rain pelting her face. Or Cord's. Thank goodness Cord had been below her and caught his hat when it tipped and blew off her head.

With rock under her toe, she used her very sore thigh muscles to get a little closer to their perch for the rest of the night. One more and she could...

No more up. Her right hand connected with a flat surface—okay, flat compared to what they'd been looking at over the past hour. "Almost there."

"Please be careful. Slow."

If I moved any slower I'd be a slug. "Got it."

Left hand. Bring up your first foot. And now the second. Almost.

"Kate!"

Oh, God. No!

Her bare hands skidded across wet, slick rock as she desperately used all ten nails to grip anything. Nothing. Her left boot found a larger rock, stopping the downward slide. She'd fallen at least three feet. The three scariest feet of her life.

"Stay where you are!"

She couldn't do anything else. She'd barely heard him with the blood blasting its thump-thump-thump to prove she was still alive. It would take her a minute to get her racing heart under control so she could climb. Her hands were torn to shreds and she had no idea how to get them to work. She couldn't get her eyes to open.

It seemed safer to keep her focus on the backs of her eyelids.

How are you going to do this, Miss frozen-in-place? There's a way. One hand. Let go and move one hand.

Search for the next handhold. Kathleen McCrea, you have to think of the baby. Move it!

She couldn't. If she moved an inch…if she let go… The sensation of falling took over. She had to hold on. Just stay put until it was safer.

But the hard reality was she couldn't manage to stay there much longer.

"Cord? I… I'm not sure I—"

"Shut up, Kathleen. You have to do this. We're going up."

Kate knew she moved. Cord talked her through every grip. It seemed that he watched every breath she took. And then they were at the ledge again.

"What now?" she asked, not certain it was loud enough to be heard but unable to maintain strength anywhere other than her fingers.

"Stay put. Don't move or talk or open your eyes. And especially don't argue with me."

He knew her too well.

And this once, she didn't object to being told what to do. She couldn't laugh about it. He was right. She had to concentrate on holding on. Staying put. Maybe after everything was over…

"Kathleen!"

"Yeah?"

"Give me your hand, hon."

Cord was above her, on the ledge. He had a death grip on her wrist. He pulled, and she braced her feet, helped as much as she could. He switched from her wrist and arms and tugged on her coat. Lying on her belly—halfway on the rock, halfway hanging—he grunted loudly and she shot onto the three-foot ledge.

Kate joined Cord's hat, placing her back to the wall,

covering her face with her blood-scraped hands. Breathing deeply and crying loudly.

"You're safe, Kate. The baby's safe. We're all safe. It's not your fault," Cord whispered in her ear. "Come on now, hon. Look at me."

"My fault?" She did look at him and sat. Water streamed across his concerned forehead, running down the tip of his nose. "Why do you think I'd blame myself?"

He grinned crookedly, lifting the right side of his mouth and slightly shaking his head. He tossed his hands a bit into the air, turning to join her by resting against the rocks. As uncomfortable as it was, she was tremendously grateful to be there.

"Oh, I know it's my fault. Everything usually is nowadays. *You* were the one saying it." He pulled his knees to his chest and obviously stretched his back.

"I didn't say…" Shoot, maybe while she was crying she had. It didn't matter. She was done with the pity party. "Do you think we'll be safe enough here to sleep?"

"That was the plan at the last ledge. You going to sleep this time?"

"Yes. You going to share your warmth?"

"Sure." He held up his arm and she slid into place. "I'll take my hat back unless you need it."

"No," she said, handing his hat to him and snuggling into the crook of his arm. "This is perfect."

And somehow…it was.

The sun rising over the ridges to their left woke him, but as stiff as he was, he didn't move. He was stretched on his side, Kate wedged between him and the mountain, her arm stuck under his. Her hands were gloved once again and snug inside his jacket pocket.

They'd shifted to lying next to each other once the rain stopped.

"Good morning," she said.

"Morning." He attempted to sit up.

"Not yet. I finally got halfway not cold."

"Halfway not cold?" he asked, giving in since he wasn't ready to move, either. They may be on a three-foot ledge, but they were close.

"Can't say halfway warm. I don't consider soggy and freezing as warm. But I'm not as frozen through with you blocking most of the wind."

"Good to be needed." He carefully maneuvered the ledge, shifting next to her. "You'll feel better with some food and water in you."

"I doubt that. How's your back?"

"Not bad," he lied, popping the top on a bottle of pain reliever. "Will two of these hurt the baby?"

She took them and washed them down with some water. Guess that answered his question.

"I'm sorry I pushed it last night, Cord."

"Don't apologize. Anyone could have slipped. Important thing is you caught yourself."

"I put the baby in even more danger."

"Don't go there," he warned. Not for himself, but her. He needed the confident Kate. The woman in charge. She couldn't be second-guessing herself.

"I couldn't bear it again," she whispered.

He grabbed her hand and removed the gloves, lacing their fingers together. They'd sat on a mountain before, just like this, the day he asked her to marry him. He knew better than anyone you couldn't go back. Life didn't give do-overs.

"Nothing happened. It worked out." Now wasn't the time to apologize for not protecting her three years ago.

"Oh, good grief, Cord." She took the last sip in the bottle and swallowed her last bite of energy bar. "Can we go now?"

It seemed the way to get Kate to be strong was to get her angry at him. But no matter what, she always wanted to talk. The shrink told him he needed to talk. He disagreed. He knew he'd failed her. Talking about that night wouldn't change anything. Their baby would still be gone.

"Wait."

"Why?" she asked. "Could you come over here? Just stand next to me. We don't have to face each other to talk."

She leaned against the rock face, clearly anxious that he'd been close to the edge. He moved closer, not wanting to cause her more hurt.

"You can't climb as upset as you are."

"I'm not upset, Cord. I mean, I didn't want you to fall, of course. But I'm not upset. You're right. Nothing happened. It's great. So we leave. I wish I could have dried out my socks—"

"My shrink says I need to apologize." He was glad he couldn't see her face. The look of disappointment had to be there. Three years and he wasn't fit for the field.

"You're seeing a shrink?"

"Regulations. I have to be cleared for duty."

"Oh," she said on a deflated sigh. "Why does he think you need to apologize?"

"It's complicated. I just… I just thought I should."

"I don't understand, Cord. What are you apologizing for, the divorce?"

"Why would I? I didn't want it." He crossed his arms, feeling as defensive as he sounded.

"You're right. So what's this apology your psychiatrist thinks you need to make?" She crossed her arms, waiting.

If she gave him an impatient sigh, he'd forget everything he'd thought about saying and just start climbing. He shoved his arms through the straps of the pack to secure it in place. Tilting his gaze, he saw where he'd grip the rocks for a quick escape. As soon as he forced the words out, he needed to get out of there fast. But his shrink had said no phones. For some reason there needed to be eye contact. His, mainly, something about it being more meaningful.

"Aw, hell." He spun her around to look her in the eyes. He kept his hands on her shoulders, but she didn't try to avoid his touch or squirm from his grasp. "I'm sorry I killed our baby girl, Kate. I wasn't there to protect you. I know you hate me for it. I also know you'll never be able to forgive me. I can't forgive myself. I should have told you a long time ago, but I was in the hospital and then it seemed…we… well, I guess I just never had the right words."

Back injury or no, her ex-husband Texas Ranger Cord McCrea turned on a dime, knew exactly where he would grab hold and leaped a foot up the rock wall. Kate stared at his jean-covered backside, then the bottoms of his shoes.

He'd thought she hated him because that monster Jorje Serna killed their daughter. She could never hate Cord. Never. And as soon as they stopped again, she'd set him straight.

It took her a bit longer to get started on this last section. She wasn't about to leap to the jutting rocks Cord had grabbed. She was kind of stunned by his sudden urge to finally talk to her. Okay, it was more of a statement than a talk. She got that. But it was Cord! A man who'd never spoken to her about any of that horrible night. He'd listened in silence while she told him what Serna had done. She'd purged all her fear, all of her shame at being so afraid, all her regret at not doing more…and he'd said nothing. Never acknowledged any part of it. She hadn't been certain he'd remained completely awake until his eyes opened, filled with a rage she'd never seen.

"Definitely a start," she said, with him completely out of earshot.

Even with the clear skies, lots of sunlight and no moisture to blink from her eyes, she still moved cautiously. Each move was deliberate and secure. Cord wasn't under her, but from the way he was shooting ahead he had confidence she was fine. At least she didn't feel left behind. It actually reminded her she'd been climbing rocks like this her entire life.

They didn't speak, and soon Cord disappeared over the edge, hopefully back to a trail. Her hands ached but she took time to secure each grip. A couple of minutes went by and she realized Cord hadn't stuck his head over the edge to check on her.

"Cord?" she yelled. "Cord!"

Had he just left her? Nonsense. He'd never do that.

"Kate. Over here." Cord was farther to her left than she'd been looking. But his voice was husky, like a loud whisper. As soon as they made eye contact, he put his finger across his lips.

She reached the ledge and just like the night before, Cord pulled her to the top. And each time, he indicated to remain silent. When he stood, she followed to where he'd dropped the backpack.

"Stay here," he whispered. "No arguing."

Taking off once again without informing her of the plan. What would she do if he ended up shot? She watched as he pulled the machine pistol to his chest and ducked behind a pinyon pine.

What had he seen?

Or heard. The distant whirling of a helicopter bounced around the canyons. Dread, adrenaline and fright all mixed together to put her stomach on edge. She stared in the direction of Cord then peeked over the rock she was backed against. All she saw was another rock.

Forget this. She wouldn't sit on the sidelines and get an update. They were a team. This was her fight, too. She removed her rifle from where it had been strapped to the pack. While she checked for ammo, Cord returned.

"Well?"

"They're searching, but it's the same chopper."

"How can you tell?"

He nodded toward the rifle and grinned. "Bullet holes."

"So what do we do now?"

"I figure it's going to take all day to cross the rest of this plateau and hit Highway 118. They still don't know for certain that we headed this way. May assume we've made it to one of the phones southeast and start to move the drugs."

"We have an advantage since we'll hear the helicopter long before it can see us."

"So we stay hidden from view and head toward the observatory."

"There are places that are closer than that," she pointed out.

"Yeah, but we can't see them. The white domes will

give us a line of sight, easier to hit our mark and end up in the right place."

"Easier for our eyes, but not our feet. And how much food did you happen to pack?"

"I'll be okay."

"It's not you I'm thinking about." She grabbed a water bottle from inside the pack, dripped some onto the cuts on her palms.

Watching Cord shift that machine pistol to his back was becoming too natural for her comfort. She really wanted this journey to be over and hiking all the way to McDonald Observatory—while it was their best option—just didn't appeal to her. She wanted to feel safe, but not just on this trip. The longer she was with Cord, the more she wanted him to be involved with the baby. Things were just easier with someone around to help.

Having a child was a new experience. One of those "unknown" things out there that she had no knowledge about.

"Remember the first time I took you to the observatory?" The thought popped into her head along with the hunger for salty nacho chips and artificial cheese. "We got the reservations for the night owl thing, but it was too foggy to see."

Cord knelt next to her, set his hat on the ground and took her palms in his hands. His gentle touch, cleaning the scratches, warmed more than her fingers. He was so familiar. So concerned about even a little thorn in her thumb.

"Isn't that when you were on a natural juice kick and they didn't have anything for you to drink?" he asked.

"I was never high maintenance. I remember you almost drove off a cliff on the way home."

"We were never in danger."

"We had to pull over."

He looked up and shook his head, laughing at her with his eyes. "The fog wasn't the reason we pulled over."

Oh, my. Every inch of her skin tingled. Every molecule was colliding with the one next to it, wanting to jump into Cord's arms. What a night that had been. It started in the car—no, it actually began at his house. A rushed dinner and a drip of salsa landing on her chin.

She'd never been so grateful for fog in her life.

"This one's pretty deep." He skimmed her right palm, close to her wrist. "It's clean, though. Wish I had first aid. Didn't think about it," he said, replacing his hat.

She wanted to tip that old Stetson and let it blow back to Valentine. The desire to mess up his hair while she made love to him on the top of this mountain was overpowering. She couldn't understand it. It was probably one of the most uncomfortable places they'd ever been but, somehow, she felt closer to the man kneeling in front of her.

He stood and took a swig of the water before stowing it in the pack. "You okay? Maybe you should eat an apple."

"Cord, about what you said on the ledge—"

"Forget it. Bad timing."

She couldn't let him walk away. After three years, he'd finally tried to talk. "But I *need* to say something."

He stopped but didn't face her. "Go ahead."

If she went to his side… She wanted to hold his hand or be held in his arms. She couldn't predict what would happen or prepare for it. How could she?

She was perched on a rock, on top of a mountain, being chased by the Mexican cartel and here's where he'd chosen to talk to her about their little girl. So she stayed where she was…longing to hold his hand and comfort him.

He was finally allowing more than a cover of indifference to show. He was grieving.

The man's timing absolutely stank to high heaven.

Chapter 14

Say it already!

Cord scanned the horizon. That chopper would be back. No question of if, only when. They should be looking for their best way down the other side. They needed an escape route, not a conversation. *Come on, Kate, just say it.*

He could listen to her tell him how much she hated him *and* look for a trail. Keeping his back to her, he moved to the place he'd last seen the chopper. He should have borrowed the binoculars when he'd lifted the ammo and pistol from Burke's gun cabinet.

Trying to look past her, he made the mistake of looking at her. She'd pulled her knees to her chest. No sighing. At least none that he heard. How was he supposed to know what this gesture meant?

"I'm listening, but we have to find a way down. You have to understand."

"Oh, I do." She jumped to her feet, pulled her gear on and joined him.

"I thought you had something you needed to say."

"I'm still debating if you're actually ready to hear it."

"I could quote my shrink if you want. She'd say it's—"

"It's a woman?" she interrupted.

"Yeah, why?"

"I'm just surprised, that's all." Her short inhale and momentary hold of its release told him she was more than surprised. "Go ahead. What would your doctor tell me?"

"She'd *advise* that you can't decide if someone's ready for a confrontation. You can't wait for perfect timing. Things just happen. Life happens."

Kate cocked her head curiously. "All right. No perfect timing. Lord knows, yours certainly wasn't, perched on a four-foot mountain ledge like we were."

"Go on then." He should have listened to himself. Talking was a bad idea.

"You need to believe me. I only blame one person for the death of our daughter. Jorje Serna is a murderer many times over."

"It's easy to say that, Kate. But I know you blame me."

"You blame yourself enough for the both of us, Cord!" Kate yelled. "I'm not angry because you were shot, near dead in a hospital and couldn't be there twenty-four/seven protecting me."

"He wouldn't have come after you—"

"Stop it! Just stop it!" She closed her mouth and began shaking her hands to calm down. "Listen to your own advice and stop thinking you can interpret everyone's thoughts or predict their reactions. I did not divorce you because of the shooting."

"Then why the hell did you?" The words were out

quickly, surprising her, if that look was any indication. "I can't remember how many times you said I wasn't there. Didn't you know I couldn't be."

"I knew you were a Texas Ranger when we met. You never hid your career goals. You transferred here because of me. I couldn't and still don't *want* to change you. I loved the man who wears that uniform."

"You divorced me."

"I couldn't do it anymore."

A piece of rock chipped near Kate's boot and flew into the air off the cliff.

"Back." He rushed between her and the open canyon, and they scrambled to where she'd been sitting earlier. "I didn't hear anything. You?"

"No," she whispered. "I'm sorry. We shouldn't have—"

"Shh. Listen."

Quiet.

Then a shot rang out from the distance. Followed by an immediate ricochet.

"He's less than three hundred yards and not a very good shot."

"Probably not, considering the wind," she stated, looking into the canyon between him and the rock. "Or he doesn't *want* to hit us. So do we run or do I cover you?"

"I'm not putting you through that again."

"And I'm not guaranteeing to hit anything, Cord. But I'm good enough to cover you."

"Did you see an animal trail, any logical switchback down?" He dropped his hat on the ground.

She reached for the rifle. "No, we're really limited. We can't go back. There's only forward. We climbed this thing right here because the ridge stretched east and west too far to go around."

She was right. "Forward. I just need to eliminate some speed bumps." He dropped his coat.

"You think the chopper spied us earlier and dropped these guys off?"

"Or they were searching already. One problem at a time." He stuffed Burke's 9mm in the small of his back, dropped an extra clip into his jeans pockets. Pulled the hunting knife and connected its sheath to his belt.

"So what's the plan?"

"Honestly, Kate, I don't have any plan. I'm going to do my best to find out how many are with the shooter. You stay here to make 'em think we're pinned down. Keep an eye open. Watch your back. You fire a shot for cover, then I'll move."

"What if there are more and they get too close?"

"That's why I'm leaving this." He hung the machine pistol around her neck. "Don't hesitate to just point and shoot."

"For the record, that's a plan," she said, grinning.

"If it makes you feel better to call it that."

It did make her feel better. He could see her relaxed demeanor this time round. Unlike at the canyon the day before. She'd realized he'd tricked her into staying. As he'd left her holding the horses, her eyes had been sparkling, deep bluebonnet-blue. He loved her eyes that way.

He tipped her chin up so their eyes met. Sky-blue. He loved them this color, too. "And for the record, I appreciate you talking to me, so don't think you caused us to get pinned down. *Here* is a lot better to have a face-off than being caught on the side of this mountain with no cover, nowhere to run and no options."

"I hate splitting up, Cord. What if—"

He placed his finger across her lips. "I'll hear you when you yell for me. That's a promise."

If he'd been closer, he would have kissed her. No question. He wanted to assure her he'd be back. He left, leaving her alone with a MAC-10 for protection.

Not the hardest thing he'd ever done...but close.

The only way to get behind the shooter was back the way he'd come along the cliff. Work his way unseen, hanging along the edge for a couple of hundred yards. Keeping his head down, he heard Kate's intake of breath. He couldn't look at her, so behind his back he held up the sign language for "I love you" she'd taught him early in their relationship.

He did. Love her. He'd never stopped. Not since the first moment they'd met. His first homecoming game back at UT. A chance meeting in the student section. She was with a date in the row in front of him. He was with loud former football players.

His grip slipped and he hung by the dang arm of his weak shoulder. "Dad blast it, keep your mind on what you're doing," he chided himself. He couldn't pull up. He swayed. The pressure on his shoulder threatening to dislocate increased with every movement. He recovered, reaffirmed his right grip and rested the wrenched left side.

Move it. You're losing time!

He could see the ledge where they'd spent the night. The cover he needed was in the opposite direction than they'd climbed this morning. Twenty more yards should do it. Sweat saturated his face but not because of the sun warming his head. The pain in his shoulder and back had been bad before this last climb. Now it was... He couldn't think about it.

Kate needed him. He'd lost track of the shots being

fired while he'd dangled in the air. He could still distinguish rifle shots from Kate—different than Serna's crew. Still only one returning fire, though.

That might lean things in their favor. Something going right? What were the chances?

The only way to see how far he'd come was to perform a chin-up. It was going to hurt like hell. Kate fired. He pulled eye level with the ground. Good cover. He just needed up. His muscles shook as he pulled himself to the top. His arm was mush.

There was no time to waste. He'd recover along the way. He didn't know what Kate was shooting at, but he watched the area where her bullet smacked near a gap in the rocks. Sure enough, Serna's crewman returned fire.

He hadn't been raised a huntsman. He hadn't served in the military. He didn't really have experience moving unseen from one scraggly bush to another. But he loved Kate and would get to that shooter. And he would take him out.

He ducked behind rocks, crawled on his belly and lay frozen to the ground, holding his breath as he unintentionally found the shooter's partner. The second man was crouched several feet below him. Kate was safe from the shooter, but not from the man near him.

No choice who his target was then. He'd lose his surprise advantage on the shooter if he didn't keep this quiet. He let the man pass him, silently unsheathing the blade, flipping it to use the hilt. If he could knock the man unconscious—

Rocks busted apart near his head, shards pricking the back of his hand. Serna's shooter alerted his partner, who stood and leaped at him. The only thing going in their favor was Serna's orders to bring them in alive. Otherwise, he'd have been shot several times over.

The second man trapped his arm—and knife—between their chests. He'd caught this guy by surprise with his gun still in his waistband while they'd been crawling. Cord used his longer legs to wrap around the shorter man and kept him from getting any leverage. He punched the man's head with his weak left hand. He grunted but that was about it. Useless. Another shot, very close to his head.

"Okay, okay. Don't shoot." Cord relaxed his body and released the man's legs. The man shoved up to his knees and gave a sign to the shooter. Cord raised his hands and dropped the knife to the ground near the top of his head.

The man couldn't reach the knife or his weapon without shifting his weight off Cord. When he did, Cord swept up his knife and sliced his side as they both rolled downhill a couple of feet and heard another shot.

He shoved the limp body off him. His blade hadn't killed him, but the sniper had miscalculated, hitting his partner square in the back. Cord used him as cover to get safely to an outcropping.

No radio. No ID. No cell. Nothing on this guy except a gun. He'd either dropped everything with the sniper or they hadn't been prepared to leave the chopper. Now for the sniper and to get back to Kate.

"Cord!"

She was in trouble and her cry shot him through his heart faster than any sniper bullet.

Chapter 15

Face-to-face, looking the stranger in the eyes, seeing the moment of hesitation there. The split-second thought wondering if he saw the same thing on her face flashed in her mind. It wasn't the first time either of them had looked down a gun barrel. She knew that just looking at him.

Serna's man showed his surprise when she didn't pull the trigger. But he also showed confident knowledge that she wouldn't.

One thought merged into the next. Just a split second hesitation. But long enough for the man to jump forward, knock the rifle aside and stick the barrel of his weapon straight under her chin.

That same split second she'd lived before—three years ago—blurred with this one on top of a mountain.

Serna had burst into her living room, having already

killed two police officers in front of her home. She'd been petrified and unable to move. It was so unexpected. Serna had wanted her to talk or maybe beg. When she wouldn't, he'd waved the gun around and walked toward the door. He didn't look where he fired his gun. If he had, she'd already be dead. The bullet only caught her in the shoulder, but the resulting trauma caused a miscarriage and killed her baby. She'd lost everything.

The man now shoving the hot barrel into her skin shouted in Spanish for a comrade's help. There was more gunfire. *Cord!*

What should she do? Fight and take a chance on injuring the baby? *Think logically.* But Serna is anything but logical. You've seen the craziness in his eyes and actions. So you're not dead. This guy didn't pull the trigger straightaway.

Serna wants you alive.

Then I stay alive and wait on Cord. He'll come. He always keeps his promises.

"Jorje, he tell us to bring you alive, but he say nothing 'bout *bambina*." He kicked the machine pistol away. Knocked the rifle out of reach. "Sit. Hands on head. I keep mouth shut if you not want kick to stomach. *Comprende*?"

She followed his instructions, first shoving loose stones from the site she'd occupy, then crossing her legs to use for protection if needed. She could pull them to her body and maybe stop a direct kick to the baby.

"Hands."

Reluctantly, she put them on top of her head. *Protect the baby* became the mantra in her mind. The last shot might have hit Cord, but she couldn't let the fear take control. Why hadn't he returned yet?

She would not allow herself to become distracted. She could defend herself. Baby or no, she just had to wait for the right moment.

The man tugged the backpack away from her, dumping everything. Never breaking eye contact with her, he rifled through the contents and brought objects between them so he could see what they were. For some reason, she couldn't look away and watched him toss bottled water and fruit over the edge.

Shots echoed among the hills again. Serna's man looked in the direction, the same as her, but there wasn't anything she could do. No weapon close enough, not even a rock large enough to throw. But the sound confirmed Cord was still alive.

After the rapid gunfire, minutes ticked by with nothing, just the wind gusting through the few trees and canyons. A shout in Spanish from a voice stating he was on his way. What had happened to Cord?

The man relaxed and continued his inspection of the backpack. He held up a small bag, and she recognized it as part of what had been under the floor at the lodge. He laughed, pocketed the drugs.

If she didn't have other things to worry about, she might be extremely angry over Cord concealing that he'd removed one. She kept watching, listening for signs of Cord. He might come back the same way he left, but he couldn't execute a surprise. To get to where the sniper was, he'd have to have gone the way this guy had come. So she kept watching, looking for movement of any kind.

"What are we waiting on?" she asked.

"Impatient to meet Jorje?" He laughed again, tossing aside an apple.

"No. Him."

Cord was fifty yards away, rifle to his shoulder, taking aim. The man faced him in time to aim his handgun. Both fired.

As soon as the man toppled sideways, Kate jumped to her feet and ran to Cord, never looking back.

"Sorry that took so long, babe," he said when she was steps away.

She threw herself at him. He lifted her into his arms and she dropped her head on his shoulder.

"I was so frightened. I'm getting really tired not knowing if you're alive or dead."

"I didn't mean for you—"

She didn't need any more words and cut him off with a kiss. A long, in-depth kiss that couldn't be misinterpreted. Even though she couldn't stay married to him she had to let him know how much he meant to her. While their tongues entwined, she remembered the other close calls he'd had as a Ranger. Were they all like this?

She only had the shooting for a comparison and that had all happened so fast. The hardest part had been dragging Cord into the car to get him to the hospital. He'd been deadweight, unable to use his legs. With every moan, she questioned if she should wait for help.

They'd never know if her dragging him into the car had caused the paralysis or if the bullet was completely responsible. Either way, if she hadn't moved him he would have bled out.

"What's wrong?"

"I'm sorry."

"Yeah, I know. You can't be close to me." He walked away for once. "Well, guess what, Kate? *I can't, either.*"

He's angry? He'd never been angry before.

"It's not that." She needed to explain. She hadn't

stopped because she was near him. She'd never told him that she'd been responsible for the paralysis.

"Stay there. You don't need to look at this guy," he commanded.

For once she obeyed without questioning. She knew where the bullet had struck. She'd seen the man's head whip back and closed her eyes before he fell.

"Ah, man, the bastard took my apples."

"He tossed them over the edge." She sank to the ground and drew her knees to her chest.

"You okay?"

"Yeah. Just suddenly exhausted." She crossed her arms and buried her face, blocking the view of Cord with the dead man.

She woke with a start and Cord's hand on her shoulder. No dead guy in sight. "Did I fall asleep?"

"I know, but it's time to get moving." He squatted in front of her, handing her a water bottle and energy bar. "You've had a rough couple of days. I don't blame you for dozing."

"What now?" The dead guy had been covered with his own jacket.

"Well, I'm not sure when the chopper will circle back around for these guys so we should probably get started to the observatory." Cord picked his too-big hat up from the ground and set it on top of her head.

"You think we can make it there without being seen?"

He shrugged and finished off his bar. "We stay under whatever tree cover we can find and we hope for the best."

"There are houses on this side of 118, Cord. They're closer."

"Do you know which way? Heading directly to a white

dome I can see from just about any hill around here is a sure thing, a definite direction. We'd be guessing about anything else. It might take even more time if we guess wrong and have to climb one of the hills between those valleys. Not to mention it's flatter where the ranch houses are, less cover than in the canyons."

"I agree." Whether he was seeking her opinion or not, she agreed. At least he'd explained why he'd made the choice. But he wasn't smiling. There wasn't a hint of a smile in his eyes, either.

No matter what happened once they arrived wherever they were going…in the end, Cord McCrea needed to know someone cared and loved him. He couldn't go through life like this current whitewashed version.

He stood, offered his hand and pulled her to her feet. Pack on his back, carrying the remaining water, energy bars and all the weapons, he led the way around another jut of rocks.

"Want your hat?" she asked.

"You need it worse than me. You're already burned from the sun you got yesterday."

She hadn't been. Not really. But she wasn't going to argue. She appreciated the shade. The sun was bright in the sky and they had a long walk ahead. "You can see the front coming from the northwest. Think we've got time?"

"I don't think we have a choice."

"Are you going to tell me what happened with the sniper? Or why you think the men were in the helicopter?" Did she really want to know the answers?

"None of them had survivor gear, just weapons."

"So the helicopter dropped off two guys to wait on us and just flew away?"

"Three. That's why I was late."

Three dead men. He'd fought and killed three men today. Three yesterday.

"Don't do that, Kathleen."

"What do you *think* I'm doing?"

"I know you're thinking about the men who died. But you can't think of them as men. They're drug runners and murderers. Would-be executioners delivering us to Serna." He faced her. "They're part of the gang and may have been the actual scum who put a gun to our friends' heads and pulled the trigger."

"Stop! I get it." She threw up her hands, wanting to cover her ears and block the images from her mind.

"No, you don't." He grabbed her shoulders, giving her the slightest of shakes. He pulled the pistol from the back of his waist and handed it to her. "Next time, don't hesitate—pull the damn trigger. Shoot the son of a bitch before he gets close enough for you to see what color his eyes are."

He didn't apologize and she didn't ask him to. Because she'd hesitated, they might have been captured. As much as she worried about him while he was gone, he worried about her. He'd showed her an "I love you" hand. The only word he knew in sign language.

He walked away from her, down the hill in a direct line to the observatory. They might just make it sometime today at this pace. If she could keep up and if Serna's men didn't find them. This side of the mountain was less rocky. Better for grazing. Easier to walk. She just wished it was easier to believe they'd actually make it out of this alive.

Damn, wet weather. The drugs and weapons had been tediously moved to a second location as soon as the storm had let up. Slower, without the benefit of the ATVs. Both engines had seized. His guess was dirt in the gas. And damn McCrea for figuring out it was the easiest way to completely halt the vehicles.

They'd barely moved the last of the shipment before the DEA had shown up and begun their search. He'd been gone all night and it was time to get back to work preparing for a doozy of a snow front. He cranked the heat up a notch, hoping that the McCreas didn't have the luxury.

God, he hated them. It didn't matter what their last names were. They were all from the same cloth. Men who thought they knew more than anyone else. Men who told you to suck it up and let your family sink into a mire. Holier-than-thou men who needed to be brought down several notches so they could be walked on for a while.

Yeah, he hated them.

And pretty damn soon…they'd be hating him.

Chapter 16

"All right. I give in. I don't want to do this anymore."
Kate stopped near a semiflat boulder and sat.

She'd tried to clarify herself each time they'd rested.
As soon as the words "what I meant" got past her lips,
he was gone. So she hadn't been able to explain about the
kiss. She'd had no luck getting Cord to listen.

"You need to stop again?"

"Again? I think we've walked for a couple of hours
since the last rest, but that's not what I'm talking about."
She understood the silence when they didn't know if
Serna's men were nearby. She especially understood the
need to conserve their energy while they were hiking up
and down hills without any solid path under their feet. It
took concentration that was becoming more difficult to
obtain with each tiring step.

But there hadn't been a sign of another human since

early this morning and Cord still wasn't answering her. He conveniently couldn't hear and asked her to repeat herself or he left and just never gave her the chance to finish.

"Actually, it's only been forty-five minutes," he said, passing the water to her.

"Right. Where are you going now?" That's the action she didn't understand—his running off. He wouldn't give her the opportunity to discuss anything that had happened.

"I need to look ahead."

"But you haven't eaten. You've barely had any water. And you aren't resting. You keep running up hills and coming back when I'm ready to go. You don't even drop the pack, so your back must feel horrible."

He pressed his lips together and shrugged. Shrugged and left.

Cord ran up the hill, blending into the lone tree trunk at the top. He stared in every direction for three or four minutes—or at least it felt like three or four minutes to her. Time seemed to be crawling by as they hiked to the observatory. Her protector came back from each of his uphill runs to give them a new landmark to aim for and keep them on track.

The pace he set didn't bother her. Cord's abandoning her each time she spoke did. She'd been so hopeful they were actually getting closer to discussing what had happened and why she'd gone through with the divorce. She hadn't been able to explain where her mind had wandered during the last kiss. As a result, he'd shut completely down. Withdrawn. Spoke to her only when needed.

"Everything looks clear," he said, hurrying down the hill. "We're in luck."

"Really?"

"Yeah. One of those houses you mentioned is just over that rise in the valley. Didn't see any cars or horses, but we can call for help."

"It might be one of the observatory people. I don't think there are any ranches this close to the state park."

"Doesn't matter as long as they have a phone. Let's go."

He took her hand and brought her to her feet. A gesture that would have brought her straight into his arms before the shooting. She missed the closeness, the love, the dependability. She even missed the dirty dishes and laundry and house cleaning. She held tight to his hand. He tossed a short questioning glance her way but didn't let go.

The closer they got to the house, the more apparent it became that it had been abandoned for some time. No satellite dish, no wires leading to the house. There was a windmill for an empty cistern, but it wasn't turning.

"We must be farther away from the road than I thought," she said as they crossed through an unlocked finished door into a half-finished building. Rock and wooden outside walls, a stone fireplace, a nice wood floor, some electrical wire and nothing else. The drywall sat covered in a far corner with visible dust caked on top of the tarp.

"Looks like someone began building this place and gave up on the idea a while ago."

"Shoot. That means no phone."

"No lights," he returned.

"No motorcar," she sang.

"Not a single luxury," they sang together, and laughed at the impromptu *Gilligan's Island* theme.

"Oh, that was funny." She caught her breath. "So I guess you're the thrifty professor. Can you whip us up a makeshift communication device with that portable radio?"

"And since you're Mary Ann—"

"Not Ginger?" She tried a movie-star pout, but began laughing again.

Cord grabbed her coat as she removed it and placed a hand on her stomach. "This has more of a Mary Ann feel to me. Besides, you're an awesome cook. Definitely a Mary Ann."

He shrugged out of her father's coat and glanced into the other rooms. All had doorways to the living area, but no doors. She crunched newspapers that were a couple of months old and dropped them in the fireplace.

"Food?" she asked.

"No kitchen appliances, empty cabinets."

"So do we push forward or hang out here awhile? I vote for defrosting my digits." She wiggled her fingers and rubbed her hands together. A fire would be nice since she hadn't really been warm since the car. "I don't know about you, but I'd love to dry my socks."

"I think there's enough stuff here to get a fire going. Nothing suspicious about a house sporting a fire. We can warm up a bit before we head out." He walked over to the fireplace. "And you can dry your socks after the fire warms up the room. Deal?"

"Deal. How long do you think we have? Maybe Serna has all his men tied up fighting the DEA. They should have found that cave hours ago, right?"

"We can only hope they were all at the cave and got locked up. Somehow I don't think that happened." He disappeared around a corner, came back with two bags containing camp chairs. "I think Serna and his men have had a fairly good warning system in place for years. The cave was loaded with supplies and crates. I wish I'd had time to look inside. But with that amount of supplies, I'd assume he was confident of not being found."

"Always the Ranger. Is that the reason you stashed a bag of drugs in your pack?"

Wrong thing to ask. He didn't look sheepish or sorry for not telling her he'd taken the bag. "Can you blame me for wanting to put this guy away? We were so close to shutting him down, Kate."

"But it doesn't matter. None of it matters. Can't you see that? He was in a federal prison for three years. Three years and that bag's the proof nothing slowed his operation. He's not threatened by you. And he wouldn't think twice about you right now or the Rangers or the DEA if you hadn't defended me and killed his brother."

"You asking me to walk away again?"

Answering his question would lead to another round of fighting and she just didn't have the strength. She couldn't explain about the kiss, either, and barely remembered why it was important to tell him. "Is that one a cot? Trade you."

He accepted her change of subject and unfolded the cot. "Lie down and I'll get that fire going."

"Orders. Orders. Orders. Oh, wow." Taking the pressure off her legs and back muscles was heavenly. "This is almost as good as the Burke's guest bed."

"Better than last night's ledge?"

She rolled onto her side to watch him build the fire and light it with a fireplace lighter he'd found in the kitchen. "This is sad."

"What is, babe?"

"This house is someone's dream and they had to walk away from it."

"Sort of fitting then."

"What do you mean?" She thought she knew and shouldn't have asked. She didn't want their dream to be over. She rubbed her belly, hoping he wouldn't say the words aloud.

"Sort of like us," he whispered. "Get some rest. I'm going to look around, keep watch and see 'bout some more wood." He pulled her father's old coat on across his broad shoulders and quietly shut the door behind him.

Kate didn't know if he was sad, too, but she finally cried. An exhausted, hungry weeping for everything. She closed her eyes and wanted to dream about a nice, safe world with no Jorje Serna or other horrible men chasing them over a mountain.

Cord pulled the door closed as quickly and gently as possible when he saw Kate was asleep. His stomach rumbled loudly, but there was nothing to eat. He was saving the last apple and energy bar for when she woke up. She needed them more than he did.

He threw some wood chips on the fire, got it going a bit stronger and threw on some dead branches. The place was warming nicely, but he added his jacket on top of Kate. His back screamed at him. His left hand still had sharp twinges and was tingling as if it was asleep. *Not good.*

Rest. They both needed it and there was nothing else he could do. He moved the chair and propped his feet on the low hearth. Man, it felt good to sit and just relieve the pressure on his back awhile.

It would be a nice house if it ever got finished. The

fireplace was made from stones they'd probably found clearing the land. Nothing fancy, just sturdy. So were the walls.

"Such a shame," Kate said softly. "I mean the house. Left unfinished, it's sort of lonely."

"It's got a lot of potential. Whoever built it put in a lot of time and craftsmanship." He twisted in the chair to look at her and couldn't hide the grunt of pain his back caused.

"Why don't you lie down awhile and stretch your back? It must be aching terribly. Come on, we need you to be able to move and get us out of here."

She stood and was already sighing a long exasperated one that meant she thought he wouldn't listen to her.

"I can take the floor."

"Fine. Be that way. But I'm ready to sit now and won't be using the cot."

She wouldn't. Stubborn, beautiful woman. And she was right. He did need to be able to move. Kate's hand was outstretched, ready to help him. He took it, determined to stand and drop her cool, silky skin as fast as he could.

And then she smiled.

Damn, she was beautiful.

In that instant he wanted her something fierce and didn't know if he could walk away. The need grabbed every manly part of him, including his heart. His insides shook. His breathing stopped when he saw the same hunger in her eyes.

He couldn't drop her hand. Instead, he drew her to him. He needed to kiss her and not be turned away. This time—if there was a this time—he wouldn't be pushed away. She came to him, her body pressing to him, tilting her chin slightly in the air, ready for his lips to claim hers.

"Don't kiss me if— I won't stop this time, Kate."

"I don't want you to."

He kissed her, starving for her closeness. He wrapped his arms around her back and anchored her to him. It wasn't enough.

"Not enough."

"Mmm."

A yes? He couldn't tell, but it wasn't a no. As much as he wanted her to stay warm, he wanted her out of that Tech sweatshirt. Wanted Burke out of the picture. Wanted anyone else out of the picture permanently. He grabbed the edges and broke their kiss long enough to pull it over her head and throw it to the far side of the room.

Her work shirt was there and then gone along with his own. She'd seen the scars and hadn't turned away. She touched the entry wound and slowly moved her hands to either side of his neck and rough, whiskered cheeks.

Her fingers then pushed through his hair, pulling his mouth back to hers. Long, excited kisses, her teeth nipping at his bottom lip, drinking in her taste, needing more. Always wanting more.

Her fingertips circled the nipples on his chest, hardened from the cold or stimulation, he didn't care. He just didn't want it to stop. Any of it. But he needed more.

Needed her.

Her hands dropped to his belt. If she got her way, this would be over way too quickly. He tugged her thermals up and off and immediately went for her pants. He slid his hands inside the waistband, easy to do with the snap already popped for her belly's comfort. She'd already kicked off her boots when she lay down, and he used his foot to push the pants to the floor for her to step out of.

It was a dance they'd done before. He'd seen her beautifully naked in front of him hundreds of times. But never like this. Her breasts were swollen, spilling over the lace of her bra. He brushed the back of his hands across the dark pink of a nipple, watched it pucker under his touch, watched her body shiver with delight.

The overlarge coat she constantly wore, and even the granny nightshirt from the day before, hid the gentle swell of their child. Without her clothes, the baby bump was just as real as the kick.

Backlit by the glowing fire, he twisted his hand in her hair, bringing her back to his mouth. He splayed his free hand across her belly hoping to feel the baby move again.

Everything about Kate made him want her more. How was that possible? How had he stayed away from her all this time? She was so much a part of him, he didn't know how he functioned without her near.

That was the thing…he'd only been sleepwalking through life without her. But being near him was dangerous—for her and the baby. He stilled his hands, wondering if making love to Kate was the right thing to do.

"Don't you dare change your mind, Cord McCrea." She tugged on his chin until he looked in her eyes. "I'm so hot for you at this very minute, I'm about to explode."

No mind reading necessary. She just knew him and could read his body language before it caught up with what he was thinking. She reached behind her back, and her bra fell to the floor.

"Well?" she asked.

Did she really expect him to put words to how he felt? He couldn't talk so he showed her by kissing as much of her pale skin as he could. She quivered in his arms as he laid her on the cot. He had to sit in the chair to get his shoes off. She laughed at him the entire frustrating time. The larger borrowed jeans were easily kicked to the floor as he stood and stopped just short of jumping on top of her.

"You're so beautiful, Kate."

"But will you still think so four months from now?" She smiled, teasing him with an image of her at full term.

"I can't think of anything prettier." Her skin had cooled and he lay on top of her to warm her back up. "You're sure about this? I know what our bodies want, babe, but—"

"Shh. No thinking. No rationalizing. Just love me."

I do and always will.

Chapter 17

Kate did nothing but feel. She'd wanted to be with Cord since the moment she'd seen him at the fencerow. For the moment, it didn't matter what was happening in the world that threatened them. There was just his naked body on top of hers. Just his strong hands skimming her sensitive skin, rediscovering the new curves she'd developed.

"I could get used to these," he said as he cupped the additional size of her breasts.

She didn't want to think about the future, that making love to him might be for the last time. Even when they'd conceived the baby, she hadn't believed it would be the final time. They still loved each other, didn't they? Love had never been their problem.

Serna was the problem and Cord was right. The madman would never stop until she was dead. He wanted to punish Cord by hurting her.

Stop it. Don't think. Just feel.

Cord's fingertips explored, stimulated and gave her courage to caress his skin. Even when she skimmed over his scars, he jumped slightly but didn't pull away.

"Does it still hurt?" She circled the bullet scar, more worried about the new bruises beginning to show on his ribs.

"They tell me it doesn't."

"But?"

"Don't worry about it."

He sealed his lips against hers, successfully stopping any words she might have said. Successfully stopping any thoughts except how much she loved being in his arms. And how much she wanted him inside her.

She shifted, moving him more into the V of her legs. His hand drifted between them, driving her to a crazy explosion. "Cord!"

She didn't need to say more. He captured her mouth again and joined their bodies at the same time. She was just as much a part of him as he was her. She knew it. Saw the connection in his eyes. Wanted to keep it forever. They climaxed together.

"I love doing that to you," she said, grabbing his biceps and attempting to get him to relax a moment. "Stay."

"I don't think so. I might pass out. We shouldn't have—"

"Please don't tell me how it was wrong. I don't have any regrets about what we did. You shouldn't, either."

He jumped up and draped her coat on top of her. He pulled his boxers and jeans on in one fell swoop. Then he was sitting and lacing up those Ranger-code shoes. "Get dressed before you fall asleep, babe." He shoved his arms into his coat and strode to the door. "I need to look around before we head out. It might be a while."

Kate's heart was still pushing the blood through her veins double time. She could feel the beating in her throat. She'd hardly caught her breath before Cord was out the door with her staring after.

She got dressed and took the time to braid her hair to keep it out of her way. She placed more wood on the fire, moved the cot a bit closer and lay back down. It seemed that she'd just closed her eyes when Cord gently shook her shoulder to wake her, but it was definitely colder and darker in the room.

"You ready?" he asked.

"There's snow on your jacket." She grabbed his bare hands he held near the fire, immediately warming them between her own. "You're like ice."

"I found the road. We should be able to make it to the observatory by seven or eight." He gently removed his hands from hers in order to rotate his body in front of the dying fire.

"What's going on?" She stood, shoving the cot backward with the force.

"Nothing. I'm just trying to get us out of here. We can't stay with no food or water. The only choice is to brave the storm for two, maybe three hours tops."

"Is that why you left in such a hurry?"

"Babe—" He stopped himself, probably because of the look on her face at his endearment. "It was irresponsible of me to make love to you here. I don't know where Serna's men are and you are far from safe."

"Bull hockey. You ran out that door and away from me. Were you trying to pay me back for leaving you like I did five months ago?"

"What?"

Protecting Their Child

"How are we ever going to move past any of that if we keep—"

"There is no moving past anything, Kate. Get used to the idea. Lord knows I had to." He slammed his hat back on his head and slammed the door behind him.

She smothered the remaining fire, slid the chairs back into their bags and returned them to the counter.

She gave the living room a longing look when the blast of cold air hit her face. She secured the door and searched for Cord while wrapping her scarf around her face for a bit of protection. She also pulled on her work gloves over the smaller knit gloves that had been sufficient earlier.

"It wasn't so cold when the sun was shining. Guess the front they've been talking about finally hit in full force," she said.

"Guess so." He removed his hat and shoved it on top of her knit cap.

She wasn't going to argue with him. It wouldn't do any good and he'd just run up a hill or something again.

"We're using the road?" she asked like an idiot after the third or fourth step toward the two rain-filled tire treks the owner hadn't used in quite some time.

"It's an easier hike unless you think we should climb the two or three hills between here and 118."

"If you're certain it's safe."

"We're out in the open either way."

"Then we better get started."

One foot in front of the other. One step at a time. They made it to the main road in less than an hour. Pretty good time for two exhausted and starving souls. It was too difficult to actually hold a conversation, but it wasn't difficult to think about what she'd like to say.

Even if they'd wanted to hitchhike, no one was out

greeting this hard-blowing storm front. But just in case Serna's men were driving the area, they chose a safe place to cross to the north side of 118.

"I can almost taste the cheesy nachos at their snack bar," she whispered on the other side.

"You can't stand those things."

"That was before." She patted the baby. "Really. I can practically smell them. And if I don't get them, I'm going to be whining a long time."

"You don't whine, either."

"Yes, I do. A lot."

That got her a relaxed smile and a soft knock on the brim of his hat.

They stayed close to the road, not having much choice since the terrain was steep and difficult. They hadn't seen a soul since the shoot-out this morning. Chances were that Serna was completely out of the area, since the DEA had planned to raid the lodge.

"I hear a car. Let's get off the road. Now."

They took cover about twenty yards uphill by diving behind several juniper trees on the downhill slope. She bent down and he covered her with an arm, keeping her face toward the ground.

She didn't see anything, just heard a car pass above their heads. "It didn't slow down. Sure wish we could get a ride the rest of the way."

They stood, brushing the snow and slush from their pants.

"Fifteen minutes and those nachos are all yours," Cord said, helping her step onto the road.

"I'd give them up in a heartbeat just to have a heater gusting hot air onto my toes. What's the plan? Who will you call to pick us up?"

"I was hoping to call in a favor, but this snow is making any plan impossible."

"As long as we get some food first. Nachos, a hamburger, maybe some french fries—oh, wow, I really want fries now and a great big cup of hot chocolate."

"What's with you and the junk food? Wait—do you hear that?"

"It's just another car. It might even be the same one if the observatory's closed."

"Too soon." He waved at her to get back to the juniper. "It's the same one, I recognize the muffler."

She slid downhill on her bottom, the cold slush seeping through her jeans. This time, Cord stayed closer to the road, gun drawn as the car zoomed downhill toward them.

"Stay there," he shouted.

"No way."

"Come on, Kate. Listen to me and stay there."

The car was upon them and she couldn't shimmy up that slope on her own anyway. So she stayed wedged between two tree trunks to keep herself from slipping farther down the incline. The snow had combined with the earlier rain and the ground was just slick mush. But stuck where she was, she couldn't see a darn thing.

A weapon discharged and she instinctively ducked. Then another. Rapid fire from another point, single shots from above her. "Cord!"

"We've gotta run for the observatory."

"Right." She tugged on her boot, now stuck inches off the ground. "Dear Lord, help me."

"Can you find a route up?" He sounded anxious, worried.

She couldn't bring herself to distract him by saying

she was stuck. *Calm down, look at it and get this done.* She removed her right foot, twisted a bit and dug her boot heel into the mud. The gunfire was less frequent but she still jerked at every discharge. With her weight on her free foot, she pushed at the small tree trunk until she could pull free, careful not to slip the other ten feet to the bottom of the gully.

"Kathleen?"

She looked up the slope. It was impossible without him pulling her like before. Maybe on a different day she could have, but now she just didn't have the strength to do it herself after walking the past three hours.

"I can't—"

The gunfire was closer. She swung herself around the juniper to see if there was another way up. The quickest way to safety was on the road. They were minutes away from the twenty-four-hour staff at the observatory. If they had to climb…even the idea of having to climb more, especially alone. She just felt defeated.

Cord slid down the hill, reaching out to catch the trees with his good arm. "Start running, woman! Let's get out of here before they notice I'm gone."

"Down?"

"Looks like the only way." He took the lead and she fell in close behind.

They hit the narrow but basically level gully. Knee-deep in water they ran, keeping the road to their right. It might have been the hardest part of the entire past three days. Her knees burned. Her overworked thigh muscles were screaming at her for rest. Her throat was so dry she wanted to catch snowflakes for moisture.

Cord held up his hand for her to stop. She bent forward, resting on those worn-out knees while he shimmied up the embankment, took a quick look and then returned. Where did he pull that energy from?

"It looks like," he whispered, his frosty breath coming in spurts as he rested, "we're about two hundred yards from the entrance."

"Then it's another quarter mile to find a human at this time of night."

"Remember those drainage pipes under the main road to the parking lot?"

"Where I just had to have our picture taken in front of the century plant?"

"Right. You can stay there while I find help."

"Normally, I'd argue with you, but my legs are like Jell-O and I wouldn't be able to keep up. So we go about four hundred yards, climb up, cross the road, use the trees for cover until the parking lot. Then we just hope no one sees us run another hundred yards to drainage pipes we hope have already drained."

"Sounds like a plan."

She laughed, caught herself, clapping a gloved hand over her mouth and watched Cord smile in spite of their dire situation. She put her hands on either side of his face and pulled his lips to hers.

"Let's go," she said quickly. "I've waited years to lie in a slush-filled drainage pipe."

Chapter 18

"You are one smart man," Serna told him, slapping him on the shoulder and tucking his phone in his pants pocket.

He hated the slap. And hated the fake camaraderie he tolerated from Serna. He wasn't like these men. He had really begun hating the so-called man walking around the empty bunkhouse. He wished he could get rid of him, but he was an important part of the Danver downfall. A downfall that would only happen if the idiot's people could catch Kate and Cord.

"Since your boys haven't checked in, they probably went head-to-head with McCrea." He leaned against his favorite post near the door. "I told you the only place those two could be headed was toward the observatory. They're smart."

Serna appeared to be high again. Pacing the room, stumbling over his own toes. "How long will it take to get there?"

"From here?" He rubbed his chin, contemplating. "The roads are going to be slick. On a normal day it might be a couple of hours. With the snowfall? Add another hour or so."

"I can't wait that long," Serna hissed through a broken tooth he'd received in prison. "Take me to the chopper."

"You're going to fly? Visibility is almost nil and the DEA is all over our asses."

Serna pulled his gun quickly for a man with such shaky hands. "Go for it, *amigo.* It saves me a lot of trouble later, I'm thinking."

His own gun was still behind his back and not a risk he wanted to take at the moment. "I can drive you to the chopper. No one will miss me."

"No. They won't." Serna dialed, talking in Spanish, most likely to his pilot.

Maybe they'd crash into a mountain.

It took a few minutes before the men in the white car stopped shooting. Cord could hear them driving back and forth along the road. "The bastards are too lazy to look for us down here."

"And I'm very grateful they are," Kate said, breathing hard and resting by leaning on her knees. "I'm *so* tired."

"How are your socks?" he teased. They were both soaked again, making their legs weigh a ton, making the walk through the water runoff even more difficult.

"Wet." She smiled and started picking her way through the brush. "Come on, Ranger Boy."

"That's my girl," he muttered to himself. Kate never gave up.

He knew she was exhausted. Heck, he could barely move. Even though they were wet, starving, aching and ready to sleep for a week, she didn't complain, didn't whine and just kept pushing forward. Those nachos—processed cheese and all—were looking pretty darn good to him, too.

The ravine followed the direction of the road fairly closely and they'd completed another turn. It should be the last before it straightened out and they could head straight for the parking lot.

Time to check things out. He stopped and watched Kate bend forward, stretching her back. He knew that sign of pain all too well. He pulled her within his arms, massaging her lower back muscles through her coat.

"I think it's been a bit longer than fifteen minutes."

"I haven't heard the car in a while and need to check our bearings. I need you to wait here," he whispered. "Take the pistol. I'll call like a dove when I come back. Shoot anything else that moves."

She nodded and he let her go. He saw a dead log and helped Kate climb halfway up the hill. She took the gun and he left. He didn't like leaving her alone. She was shivering and they needed shelter, so he couldn't delay. Down to their last option. No food, more snow and just plain exhaustion were almost worse enemies than Serna.

The men in the car were parked at the entrance and waiting on the warm hood. They all seemed underdressed and ill prepared for the cold weather. A note for the investigator in him. These men had come from a warmer climate and hadn't planned on staying long. Perhaps chasing him hadn't been in their plans, either. More important, why had two men apparently so unfamiliar with the terrain been waiting for them on the observatory road?

If Kate weren't with him, it would be the first question he'd ask after he took them into custody. Someone local was helping them. Burke? Juan? It had to be a local rancher who knew about the lodge. Someone who knew the Danvers weren't utilizing that section of their land. He knew Juan, and the more he'd thought about it, he just didn't have the spending habits of someone trafficking drugs. So what was really going on?

He stored the information for later. His first priority was getting Kate and the baby to safety. Then he'd come back and seek the answers to his questions. He followed the path to his ex-wife—a status that was getting harder and harder to remember—and whistled like a dove. He didn't need to be shot again.

She kept the gun pointing in his direction, looking past him to verify he was alone. *Yep, that's my girl.* "Getting around the bozos checking their cell phones won't be all that difficult."

"But?"

"But I couldn't see any cars in the parking lot. Activities have probably been canceled due to the weather," he answered, and sat on the log next to her.

"It's probably a skeleton crew here tonight and there are a lot of telescopes farther up the mountain," she finished on a long sigh.

"Right."

"So I hide."

"Take my coat." He pulled off her father's coat and pushed it in her hands.

"It's snowing again."

"I'll run faster and work up a sweat. Don't worry about me being warm. You two are the ones who will be stuck in a wet drainage pipe."

Her hands went protectively over the baby. He helped

get her father's coat on over her own, tucked some stray blond wisps inside her cap and wrapped her in his arms.

"We can do this, right?" Her voice sounded small and uncertain, and a tear fell from the corner of her eye.

It hurt to see her cry. "No doubts."

But he did have doubts. The McDonald Observatory had worked hard to keep the man-made light to a minimum for the telescopes. With no moon there was no way to see where a car might be. He had to physically check out all the parking lots until he found a person on duty.

They stood and his back protested with a stab of pain. He wanted to cry out with each step. He bit his lip—hard—to keep his mouth from admitting something was wrong. Kate couldn't know.

Running. Lord give him strength.

He led the way uphill and around the buffoons still sitting on the car hood, waiting. Not the brightest bulbs in the pack. He and Kate had just hiked country that included a mountain range, and successfully avoided these nimrods by walking through the rain runoff. They entered the facility on the south side. No cars in the lot. No cover to protect them.

"How long do you think they'll sit there waiting for us to stroll up the drive?"

"Head that way." She pointed east. "There's an eight-foot brick wall by the visitor center that will hide us if they drive into the parking lot. Or we can head around back."

"That's not toward your hiding place."

"I've got a deal for you, Ranger." She darted in front of him, clearly with a second wind, heading to the back of the visitor center.

"And I've got a bad feeling about this."

Cord followed. They were behind the wall. Kate led him directly to an employee entrance door. A glass door.

He pulled on the door. Locked. Just as he suspected.

"Oh, for goodness' sake, Cord. Stop thinking like a law-abiding citizen." She flipped him around and took the rifle from its spot on the side of the pack. "Step back."

She waited for him and used the butt of the rifle against the glass.

"What are you doing?"

"Going inside."

"They'll hear the alarms."

"Yes, everyone will, including the staff."

Kathleen Danver McCrea would always be smarter than him.

"Ah, got it. Everyone hears and I don't have to waste time running all over the mountain looking for nachos—or a phone."

Cord made her laugh. Now. Freezing, stranded in the snow, starving, men trying to kill them, and Cord made her laugh. And the thought of those nachos just made her want them all the more.

"Okay. Let's get this door open so you don't have to run all over the mountain looking for food." She swung back to hit the door again and he raised his hand to stop her.

"Wait. Let's think about what's going to happen."

"You want to make a plan?" she asked, excited that he'd made more than one with her over the past several days.

"I know, I know. Don't fall over. Our plans seem to be working out. I just think this is one of those times we need to walk through all the possibilities." He walked to the end of the wall.

"I agree. Can you see them?"

"No. Serna's men will get here before the staff. Stay inside until the sheriff gets here. Then call Paul Maddox and ask for an immediate evac."

"Got it. What will you be doing?"

"Getting rid of Serna's men. If I can get above them, I should be able to keep them out of the building. But if they get past me, we need to check the other entrances and see if this is the best to defend. We'll also have to deal with any staff who come down to check out the alarm."

"We'll need to make certain they can't be used as hostages. You'll need your coat back." She lifted her arm, indicating for him to tug the sleeve.

"Keep it for now. Keeping them from grabbing hostages means taking Serna's men out first."

"Cord?"

"Hmm?" He led the way around the building.

"Both of those men were checking their cell phones. Do you think they've already told Serna where we are?"

He didn't need to answer. The look on his face said it all. "We can do this, Kate."

"So he's on his way then. You can't be certain. They may try to take us to him."

"Either way, this ends tonight. The two idiots who expect us to cross the street in front of them seem to be waiting on reinforcements."

"We can't endanger anyone working here." She grabbed his upper arm and spun toward him. "And if we break into this building we'll be doing just that."

"I'll have an advantage from the roof that I can't get anywhere else. I could catch these guys while they're still in their car. We can barricade the door and wait on reinforcements."

"And if you can't eliminate all your targets? What then? Can you guarantee they won't grab the staff who will show up when the alarm sounds? What if they're caught in the crossfire?"

"So we're back to the original plan. You hide. I find the staff and get a phone."

"Or we work together to take out those two men and use their car to find help."

"That's too risky."

"We can do this, Cord. It's the best solution. The only way we can control what those men do is to take them out of the equation." She saw in his eyes that he was weighing the possible outcomes. "We work well together. We always have."

And it wasn't hard to recognize that he'd included her in the decision-making process. A first. He'd listened.

"Same as before. You stay back. Cover me with the rifle."

"If we're lucky, they're still waiting."

If there was one thing Cord could count on it was not being lucky. Luck hadn't really been on their side for the past three years.

They made the decision to take the two men out quietly at the main road, but as they began to move, the car circled through the parking lot with its lights off. They heard the muffler and ran back to the brick wall to find where they were stopping.

"They're patrolling? Why?" he asked.

"Maybe we should just hide? Together. It will take Serna a couple of hours to get here. We could make it back to the tree line and—"

Cord took her by the shoulders and shook his head. "You're forgetting he has access to a chopper. Our friends are probably driving around. They want to look busy because he's almost here."

"Then we definitely need to find the staff and call—"

"It's too late. We're it. Hear that?" He pointed to the sky. "Not thunder. It's a chopper."

He paced. Three steps away from her and three steps back. All the while shoving the snow off his head, tugging at his short hair. Worried. And if she didn't know him so well, she probably wouldn't have seen the fright in his eyes he was attempting to hide.

"Which plan do you want to go with?" she asked, reaching out and grabbing his hand. The strength she needed flowed into her even through their gloved fingers.

"We head back to the woods. Circle around and take the car when they're not looking."

"Sounds good. Just wish it included a good steak and cheesy potatoes."

"That kid must love cheese," he teased.

"Naw, this is all me. You know I'm a meat-and-potatoes gal."

"I've seen you eat your fair share of crab legs."

"Oh, my gosh, those were good crab legs," she whispered, gaining a crooked smile from her ex-husband.

They waited for the car to head to the north side of the facility before they ran. Blending into the trees toward the south, the sounds of the helicopter grew louder.

"We need to warn the staff."

"I'll do my best, Kate, but I haven't got many options." His low, soft voice shook through her as he checked the weapons and palmed the remaining bullets for his pistol.

He was right. They were low on ammo and if it came down to a fistfight, Cord was injured and exhausted.

His upper-body strength was amazing, but in his current state, she just didn't know how long he'd last.

"You need to go Rambo on these guys."

"What do you mean?"

"Cull them from the herd and take 'em out one by one."

"This isn't a movie, babe. I can be prosecuted for something like that."

She could see the possibilities crowding his brain. Normally she'd think he was cute raising one corner of his mouth and barely shaking off a bad idea, then processing another. Today she was glad he was considering it. Not stating aloud how he planned to eliminate the men determined to kill them was just fine with her. He handed her the rifle again.

The chopper topped the trees over their heads. The wind stirred the snow in a circular pattern; the running lights gave the white flakes an eerie glow as they swirled faster for a few seconds. Fortunately, the evergreens they were standing under protected their location, but they were out of time.

"Don't, Cord. I know that look." She already knew he would go back and make a stand alone. There was nothing she could do to stop him. His mind was set on one plan of action.

"It's the only way." He handed her the pack to hold while he took all the ammunition. "And don't double back and try to help me."

"It's better when we're together."

He raised his eyebrows, clearly thinking of their time together that morning. Then his lips flattened, all serious. "Don't be afraid, babe."

She was terrified. How could she be anything but? "What do you want me to do?"

"You'll be hidden in the trees all the way up the south side to the telescope. It's a longer haul. Steeper, harder, so take your time."

"Won't the observatory people come to see who's in the helicopter landing on their lawn? Take your coat back and don't argue. You need it."

"I'll do my best to keep them safe." He tugged the sleeves off and slipped back into her father's coat.

"If they're here, then why in the world are you sending me up the hill to fetch them?"

"My turn to fight." He pulled the collar up on her coat and tucked the scarf inside. Once again, he squashed his huge Stetson on top of her head. "No matter what you hear going on, Kate, I can't do what I need to do if you come back. I need you safe."

She kissed him. Or he kissed her. It didn't matter. None of their problems mattered. It would be a miracle if they got out of this alive. So she kissed him again. Long and hard, then soft and sweet.

"I'm sorry I went through with the divorce, Cord. I should have stood by you."

"Come on now, Kate. There's nothing in our song about failure. I got this covered." He gave her cheek a sweet caress and left his footprints in the freshly fallen snow as he returned to face their demons.

Chapter 19

"Ranger McCrea. Let's get this over with. No reason to hide longer. I know you are here."

Jorje Serna.

So the drug-running bastard had come himself. If they were in the same chopper that had been at the cave, that meant an additional two men, the pilot and the two already here. Six against one.

Really bad odds.

Cord listened to Serna taunt him through a bullhorn or something like it. He couldn't see the chopper from his position, but from what he could hear he assumed they'd landed in the open field or lot just east of the visitor center.

"You are surprised to see me here, I think? Your friends, they were too late and did not find a thing. I have friends of my own. Just think, all this trouble could have been avoided if you had played along like your partner."

Sad, old ploy trying to get him to give away his position by shouting back a reply. Serna wanted him dead as much as he wanted Serna *taken care of.* He might be tired, but he'd never believe Shane was on Serna's payroll. *Now, how do I take this scum down without getting killed in the process?*

He'd made it to the parking lot without being seen. Thing was, he had no clue where Serna's men were. The snow wasn't his friend making his tracks visible on a moonless night. Serna must want him bad to force a pilot to risk flying in this soup. The snow was falling steady and might even ground that chopper for a while.

Excellent for him. Not good for Serna. Serna's pilot would be antsy to take off. Hanging around to kill Cord wouldn't be worth leaving that chopper for law enforcement to confiscate. Being in a hurry might cause mistakes, work to Cord's advantage.

"Are you waiting for a rescue? No one will come," Serna continued to taunt. "Your efforts are useless. Just give up and save us trouble."

Serna was attempting to distract him. Hard to do when he didn't have any plan to be distracted from. *Think!*

He wanted to walk up to Serna, defend himself and have it all done. If he really thought that would save Kate and their baby, he'd be willing to do it in a heartbeat. But Serna wasn't an honorable man. His vendetta was to make Cord suffer and the only way was to hurt Kate.

Don't think about her. Idiot. She's fine. She. Will. Stay. Safe.

You need to go Rambo on these guys. Cull them from the herd and take 'em out one by one. He heard her voice in his head. That concept was actually his only option. Separate. Disarm. Take them out one at a time.

Two minutes and he hadn't seen anyone near the car or on this side of the visitor center. It was worth checking out. His hot-wiring skills were rusty, but might be worth the effort. If not, he'd take the car out of commission, forcing Serna to leave in the chopper. And in this weather, that didn't give them a helluva lot of time.

No one was watching the car. He kept low, approached from the trees and lifted the handle. The door opened and he slid onto the seat. He popped the casing with his knife, dug for the wires and felt cold steel at his throat.

"You the bastard that shot me?" a shaky voice asked from behind him.

There had been three men in the car? Damn. "Is that a rhetorical question?"

"Hand me the knife and then the gun. You're lucky Jorje wants to kill you himself or I take pleasure slicing your throat."

"Yeah, real lucky." He flipped the knife around and, quicker than planning what to do, he plunged it into the fleshy part of the man's arm. Once. Then twice.

The threatening blade at his neck dropped onto his lap as the howl of pain from the backseat grew loud enough to wake the mountain.

It was amazing how fast a tired, pregnant woman could climb another hill—even in a light snow—when her family was threatened. Kate ignored the soreness and shortness of breath. The air cooled her cheeks as she jogged to one of the highest peaks in the mountain range.

God, please let me get inside and call for help. And please keep Cord safe.

He's got to be safe. She heard Serna's voice echoing through the hills. As long as he was shouting for Cord to come out of the woods…she could only assume the madman didn't have him. Right?

If she could only go to the road and see if someone on duty had heard the helicopter or Serna's constant drivel. Warn them. Keep them from driving into Serna's thugs. Hopefully, whoever was in the observatory had already called the sheriff. Hopefully.

Her thighs on fire, she ached to stop with each step upward. She stepped on the high side of a small tree, put her hands on her knees and used the trunk to keep herself from falling backward. Wedging the butt of the rifle next to her for easy access, she wrapped the scarf tighter around her neck and covered her mouth, breathing the warmer air to keep her lungs from hurting as much.

A little flutter in her belly made her catch her breath. The baby moved. It gave her strength for the rest of the climb to the telescope. A powerful reminder to keep moving as fast as she could. Serna's yelling ceased and she stopped. She heard a light crunching of the snow. It could possibly be an animal scavenging for food. More likely, it was a two-legged animal hunting for her and Cord.

She stayed calm and brought the rifle to her hip. She couldn't see anything. Cloud cover and no moon equaled little visibility. What she had was blocked by the trees and darker patches next to them. She slowly raised the rifle to her shoulder. Ready.

Don't move. Steady. Aim. Don't hesitate. Cord can't rescue you this time.

Three or four trees over, she saw a puff of frosty breath. Then another. She waited. What was he waiting for? They wanted her alive!

Partner!

She turned just in time to see a body leap at her from

her left. She pulled the trigger. The man stopped, his hands covering the wound in his stomach. In that split second she looked into his surprised eyes and saw the worry that his life was over.

Oh, my God!

She wanted to drop the rifle and help him. Didn't want him to die no matter what he'd done. Then that second was gone and she turned back around. The second man was running at her. Twenty feet. Fifteen. Ten.

The crazy-wild screams and curses let her know without a doubt that he had no intention of taking her back to Serna. The knife raised high in the air would slice through her and the baby with little effort.

She didn't have enough time to raise the rifle. She swung the barrel in front of her and fired from her hip. The man took another step forward, pulling the knife back to his shoulder, ready to plunge into her when he was close enough.

Five feet.

She pulled the trigger.

The reverb from a second rifle shot echoed and faded, causing Cord to jerk as if he'd been the one hit. He couldn't let not knowing what had happened to Kate stop him or even slow him down. He couldn't allow himself to dwell on it.

After a couple of minutes of fighting, one whack with the back of his head had dazed the young kid long enough for Cord to completely subdue him. There were zip-tie handcuffs in the backseat—most likely to be used when they caught him. Now they were around the gang member, securing hands and feet to the floorboard seat frame.

"Ya gotsta help me, man. I bleed to death. You cut me bad."

"The gashes are deep, but I wrapped your jacket around the wound. If you don't move around, the bleeding will stop." He hoped. "So answer my question. Where did Serna move the drugs?"

"I don't know. I don't know."

"Then you're rather useless, aren't you?" He searched over his shoulder again, watching to see if this guy's partners were returning. He hated to do it, but he sliced and yanked electrical wiring under the dash to disable the car. Serna and his men couldn't use it to escape, but neither could he nor Kate. Then he noticed what sat in the passenger seat, another fully loaded machine pistol. Thank God something was going right.

He had to find out what was going on. Serna had stopped jabbering. Two separate shots had been fired farther up the hill. Probably Kate since the gang members had been packing the automatics. A weapon he was now thankful to have in his hands. He closed the door, swung the strap of the pistol over his shoulder and ran to the north end of the parking lot. His only cover was the drainage ditch under the road where he'd intended for Kate to hide.

He ducked inside and crawled.

Swiping the frustrating tears that wouldn't stop, Kate had to admit that no one was inside working this particular telescope. The dome structure wasn't very large, but she'd walked around the entire thing twice, pounding on the outside with a rock.

She was so exhausted she couldn't imagine a level of tiredness above this. All she could think was that Cord was facing Serna alone and she couldn't do anything to help. There was no way to break inside. No car to borrow. She leaned against the door and slid to the ground. If she didn't stop crying soon, she'd end up with the hiccups.

"Idiot!" She'd come to the large telescope, but why would anyone be here on a night with so much cloud cover? Dormitories. "Where? Where? Where? There!"

She followed the path leading past a small brick building. Lights. She ran down the steps to the road. *Please, please, please be there.*

The slush seeped through his jeans and coat sleeves. Cord glanced at his watch as he crawled through the remainder of the pipe. It had only been twenty-two minutes. Just went to show how much could happen in a short time. He listened.

Nothing. Still no chatter from Serna.

Engines he hadn't noticed before. Chopper starting back up? No, a car. But who? Too soon for the sheriff. Staffers. Had to be the staff checking out who had landed on their lawn. Took them long enough.

He ducked behind some tall grassy plant and searched for the remainder of Serna's men. Movement caught his eye. One of the men was playing sentry on the roof of the visitor center.

If he hadn't been cold before the wet had soaked through his clothes, the wind hitting him did it big-time. He waited until the man disappeared, then he stayed low and used the plants to block him from view. There was an opening at the bottom of the brick wall, and he crawled through. The headlights were closer, almost to the field. And plain as you please, two of Serna's men were waving their arms to get the car's occupants to see them.

Hostages.

What could he do? The sentry would take him out. He had no cover on either side of the brick wall. No buildings. No trees. Nothing. The car headed directly at the two men. All the driver would see was straps across their chests. The guns were hidden behind them and could easily be pulled forward.

"Damn."

Serna would use them to coax him out in the open by threatening to kill the driver. Even if the murderer didn't shoot him dead on the spot, he wouldn't need a hostage any longer and would kill them. Either way, the observatory staff would be dead.

The only choice left to him was to go out with a fight and take Serna with him.

Chapter 20

The headlights went off just before the curve at the top of the hill. The car stopped out of gun range, out of sight of the men standing in the field. Kate! She must be trying to come to his rescue and he couldn't allow that.

Very little cover in the open field. The only thing between him and that sentry/sniper was an evergreen at the corner of the building. Thin, but it might give him enough time. He needed to eliminate the threat closest to Kate first. Then the biggest threat of all—Serna.

Machine pistol on his back and knife in hand, Cord waited for the sniper to disappear to the far wall then ran toward the men. He had to disarm them both before they realized what happened. First and only priority—keep Kate safe.

He stayed as low to the ground as possible but couldn't stop to find out if the sentry sniper had seen him or not.

No shots. He was in the clear until one of these yahoos yelled out. He dug deep for the energy to run. Drew on his training and memory to attack. He threw his shoulder into the back of the man nearest to him and kicked his legs to the side, knocking the second guy to the ground.

Neither of the men had their guns at the ready. Both started cursing and talking to each other in rapid Spanish. So rapid he couldn't keep up. It was clear the guy partially under him wanted help. Cord used the knife hilt on the back of his head, close to his neck. He stopped squirming.

One down, one to go.

The second man had rolled in the snow and was on his feet, weapon ready. Predictably, the man poked the barrel at him and when he did, Cord sliced his forearm. The man dropped the machine pistol and Cord body slammed him with everything he had left.

A shot hit the snow close to his left. Then another to his right. The sentry had seen the fight and drew a bead on him. Cord raised his hands behind his head, got to his knees and let the knife slide up his sleeve.

"Before you pull that trigger, I'm Cord McCrea. I think your boss wants to see me."

"Drop your gun."

Cord gestured that he needed to use his left hand, working the knife back into his palm.

"Slowly and carefully."

Cord pulled the strap over his head and watched the car back slowly the way it had come. He dropped the machine pistol and received a hard blow to the side of his head.

"On your feet. Now. Move." He pointed the barrel of the gun toward the chopper. "You are right, *amigo*. Serna wants to kill you himself and that pretty *chica* of yours."

Protecting Their Child

Keep his attacker's mind off that car and keep Kate safe. No matter what—keep Kate safe. He wouldn't look to see where the car was, just kept working the hilt into his palm while he hid the action with his left wrist.

"Too bad. Kate's safe in the hands of U.S. Marshals by now," he said with a light shrug, faking that it mattered if the man believed him.

"That's for Jorje to think on. Get going."

Convince Serna that Kate wasn't with him. This minion hadn't seen her. Maybe it was possible. Then Serna would leave with the threat of the observatory staff calling the sheriff.

"Ah, Ranger McCrea," Serna tooted into the silence. "Bring him to the picnic area. Get the chopper ready, we can finally leave like you've wanted."

The slow whine of a chopper engine jerked his head away from the back of the visitor center where Serna waited for him. This was it. His only chance to stop the man who was terrorizing his family. One shot. Or blade.

Keep Kate safe. How? If they stayed here, she was at risk of being found. What if it wasn't her in the car? What if she was still in the trees, waiting for the right moment to take a shot. Then the sniper would take her out. He might be better than the last guy. His brain was taunting himself with the phrase "this is it" over and over again.

The shove in the middle of his back struck a sensitive nerve and made him stumble, but he managed to keep his hands in place behind his neck and the knife unseen. The trek to the picnic area was twice the length of a football field he used to run so easily and a lot farther to walk with a gun in his back.

He could use the blade on Serna if he could get close enough. But as the area where the drug lord was seated became clearer, there was a brick wall between them. His only option was to get Serna in close quarters and use the knife then. Get the enemy away from Kate.

He had time to slit the back of his jacket and get the knife inside the lining. Risky, slow, but he had the time. Deliberate movements, a few uncomfortable twists with his back to hide the drop. Now if they didn't make him leave his coat behind, he would be armed wherever they took him.

Of course, Serna could pull his gun and shoot him in the head. But, more likely, he'd enjoy beating him first. He'd want Kate's location, but Cord would never say. Besides, he didn't know and by the time he was asked it would definitely be the truth.

"This should be fun, I think," Serna said, walking toward him from the protection and warmth of the chopper.

Cord saw the left coming and braced his feet wider for the impact. Square in the jaw, the punch snapped his head to the side so fast he heard his neck crackle. Not only had he successfully stood his ground, he kept his hands behind his head instead of blocking or returning. The one to his gut put a catch in his breathing. But it was the hit from the rifle butt behind him that did the most damage.

He dropped to his knees in agony from the old back injury, the pain so fierce it made his head swim. Then a crack on his skull made it impossible to open his eyes. He could feel the blackness of unconsciousness taking hold of his senses.

Stay safe, Kate.

"What are you waiting for?" Kate screamed at the young co-ed she'd woken from a dead sleep. "Go. Go. Go!"

"But the helicopter's gone, ma'am."

"Do you think I'm going to wait here to be rescued? Drive me or get out. Every second I sit here he gets miles away."

"But the sheriff said to stay put and not move. We don't know who else is down there. They have guns."

"Can I borrow your car?"

"No. I'm driving back to the quarters and we're waiting."

The young woman put the car in Reverse and turned her little car around to head up the road again. Kate couldn't blame her. She doubted she'd believe the fantastical story of the past three days if she hadn't actually lived it.

Oh, my God, Cord, what did you do?

The young college student beside her had binoculars. Even in the low light she'd seen Cord run deliberately up to the two men in the field. He'd made a decision to get close to Serna. Probably trying to protect her. Not knowing for certain that she'd made the phone call to the Rangers, who should be headed this way in their own helicopter by now.

"May I borrow your phone again?"

The student handed her the cell from the seat next to her. "Sure, but it won't work until we get back to the house. Too many trees."

"Can you hurry?" She needed to call Cord's unit and tell them that Serna had one of their own. Maybe they could track him or something.

The woman—Kate couldn't remember her name at all—drove carefully through the snow. On a normal day, Kate would sit back and commend her for being so careful. Today was anything but ordinary.

Kate kept punching Redial even without the reception

bars, hoping and praying the call would go through even seconds earlier. Her heart was racing and her palms were sweaty. And then a wave of dizziness hit her so hard she had to put her head back on the seat.

"Are you okay, Kate?"

"Just dizzy. I haven't had much to eat or drink today."

"I've got lots of food." The student parked the car in the bare spot she'd left pulling out earlier. "Sit there and I'll be around to help you inside."

Kate was past hungry, but knew she had to eat. But first, the phone was finally dialing.

"Sheriff Barber, this is Kate McCrea." She waited, her door was pulled open and she held up a finger, too afraid to move and lose the connection.

"Are you safe, Kate?"

"They left in the helicopter, flying southwest. They have Cord. It looked like they dragged him unconscious onto the seat and then took off."

"But are you safe?"

"Yes, or I wouldn't be calling you. Get someone tracking that helicopter. You've got to do something. Please. If anything happens to him, I don't— Oh God, he gave up. He did that to save me and all I did was watch."

"We're doing our best, Kate. Stay put and calm down. I'll contact the Rangers and see if they have any choppers available."

"How long?"

"I just passed the state park, sixteen miles away. Are any of Serna's men left?"

"I really don't know. I think so."

"Listen to me, Kate. Get inside, lock the doors and protect yourself. I'm at least twenty minutes out."

They disconnected and Kate was suddenly exhausted.

"The sheriff said to make certain everything's locked up tight. We don't know how many men were left behind." She accepted the help from the young woman to get inside the building. "What did you say your name was again?"

"I'm Sharon. Did your husband kill that guy? He fell to the ground and didn't get up. The guy from the roof ran to the helicopter just before it took off. Are you sure you're okay?"

There was no reason to correct her earlier mistake of calling Cord her husband. It was easier than explaining why her ex-husband was sacrificing so much to protect her. She'd convinced Sharon to drive her down the hill. It might take a long time to change how she thought about Cord.

"I'm just very tired and hungry." Kate turned the main light off. Leaning on the wall to close curtains, she looked around the room for the best spot to defend them.

"Hey, you better sit down. I can do all this." Sharon scooted one of the sofa chairs into the hallway, away from the windows and doors.

"I'm sorry you're in danger because of me." Kate could barely walk another step, but she made it and rested on a thick sofa arm. Her mind wouldn't stop. She could barely listen to what the young woman said about it being okay and probably saving her. Kate's head was imagining all the horrible things Serna would do to Cord. She was stuck on that flying death trap with him, sending all her energy, telling him to survive, praying and then praying again.

Out of the corner of her eye, she watched Sharon in the kitchen, chattering the entire time about normally loving her job. She accepted the cold sandwich while she waited on anyone to come through that door.

"Is the gun necessary?" Sharon eyed the rifle resting across Kate's lap.

One look and a nod of her head later, Kate fingered the safety off and waited. The sheriff had reminded her that Serna's men were still out there. She didn't know how many had come and didn't know how many would still be looking for her.

"I see headlights. The sheriff made great time. It's only been ten minutes."

"Get behind me, Sharon. Stay down and don't say a word."

Chapter 21

"Sharon?" a deep male voice shouted and he pounded on the door. "Sharon, are you in there? Open up."

"Kate," Sharon whispered, gently touching Kate's arm. "That's Logan. It's okay. He works here. I'm fine." She said the last words a bit louder so he could hear.

"Thank God. You wouldn't believe what we've been hearing over the scanner. Open up."

"You can put the rifle down, Kate," she said softly.

The young woman's hands covered Kate's grip, steadying the rifle that she'd pulled to her shoulder. They couldn't be sure who was out there. Someone might be forcing him. She understood that Sharon wanted her to set the rifle aside, but she couldn't. Not yet.

A louder banging on the door caused Kate to jump. "Tell him to go away. If he's really alone, he can go away."

Sharon ran to the window. "He's alone. It's okay."

"You don't know these men. They'll do anything. They could be holding someone else hostage."

"Sharon! Answer me or open this door."

The observatory employee nodded her head. "Logan, you need to drive out of sight. I'll call you when it's okay to come back. Don't ask why, just do it. I really am safe. I'll explain later."

Kate held firm. "No one but the sheriff is getting in that door."

"I understand. We'll wait together." She returned to her place behind Kate.

Kate tucked the fright in Sharon's voice away but she didn't care. Logan must have heard it, too. His car pulled away without another word. Right now, the rifle was staying in her hand and would stay pointed at the door until she knew it was safe. That was just the way it was. Period.

When the sheriff showed up a few minutes later, Kate finally slid the safety on but still held the rifle across her lap. Her elbow knocked the sandwich to the floor and Kate got on her knees to pick up the mess. That's where Sheriff Barber found her, crying.

She couldn't stop and knew the hiccups were going to take over soon. She'd make a fool of herself, sounding ridiculous, sobbing because a simple turkey sandwich covered the floor. She didn't care. She needed to cry. And cry. And then cry some more.

Kate was right back where she'd started two days ago. Wait. What day was it? She was wrong, it had just been the night before that she'd left with Cord. How could she have added an entire day? She really was tired.

Mrs. Burke opened the door, pulling her crocheted

shawl around her shoulders for a little protection from the snow.

"I didn't know where else to take her, Juliet. She obviously needs rest and protection, but refused to stay at the observatory. Or go into protective custody. Said she wouldn't leave Valentine until we found McCrea. Maybe you can talk some sense into her."

Sheriff Barber was too young to have authority. She'd experienced so much more than this thirty-year-old Dallas ex-cop.

"I'm right here, Mike. Please stop talking like I'm not. And the last time I looked, I was a legal adult and didn't need anyone's permission to go anywhere. Nick," Kate said, looking at her friend and then his mother. "Juliet, I know this is a lot to ask. I understand it's dangerous to have me here. You can say no and I'll go to my ranch."

She spoke to Mrs. Burke, but Nick stood not two feet away. Arms crossed. Angry with each movement. Not saying a word. Typical man.

"Don't be ridiculous." Juliet wrapped her arm around Kate's shoulders and ushered her to the door. "You'll stay here until your father arrives."

The sheriff stepped across the porch toward Nick, securing his hat back on his head to protect it from the freezing air. Kate stayed in the doorway, listening, wanting to learn anything the authorities had refused to share with her, longing to fall asleep in Cord's arms and feel safe again.

"What are the chances he's still alive?" Nick asked.

"Slim," the sheriff whispered, and shook his head, his chin nearly dragging in defeat across his jacket. "I wish I could leave a deputy here, but we're all out searching. McCrea's one of our own. We won't stop looking."

"He's alive, you know," Kate said from behind the screen, feeling the cold air rush into the warmth of the living room, but she couldn't close the door until they believed her.

Nick shifted from one leg to another. Nervous? Uneasy at her being at the house or overhearing? Or just uncomfortable at the thought she was holding on to a fantasy?

"Think about it," she explained. "Serna's had more than one opportunity to kill both Cord and me. But he didn't. Not in the years he was in prison and not by any of the men he's sent after us. This is a vendetta for him and he's vowed to make Cord suffer. There's no way he's killed him without getting to me." Her voice choked on the words and she pushed them out. "He'll make Cord watch."

"So you're agreeing that as long as you're alive, Cord's alive?" Nick asked, pulling the screen open to face her.

"I think so."

"Then get into protective custody. I can't protect you here, as much as I want to think I can." Nick pressed his lips together, shaking his head. "We don't have enough hands or guns to hold off the men Serna might have."

"He's right, dear." Juliet placed a comforting hand on her shoulder.

The sheriff stepped back onto the porch and held his hat in his hand, hypnotically smoothing the rim, turning the department-issued hat in a circle, over and over and over.

"Kate, Maddox is sending someone to pick you up. They aren't taking no for an answer and may very well force you into custody."

"Fine. I'll go. Can I at least have a bath and some of those fantastic eggs of yours, Juliet?" She couldn't argue with her only hope—if she was alive, so was Cord. So she needed to disappear. No local protective custody. Wherever she went she was putting someone in danger. So disappearing was the only option.

"Nick, help Kate to the guest room while I whip up some biscuits. Mike, you're staying until Kate's ride gets here, of course."

"If biscuits are involved, yes, ma'am." The sheriff nodded. "I'll keep an eye open. Holler when it's ready."

Kate turned to Nick. "I know where the guest room is. Go do whatever you're itching to do."

He ignored her suggestion and escorted her down the hall, following her inside the room so she couldn't close the door. "Are you really okay?"

"Yes."

"Mike said you were hysterical when he found you. That you wouldn't let go of the rifle."

"For a minute, but I'm fine. It's nothing that a couple of your mom's biscuits and a good, long sleep won't take care of." She hoped. Her hand rubbed her tummy. She could only pray nothing happened as a result of the past three days. "Really, Nick. I'm just very, very tired and I'm going to force myself to take a bath before I fall asleep standing here talking to you."

She forced herself to smile, attempting to reassure him that she believed what she was saying. It was half-true. Physically, she was just tired and needed food. Mentally though, well, worrying about Cord had never been this rough. It had been a "what if" game before. This was much too real and would follow them the rest of their lives—apart or together.

"I'm here if you need me. I always have been."

"I know and thanks."

"But?" he said with a twinge of disgust.

Definite attitude that she was too tired to deal with. "Look, we've been friends since elementary school. It's never been anything other than that, so what's the deal? I'm just too exhausted to tippy-toe around your ego."

He immediately backed out of the room with a hands-off gesture. "Got it. You're still in love with McCrea."

"So what if I am? He's my husband."

"*Ex*-husband."

She slammed the door in his face.

No matter what their marital status, Cord might very well be dead. Her child might grow up without her father. That scenario was completely unacceptable and there was nothing she could do about it.

Nothing except run away and hide. And that's exactly what Cord would want her to do. Stay alive. Protect their child.

"You are one lucky son of a bitch." He spoke low into the burner cell as soon as he could get out of earshot of all the people swarming the ranch. "She came back here to wait until they found McCrea."

"Bring her to me."

"It would be better if you ambushed their car when—"

"We're out of time. The buyers are impatient and we're ready to move."

"That's stupid. Three counties are covered with feds and state authorities trying to find you. They have special units covering the mountains. The state's bringing in more choppers."

"And they won't be looking for us to move the guns into Mexico. The diversion is necessary to make it across the border," Serna said, unusually calm. "We both know they're wasting their time in the mountains. We've moved to Danver's place just like we planned."

The level tone and pleasure exuding from the drug runner's voice gave him the creeps.

"You really are crazy. What if she'd gone home instead of here?"

"You agreed she'd never do that. If it had happened, you wouldn't have to get your hands dirty."

"Was this your plan all along?" He wondered if he was dealing with a madman or a cold, calculating, brilliant mind.

"You are too curious about details, *friend*. You might want to think hard on extending our partnership before we talk some more."

"I told you I'm out. That's always been the deal. The fire's a bit too close to home and the pan's getting awfully hot around here."

"You and your sayings. You have always amused me." Serna laughed. "I like having you around."

Those words were calculated. Innocent but a threat nonetheless.

For the first time since he'd begun dealing with these bastards, a chill ran down his spine. He shook it off. Showing fear wasn't the way to gain respect. And clearly telling them he wanted out was a death sentence. No matter what the understanding had been before, now wasn't the time to remind him. It was as plain as day he wouldn't be leaving alive if he took Kate Danver McCrea there.

"You know, Serna, I've only wanted one thing and you're about to take care of that. I'll have her at your *camp* soon and I'll think hard on reconsidering. Your operation is too smooth to just walk away. When I get there, we can decide the right amount of enticement to continue our arrangement."

Like hell he would. He was dropping her close to the gate and getting out of Dodge.

It was still his plan to become a witness for the government if he was caught. He had all the evidence safely tucked in a safe-deposit box. And if he wasn't caught… that island retirement looked better and better.

He laughed out loud. He just couldn't help it. Years of planning were finally paying off. Finally.

Chapter 22

The smells were comforting, familiar. Cord knew them and relaxed. Couldn't place them for a couple of minutes until he took a deep breath—hay, manure, animals, leather. Barn. He drifted and woke with a start when a muscle in his shoulder cramped. Blasted shoulder. He must have slept wrong. He couldn't bring his hand around to work the muscle. Man, he was tired, and opening his eyes was difficult. Then he realized he was blindfolded, hands bound behind his back, face in the bottom of a stall.

No clue how long he'd been unconscious. He couldn't tell much of anything while he was blind as a bat.

This sealed it. Serna was working with a local rancher. Burke had been his first choice. But Cord wasn't gagged. Seemed to be out in plain sight, from the feel of the draft blowing across him. Serna's men wouldn't risk alerting Mrs. Burke and the hands. And every sense in him had to be totally skewed if Juliet Burke was a drug runner. No way. Where the hell was he?

His ribs were sore like he'd been kicked hard enough to bruise them. He licked his parched lips and could taste dried blood. He hadn't doubted Serna would kill him given the chance. Truth be told, when he'd let himself be taken by Serna's men he hadn't really thought further than keeping Kate and the baby safe.

Trying to get out of this mess alone wouldn't be easy, but he wasn't just giving up. He nudged his head against the ground. Slowly and painfully he inched the blindfold up so he could see and even blink. Still dark outside—at least that's what he could estimate from the nonexistent light. A dampness clung in the air from the snow outside and his muscles were stiff from the cold.

"Oh, man." His hoarse voice expressed his astonishment at recognizing the initials in the wood post of the stall. This was the Danver ranch. On their birthdays, David had notched both kids' heights into the first post, right-hand side, west door. He'd mucked this stall many times on his day off.

Serna had moved his operation here? How could the bold SOB know that no one was watching the place? It must have been Juan after all, but something more than the stall floor didn't smell right.

The door swung open, snow swirling inside along with a pair of fancy boots. No one working a ranch would wear slick dancing boots in this weather. Easy deduction that it was one of Serna's hirelings. He closed his eyes and nudged the bandanna mostly back into place. Better to play dead. Honestly, he could barely see straight, couldn't fill his lungs and had a stomach growling like a grizzly.

He could see enough to know the boots were next to

him and he was about to be kicked to see if he was conscious. He prepared for the pain and would keep his body as silent as possible without tensing. Dear Lord, the pointed toe landed in his side in exactly in the same spot, with a force that might have just cracked the rib this time around.

He almost didn't breathe. In fact, he could easily have thrown up from the pain. *Think about Kate. That'll get you through it. Thinking about her got you through all the hard stuff last time.*

Kate was safe. She had to be. They wouldn't leave him lying in a stall if they'd caught her. They'd be— *God, don't go there. You control the pain. The pain can't control you.*

He remained motionless several seconds after he heard the boots shuffle out and the bounce of the wooden latch fall into place. The desire to curl into a ball might have prevailed if his hands had been at his stomach. He couldn't take another of those kicks. Boots-man might just puncture a lung next time. Then where would he be?

Zip-tie handcuffs.

Knife. He hadn't searched to see if his knife was still in the lining of his jacket.

The secured circles of hard plastic bit into his skin and made it harder to bend his hands to search the bottom of his jacket. The pocketknife had moved around the lining but it was workable. Getting it open wasn't as difficult as fighting the burns the plastic biting his wrists caused.

Slow. Steady. He worked the blade open, cut easily enough through his coat—okay, David's coat—and got the blade into his hand. Cord was determined to saw the cuffs in half and free himself. He knew all about determination. His stubbornness kept his legs moving as he learned to walk and then run again. He had controlled the pain for two years of intense therapy. He'd control the pain now.

And when he found Boots-man, he'd make sure there was some kicking involved and not to his ribs. He manipulated the blade using his watchband for a little leverage and protection. Lying on his side, his arms just wouldn't move back and forth enough to break through the stinking plastic.

He had to risk sitting and was fortunate they hadn't taken the time to secure his feet. With his head swimming, he pushed himself up and rested against the slats separating the stalls. At least he wasn't as cold anymore. He positioned the knife again and began the tedious back and forth sawing motion necessary to escape.

A light knock on the door woke her. Just flipping the afghan off made her body scream to stay put and not move for a week. She rubbed her eyes, looking for the alarm clock across the room. Midnight and still snowing.

"Yes?"

"May I come in?"

"Sure, Nick."

He brought her a second tray with a teapot, biscuits and honey. The one before her nap had been a little bit of heaven. Then an image of Cord filled her mind. Shot, bleeding, unable to walk and passing out as she screamed at him. She covered her eyes, trying to focus on anything at all, only to see it even more clearly.

If he can survive that, he can do this. He will survive. He has to survive. Her hands dropped protectively over their baby.

"Hope you don't mind the interruption. Mom thought it important to get some more food and tea down you." He set the bed tray across her legs and crossed to the window.

"Thanks." She could tell he wanted to say something

to her. It was just like the time he asked her to the homecoming dance even when he wanted to go deer hunting. Some habits never changed. "How does the weather look and what's the latest estimate on my ride out of here?"

"Not good and getting worse on the snow. They're predicting three or four inches by morning. Choppers are grounded." He stuck his hands deep into his jeans pockets. "Mike left a couple of hours ago, before we knew there may be a problem with help coming in from Pecos."

"You're worried. I'm sorry. Your mom and dad are here and I'm putting them in danger. I should have thought things through."

"We're family. You should come to us. I just don't know how effective I'll be with the few rounds I have left. I'm assuming Cord's the one who took my ammo."

"So he wiped you out?"

"Pretty much, yeah. Glad I thought to check when the sheriff left."

"So you'll drive me into Marfa or Fort Davis?" Why wouldn't he look at her? Had they heard something else? If they had, he would have told her first thing. No, this was to do with Nick himself.

"I feel like I'm letting you down."

That was the crux. "It's my fault, Nick. I should have thought about this before I demanded the sheriff bring me here. You're the one who convinced me to reconsider. You haven't let me down and I'm sorry I slammed the door in your face earlier." She hugged him and received one back. "I'll have my shoes on and be out the door in ten minutes."

"I'll warm up the car."

It was nice knowing she wouldn't have to worry about mending fences in this weather. But she'd miss her friends. The relief only lasted until she opened the door.

The wind and swirling snow hit her square in the face and a chill spread through her body. Where was Cord? Was he out of the snow and north wind? Was he even alive?

Kate ran down the path to the waiting car. She hoped the car warmed up fast. Its exhaust formed a white cloud from the tailpipe, but the windows were still frosted. Odd. Why hadn't Nick scraped the windows clean? The little instinct that raised the hairs on the back of her neck kicked into high gear. Her steps slowed and she stopped altogether when the driver's door opened on the far side of the car.

"Oh, Mac. You sort of scared me. I was expecting Nick to drive me." She pulled the handle to open the door.

"There's a problem with a mare he's been keeping an eye on and he asked me to drive you. Do you feel safe enough with an old man?"

She pulled the door open and immediately saw the blood spatter. She pivoted to run, but the click of a gun readying to fire stopped her in her tracks.

"I should have said, you shouldn't feel safe with this old man. Get in."

"Is he dead?"

"Nick?" He put the car in gear and bounced them down the road. "Frankly, I didn't check and don't care."

The duffel from the lodge was in the backseat floorboard. So the drugs were Mac's and he'd been hiding them. Mac Cauldwell was a family friend. Someone she'd trusted. And he was the "ranch owner" Cord was certain existed.

"How much is Serna paying you?"

"A lot." He turned the corner a bit fast and the back of the car fishtailed. He laughed widely. "It's enough to finally get out of this desert and retire in comfort."

The wild-eyed look in Mac's eyes scared her into silence. Three years ago, he'd known she and Cord would be at the ranch for dinner. "Why are you working with these horrible monsters? What did we ever do to you?"

"It's all the more fun because you think there has to be a reason." His laughter grew; he was almost tearing up he was hee-hawing so much.

"You're laughing at causing my family so much pain? You're responsible for everything. You knew we'd be at Dad's that night. You killed my baby girl."

"Naw. All I did was tell Serna where'd you be."

"If you hadn't given the drug cartel access and details to our land, none of this would have happened."

It was tempting to reach out and grab the wheel, send them careening into the barbed-wire fence. Or to reach for the gun he casually held in his hand now. Mac might refer to himself as old, but he was still a sinewy cowboy. She'd seen him wrestle a cow to the ground last summer and win the senior division with the best time. Because of the baby, she couldn't risk a car wreck or gunshot wound. All she could do was hope for a last-minute miracle.

"Nothing would have happened? I wouldn't be too sure of that, missy. If it hadn't been me, Serna would have found someone else. There are plenty of people on his payroll. Just 'cause I'm helping this time around doesn't mean anything will be different when I leave. Just that someone else will be helping." He turned onto the drive to her house.

"What are we doing here?"

"The final joke's on you." He threw back his head laughing, hitting the window with the gun. "While everyone's searching for Serna and that precious Ranger of yours in the mountains, he's been running up the heating bill in your house. Probably sleeping in your bed.

But you won't have to worry about that for long. Take off your shoes."

"But it's snowing."

"Yeah, I got that. Now take 'em off." The laughter disappeared from his craggy, thin face. "I'm not sticking around to let Serna get the best of me. I'm out of here."

She bent her knee and frantically unlaced her boot, hoping he wouldn't see the string she wadded up within her fist. She got both laces down the back of her jeans before he got to the last cattle guard.

They stopped. "Get out."

"Are you going to shoot me? I thought Serna wanted to do that."

"I don't know what he'll do and I don't care. But whatever happens, I'll be long gone or making a deal for witness protection. As long as I get my cut, I'm good. Now get out."

She scooped up her shoes and pushed open the door. He reached across and knocked the shoes into the floorboard.

"Nope. These stay. Nowhere to run this time, missy. You're pregnant and barefoot and Serna will be here any minute. Hasta la vista." He shoved her out of the Jeep.

She landed hands, knees and freezing toes in six inches of snow. He gunned the engine and she crawled out of the way just before he turned and headed back the way they'd come. The icy wetness seeped through her cloth gloves and pants. She didn't want to stand, but did. The snow was cold and didn't take long to start stinging her feet.

"Now what do I do?"

She saw the familiar sight of her home about a mile away. There was nothing else around and her feet quickly screamed the only available option.

Walk home. Straight into the grasp of the devil.

Chapter 23

Cord jerked awake from a long fall in his dream. No wonder, since he was perched, hiding in a vee of the barn rafters. Another doze starting with thoughts of Kate and ending with the inability to protect her. Back to finding a way to stop Serna. Missing Kate didn't have any place in his thoughts, but it was there nonetheless.

He stretched a bit and used his right index finger to get his wedding ring from the change pocket of his borrowed pants. The silver band slid onto his cold finger as easily as the first time. His hand felt wrong without it. They'd been divorced on paper for a little over five months, but he'd never been able to leave it on his dresser more than a couple of days.

Actually, divorced wasn't the same as feeling divorced. He'd seen Kate at the fence and his first thought was to kiss her hello. Same thing had happened the night before their court date. Only then, he'd kissed her. And then a lot more.

Man, he was going to miss her. Every day and a lot of his nights he'd be thinking about her and the baby. He'd totally screwed up and there was no way out now.

She had to be in protective custody by the sheriff, marshals, Rangers—some organization that would keep her safe. Truth be told, he couldn't. He'd be lucky to keep himself alive through the night.

He had two options to get inside the house and to Serna—surprise the next one through the door and call for backup with the man's cell, like he'd been waiting in the barn rafters to do for a while now. Or wait for his escape to be discovered and sneak into the house. So far it was the first option.

While he'd been looking for a weapon, he'd raided the barn mini fridge Frank had in his office. With the setbacks Cord had caused Serna in the past several days—losing at least nine men—the criminal still seemed more arrogant than ever. No one had bothered to look in on him for at least forty-five minutes.

What the heck are they waiting on?

"Kate."

No one had left the ranch—he would have seen or heard a vehicle. That left the rancher who was working with Serna. That scum had to be delivering Kate to her very own front door. They weren't worried about Cord waking up, assuming he was less of a problem unconscious.

He couldn't wait here any longer. He had to act now. He swung down from his hidden perch in the corner. He'd thought about what to do when Kate's words came back. *"Can't you go Rambo on them or something?"*

Armed with only a pocketknife, a pair of hay tongs and the cover of darkness, he climbed from the spot where he'd waited. Since no one had come for him, it was time to take the fight to his enemy one by stinking one.

"Cull them from the herd and take 'em out one by one." Kate had told him exactly what he needed to do. He took off his jacket. There would be plenty of activity to keep him warm and the bulky coat would only hinder his fighting. He'd already cut the fingertips from his gloves so he'd have a better grip.

"Okay, babe, the threat on you ends tonight," he whispered into the darkness. He slipped out the door, away from the house. It faced nothing but the dark corral and snow-covered pasture. With no one in sight, he stayed close to the wall, breathing through his nose, limiting the puffs of frost in front of his face.

He'd heard the sentry earlier, someone walking the perimeter of the barn but doing a sloppy job of it in the cold. He stayed at the edge of the corner, waiting. Far sounds. No chatter. He slid along the next wall, hidden in the shadows, pausing again at the corner until he heard the snow crunch. He drew his palm back, ready to strike. One solid, unexpected blow to the man's face and he was done. Silent, with the thudding exception of the falling body. Serna's force was now one less.

Taking the man's hat, jacket and weapon, he walked around the corral and barn as if he were the man he'd just left in the snow. Serna's men seemed to have an endless supply of machine pistols. Cord hated to think that he'd been out of the investigation so long he didn't know if this was the real cargo coming across the border.

He wanted to take more than just one of Serna's men down before approaching the house and confronting the man in charge. But he had to find them first. The far side of the ranch buildings had a yellow glow next to the field. As he approached, the noise level grew. The sound of men hustling and issuing orders, pounding feet. They were moving cargo from or into a semitrailer.

Damn. They'd moved their operation here to Kate's ranch. The idea of her family being desecrated gave him a lump in his throat. The ranch was the reason she'd refused to leave town for so long, even after they'd been threatened the first time by Serna.

The men leaving the truck were empty-handed. The driver started the rig, warming the diesel in preparation to leave. Whatever they were doing, they were almost finished and getting ready to pull out. They wouldn't risk a semi packed with drugs. It didn't make sense. They'd break up heroin shipments, not put it all in one location. Too risky if they were pulled over. The men he watched didn't seem in a hurry, so moving everything in one shipment wasn't because they were afraid of being caught.

The last men dropped off their box and walked away from the truck. The lights went off and he heard the whine of a chopper starting, finding it on the other side of the men. He needed to get a look at what was inside the trailer to know how to deal with it. Or did he? That was the Ranger in him...the part constantly seeking the answer to the confounded questions of how Serna was accomplishing everything. Cord, the husband and father, only needed to get rid of those men and call for backup.

He picked his way around the edge of light, staying hidden. He'd counted six men warming around a fire they'd started on the ground. That meant six ways to cull each of them from the equation. Or something that would distract several.

Fire. Fire rushing toward the chopper and the truck might occupy all of them long enough to find Serna. He needed the gas Danver stored near the toolshed.

"He has to be around here somewhere."

"I saw a man wearing Edward's hat by the truck. He should be guarding the barn."

Cord darted inside the small building, just behind the door to determine how many men were outside. He raised the hay tongs, waiting.

One man stuck his head inside the shed and Cord swung the metal, catching him across his face. He dropped to the ground but not before the second man opened fire into the shed. Cord rolled to his back and pulled the trigger of his weapon, not aiming, just shooting in an arc through the open door. One shot after rapid shot.

The return fire ended and he heard a hard thump hit the ground. Cord recognized the man he'd knocked in the nose. "Hello, Juan." He dragged the unconscious slime inside the shed, calf-roping his hands and feet. "Guess that explains how they knew no one was here at the ranch. But if you're here, who's bringing Kate?"

Sliding in the snow, he rounded the corner, opened the top of the gas drum and turned it on its side. The gas splashed to the earth. All he needed was a lighter and those men would be occupied trying to save their unknown cargo in those crates.

Confused at Mac's betrayal, Kate continued the difficult walk through her property. She'd quickly realized who and what was waiting inside her home. Serna. It hadn't fully sunk in that Mac was involved with drug smugglers. She'd known the man her entire life. It was almost like having an uncle betray her family.

As Kate drew near the house, she noticed the rifle barrel. Her feet were on fire from being so cold even after she'd laced her wet gloves to the bottom of her socks for a little protection. The bits of string had come in handy after all.

The man pointing the gun in her face knocked on the front door. Serna came through, wiping the corner of his mouth with one of her mother's lace napkins from the antique buffet.

Bastard.

"Time to leave. When will the helicopter be ready?" The murderer ignored Kate.

The man shrugged. "Till it's deiced. Safe or crash. Your choice."

She thought Serna would strike him, but the man walked off toward the east pasture. She'd never felt an emotion as powerful as the hatred she had for the man responsible for her child's death. It was horrible and would consume her if she weren't careful. She had to control the rage. Harness it into energy she needed to help Cord with their escape.

Come on, man. Cord patted the pockets of the coat. Nothing. The cab of the truck was right there. He found a lighter and killed the ignition, taking the keys with him. It would defeat the purpose of lighting everything up like a Roman candle if they could just drive away.

Back in the shadows, he got close to the truck and shoved the barrel with all his strength. A trail of diesel melted a path in the fresh snow.

Lighter. Flame. Toss. Fire. Run.

Wait for it...

* * *

She and Cord would escape. There was no way they could let this evil man win whatever game he was playing. Kate wanted to claw Serna's eyes out, but the handgun in the front of his pants prevented her. If given the chance, she knew where the weapons were stored. There was a loaded gun locked in its safe in her bedside table that opened with her thumbprint, a gift from her husband.

"It's been a long chase, Kate McCrea. You got a nice place here."

Serna attempted to sound at ease and maybe a little more cultured than usual as he led the way through the kitchen. But it didn't make him anything better than the filth she scraped from the bathtub drain.

"Sit. Warm up a bit."

He'd definitely made use of her house. A kitchen chair was waiting in front of a huge fire. She sat while Serna reclined in her father's lounger with a half-eaten steak on the end table. He'd just taken a bite when the door slammed open and a short young man burst in.

"He ain't there, boss."

"Find him!" Serna shouted. He threw his plate and hit the retreating messenger. Continuing his Spanish curses, he paced the room, then peered out the window and yanked the blinds. Their crash to the floor made her flinch inside and out.

The long-bladed knife he used to slice the cord appeared from nowhere. He wrapped the cord menacingly around his fist. The evil in his glaring intent made her shiver and want to run to save herself.

"Find him!" The shouts from outside continued as Serna advanced.

The muscles in his clenched jaw twitched. He was worried. Then it sank in who they were searching for.

Cord was gone from wherever they'd been holding him. That was suddenly clear. She fought the upturn of her lips, but not the pride filling her heart.

Men began yelling *blanket* in Spanish. Something had gone wrong. At first she thought the fire was reflected in the window, but it was outside, somewhere on the other side of the barn and spreading. Quickly.

An explosion split the silence, flames shot into the sky, ridding the night of the frightening darkness for a moment. The force shook the walls of the house. The vibration burst through her thawing feet. Something big and close to the shed. Maybe the tractor fuel?

"McCrea!" Serna screamed into the window.

She was ready to run, and ready to react to however this monster came after her. She picked her route through the house. The front hallway to the bedroom and the gun box. If he followed…pull the trigger.

Chapter 24

The force of the gas explosion dropped him to his knees. He'd almost made it to the back of the shed when the hot blast of air knocked him to the ground. He sat on his butt in what used to be darkness, watching shards of the barrel burning around the field, then scurried backward until he hit the fence. Serna's men ran to the semi using their jackets to put out the flames. At this rate, they'd be successful in a matter of minutes.

On the other side of the fire, the chopper blades were still at slow speed. Cord watched the pilot open and shut the door. He tightened his grip on the machine pistol. Too far to shoot. But the semi keys were still in his fist.

He ran the perimeter shadow. The driver was in the cab searching for keys. Cord caught him across his shoulder blades on his way down. Another bad guy sprawled in the snow. To keep the truck in gear and get clear, his lone option was to shove his machine pistol against the gas pedal. It was the only way to put both the truck and the chopper out of commission. He'd pick up the driver's gun on the way back.

Cord cranked the semi, shoved it into Reverse, not caring what was in his way. If there were drugs in the back of this thing, the horses and cattle might be high for miles. He wedged the pistol into place and jumped from the truck cab.

Men began yelling. Jumping out of the way. Running. Cord got to the downed driver just as the truck backed through the major fire. It didn't stop and caught the tail rotor of the chopper as it lifted off.

The crash sent the chopper spinning into the field. It tipped, the blades digging into the ground, sending the body end over end. Time to move. The driver had a machine pistol that Cord jerked from his body. He moaned and Cord flipped him to his back, sticking the barrel in his face.

"Up."

The man staggered to his feet and Cord shoved him to the shed and roped his hands and feet behind his back like a steer. He stuffed work rags into both men's mouths to keep them quiet.

Cord draped a second gun over his shoulder and searched their pockets. Cell phone. The Sheriff's department answered on the first ring.

"This is Cord McCrea, I'm located at the Danver ranch. There's been an explosion and I need backup."

"Cord, thank God you're alive. We have every available person searching the mountains. I'll reroute everyone and send a fire truck. Wait for reinforcements.

There's a chopper at the observatory that can be there in ten."

"Can't wait. Serna moved his operation. Come in hot. I'm uncertain about the number of guns. Gotta go."

"Cord, Nick Burke was shot and we think—"

The devil could take Burke if he'd been working with Serna and received his comeuppance. He cut off the call since he didn't want to be talked out of his plan to eliminate Serna and the threat to his family. A lot could happen in ten minutes—if reinforcements could actually arrive by then.

Cord was willing to accept the consequences of all his actions.

The blood vessels in the side of Serna's neck were visibly enlarged. He was enraged about the explosion and Kate no longer knew if he'd wait until Cord was there to hurt her. She had to get to the gun.

Was an all-out run better than inching her way to the hall? She had socks—actually, knit gloves—on her feet. With no shoes on the wooden floors and stinging prickles making her feet ache, running would be a disaster. She remained in the chair. As soon as she stood, he'd know her intention. She slid a foot closer to the fireplace tools, a weapon, something to give her a fighting chance.

What would Cord do? He'd give himself two ways out. So she curled her legs to each side of the chair and quickly pushed her socks down around her ankles. She'd time her movements to get the slick cloth off her feet. If she couldn't get shoes from her bedroom, she had a set of mud boots in the barn.

Success, one bare foot.

Serna hit the wall with both fists, then spun around

to face her. She met his crazy-eyed stare and wouldn't look away. Fear of what an insane person filled with revenge would do ended up giving her strength to meet him straight on. If she made a move, she was three or four feet away from the fire tools.

Her enemy's face was the color of the bloodred middle oozing from his T-bone. His hands were still at his sides, not close to the butt of the gun. She didn't have enough time to grab the shovel or poker without his drawing and shooting her in the back. He wouldn't miss. Not this time.

Enraged as he was, he wasn't ranting around the room like three years ago. And this time, she was much more frightened. She couldn't see a way out. Armed only with shoelaces? What had she been thinking?

"Your husband has made my life hell." He cocked his head like a curious dog. "What, no response? Aren't you going to beg for your life?"

"Would it do any good?" Second sock at her toes.

"No."

"Then I'll just wait."

"Wait for the end?" He caressed the clip of his gun wedged down the front of his pants.

She choked back a laugh at the thought of him shooting himself in the crotch and ending this nightmare. She must be very tired to let her imagination venture down that road.

"You find it funny? McCrea can't rescue you. Not here."

"No." There was movement outside the window. Cord? Serna caught the direction of her eyes and began to turn. "Well, yes, actually I find it hilarious." He pivoted back to her. "After all your work, an explosion is going to bring people from miles around. But I imagine you don't find that funny at all."

"No time for games." He removed the gun and aimed it at her. The string from the blinds was dangling from his hand. "Stand up and turn around. We're leaving."

She stood, barefoot, ready to run.

Serna jerked her hands behind her, wrists on top of each other and tied. She didn't move but frantically searched the windows and mirrors trying to find a glimpse of Cord.

Gun in his right hand and his left holding her bound wrists, he shoved her toward the front door.

What would Cord do? He'd be waiting just outside that door.

Serna opened the door and pushed her into the screen. She pretended to stumble, bending her body almost in half, just in case her rescue was about to begin.

"Get up!" Serna yelled, jabbing her with the gun.

A jet stream shot above her head, aiming toward Serna's face. She was shoved forward by Cord. He stepped between her and Serna's gun just as it went off.

"No!" She fell to the front porch, rolling to her back, using her feet to slide out of the way.

Cord wasn't shot. He pushed inside, jabbing something into Serna's chest. "Get out of here, Kate."

The machine gun bounced on the floor and the men used their fists on each other too fast for her to count the blows. The screen was still propped open by her feet. She scooted, stood, got back inside.

Her gun. She ran, opened her nightstand. She heard another weapon fire from the living room. She was certain her pistol was loaded. It would be so much easier to have her hands free. No time to find a kitchen knife. She heard the click after placing her thumb in the scanner. She grabbed the pistol and ran back to the living room.

The men were rolling, punching, grunting. Serna still had his weapon. There was blood on Cord's side, across his face. Both of his hands were holding Serna's in place away from him.

With her hands behind her back she couldn't help or use her own pistol. Serna's strength seemed to be prevailing. He was lying across Cord, pinning his legs. They seemed to be deadlocked—both gripping each other's wrists. A contest of sheer willpower. She could see the determination on Serna's face and the desperation on Cord's.

"Run," Cord demanded.

She couldn't run, she had to help. This was their fight, not just Cord's job. She dropped the gun on the floor close to Cord's head. She ran to the hearth and picked up the fireplace tools. She couldn't wield anything backward, but she could drop it all onto Serna's back.

Close to both men again, Serna guessed her intention and rolled off Cord, knocking her feet from under her. She fell, unable to avoid colliding with the brick hearth. Trying to absorb the impact to her midsection, she heard the discharge.

"Are you okay?" Cord asked.

She opened her eyes, saw her gun in his hands and Serna on his back, unmoving across her father's footstool.

"Yes," she answered, still trying to catch her breath. A tight pinch started in her back and quickly spread across her abdomen. "Oh, God, Cord, what have I done? I think I'm in labor."

He was by her side in an instance. "I'm here, babe. We've got this."

Chapter 25

"We're almost there. Just hold on." Cord steered the old Ford past the city limits sign, very familiar with the route to the county hospital.

"She's only five months, Cord. She can't be born this early. What if—"

"No 'what ifs.' They'll give you something. Contractions will stop. You'll be fine. Just try to relax. Maybe that will help." He swerved back into his lane, glad no one else was on the road to Marfa during a snowstorm in the middle of the night. "Go ahead, say it."

"The contractions are about fifteen minutes apart. You're right, I just need to relax. We'll be there soon enough if you can stay on the road." She laughed, smiling at him in the rearview mirror. "But it is hard to relax thinking we'll be headed into the next gully."

He slowed and it hit him how much pain and worry

he'd caused her during their time together. It would be a miracle if she ever forgave him.

"Kate, I… I'm sorry. Whatever happens, this has all been my fault and I'm sorry."

She sighed and wrinkled her forehead for a serious look. "For the record, I blame Jorje Serna, one hundred percent. Not you. I've never blamed you."

He blamed himself and would continue to blame himself.

The last time he'd come through the E.R. doors, he'd been on a gurney, fading in and out of consciousness. At least this time he ran inside after slamming the car into Park, blocking access to the automatic doors, and began looking for familiar faces. Familiar or not, he latched on to the first person in scrubs he found and started dragging them to the door.

"Kate's in the car, five months' pregnant, contractions approximately fifteen minutes apart. The last one was about seven minutes ago."

The nurse or E.R. worker resisted and he grabbed a wheelchair and went to get his wife himself.

"Wait, Cord! We'll get her."

He heard them shouting but that wouldn't stop him. They couldn't lose this baby. They just couldn't.

Kate had gotten out of the car, holding her small tummy. It wasn't the normal E.R. pregnancy picture an expectant father wanted to see. He wanted to see her belly grow. He wanted to experience every part of life with her. Not apart.

"Good, you got a chair." The relaxed calmness evaporated as she reached out to spread his shirt wide and look at the bloodstain. "Oh, my God, Cord. Were you shot?"

He covered his side, remembering the sting he'd felt at the front door. "Must be from someone else."

"You're a horrible liar," she said, and sat in the chair for him to wheel her through the doors. "Would you please take care of Cord? He's been shot again."

Kate had stopped the first nurse who'd come to take charge of the wheelchair, flashed them a smile, a thank-you and acted as if they weren't in the fight of their lives.

Cord had a flash of that night three years ago. Maybe it was a memory or just his imagination, but the anxiety currently thrumming through his system was worse than wondering where the next shot was coming from. He could return fire, defend himself, anticipate what might happen. Here, in this hospital, he didn't have much more than the feeling of hopelessness. He'd lost everything here and each day he'd awoken here, each time he'd returned for a doctor's appointment, he'd been reminded of how much he'd lost.

He stood five feet away from Kate, refusing to move to the next curtained area. Dumbfounded? In shock? He couldn't tell. He sort of watched things happen around him and thought about everything as it did. Doctors and nurses moved around him. Someone took him by the shoulders and said, "At least stay at the head of the bed so we can work."

Needles, IV bags, monitors and voices that didn't completely register. Dozens of people helped her and he just stood there. Unable to react or help her. It was out of his control.

Was he losing it?

He'd never been an emotional man. When he said something, he meant it and he'd always assumed the person listening knew he meant it. Kate knew, didn't she? Knew that he loved her more than life?

How often did you tell her? He heard the shrink's question. And his answer had been "all the time." But had he?

"I love you, Kathleen."

Motion in the room stopped.

"I love you, too, Cord. Now will someone check under all that blood? I'm telling you, the man has been shot."

"Not shot, just cut, I think," Cord clarified for her.

They began working again and a doctor he'd never met—he knew plenty of them at this place—lifted his shirt and mumbled a curse.

"Someone get this man a bed," the doctor said.

"I'm not leaving. Do whatever you have to do, but I'm staying by her side as long as she needs me." He looked in Kate's eyes and knew she understood the full meaning of his words. He'd go wherever she needed him to. Give up anything for her. There'd be plenty of time to decide what they were doing once this baby was safe.

He also saw her love. It shot through him, energizing more than the physical part of him. She gave him the strength to conquer whatever life threw at him.

"We're getting married," he announced to the nurse squirting a stinging solution on his side.

"There he goes again," Kate said, smiling in spite of their uncertain future, "making plans without ever asking me the question."

"Is there a question to ask?"

She shook her head. "Just say when and where."

Epilogue

"Did Mr. Cauldwell tell you why he gave you a ride to your ranch?" Mac's attorney asked.

"No, he did not. And it wasn't a 'ride,'" Kate stated under oath.

It had been four months of secretive living, overprotection and major bed rest. Kate had fought the doctors about returning for the grand jury hearing. Once Mac had been apprehended, the prosecuting attorneys had pushed to get her testimony on record while she was still pregnant. "More effective and personal."

Right. She was as big as a house and her back was killing her because of the hours on a wooden chair across the hall.

"Did Mr. Cauldwell ever state that he'd shot Nick Burke?"

"Not in those words, no." Kate hated to admit he hadn't

confessed and avoided looking in the direction of where Mac sat.

"So it's possible you could have misunderstood what he'd said. And it's possible he'd received instructions from his boss, Nick Burke, to drop you at your home?"

"He drove off with my boots." She pointed to an evidence bag at the side of the room. They'd been found along the ranch's drive near the main road. "He said Serna would be there to pick me up. And let's be perfectly clear, Mac knew I was pregnant and knew that monster intended to kill me, not buy me new shoes."

A low amount of laughter rippled through the room. Kate smiled until a contraction tightened her belly even tighter than the stretched-to-capacity skin. She looked at Cord, who hadn't looked away since they'd walked in.

"Just answer the question put before you."

"Kate?" Cord stood, hands on the railing separating him from the back of the prosecutor.

"Sit down, Mr. McCrea," the judge instructed.

"I'm fine." She smiled at her husband. "Really." Cord sat but stayed on the edge of the long bench, his knuckles turning white against the dark stain of the railing.

Mac still had a smile on his face as if he seriously didn't care what she said. That it didn't matter. But this trial would determine if he went into witness protection or if he spent the rest of his sorry life behind bars.

It was the only reason Cord had finally conceded to returning to Texas for the trial. They had talked, discussed, weighed the pros and cons. Ultimately, he agreed he wanted Mac to pay for his crimes, not walk free.

"Again, Mrs. McCrea, is there a possibility that the defendant had misunderstood instructions from his employer?"

He would not walk free. She waited until the man who had betrayed her family looked at her. Waited longer while the constant smile changed to a worried frown. "There is no way Mac Cauldwell misunderstood anyone. He dropped me a mile from my home, shoeless with snow on the ground. He knew what he was doing and he stated that he didn't care."

Another contraction, much too soon after the first, made her pause long enough for the defense attorney to whine. But as soon as she could breathe again, she continued what she needed to say to keep Mac behind bars.

"He admitted that if he got caught he had evidence that would put him in WitSec. This man has no regard for the loss of life or horrible things he's done. He deserves to rot in prison, not be rewarded with a new life."

"Kate, you're going to have to restrict— Are you okay?" the judge asked.

"Sorry, but I—" She could barely talk while the contraction subsided. "I think I'm in labor."

Three police cars pulled into the Alpine hospital, escorting them to the emergency entrance. They were greeted at the door with a wheelchair and the doctor Kate had seen for the first half of her pregnancy. And yet, Cord had never been so frightened in his life. He'd just thought he'd been afraid. What if something happened to Kate? She was high risk after the past four years. Something could go wrong.

"Welcome back, Kate. Doing okay?" the doctor asked.

Kate panted, obviously in the middle of another contraction.

Cord looked at his watch. "That's less than two minutes since the last one."

"I think we should have us a baby," the doctor told Kate, who nodded in agreement.

Kate laced her fingers through his as she was wheeled straight to the maternity wing. He stood in a corner out of the way, continually turning down the offer to sit in the chair or move to the waiting area. He would be by Kate's side the entire time no matter how useless he felt. Guns he could handle. Horses he could work in his sleep. But worrying about Kate was a full-time job.

"Cord," Kate called, waving him closer. "You look like you're about to throw up. Are you okay?"

The doctor entered the room and proceeded to do her thing checking on Kate. Truth be told, he didn't know how he felt. He was about to be a father.

"Well, Kate. Things are progressing nicely and it probably won't be too long. I'll be back when I'm needed."

They were alone, something that would have scared him to death five months ago, but he loved it now. He'd spent a lot of time with his wife. Talking about what had happened in the past but, most important, how they could be there for each other in the future.

"Perfect timing, little one." Kate rubbed her gargantuan stomach—her words, not his. He was grateful for the way she looked. "I wanted our baby born in Texas so badly. I'll miss raising a family here."

"We'll be back on the ranch soon." He shook his head, baffled that his wife would continue to question his desire to run her family's ranch. "I'm done with being a Ranger, Kate. Really."

"I'm afraid you'll miss it." Her grip on his hand tightened, and tightened some more during the contraction.

This was one thing she was completely wrong about. He couldn't put his family in danger like that again, and he actually loved ranching. Even his father agreed it was time to live a normal life.

"I think you're supposed to breathe through those things, babe."

"Right. And don't call me babe. Oh, wow, here's another one."

Cord called for the nurse, who called for the doctor. They pushed, or Kate did and he held her hand. And sooner than he expected, he was a dad holding his brand-new baby boy.

"Looks like you've got that next-generation Ranger after all," Kate said. "Guess he doesn't want to be called Lorna after his grandmother."

"I love you, Kathleen." Cord kissed his son's forehead, so thankful both of them were okay. "Whoever Danver McCrea grows up to be, he'll always be protected by us both."

* * * * *

Rachel slipped her arms around his neck and kissed him back. Not shy or reluctant, it was a bold, hungry kiss that set him on fire. He swayed against her, drunk on the thrill of her lips on his, their tongues tangling, their breaths mingling.

Seconds later, she pulled away and placed an open hand against his chest, gently pushing him away. He was crazy with wanting her and was certain she could feel the pounding of his heart.

"See you tomorrow," she whispered as she opened the door and slipped back inside the house.

Tomorrow couldn't come too soon.

Dawn was lighting the sky before Rachel gave up on the tossing and turning and any chance of sound sleep. Her life was spinning out of control at a dizzying pace.

Two days ago, she'd had a career. She'd known what she would be doing from day to day. Admittedly, she'd still been struggling to move past the torture Roy Sales had put her through, but she was making progress.

Two days ago, she wasn't making headlines, another major detriment to defending Hayden. The terrors she was trying so hard to escape would be front and center.

People would stare. People would ask questions. Gossip magazines would feed on her trauma again.

Two days ago she hadn't met Luke Dawkins. Her stomach hadn't fluttered at his incidental touch. There had been no heated zings of attraction when a rugged, hard-bodied stranger spoke her name or met her gaze.

A kiss hadn't rocked her with desire and left her aching for more. She put her fingertips to her lips, and a craving for his mouth on hers burned inside her.

This was absolutely crazy.

She kicked off the covers, crawled out of bed, padded to the window and opened the blinds. The crescent moon floated behind a gray cloud. The universe held steady, day following night, season following season, the earth remaining on its axis century after century.

She didn't expect that kind of order in her life, but neither could she continue to let the demonic Roy Sales pull the strings and control her reactions.

She had to fight to get what she wanted—once she decided what that was. She'd spend the next two or maybe three days here in Winding Creek trying to figure it all out. Then she'd drive back to Houston and face Eric Fitch Sr. straight on.

There were no decisions to make about Luke Dawkins. Once he learned of her past, he'd see her through different eyes. And he'd definitely learn about her past, since she was making news again. He'd pity her, and then he'd move on.

Who could blame him? Her emotional baggage was killing her.

Don't miss
DROPPING THE HAMMER by Joanna Wayne,
available April 2018 wherever
Harlequin Intrigue® books and ebooks are sold.

www.Harlequin.com

HIEXP0318

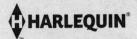

Reward the book lover in you!

Earn points from all your Harlequin book purchases from wherever you shop.

Turn your points into *FREE BOOKS* of your choice
OR
EXCLUSIVE GIFTS from your favorite authors or series.

Join for FREE today at
www.HarlequinMyRewards.com.

Harlequin My Rewards is a free program (no fees) without any commitments or obligations.

MYR17